L

The True Story of a Little Mexico City Street Dog Who Goes International

Christie Shary

Shary, Christie
ISBN: 978-0-7443-1819-7
Lucky Dog: *The True Story of a Little Mexican Street Dog Who Goes International* – 1st ed.

SynergEbooks
11 Spruce Ct.
Davenport, FL 338337
http://www.synergebooks.com

Cover art by Rahmeen Shary
Edited by Deb Staples
Contact the author at ChristieShary@aol.com

Printed in the USA

LUCKY DOG

DISCLAIMER

This is the true story of a Mexico City street dog named Lucky. All events are presented in a true manner, except those that happened before Lucky was adopted. They are, however, based on observations of other homeless street dogs in Mexico City. Some names of people and places have been changed, when requested. Certain events are also embellished and some lines are changed in order to make the book more readable. Most importantly, it is written in what the author strongly feels would be the words of its protagonist, Lucky, if only he could speak.

DEDICATION

This book is dedicated to Lucky, the best little street dog in the world – always our faithful companion, who has brought so much love, joy and laughter into our lives. Special thanks also to the Lagunita Writer's group for all their generous input, friendship and shared laughter. Also thanks to Chet and Tom for their technical support, when I just couldn't get my computer 'cranking.' And a special thanks to Deb Staples and SynergEbooks for having so much faith in me throughout the years.

Thanks and love also to my son, Rahm, always there for me with a great cover. And last but not least, special love and thanks to my husband, Tom, who has shown Lucky so much love and kindness throughout the years; the one who has been so generous to us both when money needs arose.

PROLOGUE

My name is Lucky. I think it fits me well. For I have a set of adoptive parents that drool over me like a new-born baby. I have an orange and rust-colored puffy paisley bed and a bright yellow raincoat with 'Lucky' embroidered on its hood. I enjoy custom-prepared food each night, and I even have more stamps in my passport than most Americans. Of course, my passport is an Official European Union Pet Passport, and it's enabled me to travel the world. But that's another story.

I have to tell you, though, life wasn't always like this for me. For I'm a street dog by trade – a Mexico City street dog, at that. I remember wandering the streets of the largest city in the world day after day with only an odd scrap of food or a discarded bone to gnaw on. But I was fortunate. I won the Doggie Lotto.

However, I have to admit that I'm not the most handsome of dog breeds. That's because I'm really no breed at all. I'm what they call a 'Heinz 57 Dog.' You know, fifty-seven varieties all combined into one tidy package. I think I've got a bit of Labrador retriever in me as I have nice floppy ears that got me adopted, so my parents tell me. They blow out like sails when I run, and Wendy at Mossbank Farm always said I like to do the Labrador Prance, whatever that is. I think it's kind of like marching in place when I get excited. But how Wendy and Howard came into my life, well, that's another story, too.

And I do have lots of bad hair days as I have stiff, wiry terrier hair that's not always at its best behavior. But an oil of evening primrose capsule stuffed down my throat each day by my mama has certainly made me more petable. Of course, like all streets dogs, especially

7

those of us from Mexico, I'm a yellowish gold color, I'd say about the color of freshly-harvested wheat. That's because I suppose all million of us street dogs are related in one way or another. I also have four white paws and a white chest, which is soft as rabbit fur. They say my eyes are my best feature. They are large and brown and outlined in black. I've heard some say they are 'wise-looking.' I also have long eyelashes and even a scruffy-looking beard, which Granny says is always in need of a shave.

So as you can see, I wasn't adopted for my classic good looks or my genetic background. My streak of good luck runs much deeper than that.

In fact, I'll always remember the day I got lucky. It was a cold winter night in Mexico City (that means about 40 degrees Fahrenheit) but it seemed much colder to me, as I hadn't had a thing to eat in several days. My chest hurt and I could barely breathe. I didn't know I had pneumonia. All I knew was that I was hungry and miserable, and about at the end of my 'doggie life.' And remember, we dogs don't have nine lives like cats do, so my luck had definitely run out.

Or so I thought.

CHAPTER 1
MY BUDDY

I was running down Mexico City's busy *Avenida de Reforma* that February afternoon. Horns blared as cars raced around the traffic circle like they were competing in the Grand Prix. I felt the wind from the cars blow my floppy ears in the air as I dashed in front of a bright green and white VW Beetle taxi to the other side of the road. Even though I had finally learned to fear the giant steel noise-makers, rushing between them was the only way I could cross the busy street.

I knew they wouldn't stop. They seldom stopped for maids, let alone us street dogs, us *Los Perros de Las Calles,* as they called us. After all, there were a million of us in Mexico City – what was one more of us smashed flat as a watermelon seed?

The taxi's fender grazed my tail and I felt it snap backwards, but I continued to run until I was completely out of breath. Reaching the sidewalk, I jumped onto the curb, almost bumping into a man dressed in rags who was selling deep fried *churros*, the sticky honey-coated pastries that we Mexicans love so much. I looked up at the man, pleaded for a bit of pastry. I knew my eyes were sad and lonely. *Couldn't you just pat me on the head, scratch behind my ears, and give me a bit of sweet bread?* Instead he gave me a quick hard kick in the ribs. I yelped and ran toward a graffiti-spattered wall and sank down into some tall weeds next to it. Exhausted, I lay my head on the ground, all the time watching the traffic go round and round in an endless circle like a twirling top.

I'm so cold, I thought. *And hungry. I haven't had a thing to eat in two days.* I started to cough. I could hardly breathe. Oh, how my chest ached. It was like a big bone was lodged there.

I dug a shallow hole with my front paws and curled into my street dog ball to keep warm. Although the sun was shining through the smog and haze, it was cold. Of course, it was wintertime in the high mountain-circled Valley of Mexico, home to what I had heard were twenty-four million people. And all of them seemed to like to kick me. Beginning to shiver, I looked up toward the sun, hoping to catch some of its warming rays.

Slowly, my eyes closed. I dreamed of the chicken bone I had discovered near the *carnerceria*, the butcher shop, two days earlier. I could still taste the blood as it dribbled down my snout. But the pain in my stomach knotted and woke me. I was still shivering, and I couldn't stop shaking. *I'm so hungry.* I lifted my head and gnawed on the tall grass beside me. *Maybe this will fill my empty belly.*

As I fell back to sleep, I thought of my mother, felt the warmth of her fur. I was cuddled with my four brothers and sisters in The Gully where we were born next to Chapultepec Park. It was just before the rainy season had begun. Warm milk flowed from my mother's teats and into our hungry mouths. Mama Dog was always there with us in our home – the hole she had dug beneath the underpass and where she gave birth to us. She only left on food-hunting expeditions. There was plenty of garbage in The Gully, tossed from the cars of passing motorists. But it didn't provide much of a doggie smorgasbord as it mostly consisted of pop cans, Styrofoam cups, cellophane paper and a few bits of leftover food. Of course, sometimes Mama Dog hunted down an abandoned cat or some field mice. And some days when she got really lucky, she would fetch us a fat rat to chew on. We gobbled it up like vultures, bones, fur, and all. But what we really loved most was Mama Dog's warm milk.

One morning when I was about nine weeks old, my mother didn't wake up. She was stiff and cold. No warm milk flowed from her teats, and they were hard and swollen. My siblings and I were cold and very hungry. We climbed all over her and tried to suckle. We whined and whined but no one came.

One by one my brothers and sisters died, for it was hard hunting for us pups in The Gully. Only myself and my one brother, whom I called Buddy, remained of our dog family. We knew we had to learn to fend for ourselves, as Mama Dog was no longer around to look after us. We soon discovered that mud puddles were a good source of water, as were discarded tin cans. We also found a few scraps, but not enough to keep us alive, so we tried begging for a living. But we were only met with hard kicks on our behinds from the people who lived on the street corners above The Gully. Most had nothing to give, anyway. They, too, were homeless beggars, the street people of Mexico City.

But I was the resourceful one, and knew I had to take care of Buddy and me. Even though my fur was very scruffy, I tried very hard to look cute and loveable to potential food donors. I would wag my tail so hard that it looked like I was dancing the *salsa*, and then I'd look at them with my big brown eyes. I also discovered the address of the local *carnerceria*. That meant meat for us! We could see it hanging from large hooks behind the counter of the open-faced shop. Flies danced around it like bees to a calla lily, and Jose, the butcher, continually swatted at them with the corner of his white blood-splattered apron. Somehow he took a liking to us boys, however. At least we thought he did. And were we ever glad for that. For he'd throw us an odd bone now and then, enough to at least keep us alive.

Now Buddy and I were as playful and fun-loving as any two young pups, even though we were of the 'street dog' variety. And we were growing up fast. All the seasons had passed and I figured we were about a year old. We loved to race through The Gully, then lie down in the tall grass and try to catch bugs and birds while pretending to be asleep. I became especially adept at catching flies by jumping several feet into the air, opening my mouth real wide, then snapping it shut quick. In fact, I'm still a good fly catcher to this day and it's a service I gladly perform for my adoptive family, especially when they're hovering around the barbecue. But at that time, there were no barbecue dinners in my life. I needed the nourishment of those flies to stay alive.

Buddy and I also loved to dart through the cars on *Avenida de Reforma* to the opposite side and then back again. It was kind of a dog tag game we had invented, although we soon learned that it was a very dangerous game.

One day I was running ahead of Buddy, threading in and out of the traffic, and could hear his breath behind me, his ears flapping. Suddenly, I heard a loud thud and a yelp. I saw Buddy fly into the air from the corner of my eye and plop onto the street as a huge black tire plowed over him. Immediately I knew something awful had happened to him. I raced back to my brother. He was still. I sniffed at him, put my tail between my rear legs, and whimpered all the way back to the sidewalk. I continued to cry as I lowered myself to the cold cement, where I lay for a long time, staring up at the sky.

Soon it clouded up and began to rain, as it always did during the summer and fall rainy season in Mexico City. The rain pounded down upon me, and ran into my

12

eyes. My fur became soaked and clung to my skinny frame like an old rag. Finally, I dug a hole in the grass and molded my body into it. *I'm all alone . . . I'm scared . . . and I'm so hungry.* Already I missed my Buddy. *How am I ever going to survive without him?*

CHAPTER 2
LOST AND FOUND

The next morning I awoke to see the sun shining through the haze and smog as it always did. Its warm rays crept across my body and I felt temporarily warmed. But my chest still hurt and I had a hard time breathing. The hunger pains in my stomach didn't matter any more. I was just too tired to care. Again I thought of Buddy. Oh, how I missed my brother.

I think I remained in my hole for several days. I'm not really sure. All I remember was the swirl of traffic beside me, honking horns, and the cries of vendors selling candies and newspapers.

One day in the late afternoon, I tried to stand but felt shaky. I noticed a man in the phone booth a few feet away, so I moved toward it. *Maybe he'll give me something to eat.* He was smiling, probably talking to his *novia*, his sweetheart. The melodious sound of his voice soothed me, made me want to sleep some more. I tried to wag my tail at him, but I was just too tired for begging. Instead, I eased myself down beside the phone booth and stretched out, my snout between my paws, my back legs folded beneath me.

And I dreamed. I dreamed of running through the streets of Mexico City with my siblings; of Buddy and me squabbling over a large bone. Next I was running through a grassy meadow after some bright yellow butterflies. My belly was full and it was warm and sunny. Life was so good . . . until I woke up.

Suddenly it became very cold and dusty. It was dark and the single street light nearby had just blinked on. Traffic was heavy with all the Saturday night revelers on their way to party in Zona Rosa. I barely noticed the white mini-van as it pulled onto the sidewalk nearby, or the quiet voices of the two people who stepped from it.

"Look at those ears," I heard the man say. "He's got Labrador ears!"

"Let's take a closer look," the woman said. "He's cute."

Before I knew it, she was coming toward me. I didn't move, but just looked up at her. I didn't have the strength to resist her kick or run away.

"Look at his beautiful face," she said. "A bit scraggly on the beard side, but a quick trim would take care of that."

Still no kick from her. *Is she nuts? Aren't we street dogs for kicking or else running away from as fast as one can? But then again, I really don't think she's a 'kicker.' She's far too nice.*

The man got out of the car more slowly, more cautiously. *Oh, oh, here comes the kicker,* I thought. He looked nervous, yet he had a kind face. *Maybe he won't kick me after all. He does look nice. In fact, they both do.*

"Look at that horrible fur!" the man said. "He looks like a scarecrow."

"I think he's seen better hair days," the woman said.

"And he's so old. Must be at least ten or twelve."

And to think I was barely older than a pup. *What the heck kind of an insult is that? Talk about a 'bad dog' rap.*

The woman shook her head and came closer. "I think he just might be the dog for us." She turned to the man. "Remember, you promised that when the company transferred us to Mexico City we'd get a dog."

"Yes . . . well . . . guess I did . . . but such an old dog . . . possibly a sick dog . . . and a street dog at that. I'm not so sure . . ."

He looked at me for a minute. "But he is kind of cute. I like his ears."

The woman bent down and patted my head. She scratched behind my ears and stroked my chest. I looked up at her and slowly closed my eyes and let out a little 'it feels so good' moan. I was certain I must be in 'doggie' heaven. In fact, I was sure of it.

The man's voice removed me from my trance. "Hey, take it easy there. What if he has rabies! He might bite you!"

The woman continued to pet me. "He doesn't have rabies! If he did, he'd run from us and his eyes would be red, and he'd probably be frothing at the mouth. He's a nice dog, just in need of a good home."

"Oh, I don't know," said the man. "He's too friendly for a homeless street dog." He gestured to the man talking on the telephone. "Must belong to him."

"Then why don't you ask him," the woman said, as she ran her hand down my back. Let me tell you, I just can't explain how good it felt.

I decided to stand. Stretching in my typical street-dog fashion, I reached one rear leg way out behind me, then the other, and afterwards proceeded to do the same with my front legs.

"He looks just like you do in the morning," the woman told the man.

"Except I don't have four legs." The man laughed and walked toward the phone booth. "*Es esta su perro?*" Is this your dog?" he added in English, probably hoping I belonged to the man on the phone. But I honestly sensed he liked me almost as much as the woman did. You know how guys are, just afraid to show

16

their affection. That was it. I was sure of it. I wanted to rush forward and lick him right then and there, but decided it would be too forward of me. After all, I didn't want to scare him off and mess up my good fortune. It just didn't come knocking at my 'doggie hole' every day. In fact, it had taken too darn long coming.

The man in the phone booth threw his hands in the air and dropped the receiver. *"No, no es mi perro! Por Favor, el is para usted."*

"He said 'he's not his, that he's for you,'" the woman said. They both smiled down at me. I wish I could have smiled back. But I did give my tail a few good wags with the little strength I had left.

"Let's see if he'll get in the van." The woman took me gently by the nape of the neck and led me to their car. I didn't hesitate for a moment. I was not about to lose out on this winning lotto ticket. And I promised myself to be the best dog they would ever own. *Please . . . please keep me. I'm so weary of life on the street.*

The woman slid open the side door and got into the rear seat. The man coaxed me from outside.

"Go on in, Little Guy," he said. "We're going to take you home."

I didn't need to be invited twice.

"Look, he jumped right in!" said the woman. "What a smart dog!"

If she'd only known how much of my remaining strength it took to jump up into their van. But I was soon very glad I did. The inside was warm and cozy. There was soft carpet beneath my feet. For the first time in many months, everything in my world felt so good. I sat back on my haunches, and squeezed close to the woman's knees, and stared out the front window, quickly deciding that this 'car thing' wasn't bad at all; especially when the woman gave me a good old hug.

"Everything's going to be okay, Old Boy," the man said as he started the engine. It made a nice purring sound and didn't even frighten me. *But aren't we street dogs supposed to be afraid of cars? Not this one. It's going to give me a lift home.*

"Lucky, we're going to call you Lucky," the woman said as she patted me on the head.

"Not a bad choice," said the man. "He's one lucky Mexico City street mutt, I can tell you that."

I nodded my head in agreement, liking the sound of my new name. For there was one thing I knew for sure. I was one lucky dog!

CHAPTER 3
HOME AT LAST

It wasn't too long until we pulled into the curved driveway of a pink stucco Mexican-style house, a *hacienda*. It was surrounded by a manicured soft-looking lawn covered with bushes and trees as far as I could see – plenty of places for me to do my male dog thing and for lounging in the sun. The house was enclosed by a high wall with an electric barbed-wire fence with jagged glass on top. An automatic gate closed behind the van, and I was welcomed to my safe new world. I was so happy and thankful that I let out a kind of 'doggie' sigh of relief, actually kind of a snort, and the woman and man both looked at me, startled.

"What's he trying to say?" the man said. "It sounded like he was snoring. I didn't know dogs snored." I'm afraid I would prove him right on that assumption one day.

"He's just excited," the woman said. "He's had quite the night being rescued and all."

No kidding, I thought. *It has been quite the night.* And in street dog slang that meant it had been 'quite a barker.'

Even though I barely knew them, I'd already decided on my new parents' names. I would call the man, "Papa" and the woman, "Mama." We would be a happy family, even though they spoke no 'dog language.' I would be perfectly willing to learn to understand theirs, although I had heard very little English in my life. But I couldn't rely on my Spanish. Theirs was terrible! I was certain they had just moved to Mexico. Anyway, one way or another, I knew we would learn to understand and love each other no matter what language we spoke.

"We'd better get him something to eat," Papa said. "He looks half-starved."

No kidding. I am half-starved, probably three-quarters starved, in fact.

"Yes, he does look like he could use a good meal," Mama said.

If only they knew . . . I haven't eaten in days. A half-rotten chicken bone was the last thing I remembered. I was so hungry I could have eaten a piece of cardboard, some chopped up grass, anything. But my fortune was changing fast. I could taste it already as I imagined a giant bone just inside the door.

"I found some leftover chicken and some *tortillas*," Mama said. "These will have to do." She took them from the refrigerator, which was just inside the kitchen next to the garage side door.

I peered at her intently from my place outside, not daring to move my eyes from that chicken. In fact, it smelled so good that I just wanted to jump into the house and grab it from her. But I restrained myself, remembered my manners. Anyway, I was not about to become a house dog – yet. I didn't know what lay inside all those walls with lights attached. It looked like a place without an escape route filled with strange-looking objects that I would later know as furniture and carpets, perfect places for a good old afternoon *siesta*, as we Mexicans call nap time. But for the time being, I was perfectly content to remain outside.

"What if he doesn't like chicken?" Papa said.

Are you kidding? I could eat a horse and then some.

Mama and Papa both gawked as I gobbled up the chicken and *tortilla* pieces in ten seconds flat.

"He's definitely starving," Mama said, her eyes tear-filled. "You poor little Lucky."

20

I looked up for more food, sniffed the air. A shower of chicken bits and *tortillas* from heaven landed on the paper plate before me. I gobbled it up just as quickly.

"I can't believe how fast he eats," Papa said. He shook his head. "But I think he's really an old dog. Look at his coat. It looks like a rat's nest. And his bones show right through his fur. Definitely not a picture of good health."

"He's been living on the streets," Mama said. "Give the poor guy a chance."

Papa nodded. "Yeah, guess we owe him that much. We'll have to check him out in the day light, look at his teeth if he'll let us."

"For heaven's sakes, he's not going to need orthodontic treatment," Mama said, placing her hands on her hips.

Papa looked at me again, and patted my head. "You know how expensive an old dog can be."

"He's a great dog," Mama said. "See how he looks at you. He adores you already. And you'll learn to love him, too. I know you will."

Papa patted me on the head again.

I looked at him, my eyes filled with love. *He's warming up, I just know he is.*

"Yes, he is a good dog," Papa finally agreed.

"You bet your life he is, and besides, you're making a few extra Expat bucks down here. We can afford him."

"Yeah . . . I suppose . . . but you know I'm not the dog person you are."

Mama smiled, patted Papa on the arm. "I think you'll become one with this little guy hanging around."

I looked up at Papa again, strained my neck. *I'll make you a dog lover, Papa. I promise to be the best dog you've ever had – the best little street dog in the world.*

"Oh, I don't know that I'll ever be a dog lover," Papa said, "but we have to give the poor guy a chance." He looked down at me. "After what you've probably been through."

I couldn't have agreed more. A chance to prove myself. That was all I needed.

Papa continued to talk, and I sat at attention as he spoke. "But first things first. You need somewhere to sleep tonight, Lucky." He looked around the garage and his eyes came to rest on a large stack of moving boxes. "I think I can rig something up for you, Old Boy."

It became a favorite name for Papa to call me. And each and every time he used it, I knew that it was full of love.

Now as far as beds go, they didn't know I could sleep on anything, be it a sidewalk, a pile of leaves, some weeds, or a hole in the ground. I was a street dog, after all, not some 'city slicker' Poodle-type pooch.

"You're thinking a box might have to do, right?" Mama asked, pulling one from the pile.

"Yes. It has to be better than what he had on the street."

No kidding . . . it's a heck of a lot better, Papa.

Papa took the box from Mama. It had the words **Movers International** in bold letters on its side. He filled it up with packing paper left over from their recent move from California to Mexico.

"This'll have to do."

Will it ever! I thought.

Papa put the box next to the garage wall near the kitchen door and tapped on its side to get my attention. I didn't need to be invited twice. This was the best bed I

22

had ever seen in all my 'doggie' days! I jumped into it like a jackrabbit.

"Wow, he likes it," Mama said. "It's as if it had his name on it instead of the name of the moving company."

Who cares about a personalized bed. I'm safe here. No other dogs will snarl at me and try to steal my food. No cars will run over me. For the first time in my life I can finally sleep in peace.

Mama and Papa just stood there holding hands and staring at me for a few minutes in wonder, like two little kids mesmerized over a new toy. Then they smiled at each other and kissed real quick. It made me feel good, so cozy. For some reason my chest no longer hurt quite so bad. I felt like I was already getting better. One thing I knew for sure. I was definitely a 'Doggie' Lotto winner. I had a darn good feeling that the days ahead were about to change for the better. They would be good ones. For I had finally found a home and a new family.

CHAPTER 4
GETTING TO KNOW YOU

I would soon discover that the leafy green suburb of Lomas de Chapultepec, where the wealthy of Mexico City lived, was a far cry from where I was born and raised in The Gully. This 'other side' of Chapultepec Park was indeed a different world – one filled with boutiques, sidewalk cafes and designer shops, all with machine-gun bearing policemen out front to protect their wealthy patrons.

When I awoke the first morning in my new home, I was very confused. *Where am I?* I looked around and found myself curled in the middle of a box. *Where's my hole?* It was so quiet, except for the sound of some birds in a nearby tree. *Where are all the cars that used to buzz around me each morning?* Then I remembered I was no longer a street dog. I now had a home. I was *officially adopted,* or at least I hoped I was.

It was chilly in the covered garage as the morning sun did not reach there. Of course I took care of that. I hopped from my make-shift bed, did my usual street-dog stretches. and proceeded to search for the sun. Quickly I spied it out by the front gate and headed in that direction, peeing on every shrub in sight. *Yes, this is definitely a territory worth marking.* Little did I know that my gardening mama would freak out about all those little yellow circles that I made. Afterwards I padded across the perfectly-manicured lawn. I couldn't help but lie down on my back for a few moments. It was just too tempting. The grass was soft. It felt so good, like velvet. I twirled my body around, paws in the air. I had never experienced anything so nice. In fact, rolling on the grass would quickly become one of my favorite 'doggie' pastimes.

Finally reaching a sunny spot beside the gate, I stretched out, paws before me, and soaked up the sun's warmth. *What a perfect place.* I was certain I was in dog heaven.

Soon some wonderful smells greeted my senses – tortillas cooking on the grill, the smoky smell of thick-sliced bacon, simmering *menudo*, the morning stew that Mexicans love so much. But I soon discovered that these good smells were coming from the house next door – a Mexican household – and that they were not about to be included in my morning meal. I would later learn that Mama and Papa were 'cappuccino sippers' and 'bagel eaters,' and that they lived in a *casa* where none of our wonderful fat-loaded Mexican breakfasts would be served.

Mama and Papa's heads soon poked from the kitchen door.

"Yipes, where's Lucky?" Mama screeched. "What if he's run away?"

"Are you kidding?" Papa said. "He knows a good thing when he sees it. Lucky's not about to go anywhere. Besides, this house is like a fortress. He'd never get out."

Now on that point, I was to one day prove Papa wrong. But on the other, Papa was absolutely right. I was 'dandy happy' right there in my new sunny spot.

As they approached me, I jumped right up and wagged my tail. But suddenly I had to sit back down again. I felt so weak. My chest still hurt. I started to cough and made a kind of choking sound.

"There you are, Old Boy. I didn't think you'd be far way," Papa said. *"Buenos Dias!"*

"Good morning, Lucky," Mama greeted me. She came up to me, bent down and stroked behind my ears with both hands. I stared into her eyes. Had I been a cat, I would have done some very serious purring about then. *What a wake-up call*, I thought, relaxing.

But I coughed again and had to sit up. A bunch of yellow pussy gook spilled from my mouth and I quickly licked it up. This time Mama noticed.

"He's really sick," Mama said. "We need to find a vet."

A grave looked crossed both their faces.

Am I about to die? Please . . . . no . . . not when life is just getting good. I've had such a short time in this paradise.

"I think you're right," Papa said to Mama, but first let's fix him some breakfast. He still looks half-starved."

Who cares how I look. I'm ready for some chow.

"Poor guy," Papa said. He paused for a moment, turned again to look at me. "But I was right. Look at him in the sunlight. He's really an old dog. Look at all that white hair mixed in with his yellow fur."

"Oh, I don't know," Mama said. "I still don't think he's old. He's just had a tough life."

No kidding, I thought, as I walked out onto the grass again and lay on my back. But this life here . . . why it's the beginning of something really good.

"I'm also worried about those scars and scratches he has all over his body. They even show through his fur," Mama said.

"Probably the result of dog fights," Papa said.

"Good heavens, no. I can't imagine Lucky in a dog fight. He's just too sweet."

You'd fight for any bone you could lay your paws on, Mama, if you had been starving like me. Otherwise they were stolen from you fast as a raging tornado.

"We need to get you some dog food," Mama continued. "But for breakfast today, it'll have to be more chicken and *tortillas*."

No problem for me, Mama. I don't mind the taste of that chicken one bit.

Mama and Papa had also decided it was time to "civilize me" – to teach me the ways of those city-slicker type dogs, and about the world of Lomas de Chapultepec.

"Do we have something we can walk him with?" Papa said. "It's a while before any vet will open. You know, those weird Mexican hours and all."

Mama smiled. "But life here is so much more relaxing. No one's ever in a hurry. Things just happen when they happen."

Papa grunted. "You got that right."

Mama produced a long piece of cord that I would soon recognize as a leash. It looked more like the wire the butcher had on his light bulb to me. But this one was red and had a shiny clip on its end.

"I even have a dog collar," Mama said.

Papa grinned. "Looks like you might have had a little 'dog planning' going on."

"Well, you know how it is . . . never know when you might need something." She looked sad for a moment. "Besides, they belonged to Polly. I never could get rid of them."

I later learned that Polly, a fluffy white Maltese, who was a darn lot smaller than me, had been their cherished family pet for fourteen years. She had even helped to raise their two grown sons.

"Polly Sweet Sue, oh how I've missed her," Mama sighed.

Oh . . . oh, does this mean I'm going to have to compete with a 'ghost dog' – a precious memory? I thought about it for a minute. *No, I don't mind.* For I knew there was lots of room for love in both their hearts.

But a beautiful fluffy white dog competitor? Boy, do I ever have a different look. How will I ever compete with a beauty like that? I could just imagine the 'little precious' sitting on a satin cushion on Mama's lap, her fur perfectly groomed.

Suddenly I felt the need to change my grooming habits. Mama and Papa must have had the same thing on their minds.

"Let's give Lucky a bath before we take him out," Papa said. "He doesn't smell so good."

In fact, I smelled absolutely ripe, like one of Papa's old socks after he had been working out in the garden all day. But since I still didn't seem too anxious to venture into the house, they decided my grooming parlor would be outside.

"I'll go heat up some water and get some shampoo and towels," Mama said.

Little did I know what I was in for. I just stood by Papa's side and wagged my tail like a stupid, naïve little puppy.

When the first bucket of water poured over me, I raced as fast as I could across the yard. *Maybe they were not such nice people after all!* I hated being out in the rain. Papa tore after me.

"It's okay, Lucky! We're just trying to clean you up."

After they cornered me near the flower garden, they cinched the collar around my neck, although it was a bit tight. Then they fastened the leash. I felt my fleeing freedom and protested strongly as they coached me back to the water faucet.

"You're going to be so *guapo*, so handsome," Mama said.

I was not so sure I cared for that idea, and I was certainly not in a good mood after they poured another bucket of water on me and proceeded to scrub me with a bristle brush filled with some sweet-smelling sticky stuff. It felt like I was suffering through a major Mexico City downpour as they poured bucket after bucket of water on me. But I just stood there stiff-legged and put up with it. If this bath thing was to be part of my new world, then so be it. Everything couldn't be perfect, now could it?

One thing I have to admit, however. To this day I have never loved baths. The moment my parents take out the towels, I run for cover and try to disappear. But it never works. They always find me and then it's straight to the old bathtub and all that floral-scented shampoo, no matter how hard I pull back on my collar and complain.

After my grueling grooming episode, I was exhausted. But it did make me feel a bit better. I felt kind of revived, fresh. My fur no longer smelled like auto fumes, dust and rotten food. Now I smelled like roses. *Oh, how my buddies on the street will laugh at that. At least they haven't put a bow in my hair – yet.* After all, I was a Mexican *machismo* dog. For the time being.

While I rested for a while, Papa went up to Superama, the local grocery store, and bought me some dog food, a new leash and a collar, as the Ghost Dog's hadn't been large enough for a big guy like me.

"You ought to like this," Papa said, fastening the brown leather collar around my neck. "It suits you."

It felt so strange. I had never been captive before. In fact, it made me want to run. *But I'll get used to it. I'll put up with anything for a place to call home.*

Next Papa attached that big long line to my collar. "Let's go!" he said, calling to Mama and me. "The Boy needs a walk."

I would learn to treasure the words "let's go." That meant we were headed out on an adventure, be it a walk around the block, a cappuccino break at the harbor, a camping trip, or who knows where – maybe to the other side of the world. Like my parents, I loved to be on the go.

We walked very slowly down my new street, Sierra Paracaima, as they knew I wasn't feeling at my best. It was lined with purple-blooming Jacaranda trees and Colonial Mexican houses, all behind tall walls. Mama and Papa held hands and I walked on Papa's left side, the way they had learned from all the dog magazines. It wasn't so bad being lead around. In fact I kind of enjoyed it. It hooked us all together, and boy, did I like that. That meant they were not going anywhere without me.

"He walks pretty well," Papa said. "It's as if he's always been on a leash. But it's probably because he's so old. Just can't tug any more."

"Yes, he does . . . but I think there's more to it than that. He just doesn't seem to have much strength. We need to get him to a vet right away. I'm sure he's sick." A worried look crossed Mama's face.

"I think there's one down on Las Palmas," Papa said. "Let's go there now."

We continued to walk. Las Palmas was a very busy street and I scrunched closer to Papa.

"Look, he's afraid of the cars," Papa said. "I wonder why . . ."

I briefly thought of my brother and felt so sad. I wish he could have been there with the three of us. Buddy would have liked that.

Mama interrupted my thoughts. "And he's going to need his vaccinations. We wouldn't want him to get distemper."

Little did they know that the sound of that disease had a very familiar ring.

CHAPTER 5
CLOSE ENCOUNTERS OF THE WORST
'VET' KIND

We plodded along Las Palmas very slowly. That was okay with me. I just wasn't up to jogging. Besides, it gave me a bit more time to check out my new surroundings. There were so many good smells, and maybe even some tasty tidbits to be found.

Not many street dogs in these parts, I noticed as we neared the bridge that connected *Lomas* with *Techamachalco*. But I did spy one familiar thing – the hot pink plastic tarps that covered Mexico City's 'traveling' street market. This *mercado*, as we Mexicans called it, moved all over the city, different days in different places. I remembered when it used to come close to The Gully.

Market day meant food for us street dogs. The vendors were always dropping something and we were always more than happy to help them clean it up. Quick, like a bullet, we were there to stake claim to it before they could reclaim it. Of course, it did result in some good hard kicks for us, but we were used to it, and the food we scavenged there kept us on our 'paws.'

The smells that emanated from this *mercado* were very familiar to me and I couldn't help but tug on my leash a little and move toward them.

A bit of menudo would taste great about now, or a mouthful of greasy chicheron – that's deep fried pig skin.

"Lucky seems very interested in this street market," Papa said. "His nose has been in the air ever since we got here."

"He sure does," Mama said.

32

Some laborers were seated on small wooden stools next to a counter where lots of food was displayed. Large sausages hung from a rack above it. They were dipping *tortillas* into brightly-colored plastic bowls and bringing out big pieces of meat, along with some beans.

My mouth watered. *Menudo, how'd I'd like to jump up and grab a bite of that stew right out of an unsuspecting eater's hand.* I'd done it before and I knew I was a pretty fast draw.

I tugged a bit harder on my leash and moved toward the counter.

"Hey there, wait a minute, Old Boy," Papa said. "You're wearing out my arm – and you're not about to join the dining crowd at that counter. Remember, you don't have to beg for a living any more."

Knowing it was a losing battle, I resorted to another street dog rule of mine. When walking, always keep your nose to the ground – never know when you'll run into a tasty mouthful.

And I did! Right there in front of my nose was a discarded chicken bone. I grabbed it fast as 'Speedy Gonzales' and gobbled it right up.

Mama and Papa just stood there, their mouths wide open, like I had just performed a miracle or something.

"Did you see how fast Lucky grabbed that bone?" Papa said. "He'd be a natural at shoplifting!"

Mama laughed. "Oh, come on . . . a dog shoplifter?

"Yeah, a *'dog lifter.'*" Papa laughed.

"No way. Lucky's just having a difficult time breaking old habits."

My parents would certainly find this out. To this day, no matter how tightly they hold my leash, I can't resist putting my snout to the ground once in a while and making a quick grab of whatever happens to be in my path. Sometimes I'm pleasantly surprised. There's just nothing like an old pork rib that has been rolled in the dirt. Sometimes I'm not so pleasantly surprised, however. I'll never forget one time when I reached down and got myself a bee. Let me tell you, that experience isn't one of my fondest memories.

Anyway, it still bugs Papa that I have this street dog habit, but you know, I can't be perfect, I'm only canine. We make mistakes, too.

We finally left the wonderful sights and smells of the *mercado* and walked farther down the street near the *Periferico*, a very busy road which provided an inner traffic circle for Mexico City. It was one road we street dogs never crossed. It meant instant death. It may seem strange, but no matter how miserable our lives were, we still clung to them.

"Here it is," Mama said. *"Vetrinario Manuel Ortega."*

"It doesn't look exactly palatial, "Papa said. He grimaced at the run-down weed-infested yard before the building.

"It's a vet's office," Mama said. "Not the ABC American-British Hospital. You know how most people feel about dogs down here. They're 'Expat' items they view as dirty, expensive and rabid."

"Yeah, I know, dogs are not exactly on their 'top ten' list of favorites."

Right from the start, I didn't like the smell of Dr. Ortega's office, but I had no choice other than to follow my parents inside the courtyard as we were all hooked together. Then I realized we were going inside a building and I pulled back even harder, but it didn't do me one bit of good. Finally I resigned myself that sooner or later I would have to go inside a building and that it might just as well be this one.

A dog's cry from inside really perked up my ears, however. It was a painful, sad cry. *What's going on in there?* I sensed danger and pulled back on my leash again. *Come to think of it, I'm not about to go inside a building. Bad things must happen there.*

"It's okay, Lucky, come on. We're going to get you all better." Papa pulled me toward the door, even though I sat down and tried to plant my paws into the cement. But they wouldn't stick and I was soon devoured by the structure.

Mama was standing before a counter talking to a short fat man with a *Pancho-Villa* mustache.

I didn't like his looks one bit. He looked like a real *kicker* to me. I didn't know that he'd turn out to be a real *jabber* instead. A jabber and a poker, in fact.

We went into a room that smelled like the bleach the butcher used to clean the sidewalks next to The Gully. The man slammed the door behind us. The smell stung my nose and I wanted out. I looked for an escape route. None. I felt myself begin to shake and I started to whine.

Mama bent down, stroked my head. "It's okay, Lucky. Dr. Ortega is going to help you."

I'll never forget the grin on the good doctor's face as he bent down, put one of his hands on my rear end and hooked his thumb around my tail. Then he put his other hand on the nape of my neck. Belching, he held on tight and lifted me into the air and plopped me onto a tall table like a sack of cornmeal. I was just about to bite his hands off! But no, I couldn't disappoint Mama and Papa. They had been so good to me. I wanted them to be proud. For whatever reason they wanted me on this table, I decided, it had to be a good one, so I let Dr. Ortega win the battle.

"*Macho Perro,*" Dr. Ortega said, checking out my private parts and spanking me hard on my rear end. He proceeded to force my mouth open and stick something inside it that felt like a metal rod. Boy, was I ever getting mad. But I held my teeth.

"*Mira,* look, look, his teeth are not good."

"What did I tell you?" Papa said to Mama. "He's an old dog – bad teeth."

"Distemper, he's had distemper!" Dr. Ortega said, pulling at his mustache.

Mama and Papa both looked shocked. "Oh no, not distemper!" they echoed in unison, knowing very well that it was pretty much a death sentence for dogs. Mama started to cry and Papa squeezed her hand.

"*Señor, Señora,* you not understand. This *perro* of yours not have distemper now. He had when he was a *perrilito,* a little dog. He had very high *temperatura,* look how his teeth are.

Both Mama and Papa moved closer, peered into my mouth for the first time.

"Poor Lucky," Papa said. "It must be hard for you to chew. Some of your teeth are no more than stumps."

I can chew just fine, Papa, and I'm about to show you how well on the hand of this moustache-toting vet. I started to growl real softly so as not to frighten Mama and Papa and the vet quickly retracted his hand.

But it didn't stay away from me for long. He next produced this shiny thing that looked like it was attached to a worm – a stethoscope, as Papa called it. He pressed its cold end to my chest and listened to my breathing, which was quite labored by now.

"*Muy mareeze,* very sick," the vet said.

Mama and Papa turned white again. "What's wrong with him?" Mama said, her eyes again tear-filled.

"I don't think your *perro* live even one more day."

36

By then Mama was almost ready to collapse. I was waiting for the vet to pick her up by the neck and leg and plop her next to me on the examination table.

He thought for a moment, sighed. "But I have very good idea. I think I can fix him."

Mama and Papa both smiled.

"He have pneumonia," the vet said. "He needs big injection." He stretched his arms far apart and about scared the 'doggie' daylights right out of me. *What on earth is a big injection?* It didn't sound like something I wanted to experience. I wondered if it had anything to do with the terrible chlorine smell of his office.

"Can you really cure him?" Papa asked. "We just got him yesterday."

"You should have left him on the street. He would be one of the dead today."

"Then thank goodness we saved him," Mama said, reaching out to pet me.

Let me tell you, I was in real need of her touch by then.

The vet shook his head and tugged at his moustache for a moment. "I will try. But it will cost *mucho dinero.*"

Papa looked shocked, but Mama quickly spoke up.

"Oh, thank you, *muchas gracias*, Dr. Ortega, thank you so much. It's okay, fine, whatever money it takes to make him better, we'll pay." She hugged me so hard that I thought I might break in half right there on the examination table. *Take it easy, Mama, I'm in a fragile state. You wouldn't want me to break on you, would you?*

"Hey just a minute there, we're not the Bank of America," Papa said. But then he looked at me and I noticed that his eyes were moist. *Oh, no, he's not going to cry on me, too?*

"Okay, okay, whatever it takes to pull him through."

I didn't know at the time that my papa was very concerned with the 'money matters' of our lives, especially since he always said that Mama thought it grew on trees, all hers for the picking.

When Dr. Ortega returned with a large cylinder-shaped object that was very pointed on the end, Mama got a really big smile on her face, like she'd been picking lots of money from her 'money tree.'

"You must both hold your *perro* while I give him injection," the doctor said.

Mama's smile quickly faded when she looked at the object in the vet's hand. I started to cower myself, but Mama and Papa both latched onto me as if I was about to fall off a racing train.

Then zap, something hit me like a rocket! It was like the worst bee sting I had ever had. I yelped in pain and went for the instrument in the vet's hand. He moved out fast before I could nail him.

"*Bien, bien,* you will soon be well. You are a tough *perro,* I can tell. You are a survivor. You will live many years."

I could tell that Mama and Papa were elated with his words. They completely forgot about my pain and thanked Dr. Ortega over and over again until he blushed.

"*Como se llama?* Dr Ortega asked me. "What is your name, Doggie?"

"Lucky," Papa said. "My wife named him as soon as we found him."

Dr. Ortega shook his head thoughtfully. "*Suerte, suerte,* yes, he is lucky."

"*Un lastima pregunto,*" Papa said, pretending to know Spanish.

"What is your question?" Dr. Ortega said.

"How old do you think Lucky is?"

"*Un ano, mas or menus,*" he responded.

"Did I understand you correctly?" Papa said. "He's only one year old?"

Mama piped in. "I told you so. I didn't think he was very old. Now you won't have to worry about all those vet bills piling up."

"*Si, Señor,* he is only one year, maybe one and one-half year. That's all."

Again, Mama and Papa seemed very happy.

"This *perro* will be with you for many years. *Mañana*, tomorrow, when he is better, you will see that he is still a pup.

Boy would I prove Dr. Ortega right. But for the moment, I wanted only one thing – to get back to my box bed at Sierra Paracaima and take one good long *siesta.*

CHAPTER 6
SETTLING IN

After Papa paid Dr. Ortega all that '*expat dinero*' to make me well, we went out to Las Palmas again. Boy, was I ever glad to get out of that place. And I promised myself I would never set eyes on the likes of Dr. Ortega again.

"What a strange little round man Dr. Ortega is," Mama said. I quickly seconded that under my 'doggie' breath.

Papa laughed. "You can say that again."

"But he's going to make our Lucky well and that's what counts."

We walked a bit and I was really lagging. My visit with Dr. Ortega had wiped me out. I think it had something to do with that long thing he stuck me with. Papa looked down at me and stopped walking. He hailed a VW Beetle taxi, one of what had to be several hundred zillion of them in Mexico City.

"I don't think Lucky feels well. He needs a ride home after what he's been through."

No kidding, Papa. Yes, I do think I need a lift. I wagged my tail in agreement.

When the taxi stopped, it made a horrible rumbling, tumbling sound, like it was about to fall to pieces. I didn't care. It was my ride home, so I jumped right in when Papa opened the door.

Now the driver didn't look too happy to see a dog getting inside his taxi. "No *permitte, no los perros permitte*," he kept telling Papa. But Papa pretended he didn't understand Spanish and followed me inside.

"Thank you very much, how kind of you," he told the driver. "We're very tired and need a ride home."

The driver grimaced and stared straight ahead, probably thinking about all those germs, hairs and fleas that I was depositing in his mini-shrine. For Mexico City street taxis all look the same – VW Beetles with the passenger side front seat removed, a rosary hanging from the fringe-trimmed mirror, and a miniature of Mother Mary standing on the dashboard. Of course some drivers added an extra few feet of red or gold fringe around the interior. All were painted a bright lime green.

Mama still stood outside, hesitating. She did not seem to want to get into the taxi. *Come on Mama, I thought. Before you get left.* She looked kind of pale.

"You two go ahead," she said. "I'll walk and meet you at home. I'm not about to get into another one of these taxis for a good long time."

Papa didn't complain. Later I would learn why Mama didn't like Mexico City street taxis. She'd been kidnapped in one the second week after their arrival in Mexico. But for the time being kidnapping certainly wasn't on my mind. *Who'd want to kidnap a street dog?* I wanted to get home. And besides, I needed to pee real bad.

Arriving home, I rushed straight for the closest bush I could find and then bolted for my box bed, exhausted.

"I think that injection made you tired, Lucky Boy," Papa said. "You're going to need lots of rest like the good doctor said."

When Mama arrived a few minutes later, I was already sleeping, curled in my street dog ball. I slowly opened my eyes and greeted her and then fell right back to sleep, knowing it would be the best afternoon *siesta* I had ever had. And you know us Mexicans, we love our *siestas*.

"Look how tired he is," Mama whispered. "He can sleep for a long time. We need to go shopping. Lucky needs lots of supplies."

Papa knew what that meant – tug out the good old American Express card and get shopping.

I briefly opened my eyes again as they pulled from the driveway, feeling momentarily sad. But I was just too tired to complain, so I closed them again and drifted off into 'doggie' dreamland.

It was so quiet in the garden that I must have slept for several hours. When I finally woke up, I was very thirsty and went straight to the plastic bowl near the kitchen door. It was filled with the clearest water I had ever seen. I just stared into it, thinking of all that muddy water that had kept me alive when I was on the street. Then I noticed something strange. It scared me for a moment and I jumped back. For there inside my bowl was a grungy dog that looked just like me! No matter; I quickly slurped him up.

Afterwards I looked around the garden. Everything was so green. I decided to explore it once again, this time thoroughly. I knew it would take a while – for there was an awful lot of 'marking' that had to be done and I needed to 'stake out' my territory and claim it as my own.

I must have peed on every bush and flower there, but I'm not sure it was a record. Papa once said I peed thirty-eight times on one walk. *Guess I'm just a natural at it.*

I also looked for an escape route from the garden, should I ever need one. It was a bit of street-dog knowledge that I never forgot after being ambushed by a big black dog in The Gully one day. First I checked out the front wooden gate which always opened when the van drove through. *Definitely too heavy for me to push open.* Next I padded along the fence foot-by-foot searching for openings. None. I did notice it was rusted in a few places, but the metal bars would prove too much for my poor teeth. Then I settled on the 'digging idea.' If I ever really had to get out, I could dig underneath the fence and escape. *Are you kidding? I looked around the yard. What loco street dog would ever want to escape this paradise?*

Only one thing bothered me in my new-found habitat. It was the roof dogs that lived across the street. For you see, in Mexico City people sometimes kept dogs on their flat rooftops to scare off robbers. They didn't give them very much food so they became very mean and would bark and bark and bark. I felt so sorry for them, knowing what a good life I had hopped into when I jumped into the back of Mama and Papa's van. But I did have to admit that those dogs certainly did tend to disrupt my afternoon *siesta* at times.

When Mama and Papa returned from Santa Fe Mall, was I ever in for a big surprise. I soon decided that mall must have a very good Dog Department filled with all kinds of neat things. That's because it was where all the rich people shopped, and it was filled with all kinds of wonderful, pricy stores where 'anything' from 'everywhere' could be purchased. And to think it was once the home of Mexico City's famous garbage dump, where hundreds of homeless people lived and scavenged. *What strange things happen in this world. Why, look what happened to me.*

Anyway, I was sure the shop owners at Santa Fe were not disappointed by the looks of Mama and Papa's van. It was stuffed full as a giant *tamale* with all sorts of goodies just for me. *Talk about a spoiled kid on Christmas morning.*

I wagged my tail in delight and did my best rendition of the hula when they got out of the van and opened the rear door. Of course, Mama and Papa didn't realize it was because I was so happy to see them, not because they had returned with a van load of 'things.'

Oh well, I'll pretend to be thrilled with all those sacks if it makes them happy.

"Hi there, Lucky Boy," Papa said, bending to pat my head.

"See, I knew you'd fall for him quickly," Mama said.

Papa nodded. "I just can't seem to help myself. He's so darn smart."

"And cute," Mama added.

Of course I tried to be both. I'd been working at it for a while, but I have to admit that it was a difficult task when it came to the 'looks' department.

"And he seems to be feeling better already," she added. "It's a miracle!"

"It sure is," Papa said. "In fact, Lucky himself is a miracle dog."

"I know. Imagine surviving on the streets of Mexico City day after day with no one to take care of you or feed you?"

"It must have been tough."

Little did they know . . .

"I wonder what ever happened to Lucky's mother and the rest of the litter?" Mama continued.

"There must have been more than one pup," Papa said.

It made me sad for a moment to think of Mama Dog and my brothers and sisters. *Buddy would have loved this place.* I gave Mama and Papa both a quick 'lick of

44

thanks' realizing more than ever that indeed I was one lucky dog.

"Guess what, Lucky?" Mama said. "I bought you a PPB!"

I looked at her, my eyes wide, as she pulled out a big bag from the van. It had pictures of fancy dog breeds all over it, none of which I recognized from my days on the street. I moved closer to her, wagged my tail hard, thinking that there must be an awful big bone inside.

"Look, Lucky, look. It's a puffy paisley bed just for you! A PPB!"

I think she kind of wanted me to jump up and down and twirl in a circle. Instead I just stood there, kind of dumb-like and continued to wag my tail. *Open it, would you? I'm just dying to gnaw on that bone.*

She pulled out this large orange and rust pillow-like object from the bag. I guess I looked puzzled.

"It's a *cama*, a bed, for you Lucky!" It sure looked *gigante* to me, surely big enough for a mother dog and her entire litter.

Mama put the bed on the ground and motioned to it. "Come on, Lucky, *va a en su cama*, get into your bed." It was a phrase I soon learned well – to get into my bed. Even though they didn't say it in correct Spanish, I knew what they meant. At first I thought it was neat to receive this command, and I leapt into my bed like a flying elephant. But soon I didn't like that phrase so much, as it meant they were either going to bed and would no longer pay me any attention, or that they were leaving the house and wanted me in 'my place,' neither of which I liked to hear. So I'd go to my bed like a spoiled little kid, head lowered, tail between my legs. For you see, I wanted to be in my *cama* when I wanted to be in my *cama*, like in the afternoon when I bedded down for my *siesta,* or at night when I was absolutely exhausted.

"Look, he likes it!" Papa said.

I have to admit, though, I really did love my bed. *Wow, what a place to sleep!* I sank down into its puffy top, scratched at it, then rolled over and lay my head on its equally puffy sides. *This is what I call a bit of 'doggie heaven.'* In fact, I had never felt anything so comfortable in my life. It was like I was floating on a poofy cloud when I lay on it. Why I had to force myself from falling asleep right then and there.

"Wait, there's more," Mama said. She dashed to the van and produced another sack. "Here are your new food bowls."

They were nice I suppose, white with a blue rim and covered with white spotted dogs, unlike any street dog I had ever seen. I would later learn they were the breed that starred in Walt Disney movies, Dalmatians, I believe. But for the time being I was interested in only one thing. *Where's the food, Mama? I only like full bowls.*

I sniffed at them and looked at her.

"Oh, you poor thing, you're hungry, aren't you?"

Papa had already brought another large sack from the car. "Here it is, Lucky. You're special new food, guaranteed to make you a strong and healthy dog – Doggy Delight Special Formula – imported from the USA."

I looked at the large sack, sniffed. It smelled kind of like chicken, or perhaps rice, but not as good.

While Mama filled the smaller bowl with water, Papa carefully opened the huge sack as I sat on my rear-end and waited in anticipation. Little pieces of brown stuff started tumbling out. They looked kind of like the rat droppings in The Gully except they smelled like

46

chicken. *Were they for eating? Even in my street days, I was not about to eat rat doo doo.*

"Come on, boy, give it a try. It's good for you. It's what all healthy dogs are supposed to eat."

Not this one. I didn't even want to try it. *And besides, I'm not a healthy dog, I'm sick, remember?*

"I don't think he's too excited about this new food, do you?" Mama asked Papa. "He's got to be hungry. I'm out of chicken and *tortillas.*"

"Come on, Lucky, eat your food," she begged me, bending down and picking up a handful of the dry pebbled food. I thought for a moment. *Shouldn't this begging be the other way around? Aren't I supposed to be 'the beggar?'*

"Please, Lucky, eat your food."

I sniffed at the food again and she popped one in my mouth. It was hard and dry and I quickly spit it out. *I'm not all that hungry. Remember you gave me a huge breakfast this morning.*

"I don't think he likes it," Papa said. "I guess he's not used to fifty-dollar imported dog food."

Mama shook her head. All I've got is some left-over rice."

"That might work," Papa said. "Remember, he grew up near the Japanese restaurant there on Reforma."

"You're right. Maybe he scavenged through their trash and got used to the taste of rice. *Your darn right, I did, Mama, except when they started shooting at me. I love rice, especially with a little soy sauce and meat tossed in.*

"Why don't you toss it with a bit of meat and some butter and see if he'll eat it."

Of course I'll eat it! Come on, bring it on! I waited in anticipation, my nose high in the air, sniffing wildly.

"Good idea, I know Polly always liked meat and rice."

Oh, oh, not the 'ghost dog' thing again . . .

A few minutes later, Mama emerged from the house with a plate piled high with rice and some chopped up meat.

I started to jump up and down on my hind legs, then placed my front paws on Mama's skirt, almost knocking her over in my excitement.

"Hey Lucky, take it easy, I'm going to feed you."

"Look, he's going nuts at that smell!" Papa said. "But sit, you have to sit before you get fed. And don't you go jumping up on people. It's not polite. I'll make a gentleman out of you before it's all over," he added.

I quickly got that idea right when Papa pushed on my rear-end and forced me to sit. *"Sientete, sit, Lucky."*

It's another command I quickly had to learn. That is, if I wanted to be fed. Papa insisted on it. He was absolutely determined that I obey all those dog commands he'd been studying up on.

But I had to really restrain myself when Mama dumped the rice into my old bowl after pouring the dried food by its side. I wanted that rice so badly I could already taste it. It had been a long time since I'd eaten any rice, not since the Japanese restaurant had installed new heavy duty steel dumpsters in order to keep us street dogs from having a bit of sushi.

"Get on your mark, get set, go get it," Papa said, quickly lowering his hand. I figured that was my command to go eat, and I almost dove into the bowl it smelled so good. I gobbled up the food in a matter of seconds. *What a feast!* I licked the bowl round and round again until I almost wore out my tongue. In the end, it was so clean and shiny that I could see myself in it.

"Guess we're going to be making a lot of rice," Mama said. "Lucky loved it."

"Guess so . . . but maybe he'll get used to dry food sooner or later,"

Later, I thought. *Much, much later.*

Papa put the dry food back in the bowl, just in case and I let it sit there all day long.

There was no fooling me. I was not about to eat rat doo-doo, even if it did smell like chicken.

Tired from my eating marathon and still not feeling up to snuff, I decided to take another nap.

When I awoke, they surprised me with another gift.

"Look, Lucky, we've got another *regalo* for you. You're going to love this one," Mama said, holding a small package in the air. I jumped for it until Papa gave me a stern look, so I quickly sat in place and begged.

Mama placed it before me. It didn't take me long to figure out how to open a *regalo*, a gift, and I quickly tore the wrapping paper from around it. Inside it smelled like leather. Actually they were called rawhide chews. Now these, I could get used to. Even though they were tough and hard, they reminded me of the bones I used to gnaw on from the butcher shop. And I had a feeling that these were going to be the closest thing I'd be getting to a bone in my new home as I'd overheard Mama tell Papa that bones were dangerous for us dogs because we might get a splinter caught in our throat and choke to death. *Let me tell you something, Mama, I've eaten more than a few bones in my life and I'm still walking.*

Mama and Papa had one last gift for me. It was what they called a toy. It was soft and round and bright red. It didn't have such a good smell and I decided right away that I wasn't going to eat it no matter how hard they tried to force me. *Thank you very much, dear parents, I'll stick with rice.*

Papa picked it off the ground in front of me and tossed it far across the grass. "Go get it, Lucky Boy," he yelled. "Bring it back to Papa."

I watched as it landed in the middle of the yard, then looked up at Papa.

"You're supposed go and fetch it, bring it back to me," Papa said.

That'll be the day, Papa. Why would I want to run clear across the yard just to pick up a piece of non-edible rubber? This is one trick I'm not about to learn.

But Papa didn't give up on my 'fetching lessons.' Over and over he tossed that darn ball in the air and told me to 'go get it.' Over and over again, I watched him wasting so much of his own energy, running to pick it up himself. *Boy, he must be ready for a siesta by now.* I stretched out on the grass and continued to watch him.

"If it's the last thing I do . . . I'm gonna . . ." He looked at me and laughed. "I know you're not stupid. Maybe you're not a 'born' athlete. I guess fetching is just not your thing."

Papa had finally realized I was no retriever. Good thing, as I was not about to go into a marsh and haul out some dead ducks. Didn't matter, though. Papa was no hunter. I think he just wanted someone to play with.

Okay, Papa, I'll play with you. I jumped up, raced in a huge circle around the yard three or four times, then I reversed direction and ran the other way the same distance.

"Look, Lucky's self-exercising!" Papa said. "Guess we'll never have to walk him again."

Not so fast, Papa. I love to go on walks. I'm just showing you that I'm playful. But it depends on the sport.

What a day it had been, one filled with walking, *mercado* sniffing, poking and jabbing, new beds, bowls and toys, my favorite rice dish, and finally a romp on the grass. What more could a street dog ask for?

CHAPTER 7
NEW FACES, NEW PLACES

According to Papa, there was only one more task on his 'training list.' That was getting me into the house. Over and over again he coached me, but over and over again I refused to go inside that big cave. Why I was as stubborn as a Mexican donkey.

"Come on, Lucky, come on," Papa said. "Come inside the house where it's nice and warm."

I looked inside the kitchen door, thought about it for a moment. *No . . . I like it out here where I can see the sky and roll in the grass.*

But the day finally came, when I could no longer resist. My parents were in the kitchen preparing some kind of pasta-meat dish, and boy oh boy did it smell good. Why it was so tantalizing that I answered my natural instincts for food and walked right through the kitchen door and up to the stove without thinking.

"Look!" Mama said, pointing at me. "Lucky's decided to become a house dog."

"All right!" Papa said. "My teaching methods finally worked." He looked at me, my nose in the air, sniffing all those good smells. "But he's not going to become a beggar," Papa said, as I looked at him pleadingly, even remembering to sit like he'd taught me.

That should certainly be worth a piece of meat. But it never came my way. Instead, Papa went out to the garage, retrieved my bed and placed it under the kitchen bar. I have to admit it looked kind of cozy to me there next to the stove – the food source – so I jumped right in. It was warm and inviting in their bright blue kitchen, with all the good smells and Mama and Papa working over the stove. So I decided to stay.

But soon I discovered that there was much more to explore in this new place, so gingerly I crept into the dining room. It was huge and had a great big wooden table right in the middle of it. I wondered what it was for. *Not a bad hiding place in case I ever need it.*

Next, I proceeded to the living room, but the wooden floor was slick and I almost fell as my legs spread out in all directions. It frightened me not to have stable footing like I did on the grass and sidewalk outside. But it was warm and so smooth. The living room had a big hole in the wall that I would later come to know as a fireplace. At first, I thought it would be a good escape route until I discovered it led into a blank cinderblock wall and had only a tiny hole in its top, hardly big enough for a mouse to squeeze through, let alone me. I quickly gave up on the fireplace and moved toward a wine-colored flowered thing on the floor. I would later know it as Papa's favorite Persian rug, soon to be my favorite, as well. Boy was it soft and cushy and it had a great view of the front garden, as the entire front of the house was mostly low windows. Right away, I knew it was a wonderful observation spot, and I quickly settled into my new-found territory. *Why would I want to be out on that cold cement when I can lounge away the day right here?* But I wasn't about to go up those *terracotta* things that climbed toward the sky. I'd never seen steps before. *Who on earth would want to climb up there in the air?* Not me, I'm a down-to-earth dog, that's for sure.

After my first encounter with 'house-dog life,' I more or less became a full-time 'insider' if you know what I mean. Mama loved this fact. She liked having me underfoot, following her like a little shadow. Papa wasn't quite so sure about this new full-time 'living arrangement' of mine, and he continually went around the house with the Dust Buster collecting bits of my fur, which floated all around. I'm a 'shedder'– what more can I say? I later learned that it was bad for Mama's asthma, but she happily took her medication and used her inhaler, just for the sake of my being a housedog.

I still enjoyed the garden, however, and quickly I became an infamous 'self-exerciser," so Papa called it. He'd tell everyone he met how I liked to race around the yard in large circles, running as fast as I could. After at least three rounds in one direction, I'd reverse and go the other way round and round and round like a rabid dog. All this in the name of exercise. I never knew why Papa got such a kick out of the 'changing directions' part. *Did he think I wanted to make myself dizzy by going the same direction all the time? Of course not.* I was no dumb Dashhound-type.

* * * *

I was soon to find out that Papa and Mama knew a lot of people. They loved to introduce me as their 'little Mexico City street dog' and then tell all their 'Lucky tales' to anyone willing to listen. Of course, Mama would contribute to Papa's 'almost tall' tales, as well, except she'd add the 'adorable dog' part and get all teary-eyed. *Come on Mama, I'm not all that cute. Certainly not cute enough to cry about.* I was sure many of these people got downright bored. Who on earth wanted to hear their little 'street dog' story all the time? I was even getting tired of it. So what if I was a street dog in my early years? What's the big 'doggie' deal about that?

Of course, Rosalia was the first person in Mama's and Papa's long list that I was to meet. I liked her from the moment I sniffed her scent beneath the gate from my sunbathing spot early one morning. *Buzz . . . buzz*, went the bell on the gate. *What on earth is that horrible noise that woke me from my nap?* I got up disgustingly, not even taking time to stretch. Mama hurried from the house to the gate, took me by the collar and opened it. *No free-form exploration for me today.* But I really wasn't in the mood of exploring anything but my new home as yet. There was so much to see inside the confines of those walls.

The face that greeted us was full of smiles.

"Hola, Señora, Buenos dias," said a short plump woman with salt and pepper hair. Her skin was a dark bronze and she wore black slipper-like shoes.

"Buenos dias, Rosalia," Mama answered, giving her a quick hug.

When Rosalia saw me for the first time, she looked rather surprised, but the smile still held on her lips. That was a good sign. It probably meant she was not a 'kicker.' Besides, she had on these soft shoes, so I knew she couldn't kick me too hard, even if she tried. Instead she bent down and patted me on the head.

"Él perro! El perro!" she said to Mama. Of course Mama was all smiles as she showed me off to Rosalia for the first time.

I didn't know it then, but Rosalia was our *muchacha*, our maid, and she was to become one of my best friends in Mexico City. I have to admit that at first I was surprised she honest-to-goodness seemed to like me. Most Mexicans were scared to death of dogs and would not have touched me with a twenty-foot pole. But not Rosalia.

Later I learned why. She had been raised on a farm near *Valle de Bravo*, the oldest of thirteen children. She knew how to handle any kind of animal or kid ever born, especially us dogs, as her *padre* used them to herd the family's flock of sheep.

Immediately Rosalia wanted to know where my parents got me. I think she already knew by the grin on her face. We'd both been 'there' before and it created an instant bond between us.

"Venga, Lucky, come, " she smiled. I followed her in adoration, like a little lamb being led to the chopping block, somehow knowing she would become my friend, and, you guessed it – a great source of food.

She didn't disappoint me in either area. Now that I had finally become a 'house dog – the 'Lord of the Manor,' so to speak, I liked to follow Rosalia around while she worked. She loved to dance to Tex-Mex Selena music, mop in hand, her belly bouncing. Once in a while she'd raise the mop in the air and do a kind of salute. At first I thought she was after me and I'd scamper to hide under our dining room table. But soon I decided it was just part of her Selena routine, pretending to hold a microphone.

Around noon, Rosalia always went into the kitchen to prepare her meal. Mama left her some pretty good fixins, so she'd make *carne asada* or *arachera* from thinly sliced beef, and sauté it with peppers and onions. It made my mouth water and I could hardly contain myself as I wagged my tail furiously. Fortunately, she'd share some of the tidbits with me. I especially liked it when she'd roll the flour and water into small balls and make home-made *tortillas*. Boy, were they good! I suppose they reminded me of my youth, of my days on the street with Buddy, when some people used to throw us pieces of leftover *tortilla* when we'd beg real 'hard-like.'

I loved my afternoons with Rosalia, when Mama and Papa were often away from the house. She was always smiling and singing, scrubbing away like there was no end to the wooden floor boards and terracotta tile. One thing she didn't like about me, however, was my fur. Rosalia would accumulate piles of it with her dust mop and then show me.

"Naughty Lucky," she would say, presenting me with a mound of fur half my size, yet smiling at the same time. I just looked puzzled as I sniffed it. It did smell very familiar, like me, but I had no idea where it came from. Although I have to admit that with the amount of fur she gathered, you'd think I would be one bald dog by now.

I also continued to adore my Persian rug. It lay in the living room before the cabinet which held the stereo. From my velvety vantage point, I could listen to all kinds of nice music and keep a watchful eye not only on the living room, but the entire front garden. The entry hall with the antique wooden double doors that were used for guests, and the kitchen eating area were also visible. I was close enough to catch all the good smells from the kitchen and head there whenever the scent was enticing enough.

I would often think, *What a life I have, lying here on this cushy rug, watching Rosalia work, and waiting for Mama and Papa to return home.* I really missed them when they were away and seldom took my eyes off the front gate, except, of course, when there was food involved or when Rosalia came toward my rug with the vacuum cleaner.

I hated that horrible loud monster. Too often it interrupted my afternoon naps. Whenever I heard its roar, I bolted from my rug and headed straight out the kitchen door and stayed in the garden until it was done with its onslaught.

Of course, the next best thing to my Persian rug was the front grass, where I'd roll and roll and roll like a twirling *burrito*, until my fur actually took on a greenish tint. Mama scolded me when I raced to my rug after my roll, claiming I was turning it green. Of course, I nodded in sympathy, before planting myself right in its center as she raced for the rug shampoo.

Papa, however, really freaked out when I got on his precious Persian carpet and more than once he hauled me off of it by the nape of the neck. I'd pretend growl when he did this and my sassing irritated him even more. *I'm not serious, Papa. I'd never bite you.* So not wanting to upset Papa, I started the whining whimpering routine when he pulled me away. I quickly learned this worked much better. Soon Papa would feel guilty and let me return to my rug.

"Lucky loves his rug," Mama would say. "We can get a new one when we return home."

"Yeah, right," Papa would answer. "Why not give the street dog a hand-woven Persian carpet worth thousands." Then he'd look at me tenderly and I knew he'd eventually give in.

"I know, we shouldn't let him lie on it, but he just loves this little rug so much and besides, it's really not our color." Mama looked at me sprawled on my rug and smiled. "It's pretty much worn out anyway."

"And covered with dog hair," Papa added. But he finally relented and let me have my rug to myself. Once in a while he'd scowl at me and make me feel guilty when I was stretched out on it, but for the most part he let it go. My time had definitely 'arrived.'

Except when 'Little Harold' came upon the scene. Then my life was temporarily in 'the dumps.' For you see, little Harold, the toddler son of my parents' friends, thought I was a miniature horse. From the second they entered our house, he was after me, pulling at my fur and ears and climbing aboard my back. I even tried the growling routine, but it didn't help. He just climbed right on, all twenty pounds of him. His mother and father thought it was so cute. They would tell Mama and Papa what a wonderful dog I was, that I deserved a medal. *No kidding. If only someone would get this little bugger off my back.*

Fortunately, Mama and Papa did not care for Harold's antics one bit. I was seriously hoping that Little Harold would no longer be on our guest list. Being compared to a carnival pony was not all that great, let me tell you.

But I did have one 'real' enemy – the propane delivery man. He was very dark and covered with grease and had black shaggy hair. The first time he came to the house to deliver the propane gas that we needed to cook with, I was lounging out on the front grass. When Rosalia opened the gate to let him in, I thought I'd seen a spook. It about scared the 'doggie' daylights out of me and I jumped to all fours and raced after him, snarling. I was certain he was going to abduct my dear Rosalia and I was not about to let him near her. Seeing nothing but my teeth headed in the direction of his ankle, the gas man dropped his hose and ladder and jumped on the back of his truck like a scared jack rabbit. I snarled right after him and tried to jump on board. He looked like he was going to bawl, maybe even poop in his pants, he was so afraid of me, a little thirty-pound dog. I almost felt like chuckling, but I was so intent on saving Rosalia, that I kept my snarly face intact.

Rosalia quickly came up to the truck, grabbed me by the collar. *"Bien, bien, Lucky,"* she said, it's okay. So I took the snarl off of my face and merely growled.

She told the man it was all right for him to get off the truck and hesitantly he climbed down, picked up his hose and ladder, looking like he would use them as a weapon against me. He sure did keep an eye on me as he climbed up the ladder and onto our roof. I barked and barked at him, my tail racing back and forth, as he put the propane into our tank. I might not have been so mean had I realized at the time that he was a necessary part in Rosalia's cooking routine.

Three years later, I still did the same act when the propane man arrived. Bark, bark, growl, snarl. He never did get used to me and I have to admit that I actually enjoyed scaring him. All I know is that he must have been one happy gas man when we headed north, back home to California.

Then there was Marta Eleana, Mama's Spanish teacher. She was one scared *señorita* when it came to me and avoided me like an eruption of *Popopapaketl,* the volcano outside of Mexico City.

The first time she was invited to our house for dinner with her *novio,* her boyfriend, she had forgotten about the new member of our family, namely me. Marta Eleana entered the front door, a big smile on her face. She carried a vase filled with flowers in one hand, and a basket of special Mexican cookies in the other. She looked nice enough to me and I sensed she carried food, so I popped up from my rug and ran right up to her, barking in greeting, my tail wagging. You would have thought I was Dracula, ready to bite into her neck. She took one look at me, screamed and threw the cookies and flowers into the air. Then she jumped up and flung herself into her boyfriend's arms, straddling her legs around him. I was shocked! *Was I having a bad hair day or something? Everyone always loves me – at least almost everyone.* But certainly not Marta Eleana. She screeched and screeched like a drunken coyote and I couldn't even enjoy all the broken cookies that were scattered across the floor amid the flower petals because of the racket she made.

Embarrassed, Papa quickly grabbed my collar and pulled me straight out into the back yard, while Mama tried to comfort Marta Eleana.

"Don't worry, Lucky won't hurt you. He's a very friendly dog."

Marta Elena still clung to her boyfriend, her face full of terror. "Oh, *Señora,* I hate dogs! I hate them!" She stared in the direction Papa had taken me, watched as he closed the door behind me. Boy, was I one pissed off dog, having to stand outside the back slider door and whine all night, begging to get inside. But this time I was pleading to closed ears.

"Tequila, I need a shot of tequila," Marta Eleana said, still shaking. At least by this time, she had let go of her boy friend and managed to hobble to the living room sofa. But she was still very pale.

Mama and Papa felt just terrible and Papa rushed to the liquor cabinet for a shot glass. Marta Eleana drank it all in one great big gulp. Then she looked like she was about to tip over.

"I thought you never drank?" Mama said.

"I don't, *Señora,* but I'm scared to death. "You see, I was bitten by a dog when I was a little girl and he ran away, so my parents were sure he had rabies. I had to have a series of painful shots in my stomach so I wouldn't get rabies. I will never forget them."

"We're so sorry," Mama said. "We had no idea you were so frightened of dogs."

Let me tell you one thing – Marta Eleana didn't take her eye off the dining room glass door all night long. Several times she even asked Papa if it was locked. *Like I was a trick dog who could open locks, a Dogsmith that could break right in.* I wish I could have. I think I would have given that Marta Eleana a sample of my wrath. *How could she not like me?* I just couldn't understand this for the life of me. I felt so bad. *I love everyone.* After meeting up with Marta Eleana, I was even ready to accept 'Little Harold' back into my life again.

I think I hung my head all night long, and when Marta Eleana and her *novio* finally left, Rosalia brought me into the house and gave me a heaping plate of *carne asada* and rice. At least Marta Elena had brought a gigantic amount of good chow to my life, even if I did have to wait outside in the cold all night long.

Lots of new faces, that's for sure. There were plenty of them around our place. Little did I realize that there would be ever so many more in my future.

CHAPTER 8
PAPA

I loved my Papa from the day I met him. Of course, he loved Mama and me, too. He also loved other things, especially things 'mechanical.' I even nick-named him 'the Fix-Up Man,' because he was always fixing things, like the dishwasher or the garage door or the car, even mending my bed, or gluing my dish when I accidentally licked it clean too hard and tipped it over. He always called it my "licking the platter clean routine," as my tongue went round and round and round its shiny surface. Mama didn't even have to wash my dish after I was finished, but she always did. You know her, 'Mrs. Clean.'

I'll always remember the first time I saw Papa with a hammer and screwdriver. I was downright scared. They looked like 'dog disabling tools' to me, like something he could whack me over the head with. Quickly I darted for my hiding spot beneath the dining room table.

But I soon learned Papa was not after me. But he had the funniest habit. Papa liked to hit the wall, the cabinet, or the door with his weapons, anything he could get near. I could never understand why he did this, but I began to follow him around the house on his hammering journeys nonetheless. That's because I loved it when he was down at my level on his knees. It was great having him just my height and I couldn't help but splatter him with a few quick kisses and licks.

"Lucky, stop that," Papa would say, kind of pushing me away. "I'm not into dog smooching."

Oh, you will be someday Papa, but for now I'll settle for a good old pat on the back.

63

Papa must have read my mind, for he always stopped what he was doing and patted me or scratched behind my ears.

"Can't you understand you're in my way, Old Boy?" Papa would say. Of course I didn't. All I knew was that I wanted to be as close to Papa as possible. And when he patted me so nicely, what else could I do? I'd just have to give him another good old smooch.

Of course, he'd quickly brush off its residue with the back of his hand and then back to work he'd go, singing and whistling the entire time.

I even learned to nap through Papa's construction noise after a while. I figured if I could sleep with the roof dogs' barks across the street, I could sleep with anything. But at first Papa's noise confused me when I wasn't in the same room. I thought the pounding was someone at our front door and I'd race toward it, barking furiously. But no one ever came to answer the door, so I'd give up and trot back to my bed.

"Dumb dog," Papa said, looking up from the bookcase he was fixing. "It was just me and my hammer. No one's at the front door."

I soon figured this out for myself and no longer wasted my energy door crashing.

Papa also loved another kind of work – his job, which was away from our house. He's an engineer. He designs things, whatever that means, and in Mexico, he ran his company's office.

Every morning, as a courtesy, I peeked from my cozy warm bed to nod "goodbye" to Papa and then promptly went back to sleep. He always carried a black leather bag with what he called his "laptop" inside. He also had a thing in his pocket that buzzed and its frequency hurt my sensitive dog ears every time it went off. He even had a tiny telephone like the one in our house that rang and rang, so he often had it to his ear. I can tell you one thing, it didn't take me long to figure out that Mama didn't care for all those gadgets Papa seemed to love so much. She called them his "umbilical cords to work," whatever that meant. But I did notice that whenever Papa paid too much attention to his gadgets, that he didn't pay much attention to Mama and me. That upset us both. In fact, it really hurt my feelings. Sometimes I even wanted to snatch all his gadgets from him when he was napping on the sofa and bury them out in my bone hole in the garden. I don't think Mama would have minded that even one little bit.

Anyway, even though I didn't like Papa's work things, I was dying to know where he went every morning. Eventually I got to find out.

"Come on, Lucky," Mama said one afternoon. "Let's go pick up Papa at his office."

I didn't need to be asked twice, so I jumped into the back of our van when our driver, Javier, opened the door. Quickly, I moved away from the door as I knew he liked to slam it real fast, trying to catch my tail inside. Somehow I quickly got the idea that Javier didn't really like me very much. Maybe it was all that dog fur that I 'accidentally' deposited in the back of the van. It didn't really matter why. He was smart enough to know that 'I ruled' around Mama and Papa's house, so he had to treat me nice, especially when they were around. Still, I'd never forgiven him for the time he put me in the trunk of a company car to take me to the vet. Boy, did that piss me off! I was so glad Mama and Papa found out about that one. I never had to ride like a hijacked kidnap victim again.

Anyway, back to Papa.

65

Papa's office was quite a long drive from our house and I loved looking out the rear window as we sped down the *Periferico* and then onto the *Via Ducto*, to a part of Mexico City I had never seen before. The first thing I noticed when we pulled up in front of Papa's tall office building was that a large stray dog lived across the street beside the body shop, neither in a strange location for Mexico City. For you see, here things just kind of flowed together – an office building, a body shop, some restaurants, a hotel, some graffiti, a few stray dogs, whatever . . .

Anyway, every time I visited Papa's office this dog was out front or lying beside the cars the mechanics were working on. I liked to sit in the back of the van and bark a "hello" from my safe vantage point. The dog was large and so covered with grease that I wasn't sure if it was actually white, but I think he was. And he had a mean look in its eyes. It was the kind of dog I remembered biting me during my street dog days and I was not about to meet him up 'close and personal.' I also think my parents probably thought he had rabies and we were not allowed to get anywhere near each other. Even so, Mama did have a soft spot for this dog and sometimes brought food for him and kind of slipped it out the door when he wasn't looking. And this big dog was one hungry guy. He always had his nose to the ground searching for food, probably surviving on the few scraps the workers tossed to him, so Mama's food was very welcome. It didn't even make me feel too bad that she was paying attention to him. Although I wouldn't admit it, it made me feel good. I knew what a great life I had come into and I wanted to 'share the bones,' as we say in dog lingo.

I spent quite a few hours watching this dog at Papa's office because I never did actually get to go inside since dogs were not allowed. Imagine that! But at least the guards let me sit in the car in the parking structure waiting for Papa to come out. And when he did, boy did I make a racket in greeting! The entire parking lot echoed with my "hellos" and everyone would turn and look at our van. Even the guards put their hands over their ears when Papa wasn't looking. But no one said a word. After all, Papa was the *jefe grande,* the big boss, and I couldn't figure out why he'd jump into the car so fast before Javier could even open the door for him. Quickly he'd slam it shut, like he was embarrassed of me or something.

"Stop that noise!" Papa scolded, at the same time reaching out to give me a pat.

Even though I was a chronic vocal greeter, I still got to go to Papa's office quite a few more times. In fact, one time I was very naughty and ran away. But that's another story.

* * * *

Something else about my Papa. He wasn't always working. He also liked to have fun. He loved music and often played it at our house. I grew fond of it, too and would often lie on my Persian rug before the stereo and listen to Chopin, Beethoven and the likes, all of which proved to be darn good dog snoozing tunes. But then Papa would put on some salsa or rock n' roll and completely destroy my *siesta.*

Another thing Papa loved was to go out to restaurants. That meant goodies for me in fancy 'take away' bags. The entire time Mama and Papa were away at the restaurant, I anxiously awaited their return, wondering what surprise I would receive that evening. I would be so excited that I couldn't even concentrate on sleeping or guarding, so instead I'd just roll around on our colorful soft Mexican Oaxacan rugs in the hallway until I had them in a ball and I was like a sausage stuffed inside. Believe me, sometimes it was tough getting out when I heard our van pull into the driveway.

They never disappointed. Sometimes it was pasta from Mezzanote; sometimes fried rice from Hong's Chinese Café. Or even better, I loved the leftovers from their favorite restaurant, Rincon Argentine. It soon became my favorite, as well. I loved digging into their flame-broiled leftovers and would eagerly await their return on Rincon nights out.

Yes, my Papa was near perfect in my eyes. Of course, by this time I was sure that I was the 'hot tamale' of his eyes, as well.

CHAPTER 9
MAMA

I soon came to realize Mama loved certain things, too. She spent hours typing away at her computer. Sometimes it made me jealous that she paid so much attention to that stupid white plastic thing which perched on her desk. It didn't even have a tail to wag at her. Instead it made this clicking sound which really bothered my ears. Of course, at the time I didn't know Mama wrote books – even a book about me. Can you imagine that? A street dog with his own biography?

Of course, Mama also loved Papa and, of course, she adored me. I could feel it in the way she touched me, smiled at all my little dog antics she was certain were one of a kind. I wanted to smile right back at her, but since dogs don't smile, I wagged my tail as hard as I could whenever she made a fuss over me. This seemed to satisfy her quite perfectly and she'd give me a great big hug in return. Sometimes I thought she was going to hug the life right out of me and I had to start giving her some serious slobberish smooches just so she would let go of me.

"Lucky, please, you're drowning me!" she'd laugh. "Just drowning me with all your canine love, you sweet little dog!"

I soon realized Mama loved all us critters, like when she took dog food to the stray by Papa's work. But I was soon to discover that her imagination went bigger than that. She also took lots of dog food when we went to ride the boats in *Xochimilco*, the ancient Aztec floating gardens and canals in the southern part of Mexico City. They had these boats that Mama said looked like Italian gondolas. We went there with her friends and took a

69

picnic and floated around the gardens all afternoon. It was one of my favorite 'dog outing' destinations. That's because there were so many dogs there – stray dogs, that is. My kind of critters. I'm sure that some of them must have been my long lost relatives, although I didn't recognize their scent. But most of them were a golden color and had this kind of 'Terrier/Lab' look. But I never did get a chance to really get up 'close and personal' with any of them. You see, they were not gliding through the water and picnicking on a boat like I was, enjoying a nice *siesta* on a full tummy. They were definitely on the opposite end of the 'doggie spectrum.' 'Official Street Dogs' by trade, they'd hang over the sides of the canal banks begging for our leftover picnic food.

They were so hungry and skinny, those poor dogs, their life was so tough. But still, I liked to bark "hello" to them. Of course, they barked back, eyeing our picnic basket, probably imagining it was filled with great big bones and pieces of meat. Sometimes they even had tiny pups by their sides. Mama felt sorry for them, too, so she and our driver, Javier, would open cans of dog food and toss it to them as we passed by. Boy, did they fight for that food and every bit of garbage tossed from other passing boats. It made me appreciate my life even more and I wondered how long they could survive. But every time we went back to *Xochimilco*, there they were! This 'reality check of life' like it was on the street always did me good, and I've never forgotten mine and Mama's visits to *Xochimilco*.

Of course, Mamma liked to do other things besides feed stray dogs. In fact, there was one thing she liked in Mexico City best of all – excluding me of course. That was *Hogar Dulce Hogar*, which means 'Home Sweet Home.' And it was not our home in *Lomas de*

70

Chapultepec I'm talking about. It was an orphanage. Mama really liked to help out there and she went almost every day, much to my 'doggie dismay,' as that meant I'd be left at home. But I was to learn to love *Hogar Dulce Hogar*, as well, since I soon convinced Mama that I should become a regular visitor.

"*Hogar*," as we called it, was on 'the other side of town' from our place. Here there were no purple blooming jacaranda trees and great big houses surrounded by high walls. Instead this *colonia* was splattered with graffiti, tiny shops and small stucco or cinderblock houses, often painted bright blue or yellow when their owners could afford paint. There were smells I recognized from my days on the street – of frying *chorizos*, *chicheron*, and corn *tortillas*. It made me slobber like crazy, much to Javier's dismay. Sometimes he'd just turn his head away from driving and give me the dirtiest look. If I could have told Mama about his 'looks,' and sometimes mistreatment of me, I think he would have been one unemployed driver, that's for sure.

Anyway, Mama often arrived at Hogar with a whole van load of things for the children. Sometimes there was barely room for me in the back and I'd even scowl at Javier, when he was loading all that stuff inside. Not that it did me much good. Sometimes I even wanted to growl at him, but I'd hold my tongue. Being the gentle dog I am, I just crunched into my spot by the rear window and didn't growl a thing. *At least I was going along for the ride.*

Let me tell you a little about the orphanage. A lady named Ofelia started it after her husband died. She was out hiking in the mountains near Mexico City one day and found an abandoned baby, kind of like when Mama and Papa found me. Anyway, just like Mama and Papa took me home, she decided to take him home. She named him Moses, like the baby in the Bible who was discovered along the River Nile. Well, little Moses was not an only child for long. For you see, Ofelia thought finding Moses was a sign for her to start an orphanage, so that's just what she did. Sometimes I've wondered if Mama and Papa thought of doing the same thing – bringing home lots of stray dogs and starting a 'dognage.' It was not to be. Papa has always said "one dog is plenty for us." It just made me breathe a sigh of relief when he said this, knowing I would not have to share my parents with any other dog, except the 'ghost dog,' Polly, of course.

Anyway, by the time me and Mama came onto the *Hogar* scene, Ofelia had over thirty abandoned *niños* – that's what we call children in Spanish--living in her old two-story house. And they kept on coming until there were forty children and the house was bursting at its seams. Beds were stacked in every room; there were several sets of tables and chairs in the kitchen; children were always lined up outside the two bathrooms. I always wondered why they just didn't go out and adopt a few street dogs, just to make the place complete.

It didn't matter. The first time Mama took me to the orphanage, I got a real warm fuzzy dog feeling. It was a place so full of love that even me, a former calloused street dog, could feel it in the air. And boy, were the *niños* happy to see me. I was quite the novelty as most of them had never been introduced to a 'proper' clean dog and one they could pet. Of course, at first I frightened the livin' 'doggie daylights' out of them, even though I wagged my tail and moved in for a pat or two. They'd jump back like frightened rabbits and cling to one other and just stare at me, their brown eyes wide.

But that was soon to change because Mama did not give up on convincing the children that we dogs are 'kids' best friends.

"El perro bueno, good dog," she would tell them over and over again. *"Lucky esta el perro bueno!"*

Still they were not so sure. But finally a girl named Veronica decided to pet me. She looked totally surprised when I didn't bite her hand off. Of course this started an avalanche of little hands patting me wherever they could. Why I almost thought I was going to suffocate or fall apart, but I dutifully stood my post beside Mama and let them do their thing. After all, me and these *niños* shared the same past. They, too, had been abandoned and unloved. It just made my fur stand on end to think of those little kids on the street, fighting each other for food and digging a hole to sleep in at night like us street dogs did.

But there was one thing at *Hogar* that really did bug me. That's when the very young ones got into the 'let's pet Lucky' act. When Alicia, Juan Carlos and Estefania finally decided I was not going to eat them for lunch, they really went after me. All they wanted to do was pull my ears and poke my eyes out. That was just a little bit more than I could take, so quickly I headed under a table where I thought they could not reach me. It just reminded me too much of my 'Harold experiences.' But low and behold, I'd forgotten how short they were and how adept they were at crawling. It didn't take them but a minute to join me in my hideout, their little hands ready for tugging. Oh well, what could I do? I had to just grin and bear it.

Another thing. The *niños,* and I mean all forty of them, wanted to walk me. That's a lot of miles on the footpads of one little dog. Let me tell you, when we'd load a bunch of the kids into our van and the vans belonging to the orphanage for a picnic in *Chapultepec Park*, it was one full load. Of course, everyone wanted to sit in the back with me and it was like being squashed into a can of pinto beans. But the *niños* loved it. Oh, how'd they'd shriek when we'd get close to the park. It about did my ears in! On those days I seriously wished I owned a pair of earplugs.

And then when we'd pull into the parking lot, out came my leash. Guess what that brought about? Forty pairs of hands all wanting to walk me – one dog. Of course Mama looked out for me and made them take turns. Boy, I about walked the skin off my paws on those days. But I didn't mind. It put such smiles on the faces of the little *niños*. And besides, they even shared their ham and cheese sandwiches with me, which certainly made up for my sore paws.

Back at the orphanage, there was always lots of fun in store, as well. Mama and the other volunteers had lots of *fiestas* – that's Mexican parties – for the kids. That translated to lots of leftover food for me. But as much as I tried, I was never too crazy about pizza, especially the kind with pineapple slices on top, which all the kids loved. McDonald's hamburgers didn't do too much for me either, as they were always smothered in mustard, pickles and onion, not to my doggie taste at all. Why on earth would anyone want to waste a good piece of meat like that? I just couldn't understand it.

Another thing I learned to dislike – those dumb *piñatas* the *niños* loved so much. Why they'd smack that big long stick so hard – and blindfolded at that – I was sure I was going to get it right in the snout sooner or later. Finally I learned when *fiesta* time came, I'd head straight to my hiding spot beneath a table, hoping to pick up on some dropped food. Even the little ones wouldn't join me when there was a *piñata* to be had, so I felt safe there. Besides, I didn't care much for what was stuffed inside those *piñatas* anyway – only candies and tiny rubber toys – neither in good doggie taste. Now if they'd stuffed them with sausages, dog biscuits and rawhide toys, they definitely would have captured my attention, even if it did mean receiving a few bonks on the head.

Then there were the times the orphans came to our house for a visit. It was such fun. We'd race around the front grass all day until there was a brown muddy track all across it. Of course Mama and Rosalia would make lots of goodies, and sometimes Javier cooked hamburgers on our barbecue. Of course, I'd sit beside him when mealtime came, hoping he'd drop a hamburger or two my way. Only once did that happen and I gobbled it up so fast I burned my mouth. Instead, Javier would stuff the extra patties into his own mouth, not even thinking of poor little old me. It really ticked me off.

But then Mama would come to the rescue. "Javier, please make sure you save a couple for Lucky after the children have eaten," she'd say.

So Javier would scowl and drop one to the ground for me, making sure it would land on the dirt in our flower garden. But just to show him, I'd eat it anyway and then Mama would get all upset because I'd eaten dirt. *Dirt, Mama? What's a little dirt for one with a street dog background?* If only she'd known how many dirt-covered bones I'd gnawed on in my day.

But Mama couldn't help herself. She was just one clean freak. She seriously loved to clean, even though we had Rosalia. She just couldn't help but pick up a mop or sponge when she could have spent all of that 'quality time' with me. But to tell you the truth, I didn't have much control over her when it came to cleaning. I think she really liked the smell of that pine-scented Mexican cleaner that wafted out of every household in Mexico City. But I have to admit, not once did I ever have to sleep on a dirty bed at my new residence or eat from a dirty bowl. Not with my mama, Mrs. Clean, around.

CHAPTER 10
LUPITA

Every Saturday morning Mama, Papa and I liked to go to a leafy area of Mexico City called *Polanco*. This is where the 'Juniors' of Mexico City liked to hang out. That's the rich kids. In my personal 'street dog' opinion, Juniors are one dangerous group. Not only are they real 'kickers,' but they drive around like Speedy Gonzales in their Ferraris and Jaguars and are a definite threat to maids and us 'dogs on the street.' I can't tell you how many times I raced from beneath their cars on *Avenida de Reforma*. Personally, I think what most of them need is a good old lickin' from their papas. I know my papa would never let me behave like that.

Anyway, besides the Juniors, Polanco was a really nice place, and on Saturday mornings there were few Juniors to be found. I'm sure they were all home in their fancy beds. I really liked it here because of the tree-lined streets, which, of course contained lots of marking possibilities for me, much to Papa's irritation. He hated it when I stopped every twenty feet or so to do 'my dog thing.' One time he counted thirty-eight stops in just one short walk.

It was so nice and cool here and there was no broken glass to watch out for, and no sudden holes in the nicely paved sidewalks that I could just disappear in. Yes, *Polanco* was a great place for being 'on the leash' in my opinion. It certainly was very different from most of Mexico City. Even the buildings were perfect, either Mexican Colonial or ultra-modern. They were filled with restaurants, sidewalk cafes and fancy shops – 'designer shops,' as Mama called them, whatever that means.

All I know is that in front of each one of these 'designer shops' stood a guard with a great big gun. Boy, did those gun-toting guards scare all the guests that came to visit us in Mexico City. Most of them were even afraid to go to our grocery store, Superama, or the mall for that matter, because of them. Why our visitors acted like they'd never seen a gun before. As I had not yet been to America, I just assumed that guns were standard issue outside of all stores. Yet why anyone would want to stand around all day holding a gun is beyond me. Anyway, the first time I tried to sniff one of the guard's legs as we were walking along in *Polanco*, Papa gave me a good strong lesson in obedience. Why, he about yanked my neck right off! *Don't worry, Papa, I'm not about to mark him – just checking him out.* But I've always considered myself a fast learner and certainly learned one thing. *Sniffing at guys carrying guns is not permitted.* Why, I'm not sure, but I wasn't about to test Papa in this department again.

Our favorite little cappuccino place was right on *Avenida El Presidente Mazarek*. Lots of good smells always came from its door although I was never permitted inside. There were some little tables cupped by red umbrellas out front in a tiny courtyard and I was allowed to wait beneath one of them while Mama and Papa went in to get their cappuccinos.

Mama was always looking out the door checking on me like I was about to evaporate into thin air or something. *Don't worry, Mama, I'm not about to go anywhere – I smell food in the air.* But I whined a little just so she'd be sure I was still there waiting.

"I'm always afraid someone's going to steal Lucky," she once told Papa.

He laughed and shook his head. "Who on earth do you think is going to steal a street dog?"

Mama finally smiled, too. "I suppose you're right. There are certainly plenty of them to go around in this city."

* * * *

One Saturday when we were on our weekly *Polanco* visit, something really strange happened to us and it didn't have anything to do with me doing a 'disappearing act.' I called it 'fate.' Papa called it 'coincidental.' Mama called it 'a miracle.' Who knows . . .

While walking along a shaded street near the *carneceria* and flower market, we dropped into my favorite pet store. I always wagged my tail real hard when we came close as I knew Mama and Papa would stop and buy me a treat. They also had a water dish out front for us dogs, something very strange for Mexico City. Mama and Papa had decided I needed a new bed to fit into the back of the van for when we traveled and that suited me just fine. A treat and a new bed all in one day – now that wasn't bad at all.

I jumped from one bed to the other in the pet store, trying them all out. The clerk kind of eyed me like she was irritated, but she realized Mama and Papa's frequent purchasing power, so let me go at it. *It's not like I'm dirty or something.* So over and over again I jumped in and out of beds. The pink and white bed was very cushy, but not my color. Can you imagine a 'macho dog' like me sleeping in a pink bed? Why I'd be the laughing stock of 'street dog talk.' Then there was this black bed, which Papa quickly vetoed, sure it would collect too much of my golden fur. Mama found a bed with little cats with bows on their heads but soon decided it was too 'catish' for me. Finally one got all of our approval. It was gray and white, with just about the right degree of 'dog cushiness' and it would match our van.

"Perfect size for your street dog curl," Mama said, selecting it from the pile.

"And Javier will love it for hair containment," Papa added.

Of course, I jumped right in and tested it, panting my pleasure in agreement. But I quickly jumped out when I spied a dirty white mid-sized dog outside drinking from the bowl of water.

Lupita? Is that really you? What are you doing here? It was Lupita all right! I remembered her well from The Gully, as she was quickly recognizable from the big long tear in her left ear. Why, she'd even been my girlfriend for a while until Alfonzo – that big over-grown mutt – had taken her away from me. It was not without a fight, however. I still have the bite mark on my back to prove it.

Without seeking permission from Papa, I ran outside to greet her.

"Oh, look," Mama said. "Another street dog like Lucky!"

"And a recent mother," Papa added. "Her teats are swollen and full of milk."

"I wonder where her litter is?" Mama said. "Poor things."

"Most likely they won't survive," Papa said. "Most of them don't."

"Look, Lucky," Mama said, turning to me. "What a cute dog. She's homeless, just like you were."

I was staring at her, too, love still in my eyes. We sniffed at each other, rubbed noses. I was sure she recognized me, too. *Oh, Lupita, how I loved you.*

"Lucky seems to like her," Mama said. Then she looked at Papa with the 'special' look of hers. "I was just thinking . . . "

He cut her off at the pass. "No, no more dogs. Lucky is a perfect 'only dog.' Besides, she's got a litter out there somewhere to care for."

Mama shook her head. "Yes . . . I suppose you're right . . . but I feel so sorry for her."

In the meantime, Lupita and I were getting thoroughly reacquainted. Not only had we rubbed noses, but now we were in the process of checking out each other's bottom ends. Boy, did she smell sweet. She was one 'hot tamale!' She pulled away from me, twirled around, came back close, then playfully pulled away again.

What a flirt you are, Lupita!. But I know how to flirt a bit, too.

"They act like they're in love," Mama said. "Look how Lucky's flirting with her! It's almost as if they know each other. It's like a scene from *Lady and the Tramp.*

Little did Mama know Lupita and I went back a ways. We licked each other one more time, before Papa interrupted our liaison.

"Gotta go, Old Boy," he said. "Say goodbye to your girlfriend."

But Lupita apparently had other ideas. She wasn't about to say "*adios.*"

I tried pulling on my leash and did my stubborn 'I'm not about to go anywhere' routine. It didn't work with Papa this time. He just gave me a good hard tug and I had no choice but to go with them.

However, Lupita quickly decided that if I wasn't staying, that she'd be going right along with us. She followed us about as close as any dog could get.

81

Of course, I kept looking back at her, as did Mama, but Papa kept tugging at my leash. "She's got to get back to her pups," Papa kept saying.

"I think she likes us," Mama said.

"I think she just likes Lucky's smell," Papa said. "You know how dogs are, always smelling each other in all the worst places."

Mama laughed. "Think of this – maybe they've seen each other before, like when Lucky was on the street."

"Yeah, right," Papa said. "Like she's his old girlfriend or something."

"I think she could be. Maybe he's even the father of her pups."

"Oh, come on, there are over a million street dogs in this city. Very unlikely."

"I know, but this little dog, like Lucky, is a survivor. How often do you see a female street dog?"

"Not very often. Most of them die after giving birth to their first litter because their teats become hard and infected," Papa added.

"Yes, but this little mutt following us seems to be in good health. If we could only find her litter and take them all home with us."

I wagged my tail in agreement, but it didn't do a 'doggie' bit of good with Papa. He was not about to open up an animal shelter, no matter how hard Mama and I pleaded.

"You know that sooner or later we're going to be going back to the States and there's no way we can transport a bunch of dogs – besides, it's against company policy."

"I suppose it would be difficult. . ." Mama answered, her eyes tear-filled. "But I feel so sorry for all of them."

Papa took Mama's hand in his and squeezed it. "I know you do. It's tough. But you can't save the stray dog world."

Mama said nothing more as we continued to walk the several blocks toward our van, this time faster. Believe it or not Lupita hung right in there with us. Not only was she a 'survivor,' she was also not a 'quitter.' Why she followed us all the way back to our van. When Papa opened the door, I jumped right in like I always do, looking back at her. Guess what? Lupita jumped right in there with me. Boy, was I excited! I just licked her all over.

Papa quickly intercepted. "Hey, there, wait a minute, Girl. You can't come with us. You've got a family to feed."

He nudged her gently from the car and quickly closed the door. By this time Mama had some serious tears running down her face.

"Come on," Papa said. "We've got to go." They both got inside the car.

But still, Lupita was not about to give up. She wanted to go home with us. I know she did.

When Papa pulled away from the curb, she kept on following us. I felt just terrible. *Come on, Papa, please let her come with us.* I whined and whined.

Lupita kept right on coming. In fact she followed our van for several blocks throughout *Polanco*. Boy, did I feel bad when I looked out the rear window at her. She was just racing her little heart out. *Come on, Lupita, come on Girl!*

Papa pushed down on the accelerator, speeded up and made a couple of quick turns. By this time, Mama had her head in her hands and was really crying.

But finally Lupita became a spec on the horizon, still running.

Boy, was I depressed.

Everyone remained silent all the way home. But I saw the tears in Papa's eyes, even though he was trying to be tough. I really think he wanted to take Lupita home with us, too.

"Think about her puppies," he whispered. "Just think about them."

* * * *

I always wondered what happened to Lupita, the 'marathon dog.' I just hoped she didn't get hit by a car while chasing after us. Although we never saw her again, I was certain of one thing. Lupita, like me, was definitely a survivor.

* * * *

The next morning, everything was pretty much back to normal except Mama's eyes were still red. I hadn't gotten much sleep either as I was thinking about Lupita all night.

"We're going to have to get Lucky fixed," Papa said as they drank their morning cappuccino.

Fixed? I couldn't figure that one out. *I'm just fine. Nothing wrong with me.*

"There are too many stray female dogs running around this town. He's apt to just up and chase after one of them."

"I know. I worry about that every time we open the gate. I don't know what we'd do if Lucky ran off," Mama said. "And they sure don't need to increase the stray dog population around here. They have more than their quota. You're right, we've got to get him 'fixed.' "

I soon learned that 'fixed' had something to do with the vet, definitely not my favorite topic. But it did not require mending broken bones or antibiotics. It required a scalpel and right where it hurt the worst on us male dogs.

But Mama and Papa could not find a "Fixer" to fix me, as every vet we went to said,

"Oh, no hay possible! El perro es muy machismo!

That meant it was not possible 'to fix' me and that I was considered very *macho* by all these vets. I was a Mexican male, after all! Of course I was thrilled when the vets gave my parents this sage bit of advice. I must have been considered 'very well-endowed' indeed and it made me want to stick my snout in the air and go parading around town for all the girl dogs to check me out.

Unfortunately, Mama and Papa finally had some luck. They found 'their man,' a vet by the name of Dr. Gonzales, who specialized in treating the dogs of Expats living in Mexico City. He was more than willing to perform their dirty work for a 'sufficient' number of *pesos*. So off a part of me 'went' with a slice of his scalpel. Let me tell you, never have I been so sore. I was so upset I barely acknowledged Mama and Papa on the way home. Instead I sulked in the back of the van. They both felt so bad. Needless to say, when we got home, they really spoiled me. Mama went out and bought me a new rawhide toy and Papa gave me twice my usual serving of rice and meat that night. So I decided that it wasn't all that horrible to be one of 'the wounded.' And they continued to lay the attention on all week! Of course I loved every minute of it.

Soon I didn't care whether I had all my male dog parts or not. I figured I would never have another girlfriend anyway, that Lupita was the 'only love of my life.' My new world simply revolved in and around our house in *Lomas de Chapultepec* and for this, I was one happy dog.

CHAPTER 11
THE DAY OF THE DEAD

Holidays were always special times in Mexico City. Even during my days on the street I felt the excitement, the anticipation. Somehow people seemed to be in a better mood – more generous. In street dog terms, that meant 'more food' for us.

After my adoption, holidays or *dias de las fiestas*, as they were called, became even more special. Mama always made such a big deal out of them, trying hard to participate in the Mexican culture. Of course, Rosalia was right there to help pitch in with Mama's efforts.

Dia de los muertos, or Day of the Dead, for some strange reason, was one of my favorites. That is, after I got used to it. But I have to admit, it was probably all that 'extra' food that really enticed me. Let me explain this holiday a bit better. Day of the Dead was not a one-day holiday, but a three-day holiday. It was not only a time for remembering and honoring the dead and hoping they would come back for a visit, but also a time to celebrate Halloween, whose customs had trickled down to Mexico from America.

Of course, that meant parties at the orphanage, which by now, I was always part of. The kids were dressed in all sorts of funny things like pumpkin suits and tall dark hats that kind of scared me. One even looked like a bunch of bones. But after giving him a closer sniff, I quickly concluded they were not of the 'chewing variety.' I even had to wear a costume – a little neckerchief with bright orange pumpkins splattered across its purple background. Everyone loved it and called me, *'El Perro Guapo'*, which means handsome dog. And I have to admit, that even with the 'dumb' neckerchief on, I was having fun.

That's because there was lots and lots of food. Unfortunately, I made the mistake of eating so much 'dropped-to-the-floor' discards that I got myself into a rather 'sick' mode. Papa was right when he said they never had to sweep up the floor under the table when I was around, that I was an expert 'Dust Buster," whatever that was. I'm assuming it had something to do with cleaning up dropped food. Anyway, I could barely make it to the car after the *fiesta* and on the way home I just couldn't help myself and threw up all over in the back of the van. Let me tell you, Javier was not a happy *hombre* that night, and I thought for sure Mama and Papa would be doing Day of the Dead celebrations in my honor. But Mama didn't make him clean up my mess – she did it herself – so Javier's mood improved somewhat. Why, after all that cake he stuffed himself with at the orphanage, he should have been one happy *hombre* indeed, in my opinion. In fact, he should have been the one throwing up in the van.

The Day of the Dead celebration continued at home. Mama decorated the house all in orange and black – and little white ghosts, which hung from the ceiling. It looked pretty creepy to me. In fact, I later learned that was the whole idea.

Mama, Javier and I made a special trip clear across the city to the Jamaica Flower Market and crammed the van with tons of bright orange marigolds and some bright red velvety-looking flowers. As usual, there was barely room for me to claim my spot in the rear of the van. And, oh, did it smell! Why it was so strong I sneezed all the way home. Little did I know the kind of flowers we bought had certain strong scents that called the dead back to life so they would come and visit. Now, who would want to sit and visit with a bunch of skeletons is beyond me.

Of course, it didn't help that the traffic was totally jammed. I think everyone in Mexico City had Mama's flower-buying instinct that day. Of course Mama never could pass by a Mexican flower market on any old day because she thought they were such a good deal compared to prices back home. Needless to say, our house always looked like a *tienda de las flores*, a flower shop. And poor Papa, why he was always going around sneezing because he was allergic to them.

Anyway, the traffic back-up continued. I was so miserable and squished in the back of the van I could barely breathe. Those strong flower smells were about knocking the life right out of me. And then the thought occurred to me. *Just imagine, if all of us street dogs died and we all came back on 'Day of the Dead?' Boy, what a pack of us there'd be wandering all over Mexico City. What a street-cleaning nightmare that would be after we left to go back to 'bone heaven.' Oh, would Javier really hate that!*

Arriving home, we brought the flowers inside the house and Mama and Rosalia made a huge *Ofrenda* which took up most of our hallway. They even had to push my bed way back and to the side and that really hurt my feelings. I decided to have a good sulk, at the same time keeping one eye on what they were up to. For you see, *Ofrendas* are very famous in Mexico and every Mexican household has one for this holiday. It's like a whole bunch of boxes piled on top of each other in layers and covered with white sheets. Then lots of flowers are spread all over it. Then they added all this funny candy made to look like skeletons getting married and riding bikes, and others dressed up like *Poncho Via* and *Zorro*, you get the idea. Then came the skulls made from sugar called *Calaveras,* which they placed around the entire *Ofrenda*, to make the thing look entirely 'spooky.' Next they placed a big round loaf of bread with a skeleton baked inside right near the top. It was called *pan de muerto.* Mama called it 'Dead Bread.'

Now these sweets didn't smell half as bad as the flowers to me, so I decided to go in for a closer look. But with a quick swish of Rosalia's broom on my behind, I found out that our *Offrenda* was a 'no go' place for me.

But I was not so sure I wanted to be around it anyway when they placed a clay dog on the *Ofrenda*.

"Don't worry, Lucky," Mama said, sensing I was upset to see a fake dog on our *Ofrenda* that looked a lot like me. "It has nothing to do with you. It's only a tradition that in *Mixquic*, the Indigenous people put a clay dog on their altars, which refers back to the pre-conquest custom of killing a dog and incinerating it with the body of the deceased to help its soul to cross the river to afterlife." By this time I was looking horrified. "Oh, don't worry, Lucky, we're not going to incinerate you."

I suppose I had to believe her, so I just settled in for a long autumn *siesta* in my bed in its new spot and continued to watch Mama and Rosalia do their thing. But I wasn't about to put my sulking aside. I just couldn't understand why I was not receiving the attention to which I had become so accustomed.

Next came all sorts of things from everywhere in the house to be added to our *Ofrenda*. They were tributes to those no longer with us – you know, the ones that had died. There was a hammer and nails for an uncle carpenter; some thread and needles for a 'seamstress' grandma; a bottle of Tequila for a great uncle; some whorehound cough drops for one grandpa with asthma; a pillow for another dead grandpa who liked to sleep a lot. Boy, I was hoping they wouldn't take my bed and add it to the *Ofrenda*, like they were about to remember me. *Mama, I'm still here. Right here in this very bed, waiting for someone to pat me on the head.* Then a thought occurred to me. I, too, had something to add to our *Ofrenda*, something in remembrance of my brother, Buddy. Quickly, I went out to our garden to retrieve one of my buried bones.

Returning to hide it in a good place beneath the *Ofrenda* where I was sure Buddy could find it in case he came for a visit, was I in for a surprise. For right there next to a big vase of orange flowers sat an unused rawhide chew toy and a can of chicken. They didn't have to tell me who that was for. The 'ghost dog' of course.

"For Polly," Mama said, her eyes moist.

And for a moment I almost decided I liked that dead dog since Mama seemed to love her so much.

I never did get my pat on the head that day. Mama and Rosalia's list went on and on, until there were so many things for the dead in our hallway that it about scared the 'doggie' daylights out of me. By this time, I wondered just how many ghosts were coming to visit. I was certain of one thing – I was going to find a spot to sleep in Mama and Papa's room for the next few days.

* * * *

And then another shock! On Halloween night, just as I had finished my dinner, out came Mama in her orange and black striped tights and a thing on her head with two pumpkins that looked like antennas. She also had her face painted black. Why, she didn't even look like my mama at all, and to tell you the truth, she scared me. In fact, I even jumped away when she bent down to pat me. And when Papa came home, Mama made him put on a long dark cape and a really scary face, I would later know as a mask. It had a great big mouth that looked like it could chew up my leg in one bite. I wasn't about to find out. I wouldn't even say hello to Papa when he came downstairs. Instead I ran the other way.

But soon the fun – or so they thought – began. Mama, Papa and Rosalia filled up big bowls with lots of candy and took them outside to the yard. It seemed like they were having a strange dinner to me, but I'd already had my pasta with marinara sauce, which I had now become accustomed to, as well, so why should I care what they ate? I followed them outside. Of course, Mama had tied that silly pumpkin scarf around my neck again and it was starting to itch, so I was trying my darndest to figure out a way to get rid of it. I knew it was near impossible, as Mama was one of the greatest 'knotters' in the world.

Next Papa did something even more strange for security-conscious Mexico City. He actually opened up our gate at night! Unbelievable! And to top it all off, he took three chairs outside. *Has he gone nuts?* But quickly, before I could run outside for a good look, he attached me to my leash. *Guess I won't be running to see Lupita anytime soon.* I thought of her wonderful scent. Then the minute Papa, Mama and Rosalia sat on their chairs, down the street came the biggest bunch of spooks I had ever seen in all my doggie days! I gave a great big pull on my leash, intending to race right back inside the yard and to the safety of my bed. But Papa held me firm.

"It's okay, Lucky," Papa said. "They won't hurt you. You need to be our guard dog tonight."

I was not so certain I liked that idea very much. I'd certainly forgotten how dark and cold it was on the streets of Mexico City at night. And besides, I wasn't sure if I was supposed to bite those spooks, growl at them or just sit there like a good little dog. Anyway, I decided I would just have to 'grin and bear it' and guard the ones I loved.

"They're just *niños* dressed up like trick-or-treaters." Mama said. "They're here for some treats."

They looked pretty threatening to me, whether they wanted anything to eat or not, and I watched in terror as the line of spooks grew longer and longer, until it stretched clear to the other end of the block and around the corner. But Mama, Papa and Rosalia seemed to be enjoying things tremendously, even though I was half scared out of my wits.

"I have a feeling these are not the kids who live in this neighborhood," Mama said. "Look how tattered their costumes are and many don't have any at all."

"I agree," Papa said. "And there's even a few *abuelas and abuelos,* that's grandmas, grandpas, and maids in this group."

"That's all right," Mama said. "We've got lots of treats."

Well, we sat outside in the cold for several hours until I thought I was going to freeze into a 'doggie pop.' It reminded me of my days on the street and I was seriously thinking about digging a street-dog hole for myself right in the middle of Papa's special grass to cuddle up in. To get my mind off the cold, I even tried chewing on a piece of candy one spook had dropped, but it stuck to my teeth and wouldn't go down. I finally gave up on the chewing and yanked it from my mouth with my paw. But there it stayed and I tugged at the sticky mess all night long. Let me tell you, that was the last time I ever put my snout even close to any candy bowl.

* * * *

The Day of the Dead celebration didn't end in front of our house, however. The next day there were more festivities. But at a different spot. The cemetery.

"I'm really anxious to go and observe this holiday," Mama said. "All the people of Mexico flock to the cemeteries in hopes their dead loved ones will come back for a visit."

Papa wasn't all that excited to go to an old cemetery to visit dead people, but Mama quickly convinced him they should participate in their host country's culture. So off they went. At the last moment, they decided to take me along as their 'bodyguard' just in case something were to happen. *Like if a ghost suddenly appeared.*

But they caught me by surprise once more. Since we weren't in any silly costumes, I just assumed we were going on one of our 'regular' outings, so I was more than happy to go along. Only one thing seemed strange. It was almost midnight – smack dab in the middle of my beauty rest.

Why, I'd never been to the *cemetario* before, only passed it on the way to the orphanage. From my high vantage point from the rear van window, I knew it was awful big and filled with all kinds of strange pillars and stones – and few people – live ones anyway.

Well, when we arrived at around midnight, was I ever surprised! I had never seen so many people together in all my 'doggie days.' There were parents and *niños* and grandpas and grandmas and cousins, why everyone was there! And they were carrying parcels and satchels in all shapes and sizes, many of which smelled like food! I couldn't help but thinking it was about time for a 'midnight snack.'

Although there were no lights in the cemetery, it was not dark at all. Instead it was lit by hundreds of thousands of candles, all beckoning the 'dead' back home. And the smell was very similar to our house these days. For each grave was mounded with orange and red flowers – I'd say millions of them. It just made me want to sneeze, so that's just what I did. Sneeze, sneeze, sneeze! Of course, Papa joined me in my efforts.

Well, all the families seemed to go to a familiar grave except for the tourists, who quietly tip-toed around in awe. Then the families sat around the graves and waited, like they were in a trance, anticipation showing on their faces in the candlelight. Soon they began to open up the good-smelling satchels. But was I ever surprised! Hundreds of those sugar skulls poured out. Quickly, they were placed around the grave. But I wasn't about to give up. I knew the aroma of food when I smelled it. There were more than those dumb sugar skulls inside those satchels. I was proved right. Soon all kinds of food and drinks appeared. Tons of it! Why, I had never seen so much food in my entire 'doggie' life! Nor so many bottles of *tequila* and *cerveza*.

Mama and Papa spoke softly to each other.

"Strange place for a picnic," Papa said.

"Not really," Mama answered. "They are bringing it for the dead – all their favorite foods and drink, in hopes of enticing them back here to earth for just this one night."

They were certainly enticing me, all right, and I wasn't even dead. Boy, did it smell good. The women put the food on platters and spread them amongst the flowers. By this time I was really getting hungry. I had my eye on a platter of *carne asada* and rice and was just about to go in for the kill, when I felt a huge jerk on my leash.

"Just where do you think you're going, Old Boy?" Papa held me tight, like I was a criminal or something, and I was not allowed to budge. *Come on, Papa, just a little snack. I'm sure these nice people won't mind.* But I suppose those nice people must have sensed my intentions, for soon they were dishing up the food for themselves. They did make sure to leave some on the platters, but I got the distinct feeling it wasn't like they were saving it for me. They were leaving it for the 'departed' just in case they chose to join the dinner crowd.

Mama and Papa stood at a distance and quietly observed them. Boy, was I pissed, missing out on all that good food, stuck at the end of my leash in the middle of a cemetery.

Dia de los muertos, it wasn't so bad, even if there were a lot of spooks around. But there was plenty of food. And besides, every one seemed to love each other at this time of year, both 'dead' and 'alive' and that was certainly a good thing, from my 'street dog' point of view.

CHAPTER 12
FELIZ NAVIDAD

Before I realized it, the nights were really cold. I mean cold, like when Mama wore a jacket when she went out shopping, or like when we had hot soup every night with dinner. Papa even tried lighting a fire in our fireplace, but the chimney was so crooked that all the smoke came inside. Of course, Mama put a quick stop to his 'boy scout' antics. Instead we bought some portable heaters and plugged them in, where needed, since our house didn't have a furnace. My favorite heater placement spot, of course, was right in front of my bed. Boy, was I living a cushy life. But not everyone in the Valley of Mexico was. And, at over seven thousand feet, the homeless knew what cold nights were really about. Take it from me, a former street guy. One thing I knew for sure; the colder it got, the happier I was to have been adopted. In fact, it had now been eight months since my 'discovery' date.

* * * *

Well, *Dia de los Muertos* quickly faded from my memory and was replaced by *Dia de Gracias*, that's Thanksgiving in American terms. Boy, did the Americans ever rush to Wall-Mart and Costco to get their much-needed supplies, like Butterball turkeys, cranberry sauce and pumpkin pie filling, thanks to the recent arrival of NAFTA between Mexico and the U.S.. I'm not sure what NAFTA really means, but Papa seemed to think it was quite a big deal. So did Mama from a 'shopping' standpoint.

While Mexicans thought the idea of *Dia de Gracias* was a great idea, it was not celebrated in Mexico. Of course they couldn't figure out what all the fuss was about canned cranberry sauce and pumpkin pie filling. There were plenty of fresh cranberries in the stores if one wanted them, and lots of large pumpkins, which Mexicans loved to bake and eat with rice, which made perfect sense to me. I never could understand why Americans liked to make them into scary faces, which I didn't care for much at all. Who wants to be scared out of their wits by what they called a 'Jack-O-Lantern'? Not this *hombre*. Besides, they made our house smell horrible. Of course, Americans also loved those tiny ornamental pumpkins which they piled all over the house, in what Mama called 'harvest displays.' In my opinion, they were perfect rodent food. On more than one occasion, I saw a mouse or two scurry across the living room floor from my lookout bed to attack the little pumpkins. At first Mama tried to blame me for chewing on her pumpkins, but soon concluded my teeth were not that small. I have to admit I don't have the greatest smile since I had distemper as a pup and the fever made my *dientes* stop growing. But my teeth are certainly not 'mouse-size.'

The Mexicans also had their opinions on how Americans prepared their Thanksgiving turkeys. They were certain they should be served chopped up and slow-roasted in chocolately, spicy *mole* sauce, the Mexican way. However, I never heard of a Mexican turning down any American Thanksgiving dinner invitation. That included me. For I soon learned the delights of Thanksgiving and they were not disappointing. In fact they were much better than all those Halloween and Day of the Dead sweets in my own personal 'doggie opinion' – and not nearly as scary.

98

Why, I had never seen so much food piled on our dining room table in all my 'doggie' days! It could have fed a poor Mexican family for weeks; a street dog family for a year. Of course, lots of friends came to share all that food with us and we ate and ate and ate and ate. In fact, I was so full I felt like a stuffed turkey myself after all that food. I quickly decided I liked the 'American style' turkey better than *mole* style and the potatoes and gravy, why they were wonderful. My judgment was still out on the stuffing, although I knew I would have gobbled it right up during my days on the 'street.' But I certainly couldn't understand why Mama and Papa got so excited over the cranberry sauce and pumpkin pie. However, being the good sport I am, I sampled them anyway, just to make them happy. *No, not to my 'doggie' taste I'm afraid.* Besides, Mama says that dogs shouldn't eat sugar, so they were quickly crossed off my list of edibles.

Anyway, after the eating bonanza of Thanksgiving, I couldn't wait for the next holiday. It was not to disappoint. For soon *Nacimientos* – that means Nativity scenes – were popping up all over Mexico City. That's because 'Christmas was coming' and yes, I was getting fat!

One day Mama came home with a great big box and Javier certainly didn't have a smile on his face when he carried it into the house. He even made Rosalia help him, it was so heavy. You can imagine what was going through my mind – *a bunch of huge bones had to surely be inside.* As Mama started to open the box, I got really excited and jumped up and down, especially since all the items were individually wrapped in tissue paper. That's because by this time in my adoption, I had become accustomed to *regaloes*, that's gifts, and I loved unwrapping them.

"Not this time, Lucky," Mama said. "They're not for you. Besides, they are very fragile. You see, it's time for *Feliz Navidad* – Merry Christmas!"

She gently pushed me back a bit, so I took the hint and plopped down on the floor to watch her, awaiting the arrival of my many bones. As she opened the tissue paper wrapped around each object, was I ever disappointed! No bones, not even a single one! Instead, the packages consisted of clay figures made in Guadalajara, that were hand-painted in bright colors.

"This is Mary, and Joseph, and baby Jesus," Mama said, carefully putting the figures on the floor beside her. I gave them a polite sniff to make sure they were not edible, then quietly sauntered off to my bed. Of course, I still kept an eye on what she was doing.

Soon Javier carried in a wooden house, 'a stable,' they called it. I wondered if it was a new bed for me, but quickly concluded it had no puffy cushion and that I would definitely not fit inside. They placed it on a low table covered with a brownish-colored sheet and then spread moss inside the stable. I quickly realized who this tiny house was for. It was for Joseph and Mary and their baby. Carefully and quietly Mama put them inside.

Then she continued to unwrap and I knew for certain there had to be some bones somewhere in that big box after all. More disappointment! Instead there were shepherds and sheep and some guys Mama called 'the Wise men,' *Los Reyes*, or the three kings as they are known in Mexico. Let me tell you, they didn't look very wise to me, but Mama and Rosalia seemed to think they were wonderful with their little jeweled turbans and all.

"*Bonita, bonita*," Rosalia kept repeating.

"Yes, they are beautiful," Mama said.

Well they put the figures near the stable and then placed some tiny palm trees around it and hung a big star and some angels from the ceiling. Afterwards they strung some little white lights around it. Even I had to admit it looked beautiful and much preferred it to our *Ofrenda* with all that scary dead kind of stuff. I quickly decided these figures wouldn't make bad roommates at all. They didn't frighten me one bit.

That night when Papa came home I was in for an even bigger surprise. For tied on top of our van was a great big pine tree. Now this one I couldn't figure out at all. *How on earth was I supposed to get clear up there to pee?*

I didn't have to fret for long, for Papa quickly untied the tree and carried it into the house. *How convenient. Now I won't even have to go outside.* I was quickly proved wrong.

"This is our Christmas tree, Lucky," Papa said. "So don't get any ideas."

Of course, I sat there very innocently and watched as they strung colored lights on the tree and hung a bunch of bright red and green balls from its branches. *Sure are a lot of dog toys on that thing.* Yet somehow, I had a feeling I shouldn't get up 'close and personal' right away. I'd have to wait until they went to bed to check things out. They continued to hang more items on the tree – tiny houses, silver bells, candy canes (which incidentally, I soon learned I hated), and tiny angels. I had to admit, that even from a 'doggie point of view' it was truly beautiful. Almost too pretty to pee on. As a finishing touch, they placed a fluffy white blanket beneath it. It looked so soft and cushy. I could barely contain myself from trying it out for the night.

Mama must have read my mind. "Don't even think about it, Lucky."

I looked at her innocently and wagged my tail.

"That's right, Old Boy," Papa agreed. "This tree's a 'no go' place for you. *La linia*," he said, making an invisible mark with his finger. "That's the line." It was a phrase I would hear often in my future.

I wagged my tail even harder.

Then Papa went outside again and started carrying in all these red flowers, Poinsettias, or *Flor de Noche Buena*, to us Mexicans. *Noche Buena* also means Christmas Eve, which I was soon to experience.

"No touching these flowers, Lucky," Papa said as he carried a dozen or so of them inside. *Oh oh, looks like Mama's having another 'flower fit.'* I wondered if they would make me sneeze like those orange Day of the Dead flowers, but since Papa was not sneezing, I sensed I was safe. Anyway, they put those red flowers all over the place – beside the fireplace, by the front door, going up the stairs, anywhere they felt a need for red, I guess. By this time, I'd definitely decided I would never have to go out into the garden again to do my marking. *Now how lazy can a dog get?*

I had to admit that the house looked very festive, and I was anxious to explore it in much more detail. I thought they'd never go to bed that night. For some strange reason, they were just enjoying all those Christmas carols coming from the stereo and drinking some *Noche Buena*, that's special Mexican Christmas beer. Unfortunately, I went to sleep before they did, so I never did get a chance to check out 'the spirit of Christmas,' even though I had the feeling it was pretty neat, something definitely to my 'doggie' liking.

Of course, Rosalia was up early the next morning singing Christmas carols and dusting the living room floor, so my expedition was put on another 'hold.' And Mama, why she hung around the living room, all day, too, so wrapped up in this Christmas 'thing.' In fact, that's just what she was doing – wrapping gifts. I wondered what was inside for me.

Finally late in the afternoon, she put on her coat. "I'm going to the Christmas *Mercado* to finish up my shopping," she said.

Boy, was I relieved, especially since Rosalia had taken the afternoon off. And the second I heard the front gate close, I bounded for the Christmas tree. Yes, the puffy covering beneath it was wonderful. It was so cushy, in fact, that I fell asleep almost immediately and dreamt I was floating on a cloud in 'dog heaven.'

But I didn't sleep for long – just a little 'pup power nap.' There was just too much to explore. I began with a good sniff at the tree. Let me tell you, it was tempting, but I just couldn't lift my leg. It was too beautiful. I thought about it again for a moment but still couldn't quite find the urge. *Later . . . later,* I promised myself. For the time being, I concentrated on all those colorful balls and wished that Papa was home to toss one of them to me. But he wasn't, so I reached out and quickly took one in my mouth. Suddenly it exploded and tiny pieces of glass flew all over the cushy white blanket beneath the tree. *Oh boy, was I going to get it!* I was seriously wishing I knew how to use Rosalia's broom, but quickly gave up on that idea.

Next I spied what they called a candy cane on a lower branch. It looked enticing, so I just opened my mouth and plucked it right off. Let me tell you, it went out about as quickly as it went in. A more horrible taste

I had never experienced! My mouth felt like it was on fire! I ran for my water bowl.

Returning, I decided it was time to check out the *regalos*. They looked pretty enticing to me, much better than exploding balls or fiery candy canes. There were big ones and little ones, all wrapped in bright red and green paper. *Which one should I go for first?* I decided on a nice mouth-sized box wrapped in green paper.

By now, I was getting quite good at opening *regalos* as Mama was always giving them to me, especially when they came back from America. Personally, I think she felt guilty for leaving me behind with Raul, the Company guard. But that's another story.

Anyway, this *regalo* looked pretty interesting to me. Even though it wasn't very heavy, I thought it might contain a rawhide toy or possibly a small bone. So I put the box between my paws and tore the paper off with my teeth. Inside was a velvet-covered box. I proceeded to pry it open with my mouth and out dropped a shiny gold chain. *A new dog collar?* It certainly wasn't anything I'd like to gnaw on, that I knew for sure, so I moved on to the next box. It was much larger. *Had to be a bone in there.* It didn't take me long to get it open either. Out tumbled a pair of brown house slippers, far too large for me, I must add. By this time I had the feeling I was 'barking up the wrong tree,' that there was nothing beneath our Christmas tree for me. Just the same, I continued to sniff around and finally my snout stopped short on a medium-sized, soft package. I tore it open. Bonanza! A whole package of doggie chew treats. Why there must have been about fifty of them! I proceeded to chew up every one of them up until I had a real stomach ache. I was feeling so miserable that I didn't even get out of my bed when Papa arrived home.

But it didn't take him long to get my attention when he walked into the living room and looked beneath our Christmas tree.

"Lucky! Lucky, where the heck are you?" Papa yelled, moving closer and closer to me. I was sure I was about to be 'one dead dog.' And there was no Mama to protect me.

Papa reached down and grabbed me by the collar and practically drug me to the Christmas tree, even though I dug my paws in hard. "What have you been up to?" I could tell he was really mad by the tone of his voice, so I quickly did my whining and whimpering trick. *I'm sorry, Papa. Oh, I'm sorry.*

But he continued to rant. "I told you this tree was a 'no go' zone! Now what were you doing there?" Like I understood what a 'no go' zone was. I had to admit I did, however.

But how can a dog stay away from a tree? Especially one so conveniently placed in the middle of the living room?

I pleaded with Papa some more and he seemed to soften. Still he pointed his finger at me and said, "Naughty dog! Shameful thing to do!"

By this time, I had certainly gotten the message. I stood right beside him, head hung, tail between my legs. I guess Papa decided the same thing, for he shooed me back to my bed and started cleaning up the mess.

"No more of this early Christmas stuff," Papa said, shaking his head. "Mama's gonna wring your little yellow neck when she gets home."

By this time he had discovered the empty package of rawhide bones and his expression changed. "Did you eat all of these?" He rushed over, felt my stomach. Of course I rolled over and played dead, like I was really hurting. "You're going to be one constipated dog," he told me.

I had no idea what that meant until I discovered I couldn't poop for three days. A self-inflicted punishment, I suppose. One thing I learned for sure. No more Christmas tree exploring for me.

But the 'merry season' continued. There were fiestas everywhere and people ignited fireworks in the streets. Let me tell you, I ran for my bed when I heard their loud bangs. It really set off the roof dogs across the street and they barked and barked until they were hoarse. Then on December 16th, *Las Posadas* began. These were candlelight processions that depicted the journey of Joseph and Mary to Bethlehem. They went on for a long time in a dog's life –nine days. But I quickly decided I liked *Posadas* much better than all those fireworks. It also meant I got to go to *Hogar Dulce Hogar*, the orphanage.

That's because they were doing a *Posada* and Mama was helping them out. Little did I realize, I was about to become part of the 'picture.' First of all, they dressed tiny Alicia in a long robe and put a shawl around her head. Then they dressed little Eduardo in the same manner. They were to be *Virgen Maria* and *San Jose*, that's Mary and Joseph. Then they found this old doll in the girls' room and wrapped it round and round in tissue paper and gave it to Alicia to hold.

"*Jesus*," Mama told them. "*Esta es niño Jesus*." They both smiled and Alicia kissed the doll. Of course the other children wanted to take part in the *posada*, so they dressed up in colorful homemade costumes and soon became the *pastores y pastoras*, the shepherds accompanying Joseph and Mary, and the *Santos Reyes*, the three wisemen. Some of the girls dressed up in

106

sheets and tied cardboard wings to their backs and Mama called them *"las angelitas bonitas."* By this time I was beginning to wonder if it was Halloween all over again, especially since the shepherds were carrying large sticks and paper lanterns, which I had mistaken for *piñatas*. I was about to run for cover, when Mama called my name.

"Lucky, come on, come on, it's time for your costume."

Oh, no, here we go again. Not that stupid neckerchief!

Was I ever surprised! Instead of tying a neckerchief to my neck, they covered my back with a fuzzy woolen cape-like thing and tied it around my middle. Worse than that, they put some long floppy wooly things over my ears. Boy was I mad! I started to shake them off, but they would not budge.

"It's okay, Lucky," Mama said, patting me. "You make a beautiful sheep for the shepherds."

A sheep? Why they're for eating! In fact, I started to get very nervous, like I was about to be served up for someone's Christmas dinner. But fortunate for me, that was not to be the case.

Instead Mama opened up the orphanage gate, gave the shepherds my leash, and we started off down the street. Even though it was a cold night, with my wooly sheep outfit I didn't mind a bit. I have to admit, however, that it was impossible to lift my leg to pee wearing that stupid cape.

The *niños* were very excited. They swung their staffs in the air and swirled those paper lanterns round and round, so I was continually on the lookout. Soon we stopped before a house and they started to sing a beautiful song.

Come on, let's move on. Come on, time to go.

107

Soon a man and woman answered and the children asked them if they could come in for shelter. They told us "no." Of course that didn't bother me as I wanted to get on with my walk, even though I was missing my continual 'pee spots.'

At the next house the same thing happened. But at the third house a kind-faced woman opened the door and when the children asked for shelter for the night, she kindly told them she had no room in her house but that they could spend the night in her stable. Of course, I thought of our own stable in the Nativity scene at our house. *No way we'd all fit in there,* I quickly concluded, so I pulled on my leash, ready to move on. No one budged. Instead the woman flung the door open and invited us inside.

Then the *fiesta* began! There was food everywhere – *tamales*, and corn gruel and *bacalao a la vizcaina* and *revoltijo de romeritos*, some of my favorites. I could have gobbled it all up real fast. But the kids held me back and we patiently waited to be invited to the table. While I was not given a seat, I had no fear. When the orphans were around, there were plenty of 'droppings' for me and I felt stuffed as a *tamale* myself after we'd finished.

Then I spied them. *Pinatas!* Several of them hung from the ceiling. The moment the *niños* picked up those sticks I was out of there *muy pronto!*

"*Mira, mira!*" little Maria said. "Our sheep is running away!"

Sheep or no sheep, I was not about to be caught in *pinata* crossfire ever again. Besides, I didn't even like their end result – all the fruit, nuts and candies that tumbled from them.

* * * *

Noche Buena, Christmas Eve, was soon upon us. Mama and Papa went to church and left me home alone, much to my 'doggie' dismay. After a bit of sulking I decided to plant myself before the Christmas tree and guard all the *regalos*. Of course, I also kept checking on the oven, as wonderful smells were coming from it. I suspected a turkey was inside. A huge pot of Rosalia's famous *tamales* simmered on the stove. Boy, was I ever hungry. I'd completely forgotten that Papa had fed me my rice and chicken before their departure.

When Mama and Papa arrived home, they were very happy. They both gave me a great big kiss on the head and wished me *"Feliz Navidad."* I became very happy, as well, and did my best 'welcome hula' for them. Then Papa turned on the Christmas music and we sat around the Christmas tree and unwrapped our gifts. Mama got a big gold dog collar and Papa some new house slippers, which I pretended to have never seen before. As for me, why I got a new package of red and green dog chew toys, a rubber Santa toy that squeaked, and a new wooley cover for my bed, which I rolled myself up in right way.

Then Mama and Papa moved to the dining room for dinner. Why they were being so nice to me that I was surprised I didn't get invited to sit right up there with them on a special chair. But no such luck. As usual, I had to wait in my bed until they were finished. But it was worth the wait. Afterwards, Papa filled up my dish with more turkey and *tamales* than I had ever seen in all my 'doggie' days.

Felize Navidad, Felize Navidad. Yes, I liked the sound of those words. And little did I know that *Dia de los Reyes*, Three Kings Day, was almost upon us, another day of gifts and feasting on *Rosca de Reyes*, a sweet bread with tiny figures of baby Jesus hidden inside. Oh, yes, life was indeed good.

CHAPTER 13
HOME ALONE – ALMOST

One morning when I came in from my usual 'yard exploration and marking ritual,' there they were! The thing I hated to see most. Mama and Papa's luggage was sitting in the downstairs hallway. I knew very well what that meant practically from the time they adopted me. It meant they were going away. And even worse, it meant I was staying at home. Boy, I hated those suitcases! It made me just want to whine and whine. But it didn't do me a bit of good. They'd leave anyway. I don't think they had a clue of what that did to poor little old me! Why, I was sure they were abandoning me and would never come back and that I would be out on the streets again. Fortunately, that never came to pass and I finally got used to the idea of them being gone – well, sort of.

* * * *

I well remember the first time they went away. At that time, I didn't know what suitcases were all about. I just thought they were something Papa had put in the entryway for me to sniff and perhaps do a little marking on. But I was soon to find out differently. When I finished my sniffing and was just about to lift my leg, Papa came running down the hallway like there was a fire or something. He grabbed me by the collar and about tossed me out the front door.

"Don't you even think about it!" he yelled, slamming the door shut. "Those just happen to be our suitcases, not some 'pissing post.' " I quickly got the idea. And from the look on Papa's face, I knew he was not kidding. It was kind of like the 'no peeing on the

Christmas tree thing.' Whatever . . . but spying their 'big' suitcases anywhere in the house was most upsetting to me. They might as well have put an attack grizzly bear there waiting to gobble me up. For the sight of their larger suitcases meant they were going away for a long time. The small suitcases didn't create quite such a stir in me, for they meant a short trip, not quite so depressing.

Well, the first time they were about to go away, I heard a noisy truck pull up outside. Of course, I barked and barked to warn Mama and Papa of a possible intruder, but Papa walked right out and opened up the gate for them. This I couldn't understand – especially when I saw who was behind the wheel. The vet – Dr. Ortega! It would be a good long time until I forgot about all the jabbing and poking that he'd done to me. He had his little assistant by his side – the one who always started to tremble the moment he saw me. I can understand why. If Papa hadn't held me firmly by the collar, I would have taken a piece out of both their behinds. Instead I just barked and barked and Dr. Ortega's assistant trembled even harder.

When they opened the back of their vehicle and Papa led me toward it, I stood in place like I was cemented to the ground and my paws made a big mark across the front lawn as Papa drug me toward the truck. Why, I wasn't about to get in the back of that truck for anything! It looked like a big dark cave with bars on the front to me – not exactly a cozy cuddly place at all. Thankfully, Mama came to the rescue.

"What on earth is going on out here?" she said, coming outside. "Are they going to transport Lucky in the back of that barred truck?"

Papa quickly got the idea that I wasn't about to be going in any dark old truck. "I don't think he's too anxious to get inside."

You bet your tootin' right I'm not, Papa. I continued to pull back on my leash and Papa stopped all his tugging.

"We'll bring Lucky to your office ourselves," he told Dr. Ortega.

It sure didn't take but a second for Dr. Ortega's assistant to hop right back into their truck, but I kept growling at him just to make sure he got the point. Dr. Ortega shrugged his shoulders and got inside, as well. I thought for a moment I'd been spared.

But I hadn't. For Mama and Papa soon had me in the van. Since the suitcases were not included, I had a feeling I was going someplace I didn't want to go. I was. And I was sure it was not a good place as Mama had tears in her eyes the whole way.

"We don't have any other choice but to take Lucky to Dr. Ortega's," Papa said, as I sat in my bed in the rear of the van listening to them.

"I feel so terrible," Mama answered. "He's been through so much in his life and now he'll think we're abandoning him. I'm going to find another solution the next time we travel or else I'll stay home with Lucky."

"It can't be too bad. After all, it's a kennel for dogs," Papa said.

"That's what I'm afraid of," Mama said. "Remember this is Mexico. Not exactly a 'dog paradise', if you know what I mean."

"We'll check it out."

But we got stuck in traffic. They were already late leaving for the airport, so when Dr. Ortega told them the cages were being cleaned and that no one could go in the rear of his office for at least an hour, they had no choice but to just drop me off, minus inspection.

"But everything is *muy bien,* very nice place," he convinced them, a wide smile showing beneath his mustache. Mama and Papa had to believe him.

Boy, were they wrong! It was the darkest coldest place I had ever been. And it stunk like it hadn't been scrubbed in a good long time. Of course Mama was right about the abandonment part. I did think I'd been abandoned after spending several days in a five-by-five cage in the back of Dr. Ortega's office. I barked and barked and barked until I was hoarse, but Mama and Papa never came for me. I couldn't stop shivering and I couldn't figure out what had happened to my cozy bed, which the vet never put in my cage, like Mama had told him to do. Nobody even talked to me. They just threw some scraps or crappy canned dog food inside my cage once a day, which I totally hated. Of course they gave me only a little water, so I wouldn't pee so much, hardly enough for a guinea pig. Boy, was I sad. In fact, it was so bad in there I even longed for my days on the street. At least I'd been free.

* * * *

Finally I heard the voices I had longed to hear for so many days – Mama and Papa. I barked and barked to make sure they would hear me.

"We're here to pick up Lucky," I heard Mama's familiar voice from the front office.

The assistant brought me out and both Mama and Papa looked totally shocked.

"Lucky, what happened to you?" Papa grabbed my leash. "You poor Old Boy! You stink and you've lost your voice!"

"Oh, Lucky," Mama cried. "I don't think they even fed you!" She bent down to hug me, but had to cover her nose with her other hand. "Oh, you poor little dog!" She started to cry real hard. I had a feeling I would not be coming back to Dr. Ortega's office any time soon.

Dr. Ortega's assistant just stood there with a dumb look on his face as I gave him a quick growl with the little voice I had left. Papa plunked down the money on the front counter real hard and we quickly left Dr. Ortegas's office, never to return again, much to my 'doggie' relief.

It took Mama and Papa a good long time to get over that one, so it meant I was more than a bit spoiled for the next few weeks. Of course I didn't mind it one little bit.

* * * *

The next time Mama and Papa went out of town, I got to go along. That's because some 'dog lover' friends had invited us up to their weekend home in *Valle de Bravo* – me included. Of course I loved to go up into the mountains where the air was fresh and all the pine trees grew. Plenty of places for marking up there! The only thing I didn't like about the journey was the highway around *Toluca*, before we headed up into the mountains. There was a long straight stretch there. Lots of street dogs lived in this area, as well. That meant these poor dogs provided lots of target practice for the Juniors – that's the rich people's kids, remember? They raced their Ferraris and Jaguars up to their weekend homes in the mountains, and we saw dog after dead dog along the side of the road. It almost made me cry – and I can't even produce tears. Mama cried enough for both of us, however.

Anyway, this same weekend while we were gone, we got robbed. I mean some crooks dug under the fence in the front of our house to avoid the electric wiring, then they cut the wires on our alarm system and just went right in through an upstairs window because Papa had left the ladder in the open garage. Why these robbers took our stereo and television, and all of Papa's clothes, and even the sheets on the beds. I considered myself lucky, indeed, as they didn't take one thing of mine. But as you well know by now, the typical Mexican is just not that crazy about dogs or the things that accompany them. Still, I felt so sorry for Mama and Papa because they were so sad. They even took Mama's computer. She cried and cried.

But like Papa said, "it's a good darn thing they didn't take her clothes, too, or she'd be doing a lot more crying."

As bad as I felt about the whole thing, it did turn out well for me. That meant they would never leave their home unattended over night again. Even though I would have to stay there when they were away, I wouldn't be alone in a dark cold place somewhere far from the home I loved. That's because Papa's company had decided to provide a guard to stay at the house to watch out for thieves and most importantly, to take care of me. Let me tell you, it beat the heck out of the 'doggie spa' at Dr. Ortega's office.

In fact, this plan really wasn't so bad for me at all. Although I missed Mama and Papa terribly, at least I was in my own home. Besides, Raul wasn't such a bad guy. He was a short indigenous villager from the state of Oaxaca. He always wore a police uniform and had a gun in his belt. That meant I had to be on especially good behavior as I didn't want him aiming that thing at me. For I was well aware of what guns can do. But the best thing about Raul was that he actually liked dogs. In fact, he became my good friend, my *amigo*. He even shared his food with me at Mama's insistence, but they left so much in the refrigerator that one little guy like Raul could not possibly have eaten it all. Papa also told him I was to sleep inside the house and should watch TV with him at night.

I remember many nights when Raul cooked us up some tasty *carnitas* and *tortillas* with refried beans and we both ate so much we looked like two stuffed sausages. Afterwards, we lounged on the sofa in the maid's quarters and listened to *Mariachi* music and Mexican love songs. Raul would cry and cry and sometimes I'd even howl along with him. Then he'd turn on the television in the kitchen and we'd watch *Telenovelas* – that's soap operas – almost all night long. Actually it was kind of fun, although I didn't get a lot of sleep on those nights and felt pretty much sleep-deprived. When my parents returned home, they never could figure out why I slept so much the first few days.

As you can see, Raul actually did comply with Mama and Papa's wishes to take good care of me. Of course, I'm not sure if it was because they gave him a big *propina* – *a tip* – when they got home, or just because Raul really did like me. I liked to think it was because of this.

Only one thing I didn't like about Raul. He always gave me a bath before Mama and Papa arrived home. But it was not the nice warm kind with perfume-scented shampoo like Mama and Papa gave me; it was with cold hose water and Tide detergent! I smelled like Clorox for a week after and my fur started to turn white. At first Mama thought I was just getting old, until she discovered that Raul was bathing me with laundry detergent. Of course, she put a quick end to that. Oh, boy, the things we dogs go through.

Raul also liked to give me training lessons, not that I thought I needed them. I much preferred to sunbathe in the front garden rather than run to Raul when he whistled in his funny little whispery way. I got used to it, however, and since he was so good to me, I decided to comply. Why, there was nothing that made Raul grin more widely than when he showed Mama and Papa the new tricks he taught me during their absence. That, and the fact, he had cleaned up every piece of poop in our yard, which for some reason he was so proud of, as well. Now who would love to go around cleaning up dog poop all day just for a bit of special recognition is beyond me. But it sure made Raul happy.

Yes, come to think of it, Raul, was a good friend. I even missed him when he was not around our house, and even more so when we moved to America. But still, the best times of my life were when Mama and Papa were there with me. And when they put those suitcases in the attic, why I was one very pleased pooch indeed.

CHAPTER 14
HI HO HI HO IT'S OFF TO CAMP I GO

"Maybe Lucky should go to dog training school," I heard Papa say one day when we were walking through *Chapultepec* Park. Now, I loved this park, the largest in Mexico City, so I wasn't paying too much attention to Mama and Papa's conversation. Instead I was busy sniffing out all the good park smells – leftover *tortillas*, dumped ice cream cones, popped balloons, the markings of other dogs. It all made me one happy dog.

"Not a bad idea," Mama answered. I figured they were talking about something that would be in my best interests, as Mama always sided with me.

Was I ever in for a surprise! For going to school meant I would not be with Mama and Papa for quite some time. And I never have learned to care for that idea much at all, even to this day.

We kept on walking and I continued to tug on my leash, trying to go all the places I wanted to go and not where Papa wanted to lead me. It had definitely become a 'war zone' between us. It seems I always wanted to go one way – Papa the other. I just couldn't understand why he didn't want to give me the time to take in all those 'good' smells.

Papa gave a hard tug on my leash and I yelped, mostly, of course to get Mama's attention.

"Hey, don't hurt him," she said.

"I'm not, but he's got to learn to obey. An untrained dog is a useless dog," Papa said, in his most authoritative tone.

"He's not a puppy anymore, remember? And you know the old saying, 'you can't teach an old dog new tricks,' " she added.

"I'm not so sure about that," Papa said. "Lucky's very intelligent. I think he can learn anything he puts his mind to. He's just got a stubborn streak that needs a little tweaking."

'Tweaking,' I hadn't heard that word before, but I had a feeling it had something to do with fixing me. Suddenly I remembered the last fix-up job they had done on me, compliments of Dr. Gonzales, our current vet. I wasn't about to go through all that pain again. It had changed me for life; that I knew for sure. For some reason I wasn't much interested in chasing after the girl dogs anymore. *Who cares . . . as long as I have Mama and Papa, I'm happy.* I thought briefly of my first love, Lupita, and wondered what had happened to her since our encounter in *Polanco.* I had a feeling it wasn't all that good, that she hadn't won the second 'Doggie Lotto.'

"I heard about a dog training school at Newcomer's Club," Mama said. "I believe it's called *Hacienda Campus Canino.* It's run by a British woman. Lots of expats send their dogs there."

"Sounds good," Papa said. "It seems as if the British should be good dog trainers, as they're specialists in the 'manners and etiquette' department."

"That's what I was thinking, and they also seem to like animals."

Well, Mama went home and found their fancy brochure, which showed pictures of happy dogs being led around a lake and sleeping on fluffy beds in a beautiful old *hacienda.* She even showed me the brochure, like I would be impressed or something. I wasn't. That's because all the dogs pictured were not with their mamas and papas and it really scared me. No matter, it wasn't long until off I went to *Hacienda*

Campus Canino, which means the house of dog training, I think. I wasn't sure what that was all about, but I was soon to find out.

Of course, it all started out perfectly well. Mama and Papa loaded me into the van with my bed and headed north to *Zumpahuacan,* where the school was located.

"I thought I'd bring along a picnic," Mama said, "so we can stop in the mountains somewhere along the way and relax. It's always feels so good to get out of the Mexico City smog."

"I think it will be good for Lucky to be away from it for a while," Papa said. "He's spent his entire life in this gray haze." He looked up at the sky, shook his head. "A little 'lung purification' will do him good."

"I know it will, but I can't believe that he has to be away from us for six weeks."

I saw this 'sniffly look' on Mama's face and figured I was headed for trouble.

Oh well, I'll think about that later. Instead, I looked out the window at the pine trees whizzing by. There was one thing I became especially interested in – these huge dog-like creatures in large pens. People were even on their backs! Now this I could not understand. *Who would want to ride a dog? Oh yeah, Little Harold would.*

"*Mira*, Lucky, look!" Mama pointed at the animals. "Those are horses."

I squinted to get a better look and Papa slowed down. *Nope, I'm not too excited to meet any of them – they look like they could swallow me whole.*

I started to bark and wag my tail furiously, like I was going to frighten them off or something. A strange odor crept into the car and it smelled like weeds and grass. Of course I had never been exposed to the smell of horse manure. However, in my future I would come to know horses well. They were always in Hyde Park on my outings there, going down the bridle paths, their riders dressed in funny black hats, tall black boots and red coats. Once in a while I'd snatch a bit of their dried up poop and carry it around. I'm not sure why, but it didn't taste so bad. It sure infuriated Mama and Papa, however, and they'd quickly make me spit it out and put me back on my leash. *Now what harm can a little horse poop do a dog?* I always wondered. But as usual, that's another story.

As we climbed higher into the mountains, I completely put horses out of my mind. There were so many other interesting things to see – especially those bright green and red homemade sausages – *chorizos* – that hung from the little wooden stands along the roadside. Boy, did they smell good! I think I could have eaten about a dozen of them in two minutes flat! But Mama and Papa didn't give me an opportunity, since Mama quickly produced sandwiches from her picnic basket when we stopped. I'm sure she didn't think those hanging sausages were safe to eat. But I didn't agree. I saw a lot of chubby people sitting on the log benches in front of the shops and they sure didn't look like they were dying of salmonella to me.

After we finished lunch – I got the leftover cheese and bread – we proceeded up this tiny little road that clung to the mountainside. It looked darn scary to me as our van barely fit on it. In fact, I was so scared I quickly fled to the other side of the van.

"Look, *Nevado de Toluca*," Papa said, pointing up at a giant volcano-type mountain. "Let's give it a climb, should we?"

"Climb," now that word wasn't in my vocabulary as yet. But I was soon to like its meaning very much, for I quickly learned it was connected to one of my favorite pastimes, 'walking."

"Sounds good to me," Mama said, as they parked and got out of the car.

Papa put my leash on first as I think he was afraid I'd go scampering right up to the top of the mountain and leave them both behind. I have to admit, I'm a pretty fleet-footed pooch.

We hiked up a dirt trail for quite a while. There were only a couple of other hikers on the mountain. It was so beautiful and peaceful. The air smelled like pine and the sky was bright blue. There was even a little lake where I got a drink – at least a brief one – as Mama quickly produced a water bottle and poured some in her hand for me to drink from instead.

When we were almost at the top, Papa did something very strange indeed. He undid my leash. Why, I couldn't believe my 'doggie' eyes! Why, I was so surprised I didn't even run away. I stood right by his side. Now that really surprised Papa.

"Can you believe it?" he said. "I thought Lucky would be two blocks away by now."

I didn't disappoint him for long. The sight of a squirrel running up the mountainside spurred me to a fast trot in its direction.

"Lucky, you come back here right now!" Papa yelled. But I was out of sight, thinking only 'squirrel.'

Mama and Papa chased after me. By then the squirrel had disappeared into a hole. I stood there sniffing until they caught up with me. Needless to say, that was the end of my freedom.

"You're staying right here with us, Old Boy," Papa said, clipping the leash back on. "At least until you're trained."

Well, we kept on hiking until we ran into this cold white stuff. Why it about froze my paws off! In fact, I was wishing real hard that Papa would pick me up and carry me. But he didn't.

"That's snow, Lucky," Mama said. "You'll be seeing plenty of that when we visit Utah some day."

In the meantime, Papa picked some up, made a big ball, and tossed it toward me and Mama. It hit me smack in the middle then exploded before I could even catch it. Papa quickly threw another one and this time I caught it mid-air. Why, it tasted just like water, but much colder. I gobbled it up.

"Look! Lucky likes snow," Mama said.

I decided to give it a roll as I was hot from our climb. I soon came to find out that this 'refrigerator treatment' worked quite well, for I remained one cool dog until we reached the top of the mountain.

The view was beautiful. We could see clear back into the huge sprawl of Mexico City and even farther, to the other two volcanoes, *Popocatepetl* and *Iztlaccihuatl*, both over 17,000 feet tall according to Papa. I wondered if we would someday climb all of them. I sure hoped so as I had quickly decided hiking was my new favorite pastime and I loved the thrill at being over 15,000 feet high. It was a bit harder to breath up there and I noticed I didn't have my usual 'doggie pep.' That was okay with me. It was great fun.

But all fun things have to come to and end. Soon we were back in the van and headed to my dog training school.

The second we drove into the long driveway and saw the big sign which read *Hacienda Campus Canino*, I got this funny feeling in the pit of my stomach, like I was going to be at this place for a long time. I quickly took note of the many bushes and flowers for peeing purposes, and lots of grass for running. That much was good. *Then why did I have such an uneasy feeling?* I think it was because Mama was so quiet. I could tell she was feeling sad. But not Papa, he was just whistling away, like always.

Well, they took me inside this beautiful *hacienda*. The *saltillo* tile floors were so polished that I started to slip and about fell on my face. A woman with a strange accent greeted us from behind a tall desk. I didn't know at the time it was 'British,' and that there would be plenty of British accents in my future.

"I'm Suzanne," she said. "And this must be Lucky." She bent down to greet me, and scratched behind my ears. *Now this can't be such a bad place, can it?*

She proceeded to tell Mama and Papa all about her training school and how they used praise, motivation, calmness and consistency to train the dogs. Mama and Papa had big grins on their faces, so I decided everything was just peachy fine.

"We don't use punishment," she continued. "Only a quick jerk on the collar to remind the dog of his errors." *Now a jerk on the collar, I knew what that was all about.* I quickly decided I was about to have 'one sore neck.'

Mama and Papa nodded.

"And when I say 'correction' – one good correction is far better than twenty light nagging corrections."

Now what a 'light nagging correction' was all about I had no idea.

125

"And we always end each training session on a very positive note," Suzanne said, with this big cheery British grin on her face. "So I'll just need Lucky's vaccination record. Of course we'll need to give him an additional rabies vaccine and kennel cough injection," she added.

"That's fine," Mama said. She pulled an envelope from her purse and gave it to Suzanne. "Here's his immunization record."

"Well, Lucky, let's go," Suzanne said, taking my leash from Papa. "You'll be a fine dandy trained canine in six weeks when you next see your mama and papa."

Of course, by this time, tears were streaming down Mama's face. She bent and hugged me so hard that I thought I was going to break in half. I planted my feet firmly on the tile. But little did it matter. I slid right across on my behind when Suzanne pulled on the leash and I had no choice but to follow. I whined all the time, however, making darn sure Mama and Papa knew just how displeased I was.

"I'll return shortly and take you on a tour of the premises, just as soon as I deliver Lucky to his trainer, Miguel."

Miguel, I thought. *Sounds Mexican.* I wondered if he'd be a 'kicker' or if he was the one to apply all those 'nagging corrections' they'd been talking about.

"*Adios,* dear Lucky," Mama called out as they turned to leave. "We'll miss you terribly."

Even Papa looked kind of sad.

But what about me? Where on earth am I being led?

We soon met up with Miguel, a small young man with long dark hair. He reached down and actually patted my head. Boy, was that a surprise! He kind of reminded me of Raul, which was reassuring. *But where*

126

are my Mama and Papa? Where's my fluffy bed? The entire place smelled like the green pine disinfectant Rosalia loved to use. At least that was reassuring. Mama would be happy with its cleanliness.

"Venga, Lucky, come," Miguel lead me down a long hallway with large pens on both sides. It looked like a jail to me. Several other dogs were inside them. They barked and barked as we walked by. I didn't even get a chance to stop and exchange sniffs with them.

At the end of the hallway, Miguel paused and opened the latched door. *No way I was going inside that trap.* I stood firm. He gave a tug on my leash and pulled me inside. I spied a bed. It was fluffy all right, but it wasn't 'my' bed. An aluminum bowl filled with water was beside it. Miguel told me to take a rest and that he would begin our training sessions in the morning. He quickly exited and closed the gate before I could squeeze out after him. I knew he'd done that trick a few times. Boy, was he fast. I looked around my 'run' as they called it. *Run? Where was I supposed to run in here? It was only about the size of my Persian rug. And where are my Mama and Papa?* I raced back and forth inside the pen, barked for my parents. But no one responded.

About sunset, Suzanne brought a bowl heaped with dog food and placed it in my run. I took one sniff and put my snout in the air. *No way am I eating that stuff. Where's my rice or pasta?*

She looked puzzled. "Whatever is the matter with you, Lucky? Aren't you even a wee bit hungry?"

Obviously, she wasn't familiar with my food requests. *Actually, Suzanne, I'm starving. But there's no way I'm eating this stuff.*

"Maybe I can find you a different kind of food." She placed a bowl of dry dog food next to mine. Do you prefer this?"

127

Again, I refused it.

"I'm sure you'll decide to eat when you're hungry enough," she said, smiling at me, like she was reading my mind.

Boy, did I prove her wrong! Even though I was starving, I refused to eat her dumb food.

By morning, I'd changed my mind. My stomach was twisting in pain like my days on the street and I remembered that I would have eaten anything back then. *Perhaps this food is not as bad as I think.* So I pretended it was spaghetti and meatballs and gobbled it down, at the same time trying not to taste it. But I couldn't help myself. It tasted like mud to me, maybe mixed with a bit of meat flavoring. Then again, what choice did I have? *Eat or become a 'ghost dog' like Polly.*

Then the training began. It went on and on and on and on. I'd never walked around in a circle so many times in my life. In fact, it made me downright dizzy, and my paws hurt.

Miguel kept lifting his hand in different directions saying: "heel position," "sit," "down" and "stay." The list went on. And he was talking to me in English. This I definitely couldn't figure out as I knew darn well he spoke Spanish.

Anyway, it didn't take me long to figure out what he meant by his hand signals and voice commands. Certainly not six weeks! *What kind of a stupid dog do they think I am?* It didn't matter.

In fact, I was getting darn good at it – when I wanted to, that is. I could see the look of frustration on Miguel and Suzanne's faces when I didn't do as they commanded.

"Now, Sir Lucky," she would say. "Please obey the commands."

Like I was going to do exactly as she said every time. I did have a mind of my own, you know.

* * * *

The long six weeks of my confinement finally passed and it was time for my graduation. I was sure ready to go home and I was certainly ready for a good old plate of Mama's famous spaghetti and meatballs or some chicken and rice or a slice of beef from my favorite restaurant, *Rincon Argentine*. It made me salivate just to think of them. But most of all I missed Mama and Papa. In fact, I dreamed about them every night.

On graduation day, we woke up early and Miguel gave me a bath. He put a red scarf around my neck and told me I looked real *'guapo.'* By the smile on his face, I could tell I was 'one handsome *perro.*'

They took me into the inside training ring, which had mirrors all around it. Little did I know that Mama and Papa were on the other side looking at me through the one-way glass. They must not have spoken, for I know I would have heard their voices from any distance. Again I did my thing, going round and round and round the ring, led by Miguel. Then it was sit and down stay and heel and more heel. Guess what? I passed! I had a feeling it was about time to go home.

It was. When Suzanne led me into the front reception, Mama and Papa stood there beaming at me. Why I've never done my hula dance so hard, I was just so darn happy to see them. Of course, I jumped right up on both of them and Suzanne's face froze in horror!

"Lucky, Lucky! Remember your training! Sit, sit!" I tuned her right out and yelped and yelped a warm 'doggie' welcome to my parents.

"I wish to apologize," Suzanne said. "Lucky is really very well trained. I don't know what got into him."

"It's just seeing us after so long," Mama said, hugging me. Papa hugged me, as well. Why we were one happy family once more. And this is even with my training costing them a bundle.

"I must admit that we had several problems during Lucky's stay," Suzanne said. Mama and Papa both looked up. "He certainly missed the two of you and he did not seem to care for our food."

Bingo, Suzanne, you won the thinking prize!

"And furthermore, it seems your husband has been vaccinated for kennel cough and rabies."

Mama and Papa both looked puzzled.

"You see, you gave me the incorrect Vaccination Card, which I'm afraid did not belong to Lucky, but to you, sir." She looked at Papa apologetically. "After we gave Lucky the required injections, we entered them on your card, thinking it was his."

Mama started laughing hysterically, but Papa wasn't quite so sure it was funny.

"Now when you travel for business, you can show everyone your rabies vaccination and kennel cough proof," Mama laughed. He decided to join in her laughter.

So we said *"Adios"* to *Hacienda Campus Canino* and this time headed in the opposite direction – back to Mexico City. I could already taste Rosalia's *carne asada*.

CHAPTER 15
NORTHWARD BOUND

"Guess what?" Papa said rushing inside the house after work one Friday night. It was my 'lazy time of day' so I was taking a good old snooze and he about scared the 'doggie daylights' out of me with his loud voice. I wasn't used to Papa yelling unless, of course, he was upset with me, and I knew he couldn't be upset with me as all I had been doing was sleeping on my Persian rug. Anyway, I quickly jumped up and ran out to the kitchen to greet him.

"You've been sleeping on the job again, Old Boy," he kidded me, watching as I zigzagged toward him, still half-asleep. "You look like you've had one too many."

By this time I was awake and doing my 'welcome hula.' Mama had joined us by then.

"I could hear you from upstairs," she told Papa. "What are you so excited about?"

Papa had a broad smile on his face and began talking even more excitedly. I was certain that we must be going for a really great walk or something extra good, maybe even for a hike up another mountain.

Boy was I ever wrong! Instead Papa grabbed Mama real fast, gave her a big kiss right on her lips. She gave him this kind of funny look.

"What on earth is wrong with you? Have you gone *loco*? I think maybe you've been breathing this Mexico City smog far too long."

"You're right about that," he answered. "And all that's about to end."

"Are you saying what I think you are?" Mama asked.

"You better believe it. We're going home!"

Home? I thought we were home. What does Papa mean?

"My boss called me from California today and said we are being transferred back to the home office, effective at the end of the month."

Mama started to cry, but she was smiling at the same time. Now this I just couldn't figure out.

She grabbed Papa by the shoulders and hugged him real hard. Then I saw her coming toward me.

Oh, oh, I'm in for a real squeezing job. I didn't know whether to run, howl, or just sit there and wait for the results, which I more or less guessed would be a big smooch. I waited.

"Oh, Lucky, you're going to move to California with us! We're going back to America!" Mama said, hugging me so tight I could barely breathe.

Boy, this California, America, whatever, must be something to really get excited about. Now where in the heck is that? I had no idea, but I soon decided it must be a very special place to make both Mama and Papa so excited. Little did I know that things were about to change 'big time' in my life.

* * * *

And then the *fiestas* began. Mama and Papa had several at our house and then on other nights, off they went and left me home all alone. Boy was I depressed. If 'California' meant I had to spend almost every night alone, then I didn't like it even one little bit. The only good thing about all their nights out was that they would come home with lots of *regalos*, some of which were in the form of food. That meant plenty of *carne asada*, *mole, tamales* and the likes for me. I was almost popping out of my fur with all that leftover food Mama and Papa seemed to be bringing from some 'bottomless pit' in the middle of Mexico City.

"Everyone has been so kind to us with all these goodbye *fiestas* and all," Mama said, one night as she dished me up a big pile of meat and rice which they had brought from a *fiesta*. "They must think we're going to starve when we return home."

"I think they just want us to remember their famous Mexican hospitality," Papa said.

"Yes, it has been a great four years, despite some of the crazy things that happened to us down here," Mama answered. "The Mexican people have been very kind to us."

I noticed that her eyes were starting to water and prepared for the worst.

Oh, oh, there she goes again . . . her crying thing.

"Yes . . . they have and we've had some great times," Papa said. "It will be hard to leave Mexico in many ways."

"I know it will, but thank goodness we're taking our most precious bit of Mexico back with us." She looked at me, bent down and gave me one of her 'bear hugs'. "Lucky, what would we ever do without you in our lives?"

"Maybe we should just turn him out on the street again," Papa said, trying not to laugh.

Mama bopped him one playfully. "No way!"

"Of course we won't leave Lucky. I've gotten kind of attached to the Old Boy myself."

"Kind of? Why he gets a kiss before I do when you come home from work!"

Papa laughed. "Well, like I've always said, Lucky's always happy and he never asks for money. What more can I add?"

Then Mama laughed, too, and touched Papa on the check. He hugged her back.

I had a feeling things were about to get a lot more mushy, so I crowded between them, hoping to get in on some of the action. They both gave me a big 'smacker' right on top of the head. Boy, was I one happy dog! But not for long.

That's because early the next week, all these strange men with dark hair showed up at our house – definitely 'kickers' I feared, so I ran and hid under the dining room table real quick-like. But I kept an eye on all of them as they carried box after box into our house and rolls and rolls of white paper and great big pieces of cardboard.

Rosalia, mop in hand, watched them, too. Why, they must have frightened her as well, for all she did was cry--and Rosalia was always happy and smiling. I couldn't figure out for the 'doggie' life of me why she was so sad. Those *hombres* weren't all that scary. And I hadn't done a thing to mess up the house in days. Anyway, I went up to her, gave a little yap and placed my front paws on her legs. She cried even harder.

"Oh Lucky, *mi perro*," she sobbed.

I just didn't know what to do, so I tried licking her leg to see if that would comfort her. She cried even harder and ran into the bathroom. Now I finally realized what Papa was always saying about 'those emotional women.'

Well anyway, these guys started to take things out of all our cupboards and wrap them in paper and put them in boxes, but I growled real hard at them every time they got even close to my dishes, which were on the floor beside the refrigerator. They even took the cushions off the sofa and then wrapped them up in cardboard like big

Christmas presents. Then they started rolling up the rugs. I rushed to my Persian rug to defend it but it was rolled up and wrapped before I could pounce on it. Was I ever mad! I even growled at them, and all the men stood in the corner, hands held high in the air. Did I ever know how to control them! They didn't dare go near my bed after that, because each time they got even close, I let out a loud growl followed by a big bark. They soon learned that they were not about to mess with 'this *perro*.'

By the end of the day, our house was empty and all of our things had been loaded into a giant truck half the size of our yard. It was parked in the street out front. Only two things remained – my bed and my dishes. I was frightened out of my wits! My world as I knew it had been packed away into that truck! *How was I ever going to get it back?* I started to whine real loud and Mama came running in from outside.

"Oh, you poor Lucky," she said. "It's going to be okay. They're going to take everything to our new home in California."

Oh, no, not that 'California' word again. What in 'doggie daylights' does it mean?

"Javier is here to take you to the airport to make sure that your traveling papers are all in order so you can be on the plane with us tomorrow. I'm going to meet back up with you at Papa's office."

When Javier entered the room I became even more upset. I was seriously afraid I was being sentenced to his care forever! I never did forgive him for the time he put me in the trunk of the company car to take me to the vet, or when he threw my food on the ground or all the other mean things he had done to me. In fact, I didn't like that Javier even one little bit and I wanted to bite his hand off when he tried to put my leash on. But Mama came to his rescue and quickly secured me.

"Your bed will be right here when you come back, Lucky. I promise."

I wasn't quite so sure, but Mama had never lied to me before so I had to believe her.

Begrudgingly, I let Javier lead me from the house and to our van, my tail between my legs.

* * * *

Things at the airport didn't get much better. Javier tugged me into this office against my will, cussing me the entire time. He slapped a pile of papers on a desk. We waited and waited for about an hour until I thought I was going to pee on the floor while the fat bearded man smoking a cigar who sat at the desk looked up at Javier and then down at me. Finally, he held out his hand and made a motion with his two fingers, so Javier dug into his pocket and pulled out a fistful of *dinero* and gave it to him. The man smiled and finally stamped the papers.

"*Adios, el perro,*" he smiled, pocketing the money. Javier scowled, grabbed the official exit paper, and then off we went toward Papa's office.

"Like they need another street dog in Mexico City," he yelled at me in English. He didn't even give me time to pee, and boy was I one miserable pooch all the way to Papa's work. *Javier, you just don't have a heart when it comes to me, do you?* I had a feeling he was one *hombre* I was not going to miss when I went to California – America – wherever it was we were going. I wanted to give him one last bite so bad, but I refrained, concentrating instead on my urge to relieve myself.

136

When we reached Papa's office and parked several stories up in the parking garage, I figured that I would finally have my chance. For some reason, Javier forgot to close the window on the driver's side of the van when he went in to find Mama and Papa, so I made fast work of my opportunity.

I jumped over the seats and to the front of the van, then hopped right out the window to freedom.

Of course, I did 'my thing' on the first post I found, and as an extra bonus for Javier, who was responsible for keeping our car spotless, I let it go once on each tire. *That'll show him – wait until he gets a whiff of this!*

Enjoying my freedom, I decided to go for a little walk while I was at it. The parking ramp was pretty large and there were lots of good smells in there, so I continued my trek downward toward the entrance, my nose to the ground in perfect street-dog fashion. *Not much to eat in here – they must have lots of sweepers.* But I wasn't hungry anyway, after all the stuff Mama had been feeding me for the past week. But still, there was so much to explore.

When I reached the entrance to the garage, I met up with four guards. I was trying to figure out what to do to get around them when I noticed that they didn't care a 'doggie diddly' whether I left the garage or not. *Bet they don't know I'm Papa's dog – probably think I'm just another street dog.* I pranced right by them and out onto the street. I was later to be proved correct about that prediction.

Anyway, when I reached the street, I was met by a pleasant surprise. For right across from Papa's work was a lunchtime food market. Of course, several other street dogs had already laid claim to it and about bit my head off when I approached. *Don't worry, don't worry, I'm not about to steal your food.* I looked at the boney creatures for a moment, felt so sorry for them. It had been a good long time since my days on the street, but I still remembered them well. In fact, they were chiseled in my memory, and every time I thought what a cushy life I now had, I forced my mind back to those days just to keep myself humble. It wasn't fun to be hungry all the time or to sleep in a dirt hole and wonder when you'd be kicked or attacked. I decided I'd better get out of there before I really broke down and led a couple of those poor dogs up to our van. *Now Papa wouldn't like that even one little bit, now would he?*

I was soon to learn there was a lot more to explore besides the food market and thinking of my painful days on the street, so I hastened my clip and went right across the footbridge which crossed over the *Via Ducto*, the big road which ran beside Papa's work. *No sense going onto that street.* I briefly thought of my brother, Buddy, and how he had fallen victim to a busy street. *That's not about to happen to me – especially the day before I leave for California – America – whatever.*

While crossing the bridge I noticed this girl looking at me kind of strange. I even thought I heard her call my name, but decided I was imagining this since I didn't know anyone in this part of town, so I just kept on my merry exploring way. Then I remembered her. She was from Papa's office and had come to our house that morning to check on the move. I decided what a small world Mexico City really was. *Imagine, running down the street and seeing someone I know?* But I don't really think she had any idea of who I was, even though she had patted me on the head not more than three hours before.

I was to learn later that back at Papa's office, things were really getting exciting. For I'd been missed. When

138

Mama came down to the car and discovered I was missing, she really flipped out. They said her screams could be heard clear the other side of Via Ducto, which was a very noisy road. Anyway, I guess Javier came running and discovered what he had done, and when he met up with Mama, she really let him have it. And let me tell you, my Mama seldom lets anyone 'really' have it. He was probably so scared he about wet his pants, definitely afraid of what Papa would do to him when he found out. And to think I was having my revenge on Javier and didn't even know it.

By this time, Papa was on the scene and he was not a 'happy *hombre*' at all.

Then the action of finding me really began. Why, you'd think the building was on fire, the way everyone came racing from it, Mama later told me. The entire guard force of twenty was alerted and they went running around the parking lot and the streets surrounding the office like a bunch of crickets doing the *kooka racha,* like some ants searching for a sugar bowl. I wish I could have seen Javier's face at about that time. It must have been plenty red. I would have loved seeing him squirm. Of course by then Mama was crying and crying, saying that she had lost her Lucky for good. In fact, everyone was just going crazy and all because of one little street dog – yours truly.

And here I was out merely having a good old time. I was planning to come back anyway – I knew I had a darn good thing going. I was just out for a little 'self-exercising,' didn't they know? I knew how to find my way around town. I was once a 'street dog' after all, and I had a pretty keen sense of smell – that I knew for sure. And besides, I figured I needed to take one last look at my 'homeland,' since I was leaving it for good.

But I didn't get the chance to sniff my way back to Papa's office. I was found. For you see what happened was that the girl I had seen on the street noticed all the commotion when she walked into the parking garage and asked what was going on. When they told her Papa's dog was missing, she got this enlightened look on her face and finally remembered who I was. She told them she had just seen me crossing the *Via Ducto* bridge. You can imagine what happened next.

They got me! Before I even got to finish my adventure, this whole group of guards pounced on me like I was a pot of gold. Why, I thought I was going to suffocate. Afraid that I would escape again, they formed this circle around me, all holding each other's waists, standing hip to hip. Why I felt like I was in a cage and I didn't care for it one bit. I looked and looked for an escape route but there was none. Then I saw Javier push through the circle, my leash in his hand, his face very red. I was sure I was about to be one 'dead dog,' that he would surely strangle me with it. Instead, he called me all these names in Spanish that I can't repeat and slung my leash around my neck like he was roping a bull. Boy, did that hurt! The guards all parted ways and he tugged me back to Papa's office with the force of a bullfighter. But, of course, when he saw Mama and Papa at the entrance to the parking lot, he let up on the leash and led me inside like we had been on a nice spring-time walk through the flowers. Boy, did I hate him! In fact, I promised myself that if it was the last thing I did, I would give Javier a good bite before I got onto the airplane.

"Oh, Lucky," Mama said, crying. "They found you! I could have never left Mexico City without you!"

Of course, I hadn't planned that she would, but I figured I was going to have a hard time convincing her of that. Instead I licked her face and she cried some more and hugged me.

Papa looked pretty relieved. Even though he didn't cry, I knew he wanted to. "We're going to keep a close eye on you for the next twelve hours," Papa said. "You're not getting out of our sight again until we see you loaded onto that airplane."

They did exactly what they promised. Even though I had to spend the night alone in the house while they stayed at a hotel, I wasn't really alone. Believe it or not, Javier was my 'special' companion. That's because Papa made him sleep in our van that night, which was parked in our driveway. He was to be my personal bodyguard. Now, I can imagine how pleased he was with that. But for once he wasn't so bad. Why, he must have opened the kitchen door about a hundred times during the night to make sure I was still there. I think it might have had something to do with him keeping his job. Actually, it was kind of reassuring to me, even though I barely got a wink of sleep. Our *casa* was just so lonely and empty and I was afraid Mama and Papa would forget me in the morning, so I didn't mind Javier's eavesdropping all that much. Anyway, he'd be out of my life for good in the morning, so I decided to be a good boy. In fact, I didn't growl at him even one time.

Early the next morning, Javier loaded me and my bed into the van and off we went to the *El Presidente* Hotel to pick up Mama and Papa.

Arriving at the airport, the man at the counter took my bed and put it into a big box and replaced it with a green cage with bars on its front. Now let me tell you, I didn't like the looks of that one little bit. But I was so tired from lack of sleep that I let Papa push me inside.

To tell you the truth, I was also feeling a big drowsy after eating that little candy Mama had given me on the way to the airport. One thing I knew for sure, all I needed at the moment was some sleep. In fact, I was so sleepy that I didn't even have the energy to bite Javier when he told me 'goodbye,' with a big smile on his face, even though I had promised myself I would. *Oh, well, he would be out of my life for good now.*

Then it was 'up up and away' to California, and my new home in America – to my new life.

"Adios, mi Mexico!" I thought as I curled into my 'street dog' ball inside the cage, which was in the cargo compartment of the airplane. For some strange reason I wasn't afraid, even though the jet was bouncing around in the air turbulence caused by the afternoon thunderstorm. I was just too tired to complain, or to call out to Mama and Papa, wherever they were. Besides, I sensed that even better things were about to happen in my now 'non-street dog' 'non-Mexican' life.

CHAPTER 16
WELCOME TO AMERICA

I'd like to describe my airplane ride in the big jet from Mexico City to California – the first of many to come, by the way – but to be truthful, I can't. That's because for me, it was one great big *siesta*. Like I said before, I'm sure it must have had something to do with that little candy Mama gave me on the way to the airport. Anyway, after hearing Mama and Papa talk about it, I'm glad I missed it. Apparently, the baggage handlers put my traveling kennel – and that, of course, included me – in the very belly of the airplane, down next to all the luggage and mail and such. Like I was a piece of cargo or something – can you imagine that? Apparently, there were two other dogs down there, as well. We were in what they called a 'special' climate-controlled place for live cargo.

Mama said they could hear barking all the way from Mexico to California, a journey of three and one-half hours. She was afraid it was me, but Papa assured her it wasn't my bark. It was actually the other two 'passenger' dogs. Let me tell you, they must have been very hoarse *perros* by then. All the other passengers in the plane must have wondered what was going on with all that barking. Most of them were Mexican, and you know how they are – definitely not the world's number one dog lovers – so they must have been frightened out of their reclining seats when they heard all that racket below them. As for this doggie, I saved my barking to greet Mama and Papa and about every other person at Los Angeles International Airport, so I've been told.

About the time we were ready to land, I began to wake up. *Where am I?* It was kind of dark and all I could hear were the airplane engines and, of course, barking from the two kennels next to me.

"Give a guy a break," I growled at them. "Can't you see I'm trying to sleep?" Of course they couldn't see much of anything in our tight quarters either, so I gave up on it and dozed a bit more. But I certainly got an abrupt wake-up call when the plane landed on the ground and I bounced up to the roof of my kennel. "Ouch!" Man did that ever give me one big headache.

Two *hombres* with very dark skin removed me from the plane. One stuck his finger inside the cage and began talking to me. "Hi little Mexican puppy," he said.

I'd never seen the likes of him – a Mexican who actually liked dogs? I couldn't even bear to growl at him I was so shocked. I later learned that he was no Mexican at all, but a person called a 'Black' in America. In fact, I soon learned I was no longer called a Mexican. I was a *Latino*, or *Hispanic*. I couldn't believe that in a little over three hours I had actually changed my nationality. Now that's called a *Speedy Gonzales* transition, if you know what I mean.

Anyway, these guys took me inside a huge building with a big photo of a handsome man hanging on the wall and a sign which read: WELCOME TO THE UNITED STATES OF AMERICA. By this time I was wide awake and looking all over for Mama and Papa. *Where are they?* I started to get real nervous and began pawing at the bars on my cage. But they didn't budge even one little bit. I wondered if I was to be captive for life.

Finally I heard familiar voices. Mama and Papa were standing not twenty feet from my cage. Mama held our video camera and was catching the whole moment on

144

film as she hadn't noticed the sign on the wall which read ABSOLUTELY NO PHOTOGRAPHY.

"Welcome to America, Lucky!" she zoomed in on me – behind bars at that! Definitely not a photo I wanted for my album. In fact, I wasn't all that keen on hearing her greeting at the moment. I wanted to get out of my kennel – immediately. Besides, I had to pee real bad. So I started barking as loud as I possibly could.

Let me tell you, it certainly got everybody's attention in the entire luggage reclaim area. When I wanted to get my message out, I had no trouble doing it. My bark could be about as loud as an afternoon thunder storm in Mexico City if I wanted it to be. This time that was the whole idea and I barked and barked until Mama and Papa came dashing up to my kennel. A U.S. Immigration Agent was right behind them.

"No cameras! No photography permitted!" he told Mama, a cross look on his face.

She looked perplexed. "I was just welcoming our Mexico City street dog to America. I didn't realize . . . Believe me, I'm not a spy." She quickly popped the camera into her carry-on bag before the officer confiscated it.

"Take it easy," Papa whispered to her, "before we get arrested."

Of course, I wasn't one bit interested in their conversation. I was just so happy to see my parents that I even peed in my cage, but only a little. After all, I was no longer some dumb little puppy.

"Can we let our dog out of the cage?" Papa asked the officer.

"Absolutely not. We need to see his transport papers first," the officer said.

Mama dug into her bag and came out with them. "Here they are, Officer, our dog is totally legal."

But still I was not permitted out of my cage, so I kept barking and barking. By this time, a large crowd had gathered around us. They probably thought someone was beating me or something by the racket I was making. Some of the people looked totally shocked. Perhaps they were animal rights activists, which I soon learned were quite a powerful group in America. I know whenever Mama or Papa ran into one of those 'animal rights people' when we were out walking and they asked about me and Mama told them they had adopted me from the streets of Mexico City, why they would look at me like I was a dog who could fly or something else really incredible. Then they'd about break down into tears of joy they were so happy. Believe me, they weren't the only happy ones. I was more than happy to have been adopted myself.

Anyway, finally the Immigration Agent nodded his head. "The papers look fine," he said, barely glancing at them. "You can take him out of the cage but you must remove him from the building immediately. And can you please get him to stop barking."

Like they could do that. When I made up my mind to bark, let me tell you, I did just that.

But the officer didn't need to ask Mama and Papa twice, for we were 'out of there' like a streak of lightning, rushing until we reached the sidewalk out front. I must have peed on the big cement post for about five minutes while Papa went to pick up the rental car.

By this time, I had noticed a little patch of lawn near the terminal entrance. I tugged on my leash toward it, knowing that a good 'roll in the grass' was what I needed after the long flight. But Mama didn't seem to understand.

"Lucky, are you okay?" Mama asked. "You were such a brave boy, riding all by yourself in the cargo hold of the plane." I suppose she'd already forgotten about those two 'barkers' that traveled right next to my ear. "Are you still sleepy Yellow Boy?"

I gave her a quick 'love lick', then sniffed the air. It smelled so different from Mexico City. *Where were the automobile fumes? The smell of cooking fires? Where was all the noise?* I just stood there by Mama's side and took it all in, having given up on reaching the grass for the time being.

Of course, the people puzzled me, too. Almost everyone who passed us, bent down, patted me, and said "Oh, what a sweet dog." I never even got one good kick, and for this I was very pleased. *I think I'm going to like it here in America*, I quickly decided. *They seem to really like us Mexican perros.* In fact, I had a definite feeling my days of 'kickers' were over.

Papa pulled up in a big green SUV a few minutes later. It kind of looked like a van but was not as long. It was certainly taller, and I had to really jump high to make it inside.

"Good jumper, Lucky," Papa congratulated me when I finally made it high enough to get inside on my second attempt. Boy, was it ever cushy in there – lots of nice dark fluffy carpeting – the better to collect my fur, I suppose. Besides, by this time Mama had taken my bed and water bowl from their box and I jumped right in my *cama*, like I had been separated from it for months. She quickly filled my bowl, knowing I would be thirsty. *But wait a minute, this water tastes funny, very different from Mexican water.* I drank it anyway.

So off we went down the San Diego Freeway toward my 'new world.' And boy did the cars ever whiz by us. It was like they were all in a hurry to get some place, very different from the way traffic barely crawled in Mexico City. I noticed something else very different from Mexico – lots of the cars had dogs inside. Now this was really exciting! I wagged and barked all the way to Orange County and to Dana Point, the beachside community where Mama and Papa lived – the place that would soon become my new home.

"We're going to take you to the beach first thing, Lucky," Mama said. Now what that was, I had no idea, but I'd noticed that the air here smelled different, even different from the air at the airport. It was fresh, kind of salty, in fact. Of course, at the time, I didn't realize this smell would become my signal that we were almost home, and I could start getting excited. But for the time being, it was just 'different,' and I looked forward to discovering everything in my new world.

Soon the cobalt blue Pacific Ocean was before us. Why, I had never seen anything so big and blue in all my 'doggie days'. It was one big beautiful water, that's for sure.

"Do you want to go for a walk on the beach, Lucky?" Mama asked. The word 'walk' certainly got my attention and I let out a quick whine.

"I think we'd better drop off our things at the apartment first," Papa said. "Then we'll go to the beach and get some lunch."

You see, we actually weren't going to go home to our house just yet as someone else was still living there and Mama and Papa wanted to remodel it before we moved in. We would be moving into what they called an apartment for a couple of months. It didn't matter to me where we lived – just as long as I was with Mama and Papa.

Anyway, we drove up this long steep road to the top of a hill and into this big grassy area where houses were stacked one on top of one another. I had never seen such a sight. This lady came out of one of them and met us with a little tiny car with no top, which I later learned was a golf cart. I soon discovered this was a great vehicle for what we dogs like to do best – smell the air and hang our heads out and take in everything. As we drove along. I sniffed the ocean air and looked at all the grassy areas filled with trees, so different from Mexico City. *Am I ever going to have the time of my doggie life here.* The woman stopped at a building and up we went to the top floor. Not being used to steps, I huffed and puffed all the way up. I would have preferred to stay down on the grass out front for a bit, for by this time I had to do my 'big number.' But no one seemed to notice my attempts to stop, so up I went with them, anxious to explore my new home.

"Good exercise for all of us," Papa said. "But Mama will hate taking you to potty at seven every morning."

"You got that right," she said. "But it's only for a couple of months."

The lady showed us around the nicely furnished apartment, gave Papa the keys, and left. Since they needed to move our car in front of the building and unload it, they left me inside the apartment and went downstairs, forgetting that I hadn't gone potty for a good long time.

When they returned, boy did I have a big surprise for them. For there in the middle of the living room was a big pile of you know what! Boy, was I embarrassed! I'd never done such a thing before in all my 'doggie' days.

Papa almost stepped on it when he came inside the door, carrying a big box.

"Watch out!" Mama said, just as his shoe was about to tread upon forbidden territory. "Lucky's had an accident."

Papa dropped his box and looked down at the nice new beige carpet. "Lucky, how could you!" His face was very red and I thought for a moment he was about to kick me. *No, Papa wouldn't do that.* But he certainly did a lot of screaming.

In the meantime, Mama made a dash for the bathroom and came back with an armful of paper towels, like she was about to clean up a pile the size of my kennel. "Oh, poor Lucky," she said. "It wasn't your fault. We forgot to take you for a potty walk before we came inside."

But Papa still didn't look convinced. "Damn dog! We shouldn't have brought him back home with us. Look how simple our life would have been."

"Don't you dare say that," Mama said, quickly cleaning up the mess and disposing of the evidence.

Of course, I just huddled in the corner, feeling very bad indeed.

"He won't ever do it again," Mama said. "Look how horrible his feels. You know it wasn't his fault. And don't you ever dare say that we shouldn't have brought Lucky back with us."

By this time, Papa had softened. He even hung his head a little, which he seldom does. "You're right . . . I'm sorry Lucky . . . but if you ever do that again, I'm going to . . . ."

Mama never let him finish. "Come on, let's go to the beach. I want to see how Lucky likes to play in the surf."

Believe me, I was about to surprise her in that department.

It only took us a few minutes to drive down to Laguna Beach, which was filled with quaint little shops, restaurants, and lots of artists and animal lovers, as I would later learn. That's because whenever Mama, Papa and I went there, everyone would love me to bits and they all wanted to paint my portrait. Now how lucky can a dog get?

My first time in Laguna I think I disappointed my mama. For I was far more interested in the smells coming from the restaurants than I was to romp on the beach – that's this big sandy place in front of the ocean. The first thing we did was stop at Starbucks for a cup of cappuccino.

"Oh, how I've missed Laguna." Mama's eyes misted as she looked across the street at the ocean.

"Oh how I've missed this cappuccino," Papa added. And Mama agreed.

I stood outside the door and waited for them, whining the entire time. For I was more interested in exploring the smells coming from Johnny Rocket's, the hamburger diner next door. In fact, I was starved as I hadn't eaten all day. Mama remembered this fact at about the same time.

"We'd better get Lucky something to eat," she said. "Guess a hamburger will have to do."

"They cost ten bucks," Papa said. Still he moved toward the door of the diner, for he knew he wasn't about to win that one.

Anyway, it was the best darn hamburger I ever had, for Papa ordered it with only the meat and bun. Why I gobbled it up like I hadn't eaten in a week. *Now this American food is good!* I looked up at both Mama and Papa, wagged my tail. *I'm ready for another one.* But my wish was not granted.

Instead, we crossed the road to the beach and found a bench on the boardwalk, which ran alongside it. It was a bench I would spend many hours of my future on, as Mama and Papa drank cappuccino and gazed at the

Pacific. I lay down beneath them and took in all the sights and smells. *Now this is the life. I have to admit that. How lucky can one little Mexico City street dog get?* Of course I would have liked a little cushion to lounge on, but you know, one can't have absolutely 'everything' in life.

I gazed at the waves rolling in and out and across the beach. Why, I had never seen so much water in my entire 'doggie days' and was certain I was about to be given one big bath when a big piece of water jumped over the boardwalk. And you know me and baths – something I never have really learned to enjoy. I jumped to my feet and hoped real bad that Mama would invite me up on the bench with them, but she didn't.

"Lucky, look at the waves!"

Like I really wanted to see something that was about to come and crush me.

"Let's go down on the beach for a walk," Mama stood and beckoned to me.

Papa polished off his cup of cappuccino and joined her. I stayed firmly in my spot until he tugged at my leash and forced me down the stairs and onto the sand.

Hey this is not so bad at all, I quickly decided. *So nice and cushy.* Immediately I lay on my back, and rolled around in the warm softness.

"Lucky likes the beach!" Mama said.

"I think he likes to make a big mess," Papa said, studying my sand-covered body. "He's going to make a disaster out of the car."

Little did I care, for I rolled around in the sand until a giant wave about crashed over me. Boy, was I the first one who wanted to scamper back up the stairs. But Papa held onto my leash and led me closer to the water. I was about to have a heart attack. Why those waves were taller than I was!

152

But a few minutes later the water was calm again, so I decided to get closer to check it out. Besides, I was thirsty.

Gingerly, I put my front paws into the water. It was cold! I stuck my snout in, took a quick sip. Salty! I spit it out as fast as I could.

"Oh no, Lucky, you can't drink the ocean," Mama said. She quickly pulled a bottle of water from her purse. I lapped the water up from her hand real fast like, trying to get rid of the salty taste. It was the last time I would try that stupid trick.

"Let's walk along the beach," Papa said. "Do you want to go for a swim, Lucky? *Does Papa think I'm stupid or what? There's no way I'm about to set paws in that salty, cold water.*

I proved myself right on that point. I never did go into the ocean as long as I lived in California. True I saw lots of other dogs on the beach who loved nothing better than scampering into the waves after a piece of driftwood thrown in by their owners. But not this street dog. *Boy, these California dogs can be dumb at times.*

For me, I liked to walk along the beach with Mama and Papa just fine. There were lots of good smells there for me to check out, and the sand felt wonderful beneath my paws. I also liked to watch the other dogs swimming and such, but for me, I knew very well I was not about to become a full-time 'beach-bum' type of dog.

Lucky in Belgium

Granny, Mama and Lucky during
Tulip Time in Holland

154

*Lucky & Parents on the top of
Nevada de Toluca Mexico*

Lucky camping in Colorado

155

Lucky at Laguna Beach, California

Lucky at the Grand Canyon in Arizona

A housedog at last!
Lucky on his favorite Oriental Rug in Mexico

CHAPTER 17
LIFE AT THE BEACH

Even though I never became an "Official Beach Bum," of the get-in-the-water variety, I certainly enjoyed life at the beach. Mama and Papa even began calling me "Lucky the Yuppie Beach Bum," which I actually thought kind of silly, but cute. They also liked to call me 'Golden Guy,' 'Yellow Dog,' 'Yellow Boy,' 'Old Boy,' and 'Lucky Dog.' Mama even called me 'Sweet Pea,' sometimes and why she thought I looked or smelled like a pea I could never understand. Now how a dog can have so many names, I'll never know; but I answered to each and every one of them just as faithfully as a little dog could.

Well, we lived in the apartment for two months, going up and down, up and down all those stairs several times each day. But I didn't mind apartment life half as much as Mama and Papa did. They hated all the 'comings and goings' by other tenants late at night and the loud music from adjoining apartments. I kind of liked it. It reminded me of my homeland in a way. And the stairs, why I learned to go up and down them like a robotized rabbit, and about took Mama's arm out of joint every time we climbed them. In fact, far into the future she suffered from what she called 'Lucky elbow,' complements of little old me.

"Hey, Lucky, wait for me," she'd scream, struggling to hang on to my leash.

Well, Papa took care of that problem. He bought what is called a 'choke chain.' And boy did it ever fit its name. It had a bunch of little rounded things all hooked together to form a chain. I didn't like it even one little bit, but since it was the only way I was going to get

159

outside, I had to sit there and wait while they placed it over my head and cinched it up. Sometimes it even got caught in my mouth on the way down and Papa always told me it was like having 'doggie braces' on my teeth, whatever they were. I hated having a mouth full of steel, so I quickly shut my trap and the chain slipped out of my mouth.

But that darn chain created other problems for me, as well. For you see, my choke chain worked like this. When it was placed over my head correctly and attached to the end of the leash and pulled tightly, it kind of formed a noose around my neck. I'm not kidding – a noose – you know, like they use to hang people. But I wasn't a criminal like *Poncho Villa* or anything, and I just could not for the doggie life of me understand the reasoning behind it. But then I got the idea – its purpose was to keep me 'in line' – which means well behaved and obedient.

Well, guess what? It worked, much to Papa's delight. For each time I pulled on it, that darn chain cinched right up and about gagged me. It also pissed me off, but I was so excited to get out into the fresh air that I learned to ignore the chain's pressure and gagged all the way down the stairs the first few times Mama or Papa put it on.

Of course, Mama felt terrible about the entire thing, telling Papa it was a form of animal cruelty, with which I fully agreed. But Papa said it was the only option they had for getting me to be well-behaved on my leash – that if I didn't like it choking me, I didn't have to pull. Of course, he promised Mama I would only have to wear it for a short time. And come to think of it, Papa was right. For after I quit pulling against my choke chain, low and behold, it stopped choking me. Besides, I soon learned good walking etiquette and that 'choke chain' went right into the old garbage can.

Anyway, Mama and I took many long walks during the day, as there were lots and lots of paths around the apartment buildings. When we went by the playground, we'd see some Mexican maids playing with children. Boy, did they jump up on the jungle gym real fast when they'd see me coming. *Guess I still had that special touch with Mexicans.*

The paths in our complex also went into kind of a wooded area filled with all the native California plants, like sagebrush and chokecherry. It was beautiful and very wild. I loved all the smells. There was one that especially attracted me and I was very determined to find out what it was. I soon did. For out of the underbrush ran this small gray furry animal with a fluffy white tail, a miniature one right after it.

"Look, Lucky, *conejos!*" Mama cried out. "Rabbits. It's a mother and its baby!"

Well let me tell you, I about lost it because I was so excited. I barked and barked and made such a racket that I saw the maids in the distance running toward the apartment building like I was a bull escaped from a bull fighting ring and was about to eat them whole. But I wasn't going to take my mind off those rabbits for long, and decided I was going to catch up to them no matter what, choke chain or no choke chain! I pulled so hard that I'm sure I about took Mama's arm out of its socket, but she held firm and slid along the grass after me. And to think I could pull over a hundred pounds – why I was amazed at myself!

But I never caught those *conejos*, much to my serious disappointment. I'd never seen anything so fast, especially with 'yours truly' barking at their heels. Only one time did I almost catch one by its cotton ball, but I missed. I'll never forgive myself for that one, let me tell you. And I have to admit I've had many chances at *'conejo* grabbing' over the years, yet it's one task I just can't seem to master. But I'll never give up on it, for I've promised myself that one day I will have a rabbit right between my jaws. And I can just imagine its wonderful wild taste.

* * * *

Finally, we moved to our peaceful house on San Raphael, much to Mama and Papa's delight. I think that was because it was within walking distance of the beach. And walk, walk, walk, that's what they loved to do. That didn't bother me one bit and I was always happy to join in their exercise routine.

Of course, my first thought about moving into our Dana Point house was whether or not there would be rabbits. My wish was granted, but that's another story.

I'll never forget the day we moved in. Mama had to drive me down from the apartment in Papa's restored 1966 Mustang Convertible – definitely one of the loves of his life besides Mama and me. That's because our new Jeep was at work with Papa. Now I thought this was great as she put the top down and I had all the fresh air I could ever wish for all the way there. Why the wind whipped through my fur and gave me the total 'air conditioning' treatment. My flying fur also did a treatment on the black interior of Papa's car. It flew all over the place, landing in every little crevice there was. To tell you the truth, Papa was not so happy when he saw his car crammed with my fur. In fact, two years later he was still finding bits and pieces of me stuck beneath the seats and in the door handles. Needless to say, I was never allowed inside the convertible again. Oh well, guess I can't have it all.

Anyway, when we got to the house I was really excited. It looked pretty big to me and first thing I did when Papa opened the door was race inside and across the floor to discover my new home. Well was I ever in for a surprise! I didn't know the floor was marble, and newly polished at that. Why, I started to slide like I was on an ice skating rink and I couldn't stop until I slid right across the living room and kitchen to the back sliding door. I practically flew right through the glass! Let me tell you, I quickly learned to tread very slowly on those marble floors, although my paws never did seem to be able to grip them, no matter how hard I dug my nails in, much to Papa's dismay. One other thing, that floor was cold as ice. For some reason, they put my bed on top of my Persian rug and then right on the marble for the first few nights. Boy did I freeze – I mean they might as well have just put my bed in the refrigerator – and this was in the summer time. Did that floor ever make my bones ache!

Of course, I started complaining about my sleeping arrangement in my own 'doggie way' and Mama finally figured out I was not too crazy about my bed spot. Guess what she did? She moved me and my bed to the nice cushy carpet in the living room, not so much to Papa's delight. But after she explained to him that I was getting middle aged – about five in dog years – he agreed that I should sleep on the carpet. Of course, the first thing he did was go out and buy a brand new carpet cleaning machine. Now just what he thought I was going to do to his new carpeting, why I had no idea. All I wanted to do was have my little bed there. And do a little 'doggie rolling' on occasion, of course.

But this first day at our new house I wasn't interested in sleeping. I was interested in exploring. The second Papa opened the rear sliding door I was out, searching for *conejos* just as fast as I could. My 'rabbit wish' was eventually granted, although I didn't find any that day. But as soon as Mama planted her flowers and the grass started growing back, boy did we have loads of them! It was like a regular rabbit colony. Now by this time, Mama had decided she didn't like rabbits even one little bit as they seemed very fond of her petunias and impatiens. I certainly had an interest in them, however, and first thing I did when they let me outside was to do a quick bit of 'rabbit hunting.'

Anyway, back to my first back yard exploration. No, I didn't find any rabbits that time, but I did discover other things. I could see the ocean very clearly, but I liked it much better at this distance – no chance of waves jumping up here. And there was this big covered thing – something I had a feeling was a big pool of water – not like the ocean, but much smaller. But I wasn't certain since I couldn't see beneath the cover. But I could smell water. Now in large quantities that meant 'bath' to me, so I quickly got away from it. I was just not in the mood for one of Papa's baths.

I quickly noticed that the entire yard was fenced, which meant there was no escape route to provide me with further hunting grounds, so I scampered to the side yard by the kitchen to look for one. There stood a big tall structure, which Papa called a built-in barbecue. Now, I didn't know at that time that it was a place for cooking food. It looked to me like one big step to get me up and over that six-foot fence. I quickly placed my front paws on the small wall beside it, jumped up, and then one more jump and I was on top of the barbecue, and then a final jump and I was over the fence. *Now that was slick. But where are the conejos?* There were none. Instead, I found myself captive in someone else's back yard. And there were no barbecue steps over there to get back over to our yard. I was stuck. And Mama and Papa were no where to be found as they had gone upstairs. How I was going to get myself out of this one, I had no idea. I decided to call Mama and Papa.

Of course, they quickly answered my distress calls and ran outside.

"Lucky, Lucky, where are you?" Papa said, racing around the yard. Mama ran right after him.

They couldn't find me anywhere. *Hey, dummies, look on the other side of the fence!*

Mama was in one of her panics by then. "Lucky was probably eaten by a coyote!" she screamed.

Whatever that was, I didn't want anything to do with it by the sound of her voice.

"Don't be silly," Papa yelled. "The entire yard's fenced and there's no way a coyote could carry Lucky away!"

"But they did that to our old neighbor's dog! They never found even a bone!"

Now Mama was really upset.

"Come on, Lucky's forty pounds. He certainly doesn't fit into any coyote's jaws."

Mama settled down a bit and continued looking for me. I barked even louder and finally they spied me in the neighbor's yard.

"Oh, Lucky, there you are! How on earth did you get over there?"

Papa quickly did one of his engineering assessments and figured out exactly what I'd done. "Lucky, the escape artist," he laughed. "Now there's nothing over there you need to discover, so get on back over here, Old Boy."

He soon concluded there was no way out other than the front gate, as all I did was pace back and forth along the fence and howl.

"Okay, okay, I'll come and fetch you, but don't you try that trick again, or I'll leave you there to be eaten by Norma's Big Tom."

I would have agreed to any condition, and besides, I had no idea of who Big Tom was anyway. One thing I can tell you; I never did jump over the fence again.

The remainder of the afternoon I napped away, totally enjoying the ocean breeze, which blew through the back slider. *Now this is the life, I have to admit it.* I thought briefly of my days on the streets of Mexico City, not missing them even one little bit. In fact, the breeze soon lulled me into the best *siesta* I'd had in a good long time.

When I awoke, I found Mama and Papa out in the backyard taking a bath. *I was right! It is a bathtub and I'm not getting anywhere near it.* I did find it strange, however, that they were taking their bath outside – and in their clothes – clothes that I later learned were called swimsuits! And I was seriously hoping they'd never be getting me one of those. They also had some candles lit and they were drinking champagne. Then I caught sight of some food and I just couldn't keep myself away any longer.

So I walked outside and to the steps that led up to the 'spa,' as I later learned it was called. Why, Mama and Papa were banging their glasses together and didn't even seem to notice me.

I'm here! I'm here.

Mama finally looked up. "Oh, Lucky, there you are. We thought you were going to sleep all night long."

Are you kidding, Mama? I'm hungry. I could see that they were munching on some sushi and I was hoping a little lost tidbit would float my way. That's because by this time I was really getting brave. I had made it up the steps to the wide raised brick ledge, which ran around the tub. I pulled back for a moment. The water was really steamy and bubbly. It looked like one big cooking pot to me. Now who would want to sit and lounge around in a boiling cauldron of soup was perplexing. But Mama and Papa certainly seemed to be enjoying it. And during the second glass of champagne, why they seemed to enjoy it even more.

"Wanna take a dip, Lucky Boy?" Papa asked.

Oh, no thanks, Papa, not me. I pulled back a little, settled down on the ledge as far away from the water as I could get without falling off, still hoping for a bit of sushi. I have to admit that the view of the sunset was wonderful. In fact, it soon became my favorite spot for sunset gazing. Besides, the water in the spa actually warmed up the air and it was about as cozy a spot as could ever be found in our back yard.

Boy, I sure could have used this place during my days on the street, I thought, rolling tight into my street dog curl. Oh well, I had it now and I was going to take full advantage of it and appreciate it to the fullest. In fact, I had decided I was going to appreciate my new American life to the hilt, as well. And believe me, I did.

CHAPTER 18
IT'S A BEAUTIFUL DAY IN THE NEIGHBORHOOD

I have to admit that life on San Raphael was splendid indeed. Why, I even got to meet the neighbors, something one didn't usually do from the high-walled houses in Mexico City. It was a pleasant neighborhood with palm-lined streets and stucco houses with red tiled roofs. 'Very California,' I later learned. It looked very 'Mexico' to me except that the eight-foot walls and barbed wire fences were missing. I didn't mind that one bit, for when I went into the front courtyard I could actually see out through the wrought-iron fence and watch the neighbors go up and down the street. Most had dogs with them and that really got me excited. Why, I'd never barked "hello" so many times in all my doggie days.

There was one neighbor I became especially close to. Her name was Nori. She was the widow who lived across the street. I came to know her as the '*galleta* lady,' as she always had a cookie in her pocket for me. Now let me tell you, that lady really knew how to make friends, and every time I saw her come out of her front gate I'd bark and bark like crazy until she came over with a *galleta* for me. I was just so proud of this attention-getting tactic I had developed. Of course you can imagine how Papa felt about it. And Mama, she said I was just being friendly to the neighbors.

Nori never ever let me down in the 'cookie' department. She was also very kind to me. She'd rub behind my ears and tell me what a lucky dog I was. Duh? As if I hadn't realized that already. Well, Nori and I became quite the pals. In fact, I thought that if I ever had to live with any one else, Nori would definitely be my pick. Why she'd actually give me Christmas presents each and every year, like I was her grandkid or something. One year she gave me a big glass jar with a picture of a dog that was for my dog biscuits. It still sits on our kitchen counter top and every afternoon about 3:00 p.m. I go and sit before it and Mama gives me a couple of doggie treats. It's kind of a special ritual the two of us have. She gets a biscuit from the jar, I slide down to the floor, all four legs spread, and look up at her with adoring eyes and 'bingo' down drops a biscuit between my two front paws. But I hold my position, for I know there will be another one coming. It's a tactic that has worked very well for me throughout the years.

"Aren't you smart, Lucky? Mama says. "You really do know how to count, don't you?"

I tried counting to three, but the third *galleta* never came my way, so I decided that I need not pursue any further math lessons.

I also got to meet our other neighbors. There was Lisa next door. Oh, was she a sweetie. She loved me and her four little fluffy Maltese, which, incidentally, I didn't even realize were dogs at first. They looked like five white mops running around to me. So until I heard them bark from beneath all that fur, I had no idea they were my kind of species. But Lisa loved us all, like we were about to go out of style or something. She just couldn't get enough of us. Now this I liked. Whenever I'd go by her side of the fence, she was 'all loves.'

"Oh, Lucky, you're so cute!" she'd tell me over and over again until it about went to my head. "And I love your little beard."

Now Lisa I really loved, but her yappie little Yuppie puppies with bows in their hair, I was never so sure about. There was more than one afternoon that they

169

woke me up from my *siesta,* and they didn't seem to like me all that much anyway. I'm not so sure her husband loved them so much either, for I often heard him call them the 'little . . . "(sorry, but I can't say this word) whenever they got anywhere near him. Of course, that was when Lisa wasn't around. But he was kind of an athletic 'football' type of guy and I just don't think 'lap dogs' were his thing. I always pictured him more with a Lab or Golden Retriever sitting beside him on the sofa watching a ball game.

Oh yes, and then there was Norma, the nice lady who lived next door on our other side. I don't think she was much into dogs, but she always treated me fine and said "hello" whenever she saw me sunning myself on the hot tub ledge.

"You've really got it good over there, Lucky," she'd tell me. Like I didn't know. Of course I did.

There was only one thing I didn't like about Norma. That was Big Tom – her enormous black cat. Why he'd snarl at me every time I came out of the house when he was sitting on top of our barbecue taking his 'cat nap.' He was a 'real trespasser' and I wanted him out of our yard real bad, but I wasn't about to let him test his claws on me, so I more or less kept out of his way. I knew they would be long and sharp and capable of tearing me into a lot of furry pieces, although I certainly didn't like him 'cat napping' on our barbecue and teasing me. Actually Big Tom and I finally reached this truce. I wouldn't bark at him if he'd get his furry self out of our yard when I came outside. It seemed to work. Of course, once in a while when he'd refuse to budge, I'd give him a little bark just to let him know who was in charge. Still I know that Big Tom got a kick out of teasing me, sitting up there just out of my reach. But I could have fooled him. He had no idea I could jump up there and pounce on him real fast. I never did let on, however, always aware of his 'clawing potential.' Anyway, we both stayed on what came to be known as 'our territory.'

Soon I came to discover that we also had friends who lived out of the neighborhood, some of them very far away. Nelson and Judy lived clear across the country in Virginia, wherever that is. They usually came to our house for Thanksgiving. Boy, was that an event. They were dog lovers like Mama and Papa and even had three black Labs and a Golden Retriever of their own, which they called 'the kids.' I never did get a chance to meet them, as Papa didn't allow 'dog visitors' as he was afraid I'd mark my spot over their scent after they left. They were probably right about that one.

Anyway, I'm sure Nelson and Judy spoiled their dogs, as they certainly spoiled me. And they just thought I was so cute, so unique.

"Imagine owning a street dog," they'd tell Mama and Papa. "That's really something."

Why you'd have thought I was a circus freak or something with the big deal they made out of it.

"Remember the time we came to Mexico, Lucky?" they'd ask. "It was when you were first adopted and you were an absolute 'bag of bones.' "

I didn't need to be reminded. I well remembered those boney hungry days.

I think Nelson thought I was still in the hungry mode. For every Thanksgiving dinner, he'd sneak me bits of turkey under the table when he thought Papa wasn't looking. That's because I wasn't supposed to be anywhere near the dining room table during meal time, let alone under it. I was supposed to be waiting in my bed. Boy, would Papa have been upset. But through it all I still remembered my 'table manners' and never begged – except when Nelson came to town.

Then there were all the relatives that came to visit. Papa had a whole mess of them here in California. Why, they just kept coming and coming and coming. Often they came for a barbecue on Sunday afternoons. Of course, to me that translated into lots of 'doggie' leftovers, so I was more than happy to miss my afternoon *siesta*, due to all the chaos. That's because Papa's younger brother brought his two little kids, Nico and Isabella. Now I hadn't been around too many kids except for those at the orphanage in Mexico City and those kids happened to like me. These kids didn't.

Why when Uncle would carry Isabella into the house, she'd take one look at me and scream, like I was a big black bear about to gobble her up! She screamed and screamed and turned all red in the face and clung to her dad like she was glued there. I just couldn't figure this out at all. Why I remember the first time she met me, her papa had to sit her on the kitchen counter top so she'd be out of my way. Of course, I was very curious about Isabella, so I kept sniffing at her little red shoes. Boy, did that set her off! It set me off, too – right to the back yard.

Their next visit, Isabella moved a little closer to my level. She sat on the sofa all night next to her mother, legs clamped together and screaming. Now, that really upset me. Here she was where I could really sniff her out and she wouldn't let me anywhere near 'sniffing range.' *Now, I'm not that scary, am I?* Let me tell you, Isabella gave me a real inferiority complex for a while there.

Now her older brother, Nico, was a bit more friendly – just a bit. He walked around with his hands in the air so I couldn't even move in for sniffing purposes. That's okay, I've always preferred sniffing people below the waistline anyway. Nico was to have none of that. The second I got within about two feet of him, he'd run up to his dad and grab his hand, all the time pretending to be brave. I guess that was because he was eight and didn't want to appear a sissy. I didn't care. I just left him alone and went to my bed, sensing that sooner or later he would come to like me.

He did. Why before long he was telling his parents that he wanted a puppy – probably to scare his little sister – and that I was his 'best friend.' So he said. Still I wasn't so sure of this. But Nico did begin to reach down gingerly and pat me lightly on the head real quick before he'd jump away from me like a frightened bunny. I appreciated the fact that he did even that, as he'd never been around dogs before. So I knew I would have a future with him. Now Isabella I wasn't so sure about.

In fact, after a couple of months, the second Nico got to the house he wanted to put me on my leash and walk me round and round or throw a ball for me to fetch. Why that family brought me so many new doggie toys I couldn't count them. However, they soon realized I was not a 'fetcher,' so that ended that. Instead, they started bringing me rawhide chew toys. Now these I could relate to.

Little Isabella was another story when it came to the 'establishing a dog friendship' department. She was not about to like me one little bit. It didn't' matter if I just came from the doggie groomer and smelled like lilacs, or if I looked at her adoringly and didn't bark at all. I felt so bad each time they came as she would cry and cry. As a 'last ditch' effort for affection, I even tried to lick her and wagged my tail to tell her how much I liked her. Why she cried like I'd bitten one of her fingers off! Even Mama and Papa came running. Like I was going to eat their niece or something, right? I didn't think that would be a good idea unless I desired a place on the street again.

"Lucky, leave Isabella alone," Papa said, grabbing me by the collar. I finally got the message – Isabella was 'off limits' to me. I had no choice but to obey my parents, but still I'd often look at her from a distance as she was eyeing me from the sofa and thought what wonderful chubby cheeks she had, all the better for doggie smooching.

This went on for about two years. Suddenly when Isabella turned four, things changed. She decided she would like dogs – at least me. Why the first time she reached down and petted me from the safety of her father's arms, I about fainted. But I liked her touch and was determined to win her love. I knew there would be a little smile on her face for me one day. And I knew it would be soon. It finally happened, and to this day, she even gives me a little hug around the neck each time I see her.

Now Papa's mother was still another story. Grandma was clearly 'head of the family.' One thing I know for sure about her – she made about the best rice with sauce that anyone could ever make. She also saw to it that there was plenty left over for me whenever we went to her house. Now I have to admit she was not so much into 'dog touching.' Only occasionally did she reach out and barely tap me on the head, and then run to the sink to scrub her hands with her antibacterial soap. It was like I was covered with arsenic or something. But that was okay with me if Grandma wasn't into the 'dog touching' thing. For Grandma was into 'dog feeding,' and that suited me just fine.

Oh, and I almost forgot one more relative. That's Uncle Rocky from Albany, New York. He's Papa's older brother. Every once in a while he'd jet in and visit us for a couple of days. Of course his visits were always fun for me because it meant more parties, thus more food. It also meant more trips into Laguna Beach and down to the Harbor, places I adored.

Uncle Rocky was something else. He looked a lot like Papa and sometimes I almost got them mixed up. But Uncle Rocky I had to beware of. That's because he's very clumsy and practically stepped on me every time he moved. Yet he was always a jolly sort when he came to visit and smiled and laughed all the time. He also said he was allergic to dogs. But then so is Mama and she loved me anyway. So Uncle Rocky would have to adapt – sneezes and all – as I was here to stay.

Of course, Uncle Rocky realized I was not going 'anywhere,' so he made his best attempt at liking me, although he had never been around a dog in his life. I liked to tease him. I'd lean up against his black trousers when he'd arrive, and he'd have quite a fit when he discovered his pant leg was golden – my fur color to be exact. Or I'd go up and give him a big lick and then he'd rush to the sink to scrub his hands.

"Lucky, stop that," he said. "It's not sanitary."

But Papa would tell him to 'chill out.' Of course, Uncle Rocky had a hard time doing this, as he was the type who would wipe down all the utensils at the restaurant before he would use them. I even saw him do it myself down at the Harbor one day. I guess he was actually pretty smart, washing his hands after touching me. He seemed to know all the places dogs like to put their tongues.

Life was always such fun with Uncle Rocky around. Now his little Grandaughters, Lindsey and Sophie, well they're another story in my future. In fact, we all liked Uncle Rocky's visits so much that Mama even got our names confused. She started calling me "Rocky" and Uncle Rocky, "Lucky." Boy, did they have a few good laughs over that.

"Do I remind you of Lucky?" Rocky would ask my parents.

"Well . . . you know, you're always happy and like to snooze a lot. Only one difference – Lucky's not addicted to CNBC."

I personally didn't see what was so funny. But since they were all laughing, I had no choice but to wag my tail really hard and join in on the fun, even though I never really did enjoy being called "Rocky."

Families – close friends – they're so important in one's life. I certainly got a full dose of them on our return home. But let me tell you, I loved every minute of it. It was just like there was always someone around to pat me on the head, rub my tummy, slip me a bit of food before dinner, which was never permitted when only Mama and Papa were around. Yes, they were great. And I'm only talking about the ones I met in California. I had yet to meet the Utah contingent. But visiting them was on my list of 'Things To Do' I can assure you of that.

CHAPTER 19
EXCURSIONS, EXCURSIONS, EXCURSIONS

Our new life in California went by very quickly. That's because we were often 'on the go.' Why, sometimes I barely had time to get in my 'doggie beauty sleep,' although I have to admit my coat was getting better and better by the day. Personally, I think it had something to do with the clean air and all of Papa's baths, which had now become a real ritual, much to my dismay. Mama swore it was due to the fact that she was giving me an evening oil of primrose capsule every day – that if it was good for her skin, why it had to be good for my coat, as well. Besides, the vet had also told her this. Anyway, I was looking quite handsome indeed, a far cry from the scrawny little street dog they had adopted. Let me tell you, I got quite a number of 'looks' from excited dog chicks when they walked me around town.

Our excursions went in different directions. Most often we made the drive to Dana Point Harbor – definitely one of my favorite places in the world. I could hardly contain myself in the rear of our Jeep until we got there. Why I'd whine and whine like I was going to the vet or something. But these whines were different – they were the whines of one happy and excited pooch. That's because it was so wonderful, once we completed our five-minute drive. You see, we'd park high above the harbor and hike the path which led along the cliffs and down to the waterside. There we could watch all the boats on the ocean, their sails furled, as well as those tied up at the dock, which looked like little toys from the path. The smells were great, too, for there were a lot of seafood restaurants below. Now I'd really never been much into seafood – until we moved to California – and then it was 'one fish after another' in my diet. Mama always said that "if seafood is good for us, then it has to be good for Lucky, too." So, fish I was to eat. Actually, I think she was worried about my cholesterol after eating Mexican food for all those years. But I have to admit, it was still my favorite, and I much preferred my *tortillas*, rice and pasta over any old sautéed trout.

But one of the best things on our harbor view path was the park we went through. It also overlooked the harbor. Here a group of dog owners always gathered at the top of the hill on their lawn chairs – with their dogs, of course. Why there were big ones and little ones and fat ones and skinny ones, and long haired-ones and short-haired ones – dogs that is. I never paid much attention to the people they were with. Why Papa said it was a regular kennel club show, not that I'd ever heard of such a thing as a 'kennel club' although I'm sure it has to be a place where dogs hang out and sniff each other.

You can imagine the great smells that were present. My sniffer was going ninety miles per minute. And these dogs were not on leashes. They were running all over the place, like a bunch of street dogs. But I was smart enough to know that they weren't – just not bony enough. They sure were having fun, though, and I wanted to jump in and join them. But as much as I begged, it never happened. I finally figured out Mama and Papa were too excited to get to their cappuccino down at the harbor.

"No, Lucky, you can't get off your leash," Papa said. "It's not legal."

Whatever that word meant, I didn't care for it so much, but I always did manage to get in a few good sniffs and kisses as we passed by.

But one day the dogs all disappeared. You see, a local sheriff had discovered their secret play place and shut it right down. Boy was I disappointed! The dogs and their owners had to move to the bottom of the hill where the city had built a small, high-fenced play area where they could run free. Looked more like a prison to me and I wasn't about to get anywhere near it. For you see I preferred a leash to total bondage any old day

Anyway, when we finally got down to the harbor, we'd walk and walk some more. It was so much fun. Why, I must have lifted my leg at least a hundred times before we were through. And all those dogs! On Sunday mornings it seemed as if every person had a leash in their hand, with a dog leading them around. It was a real 'dog jam,' kind of like a Mexico City traffic jam, come to think of it. I sometimes wondered if the non-dog owners in the crowd were not too crazy about getting tangled up in all our leashes, and were afraid we'd bite their little kids. But for some strange reason, they didn't seem to mind us dogs, as more often than not, I'd get a nice pat on the head from them and they'd say, "Oh a dog with a cute little beard! How strange. What kind of dog is he?"

Of course, Mama would insist on giving her usual answer. "Why he's a Mexico City street dog."

Papa would shake his head with a 'here we go again' expression, but smile nonetheless.

Then the person would look kind of surprised, like I had come down from the moon or something and say, "A what? Did you say he's from Mexico?"

"Yes. We adopted him when we lived there."

Then they'd look at Mama and Papa as if to ask why on earth they were living in a place as far away as Mexico City? "Oh, how wonderful of you to adopt a little homeless dog. Where did you ever find him?"

Duh? On the street, you dummy. I was a street dog, remember? Weren't you listening? Did you think I was waiting around to be adopted at some pet spa or something?

Then, if Mama really thought they were interested, she'd tell them my story – in brief, of course. Most of the time they'd look as if they couldn't believe it, and then act like they were just going to run down to Mexico City and save all million of us street dogs. *Sure thing. Why that would take an act of epic 'doggie' proportions.*

Anyway, by this time in Mama's story I was getting a little restless. After all, this was in the middle of my walking time – my special time – so I'd tug on the leash a bit and let out a little groan, like I had to go potty real bad. *Come on, Mama, let's move it.* It seemed to get her attention, so on our merry way we'd go. Why we just had so much fun that it would be totally impossible to explain it in 'doggie terms.'

There was only one thing on our Harbor walks that bothered Mama and Papa – the uncollected dog poop we'd sometimes see. Of course, it was always right smack in the middle of the sidewalk, where even a person with 20/20 vision would have to step right in it – creating one big squish. Of course, since it was all smooshed out, more people would step in it and pretty soon it would be spread all over the sidewalk in 'people footprint format.' I even found that disgusting.

"And to think there are doggie clean-up bags in receptacles every fifty feet," Mama said. "Unbelievable!"

"Oh, shit!" Papa said the next moment. For he had stepped right in the middle of a pile of 'you know what.' Then he'd give me this look, like I was the proud owner of all the dog poop in the world.

180

Not mine, Papa. You can't blame me this time.

Even so, Papa certainly wasn't happy about this, so he blamed Mama for making him step in the poop because she was talking to him. Of course she wouldn't take that for an answer, so then Papa swore and swore at himself for stepping in it, all the time rubbing his foot in the grass at the edge of the sidewalk, then dipping it right in the middle of a mud puddle, like the poop was going to make his shoe disappear or something. For a minute I thought he was going *loco*, as this was not the fussy Papa I had come to know – he was just not one who would put his foot in a puddle, let alone a muddy one.

"Damn dogs," he said.

"No, damn owners," Mama corrected him.

Still the harbor really was a beautiful place filled with cute shops and fine-smelling restaurants, and really very little dog poop, now that I think of it.

Of course, my favorite restaurants to walk by were Jon's Fish Market and Turk's.

That's because they smelled so good. And besides, they both had a nice waitress who often brought me some leftovers once they learned I had been a street dog, like they thought I was still starving or something. I suppose I'll never live down my past street dog title, but I have to admit, it has come to serve me well over the years. I finally figured out that people still think I'm hungry and lonely, and so they really load on their love and food when they meet up with me.

And let me tell you, a little snack right in the middle of my exercise time always came in very handy. Although Mama and Papa really didn't want me to eat it, they were too polite to say "no" to my generous benefactors. Except when it came to bones. Then Mama would put her foot down and tell the giver I was not

181

allowed to have them, that I had bad teeth. Why, I thought my teeth were just fine and perfectly good for gnawing on bones. But I could never convince Mama and Papa of this, unless the bones were the size of a baseball bat and no where near my mouth size. Why, I chewed up many a bone for dinner during my 'street-dog days.' Oh well, a dog just can't have everything I suppose.

Another favorite 'stopping off' spot of mine was a gift shop right across from a restaurant called Seafood Grill. Even though I had to wait outside while Mama and Papa checked out the store, I felt totally happy. That's because of the good smells coming from the restaurant. Why one day I tugged on my leash so hard while trying to get a good whiff of their charcoaled fish and steak, that Papa's knot on my leash gave way and I found myself free. Of course I didn't waste any time getting across the sidewalk to check out all those good smells 'up close and personal.' The door of the restaurant was wide open, so I figured I might as well just venture inside, dragging my leash behind me. I didn't get far. Why from the commotion my presence caused inside the restaurant, you'd think I'd bitten someone's head off or pooped right in the middle of their cooking griddle!

"A dog! A dog!" everyone yelled.

"The Board of Health might come!" the man at the cash register screamed, rushing to intercept me, just as I was about to enter the kitchen.

Why, he grabbed my leash and about threw me out the door. Of course Mama and Papa heard the commotion and came running real fast, like I was on fire or something. Well, they rescued me just in time, apologizing to the owner over and over again. Of course, that was the last time I was allowed to visit

Seafood Grill. But later in my life I would learn that dogs do sometimes get to go to restaurants. Little did I know I was to become a frequent 'restaurant diner' in my future. But that's another story.

Of course, our outings included more than the harbor. Laguna Beach was often on our 'calendar of events.' Whenever we went there, it always reminded me of my first day in America. I loved the people of Laguna – artists, granolas, homeless, Yuppies, and all – and boy, did they ever love me! But I think they were of the 'dog-lover variety' of people – all of them. Why, I've never seen so many dog owners in my life, all walking along the beach and playing with their pooches. It was kind of sentimental actually – like it should be in a painting or on a postcard. I was sure the local famous artist, Ruth Meyer, would surely do something about that one day. Why, I bet my mama and papa would buy her first dog painting of Laguna.

Of course we always had our cappuccino while there – at least Mama and Papa did – and I always looked at the diner next door, hoping for another hamburger. Now that never happened, as you can imagine. But I'd learned in my life long ago to never give up hope.

After our purchase, or lack of it in my case, we walked across the road to the boardwalk beside the beach and sat on our usual bench and stared out at the ocean.

"It's just so beautiful here," Mama always said, her eyes moist. "We're just so fortunate to live in such a wonderful, peaceful place."

I'd think of the buzz of traffic in Mexico City and the stench in the air. *No kidding, Mama, we well know that.*

Papa always nodded his head in agreement and took her hand in his.

Why, I almost choked up at those moments. Careful not to destroy their cuddly mood, I moved to squeeze between the two of them in front of the bench. Of course their hands would fall to my head and they'd pat me so gently that I'd almost doze off.

Why, I'll never forget one special evening when the three of us were sitting on our bench overlooking the beach. A young barefoot boy was walking with his black Labrador along the shoreline. They were back-lighted by the sun, which hung like a huge orange ball as it sank into the glowing sea. The beauty of the moment even made my eyes water. And let me tell you, dogs don't cry very often. But it just looked so beautiful and perfect, the way I imagined dog heaven to be. As my papa would say, "That's a perfect 'Kodak' moment."

CHAPTER 20
BROTHERS CAN BE QUITE FUN

Several weeks after our arrival in California, I was in for a big shock. I was to discover I was not an 'only child' as I had always believed. Of course, that was not counting my original dog family, whom I had lost. It still brought tears to my eyes when I thought of them, especially my brother, Buddy.

One day while I was snoozing, the doorbell rang. As usual, I raced to the door, barking wildly. I loved receiving visitors and I couldn't wait to see who it was and greet them in proper 'doggie style.' Of course, Papa never cared much for my type of greeting, but that's one thing he could never convince me not to do, no matter how hard he tried.

Anyway, when Mama opened the door, she started kissing and hugging this young man who stood outside. "Matthew, Matthew, welcome home! How was the drive from San Diego?"

I couldn't figure out who the heck this guy from San Diego was, but I could certainly see Mama was crazy about him, so I decided I should certainly participate in her welcoming ceremony and be crazy about him, as well. Quickly, I jumped up on my hind paws and proceeded to lick his Levis.

"Hey there, boy, what's up?"

Mama quickly introduced us.

"This is your brother, Matthew."

I took a second look, and for a moment crinkled the fur on my forehead as I was accustomed to doing whenever I was thinking about something very seriously. *Was I being replaced? He sure didn't look like any dog I had ever seen, certainly not like me. And he was nothing like the 'ghost dog' with her fluffy white fur and pink bows and all.*

Matthew bent down and gave me a quick hug and rubbed his hand up and down my back. "It's great to finally meet you, *Amigo*, sorry I didn't make it down 'Mexico' way."

I immediately liked his style and quickly forgave him for not coming to visit us in Mexico. For I knew I was gonna like this guy, no matter what he was going to be to me – brother, *amigo*, whatever.

Papa came onto the scene about then and quickly scolded me for jumping up on my new-found brother. *Why Papa, what do you want me to do, just roll over on my back and play dead? Now how often does one get a new brother?*

But in the excitement of Matthew's arrival, Papa quickly forgot his chastisement and also did a lot of hugging and kissing of this new person in my life. Now this I really liked; it was right up there with all my 'doggie expectations.'

"Hi son, welcome home," Papa said, hugging Matthew again.

Now I was even more happy to have Matthew around, knowing Papa liked him, too. He seemed to complete our little family. Before I knew it, I was wondering if Matthew was going to live with us, and maybe even share my bed with me. Now that would really be fun – someone to keep me warm and cozy at night. But this was not to be so, even though Matthew was certainly on 'the scene' a lot while we were in California.

"How about let's go fire up the barbecue," Papa said.

Now that idea I could always go for, so I followed them outside to the patio.

"Hope we're having ribs, Dad," Matthew said. "My favorite."

Now this was a guy I was definitely going to like, as I had quickly learned that ribs were one of my California favorites. Of course Mama was always saying that I shouldn't eat the bones, that they were dangerous for us dogs. But this is one argument Papa often won when he promised to only give me the largest and toughest bone; one that I couldn't possibly chew up. *Like I hadn't chewed up a few bones in my days. Come on, Mama, 'lighten up.'*

Soon Mama came out with this huge pile of beef ribs on a tray. It looked like it was enough to feed the entire Mexico orphanage. I thought maybe we were planning on guests, but no one else arrived. Later I learned that Mama liked to send home lots of leftovers with my brother. In the future, when I saw his fridge, I could understand why.

Of course, I didn't move far from the barbecue all afternoon, as Papa slowly cooked the ribs for that night's dinner. I especially kept an eye out for Big Tom next door, for I wasn't about to share even one bite of our ribs with him. *Darn cat, anyway. I don't know why he has to interfere with my perfect little life here.*

During my stakeout, Matthew sat at the table and watched me in amazement. "He's such a cute dog," he said to Papa. "I can see why you and Mom adopted him."

"It was his floppy ears that got to me," Papa said.

Mama laughed. "Not only his ears. You just couldn't resist him." She bent over and ruffled my fur. *"El perro bueno,"* she told me. "You're such a good dog."

Matthew looked at her warmly. "Wow, I just can't believe I've been replaced by a dog – and a street dog at that."

"It's hard to believe isn't it?" Papa laughed. "But one thing you've got to know. Lucky's always happy, he loves us unconditionally, and he never asks for money."

Matthew couldn't help but laugh, too.

That afternoon was the beginning of a long friendship between Matthew and me. In fact, we soon became the best of buddies. Besides being a great guy, Matthew was also a 'lounger' and a 'snacker' as I was soon to find out. For he loved nothing better than to lounge on the sofa and watch TV, often with a little snack in hand. Now this was definitely my kind of guy. Of course, he'd also slip me a little piece of his sandwich from time to time, even though he knew I was not supposed to beg. And sometimes when he'd leave the scene for a few minutes and his full plate would still be sitting on the coffee table, I had 'to do' what 'I had to do,' if I was 'any' dog at all.   Why, I just couldn't resist the temptation of food so 'in my snout,' so I'd help myself to a bite or two, knowing Matthew wouldn't mind sharing his meal. After all, he was my brother. Besides, what he didn't know wouldn't hurt him, now would it?

Matthew and I also did other 'brotherly' things together, like go outside and play Frisbee. Of course he did all the throwing and I was supposed to do all the running, but it didn't quite work out that way. As I've told you many times before, "I'm no fetcher." He didn't seem to mind. He was not so much into the 'running' thing himself.

Instead, we'd just sit on the grass together and 'gel,' and watch the Pacific. It was something I absolutely loved, especially when he rubbed my tummy and scratched behind my ears.

"Good boy, Lucky," Matthew said. "Mama and Papa sure love you. It's great to have you around."

No kidding . . . it's good to have you around, too.

Now Matthew had two other habits I enjoyed, equally well. Number one, he loved to play the classical guitar, which I totally thought of as a Mexican instrument, so I decided he must have a little bit of 'Mexican' in him, after all. For hours I'd sit and listen to him strum that thing, which I found to be perfectly good snoozing accompaniment.

Another thing about Matthew that I really liked was Amy, his girlfriend. Why, when they'd come up from San Diego the three of us would have such great times. Amy was the active type and she'd hitch me up to the leash and drag my brother from the ball game on T.V. and off we'd go down the pathway from our neighborhood to Salt Creek Beach. Only one problem with this plan – neither liked to pick up my poop – and that's even with the cute little pink scented bags provided in the holder attached to my leash.

"You have to do it," Matthew said to Amy.

"No, you have to do it," she replied.

Well, this went on and on and on until I wish I hadn't pooped at all. But it was a 'done deal' and I couldn't exactly clean it up myself, so I just stood there waiting to see who would do the noble deed.

Usually, Matthew won this contest. Amy would finally resign herself and clean it up after he turned green in the face and acted like he was about to lose his lunch.

"You're such a sissy," she said, scooping it up with the bag, at the same time making a horrible face herself.

Man, I couldn't help it, you two – I had to go.

Then off we'd go on our merry way to the beach. I remember those days so fondly, the three of us walking down the sunshine filled path, the blue Pacific before us.

Little did I know that there was a lot more of Matthew and Amy that I would see in my life, but it was to be far across another ocean in a cold and damp place.

* * * *

I always missed Matthew when he left and the next day I'd keep looking out the window for his return. Sometimes when he didn't come up to visit for a while, we'd head south – that means we'd drive to San Diego. I enjoyed nothing better than that.

In fact, our excursions to San Diego became a favorite of mine. I'd always know we were going when Mama put my bed in the back of the Jeep, along with my water dish and the small cooler. This meant it was not an outing to Laguna or the Harbor, but much farther.

Why, I'd be so excited when we first started out. I'd sniff the air and look out at the Pacific Ocean as we drove down the San Diego Freeway. But for some reason, I was soon asleep. I finally figured out it was the motion of the car that did it to me. I just couldn't help myself. Whenever we would travel, I missed most of the scenery because I was napping. It really upset me. But at least I always woke up before our arrival.

In fact, I knew when were near Matthew's house by the smell in the air. That's because us dogs' noses never let us down. Why, our smell is one million times more sensitive than a human's. Can you imagine that? Anyway, when we neared Matthew's house I really put my smelling expertise to work. Here the air was not as wet smelling nor as salty as at home, and this was my first signal we were near my brother's house. And the second we turned into Matthew's street, I was 'all barks.'

"Lucky, be quiet, would you?" Papa said. "You're going to break our eardrums!"

But Papa, I'm just so excited to see my brother that I can hardly contain myself.

As soon as they opened the rear door of the Jeep, out I'd jump and race for the front door, Mama trying to catch up with me and grab my leash. I was determined to get to that Uma – my brother's cat – just as soon as I could. But Uma always outsmarted me. Perhaps if I had approached a bit more quietly . . . but by the time I was inside the house, she was under the bed in her 'safe zone,' which was 'off limits,' even to me. So just to get back at her, I'd head right for her dishes. There I proceeded to lap up her water and chomp down her 'Meow Mix.' Now those little bits of chicken-flavored morsels were good, but the entire bowl barely made a dent in my empty belly. They were just an appetizer and I wanted more. But that was never to happen, as Matthew always grabbed her dishes and put them up on the counter, like I was going to gobble them up, as well.

"Please, Lucky, don't eat Uma's food," Matthew said. "She won't go near her dishes when she finds out you've been at them."

Of course, I didn't have a lot of say in the matter, so I'd just leave them alone and race out to Matthew's back yard, one of my favorite places. That's because it was big and had lots of room for running and rolling. Believe me, I did lots of both there. And better, still, there was no water, like in pool or spa – only a Buddha, who sat in the corner of the patio and looked at me all the time. Once I went up to him and gave him a good sniff, but he didn't seem to want to play. In fact, his eyes had kind of a closed look, so I decided he must be sleeping. I thought of lifting my leg to see if that would get his full attention, but decided not too, as he seemed pretty special to my brother.

One thing we didn't do at Matthew's house was eat. That's because his refrigerator was mostly empty. Of course, this always made Mama and Papa feel bad, so they insisted on taking my brother out to lunch. *I finally know why Mama was always sending all those leftovers home with Matthew.*

Most of the time we went to Old Town San Diego. Now I really liked this place. It smelled like *tacos* and *burritos* and had all these old adobe houses with red tiled roofs. It reminded me of Mexico. But guess what? I never once met a 'kicker' there. Instead there were lots of 'petters' and 'patters.' Now these, I liked just fine. For you see, while Mama, Papa and Brother were in the restaurant eating, I snoozed outside under the giant Jacaranda tree and waited for their leftovers, meeting up with many 'pets' and 'pats' from passersby.

Of course, Mama came out several times to make sure I hadn't been 'dog-napped' or anything, and to check on my water supply. Believe me, I had plenty; for every person that walked by seemed to pour some of their bottled water into my dish, like they thought I was really thirsty or something. Why in Mexico I'd been accustomed to drinking water from muddy puddles and no one seemed to worry about that even one little bit. Oh, had times changed.

When my family came out of the Mexican restaurant, boy was I one happy pooch. I wagged my tail and barked at them as if I hadn't seen them for an entire month!

"Quiet, Lucky, quiet!' Papa always ordered, but I barked all the same.

Of course, their leftover rice and beans were wonderful; all smothered with cheese and salsa, just the way us Mexicans like it.

On other days when we visited San Diego, we'd go to a place called Sea Port Village for lunch. This was a nautical village on San Diego harbor filled with lots of seafood restaurants and gift shops. Now the restaurants I liked. The shops were off limit for dogs, but I didn't want to visit them anyway, although Mama sometimes led me from one shop to the next and tied me outside while she went inside. What she did in there I'll never know, but Papa wasn't much interested in those stores either, and told me it was a 'woman thing.'

So Papa, Matthew and I would just sit on our favorite bench and watch the world of San Diego Harbor go by. And it was one big world, by the way. There were boats as big as bullfighting rings and even ones that looked like floating houses. But definitely not the type of house I'd like to live in, not being much of a 'water lover' kind of dog.

Then there was this big thing in the middle of the village covered with brightly-colored animals, that didn't even look up when I barked at them. Well, this thing went round and round and round and had very loud music coming from somewhere inside it. It really bothered my sensitive dog ears. In fact, I didn't like it much at all, and always pulled on my leash when we got near it. I much preferred the fast-food stands that were nearby. Why, they reminded me of a street market in Mexico City, except there were not as many tasty tidbits dropped on the ground for me to gobble up. Instead, people threw their leftovers in big cans that were far too large for my prying snout to reach inside.

Still, we had quite a time during our visits to San Diego and I loved being around my brother. In fact by this time in my life I had definitely decided I liked the idea of travel a lot. But little did I know I would be doing a heck of a lot more of it in my future.

CHAPTER 21
PET CARE – AMERICAN STYLE

Now I have to admit that all my days in California were not as exciting as our excursions to San Diego and our outings to Laguna Beach and the harbor. Many days, my life consisted of lounging around the house all day, moving from one sunny spot to the next. Of course every day I did two very special things – take a walk with Mama and receive a treat of two *galletas*, that's cookies, remember?

Every morning at about 10:00 a.m., Mama would put on her jacket. That meant 'walk time' for me. She didn't have to ask me twice. I was up and running at the sight of her blue zip-up sweatshirt. And when she took my leash off its special hanger next to the garage door, I was all 'jumps.' In fact, I was so jumpy that she had a hard time getting my chain over my head. For some reason she could never understand why I kept yapping, my mouth wide open, so she couldn't get that contraption over my mouth. *It was because I'm so excited, Mama.* But it took me a while to figure out I would not be going anywhere without my leash on and that Mama couldn't put it on until I closed my mouth. Now how stupid can a dog be?

Well, I finally figured it out and then off we'd go down the street, just as soon as she grabbed a poop bag from my special drawer.

I loved our walks. Why, we'd greet almost everyone in the neighborhood, as all the dog owners were usually out walking their dogs at about the same time. I especially liked Jake, the big yellow Labrador a couple of doors down. He limped a lot because he was so old. I was seriously hoping that I wouldn't be limping when I got to be his age. And then there was the Golden Retriever, Calli (short for California Dreamin') two streets away. Why his Mama had a van parked out front where he was taken for a weekly bath. I was sure hoping Mama wouldn't get any ideas about that one. The next door neighbors had four little white Chihuahuas, which Mama told me were Mexican, but they didn't look very Mexican to me and they barked and barked and often woke me from my *siestas*. And then there were Lisa's batch of Maltese, which I already discussed, and Norma's 'Big Tom,' who I still detested. But I knew he'd be around for a good long time since cats have nine lives.

Oh, yes, and then there was precious Boo Boo, the Chow that lived down the street. One thing I know for sure, Boo Boo was another dog I would certainly have to call 'lucky,' even though her name was not 'Lucky,' like mine. That's because she belonged to Rose. Why she loved her fluffy Chow more than any old dog has ever been loved. She was fourteen years old – but I certainly couldn't tell. That's because she was so well taken care of. Now I don't know if her mama made her rice and pasta every night – maybe she did – I know she was from Italy. But believe you me, I've never seen such a well-brushed Chow in all my 'doggie' days. Why each one of Boo Boo's fluffy long hairs was perfectly combed in place. And each and every time we sniffed at each other, why, I was almost afraid to sniff too close as I thought I'd ruin her 'fur-do.' And that I'm afraid would not have made for a happy Mama Rose. I soon learned it was much better to bark Boo Boo a 'hello' from a distance while she was sunning herself in her favorite spot beside their lemon tree.

Anyway, while our owners were visiting, all us neighborhood dogs sure had some great 'dog chats' together – with plenty of sniffs thrown in, of course.

I well remember the first day we went for a walk in our neighborhood. I started out really peppy as I was so excited. Why, I just about pulled Mama's arm out of joint the first couple of blocks. Then as we moved our way down the hill to the lower street, I really started moving. Mama was yelling at me, but I just kept on tugging in one direction like there was a big landslide coming right after us.

"Lucky! Stop, Lucky!" Mama yelled, stumbling after me. But I was barely in control of my paws. Instead my nose was in control of me. Mama was sure there must be a female dog in heat somewhere on the street. But that wasn't it at all. For you see, some Mexicans *trabajaros* – that's workers – were doing some construction work on the street landscaping, and in the back of their pick-up truck sat a big cardboard bucket. Guess what it was filled with? *El Pollo Loco*, my most favorite food in the world! Why the smell of it took me right back to Mexico, and there was nothing I wouldn't do to get a big bite of that chicken, along with some beans and Mexican rice, even if it meant dragging poor Mama down the street. When she finally figured out what I was after, she started to laugh.

"Lucky, why didn't you tell me you wanted some *El Pollo Loco?*" she said. "I can't believe you could smell it clear down the block. Now we'll have to go out and get you some, won't we?"

By this time, the workers were at full attention, after seeing me rushing down the street barking. Probably thinking I was a rabid dog which was going to gobble them up, they jumped into the back of the pick-up and grabbed the food and held it high above their heads.

Boy was I disappointed. They didn't even throw me a bone. But Mama kept her promise, and right after our walk, she took me to *El Pollo Loco* and bought me a three-piece meal. Oh, how I loved my mama. In fact, our weekly visits to the fast food restaurant were a very special time for Mama and me, something we decided Papa really didn't need to know about as Mama was sure he'd say, "Why the heck are you taking the dog out to a restaurant?" Little did he know that there would be many restaurant meals in my future.

Of course, in California I didn't get to go inside, but I'd wait patiently in the Jeep until Mama brought out the chicken and then boy, would we feast. What a life I had.

And to top it all off, when we returned home Mama gave me *gayettas* from the special little dog cookie jar on the kitchen counter. It was never just one. Quickly I learned that if I stayed in my 'down' position there would be another treat for me. These were certainly some great new things about my new 'American' life.

In fact, it wasn't long until I learned that almost everything about life in America, my adopted homeland, was very good indeed. One thing for sure; we dogs certainly had a much more 'cushy' life than we did in Mexico – especially those of us of that are of the 'street dog' variety.

Unfortunately, however, baths were still part of my agenda, even here in America. But now they were conducted at the Pampered Pooch Palace since Papa got tired of bathing me in our bathtub – and there was no Raul here to bathe me out in the garden, thank goodness. When Mama took me to the groomer, I came out smelling like a bunch of calla lilies. The smelling part, now that wasn't so bad, but what it took to get me there, that was something else. I well remember the first day Mama delivered me to the grooming parlor.

"We're going to get you groomed, Lucky, and I don't think Papa will be sorry to give up that job," she said, putting on my leash. Of course I thought I was going for a walk, so I was really excited. Wrong. I was going to the Pampered Pooch Palace which, unfortunately, I came to know quite well. And let me tell you, it was nothing like going for a walk at all.

"There's nothing quite like a good bath," Mama said, walking me toward the car. By then I was really excited, thinking for sure that we were going to Laguna or some other fun place. But her mention of the word 'bath' caused me to stop in my tracks and put my tail between my legs. I started pulling hard on my leash in the opposite direction, but it didn't do one bit of good.

"In the car you go," Mama said, holding my leash tight.

Well, maybe this won't be so bad after all. There's certainly no bathtub in our car, now is there?

Joyfully, I jumped in, my tail racing like a whip.

We have to be going to the harbor. Come to think of it, I don't think so. Papa's not with us. We always go to the harbor with Papa.

We didn't drive very far and soon pulled up in front of a big pink building with pictures of poodles with bows on their hair crowding its front.

Dogs . . . this place must have something to do with dogs, I observed. *That must mean me.*

"Come on, Lucky, in we go," Mama said, opening the rear door.

Of course, I just wagged my tail and followed her right in to what I later came to call 'the torture chamber.' That's because it's what they did in there – torture us dogs. And all in the name of vanity.

That's right. They tortured us so that we would come out looking beautiful, handsome, whatever. It's a funny thing about these Americans. They always have to look and be just perfect – at least in our 'neck of the beach' they do.

But before they could get started with their miscellaneous 'torture tactics,' Mama had to check me in and sign all these forms, like she was going to be leaving me there for life or something. Let me tell you, it certainly had me worried. I was afraid I was going to dog training school again and I'd had enough of that in my life. Besides, I didn't ever want to be separated from Mama and Papa again.

Well, the lady at the reception desk looked a lot like the poodles on the front of the building. She was dressed all in pink. She even had puffy hair topped with a big pink bow – a real 'poodle' look in my opinion. She even had poodles all over her skirt, with little black leashes on them. Had I been able to laugh, let me tell you, I would have done so. Of course, we dogs can't laugh or smile, so we just wag.

"Welcome, Lucky," she cooed. "What a cute name." She drooled over me until I thought she was going to kiss me right on top of the head, so I pulled back. That's because I didn't want just anybody kissing me, especially someone dressed like a poodle.

Of course, Mama had to tell her my whole life story and the lady actually got tears in her eyes. But I wasn't interested even one little bit. For I had spotted the doggie cookie jar on the counter and up went my paws. I didn't have to beg twice as my street dog story had already won her sympathy. Quickly she popped a cookie right into my mouth, liver-flavored, I believe it was. Of course I would have preferred something more in the *jalepeno* or *carne asada*-flavored range, but it would have to do.

Soon I was whisked away by a young man dressed in tall rubber boots and an apron and lifted onto this great big shiny white counter. One major problem with it – it had a big sink with a sprayer on the nozzle. I knew what that meant – bath time! And before I could jump and run, he clipped a big collar-like harness-thing on me. I felt like one of Santa's reindeer.

I should have recognized that I was in for a bath when he removed my regular collar. *How stupid can a dog be?* I just wanted to bite myself for being so gullible.

Before I knew it, I was in the sink and covered with sweet-smelling suds – the kind that don't cause tears, of course. In fact, I had to admit they were much more pleasant than the Mexican detergent Raul had always used for bathing me.

Raul – I hadn't thought of him for quite some time and briefly wondered how things were down 'Mexico way,' but a big scrub brush quickly brought me back to the moment. Why this teenage groomer was scrubbing me so hard I was certain all my fur would be washed down the drain.

Then the rinsing began. When he pointed that spray nozzle at me like he was going to shoot me, and turned it on full-force, I knew I was really in for it. I thought I was going to drown for sure. I tried to jump from the sink, but he kept on pulling me back and sprayed and sprayed and sprayed until I tried to bite the end of the nozzle right off.

It must have frightened him. For he finally stopped his assault and lifted me onto the counter top. To get back at him, I shook as hard as I possibly could and soaked him with water until he looked about as drowned as I was.

That didn't stop him, for it was on to the next 'torture session – the cutting and beard trimming. Before I could protest, off went my little beard real quick like and 'zip, zip, zip' went the clipper down my legs, as if I hadn't lost enough hair under the scrub brush. He even started messing around with that thing on my eyebrows, and let me tell you, this I didn't like one bit. So I started growling at him.

To punish me some more, he opened this glass door below the counter, which was the opening for a hot little chamber. It looked like Mama's oven. He put me inside and I was sure I was about to get baked. Imagine . . . baked Lucky for dinner. *Now how would Papa go for that?*

Thankfully, I didn't get baked. For the groomer had put me into what they call a 'drying chamber' and it was full of nothing but warm wind. But it was like being placed in the middle of a hurricane, and I watched horrified as my fur flew in every direction. I wondered if he'd ever been in that thing. Of course, by this time I was really fed up, so I started to call for Mama as loud as I could, but she didn't even come.

Finally, I resigned myself to being one bald dog. Just to make sure, I looked down at my paw – *still some fur.* Boy, was I relieved. I almost wanted to wag my tail. That is, until I saw this lady come toward me with a big pair of shiny steel things. She led me from the drying hut and before I knew it, she had my front paw in her hand and I was certain she was going to cut it right off! I soon discovered, however, that she was merely going to trim my nails, something I had never had done before. That's because I'd always worn down my nails by walking Mexico City's streets. *Now she's not going to paint them red like Mama's, is she? How totally embarrassing.*

She didn't. But she did bring out this stick with cotton on both ends. Why she flipped my ear over my head and dug right in. Now what she would find of interest in my ear was beyond me, but there was nothing much I could do about her digging as I was still harnessed in place. I just didn't like this 'harness' thing even one little bit, but a prisoner I was still to be. Let me tell you, I thought it would never end.

But the final insult soon came. She put a pink scarf around my neck with tiny poodles all over it, if you can imagine. *Me in a pink poodle scarf? What kind of a macho dog am I now?* To top it all off, she sprayed me with some rose-scented stuff that made me sneeze. *How will I ever hold my head high again?* I was more than ready to go home, curl up in my bed and have one good sulk.

In fact, I was so exhausted after my ordeal and more than ready for my normal afternoon '*siesta*' time. But that wasn't to be. Instead Mama took me to the harbor for a walk and all was quickly forgiven for my 'torture chamber' experience.

However, a few days later, came my next California 'doggie' experience. For I was soon to find out that California did have at least one thing in common with Mexico – vets! This I didn't like too much at all – especially if it meant I would be visiting one of them. But on this matter, I didn't get to vote.

"Let's brush your teeth, Lucky," Mama said one morning. She pulled out my red toothbrush and chicken-flavored toothpaste from under the sink. This I really liked, even though I couldn't quite figure out why she enjoyed scrubbing the inside of my mouth. Actually, it didn't feel so bad and I sure liked the taste of it all. Why, I slurped it up real fast and Mama could hardly get it on my teeth.

"Now it's time to go and meet Dr. Saunders," Mama said. So when she got my leash from its hook and I noticed that she carried her purse, I thought for sure we were going to *El Pollo Loco*. But then I thought again, *what if I'm going for another 'torture session' with this doctor, whatever his name?* I didn't know whether to stand firm or jump in the car. I decided to 'jump.'

We were soon headed to Golden Lantern Veterinary Clinic – another fancy-dancy name for 'vet,' I was soon to learn. But when we got there, I discovered it wasn't so bad. There was a big waiting area filled with – can you believe – dogs? Why there were big dogs and little dogs, and fuzzy dogs. There was even a funny-looking dog covered with big black spots and one with an umbrella around its neck, which I would one day learned is called an 'Elizabethan collar.' Why I sniffed and sniffed. I sure wanted to lift my leg a couple of times, but figured out it might make Mama real mad, so I didn't. Besides, I hated to disappoint her because it made her so sad, and then she'd go ahead and do her 'crying' thing. Instead I continued my 'sniff and greet' routine. Why, there must have been ten dogs in that waiting room, some barking, some frightened and sitting in their owner's laps. Now me, I was no lap dog, so I just stood by my Mama's side, real brave-like. There was even one cat in a cage and let me tell you, it didn't look like a very happy 'Walt Disney' kind of cat at all. It just sat there and hissed and growled and humped its back in the air, its ears flat to its head. I wasn't about to tamper with that cat, not after my experiences with Big Tom next door and Uma in San Diego.

When the receptionist called my name, I stuck right in my spot. This place had a suspicious smell to it, even though it was filled with dogs. But Mama convinced me with a *galleta* from the jar on the countertop that I should follow her and I was soon in the examination room. Yes, it definitely had a kind of 'vet' smell to it, but everything was very clean and shiny, the Orange County way. There were even photos of all breeds of dogs on the wall, all looking very happy. And there was a cushy dog bed in one corner – it was all very homey, come to think of it. Then I discovered a second cookie jar on the counter next to a big shiny-topped table and I got all excited.

"No more cookies, Lucky," Mama said. "You're going to get fat."

Like I really cared. Come on, Mama . . .

Little did I know I would soon be on a diet.

Then in came Dr. Saunders. Why he was nothing like Dr. Ortega in Mexico at all. He didn't have a mustache, like I had supposed all vets must have. And he didn't pick me up like a sack of cornmeal and plop me on the examination table. Even better, I didn't see that 'shot thing' in his hand – no scalpel either. It was pretty good news for me. Instead, this new vet of mine got down on his knees at my level, patted me on the head and ruffled my fur.

"Hello, Lucky," he said. "I'm Dr. Saunders. How about checking you out?"

Gently he picked me up and placed me on the examination table. There he looked me over really good. Why, he didn't even hurt me one bit. Was I ever shocked! *Now, this I could get used to – a nice massage by a kind and gentle guy. Much better than that Pampered Pooch place.*

That was until the needles started coming at me. But the vet was gentle with them, too, and I only felt a little pinch each time he pointed one in my direction, so I decided to forgive him. Besides, Dr. Saunder's office was right across the parking lot from my favorite fast food, so I thought if I was good, we would certainly head in the direction of *El Pollo Loco* for lunch.

Wrong! He told Mama I was getting a bit chubby and needed to go on a diet, like no pasta and rice, not even chicken. Little did he know that I'd done more than my fair share of dieting my first year of life. He told Mama that I was to eat this especially prepared 'adult dog formula,' that would make me very thin and trim. I wonder if he realized that it tasted like sawdust. Why, Mama was always on a diet and I didn't see her eating any of it. Of course I wasn't about to put up with that stuff either, so I immediately went on a hunger strike. It was not long until I was back to my 'rice and pasta' routine, with a little *El Pollo* thrown in.

Wow, the things I was experiencing in America. Most of them were wonderful, of course, a few of them not so great. But I have to admit, I still considered myself one very lucky dog indeed.

CHAPTER 22
STARRY NIGHTS AND PRICKLEY PEARS

One Friday afternoon during my *siesta* was I ever in for a big surprise. Papa came home with this big white box hooked to the back of our Jeep. I could not figure out for the 'doggie life of me' what it was. But Mama and Papa seemed plenty excited about it, so I decided I would be, too. Little did I know it was about to become my temporary home. That's because I was about to go camping for the first time in all my 'doggie days.'

Soon Mama and Papa were carrying out boxes of food to the big white thing. It had a tiny 'dog size' door and they shoved the boxes inside, along with some sheets and towels. Now the towels, they frightened me as they meant one of two things in 'dog lingo' – bath or footwash, neither of which I was too keen about. But I figured out there was no way Mama or Papa would fit inside that little door to give me a bath, even if there was a bathtub inside, which I was to later find out did not exist.

Soon out came my bed. *Oh, oh, am I about to go to Camp Laguna?* That's the kennel they always took me to in Laguna Canyon. It wasn't actually called 'Camp Laguna,' but Mama called it that so I would think I was going to a really neat place. Actually, as far as kennels go, Coastal Kennel was darn good. The young people who worked there actually liked us dogs. Monica and James and Mike and Aaron, and Chris and Jason were real good to me. They even called me their 'pal,' whatever that is. I think it's something like *amigo*. And they played with us dogs and took us for walks. Of course, Monica always thought I was going to bite her. But I wasn't. For I was only giving her 'butterfly kisses,' as Papa called them. One thing I can tell you, Camp Laguna was certainly nothing like Dr. Ortega's kennel in Mexico City. The food wasn't so bad either, even though they didn't serve me rice or pasta. But they had some pretty darn good *galletas*, which they gave me as often as I begged for them. Of course, they didn't have Persian rugs for me to lounge around on either, much to my displeasure. But the main thing wrong with 'Camp Laguna" was that it didn't have Mama and Papa – so I spent more than a bit of my time there calling for them.

I was soon to find out on this particular occasion, however, that I was not going to the kennel, but that we were heading far away from home, clear out to the California desert and to Southern Utah on a camping vacation. Whatever it was we were going to do, if I was going to do it with Mama and Papa, it was fine with me.

"Come on Lucky Boy," Papa said. "Jump in your bed in the Jeep."

I looked at him for a minute and wondered how I was going to get inside. This big old iron bar that hooked the box to the car was in my way.

"Come on, Lucky," Papa said again. "You're not going to let a trailer hitch stop you, are you?"

Of course I wasn't. I soon figured out I could jump onto the hitch first and then into the car. Actually, it turned out to be a great step. I figured out I might need a step to get in the car some day. But for now – even though I wasn't getting any younger – jumping inside the Jeep was always a favorite pastime of mine.

"We won't be needing one of those dog ramps for you anytime soon, will we Old Boy?" Papa said, giving me a good hair tussle. "But I worry about you breaking a leg when you fly out of the back like the Acapulco cliff divers in Mexico. You could get hurt."

Don't you worry about me, Papa. I know what I can get away with.

But was I ever surprised when I jumped inside the car. Most of my usual dog territory was taken up with lots of other things. Why, there was barely room for my bed. *Thank goodness, they squeezed it in.* For right next to me were two suitcases, balanced on top of one another and a box filled with canned food. They looked kind of tipsy to me and I wondered how much they weighed, as I didn't want to become some sort of 'doggie pancake,' if you know what I mean.

Mama must have thought the same thing. "Those suitcases have got to go in the back seat," she said. "I well remember the last time we put something heavy beside Lucky. You made that quick turn on the *Autopista* and Lucky ended up with a large terracotta pot in his bed. Why it practically smashed him!"

"Yeah, you're right." Papa quickly moved the suitcases and replaced them with a small ice chest and some extra coats. I figured out there must be something good to eat in the ice chest, so I was more than happy to look after it.

"Okay, let's go!" Papa said. That was all I needed to hear. We were definitely headed for another family adventure and I was going to be part of it.

We drove for several hours, far away from the beach. We even went up over some mountains and I was hoping we'd get to stop and hike to the top of one of them like we did in Mexico. Nope. Papa whizzed right by them. From my lookout point in the rear of the Jeep, I noticed lots of new and strange things. I could see such a long way since there were very few trees. The air smelled different, too. It was hot and dry. It didn't look at all like San Diego, so I was sure we were not going there.

Finally, just before sunset, we drove into this dirt road in a great big valley with a sign that read 'Mojave National Reserve.' All the trees were short and fat and very round; others were tall and slender with great big arms, and all were very prickly looking. Later I would learn they were cactus and not the best thing for me to do my 'pee job' on.

"Isn't it beautiful out here?" Mama said. "You're going to love camping, Lucky."

Now I wasn't so sure about that because I didn't know what camping was. And when Papa opened the rear of the Jeep and let me jump out, I was even less sure I was going to like it. Boy, was it ever hot! I thought my paws were going to melt right from under me. In fact I would have jumped back into the car, except that I just happened to see a flash of gray whiz by me and into the manzanita bushes.

Conejos! Wow! Rabbit hunting time! But Papa had me on the leash faster than that fleeting rabbit. I barked at it just the same and smelled the air. *Lots of good smells out here, that's for certain.*

Just to make sure I would stick around, Papa got this long chain from the Jeep and put it around the table leg, which was in the middle of all these prickly things. I couldn't imagine who would want to sit at a table out in this heat, but I quickly crawled under it and found it could provide me some nice shade.

I watched as Mama and Papa unloaded the car. Then this funny thing happened. Papa took out a tool and put it in the front of the big white box and it started to grow! Soon the door became big and some windows appeared.

Wow, a growing miniature house. How about that? I couldn't wait to go inside and explore it. After calling several times, Mama came to my rescue and led me to this new house on wheels.

"It's our tent trailer," Mama said, opening the door. I jumped right in. Why it even had a table and chairs and a bed. I couldn't believe it! I sniffed the whole thing out. There were no Persian rugs, so I decided the bed would have to do. Just as I was about to jump up on it, Papa stopped me in my tracks.

"Oh, no you don't, Lucky. You know you're not allowed on beds." *Of course I did, just wanted to test you, Papa.* Since I knew it was a 'no win' situation, I gave him this kind of dirty look and curled up on the braided rug in front of the stove. *At least it's cooler in here.*

My bed was soon to arrive on the scene and I jumped into it quick as a jackrabbit.

"We'll put it here in front of the heater for you in case it gets cold at night," Mama said.

Yeah, right, Mama, I hardly think it's going to get cold here.

Was I ever wrong! After we watched the sunset, which was red and orange and purple, I was actually in the mood for my red 'doggie sweatshirt,' and that didn't happen very often, let me tell you. Mama saw me shiver and put it on me.

"Lucky, you're so *guapo*, so handsome in your red camping sweatshirt," she said.

Frankly, I didn't care if I was handsome or not, all I knew was that I was finally warm. But I did wonder how I was going to manage to pee with that thing on.

Soon Papa put some wood in this hole in the ground. He lit it and we had a fire, just like in our fireplace at home. Now this I really liked, especially when Papa put

211

my bed near enough for me to feel the heat. *Now this camping thing wasn't so bad after all.*

It became even better. For it wasn't too long until Papa took the shish kebab meat from the ice chest. It was always my favorite meal, but we only had it on special occasions because Mama and Papa thought that red meat wasn't so good for us. *Well then this had to be a special occasion, now, didn't it?* Mama and Papa certainly looked like they were enjoying it. Why they opened a bottle of wine and put candles on the table, even a tablecloth. They also had a portable stereo and they put on some of my favorite Mexican love music. *Now this is definitely going to be a good night.* I just lay back in my fire-warmed bed, listened to the music, and sniffed all the wild smells.

It smelled even better when Mama got the rice boiling on this little green stove and Papa put the meat on skewers and placed it over the charcoal briquettes. And there's no better smell in the world than Papa's sizzling shish kebab. I couldn't wait to have my fill of it.

I did. As a special treat, they put this big plate of kebab and rice in front of me. I truly thought I was in dog heaven. Why I ate so much I seriously thought I was going to pop wide open. And the rice made me so thirsty, I drank two full bowls of water. Little did I know all that liquid would come back to haunt me in the middle of the night.

After dinner, Mama and Papa joined me by the fire and we looked up at the ebony star-crowded sky. Even I had to admit it was the most beautiful thing I had ever seen in all my 'doggie days.' It was like I could reach right out and touch them with my nose, they seemed so close. Papa had turned off the music and we listened to the sounds of the night. They were wild unknown sounds.

Just as I was about to doze off, I heard this loud howl and up went my ears. I quickly sat at attention and whined.

"It's a coyote, Lucky," Papa said. "A big wild dog, kind of like you."

Well, I didn't care so much for the sound of it, and let me tell you, I was one happy 'tame' dog when Papa put out the fire and we went into our tent trailer. It was warm and cozy in there and I just loved sleeping right next to Mama and Papa's bed. It was a first for me and something I knew I could get used to real fast, especially with that little heater right next to my bed. It turned on every so often and kept me totally nice and warm. And I didn't even care if my parents snored a little. It was a comforting sound, much better than the howl of that old coyote.

In the middle of the night, I awoke, however. I needed to pee real bad. I went and stood before the door and called Mama and Papa.

"What's the matter, Lucky?" Papa asked

I continued to whine and he quickly figured it out. So he put on his shoes and my leash and out we went into the wilderness. It couldn't have been soon enough for me. I raced to the first tree – I suppose I should say cactus – I could find, and up went my leg. *Ouch! What in the heck bit me?*

I drew back my leg and yelped.

Papa looked at me, then laughed. "Stupid, dog. You can't pee on a cactus, especially a *cholla*, a jumping cactus."

Well, Papa, how would I know? I'm not a 'great outdoorsman' like you. I'm just a pampered pooch.

He led me to a small shrub without any leaves and I quickly did my thing. Relieved, I was ready to go back to my cushy bed. I promised myself one thing – I would not be drinking any water before bed next time. I was not about to have another thorny experience.

The next morning, Papa cooked breakfast outside. We even had bacon and eggs, a rare treat for us. And boy did I gobble them up. Why, I didn't get breakfast very often, only when we were camping. Then it was 'on the road' again and heading for our next destination.

That evening we arrived at what they call the Grand Canyon. It was in the state of Arizona, a very long way from California and the beach. It looked like one very big hole in the ground to me and made me dizzy when I looked down into it. But Mama and Papa thought I was so cute when I got up on my hind legs and looked over the wall. Why, they must have taken a hundred pictures, just like I was their one-year-old kid.

There's one thing certain about me. I can't stand to not know what's going on. If Mama and Papa thought something was worth looking at, then so did I. But after a while, I had to admit all the viewpoints were looking pretty much the same – lots of red rocks, pine trees, and a tiny river at the bottom of the canyon. The one thing I really appreciated, however, were the gray squirrels running around at the top of the viewpoints begging for food from the tourists. They looked like they would make excellent snack items themselves. Needless to say, I never got to sample one.

Of course, Mama and Papa made up for my lack of squirrel meat, because every night at our campground they made some great camping grub for us. Why we had chicken and hot dogs and hamburgers, and steak and fish, all my favorites. Why if it hadn't of been for the hiking we did during the day, I would have turned into one very fat pup.

Soon we headed north and stopped at a place called Monument Valley. It was filled with bright red clay towers, which Papa called 'formations.' Some of them looked like giant hotdogs to me, but I didn't think they would taste very good, as Mama said they were made of sandstone. I wondered if we were going to climb any of them. But Mama said they were protected, so a climbing expedition was out. We merely enjoyed their beauty from a distance, and I have to admit, the bright orange and red sunsets there were the best we had ever shared as a threesome.

Nearby Lake Powell was next on our travel agenda. Of course, I didn't get anywhere near it as I wasn't so fond of water, but I enjoyed it just fine from our campsite. I certainly couldn't imagine why Mama and Papa kept jumping in the water and getting all wet. Not this pooch.

Finally, we reached Bryce Canyon, Capitol Reef and Zion National Parks in Utah. Now these places were great – very little water in sight, except for one river. And I liked all the big red rocks and viewpoints. Why, we could see forever. The sky was so blue and there were wild flowers everywhere. But Mama wouldn't even let me pee on them, telling me that they were only for looking at and smelling. Now why I'd want to go around smelling some stupid wild flowers when I could go around smelling deer and squirrels was beyond me. And let me tell you, there were plenty of those critters. But the first time I saw a deer, it about scared the 'doggie daylights' out of me. At first, I thought this big dog was coming into our campground. I jumped up from my cushion and barked and barked. It took one look at me and off it raced, its white tail high in the air. Of course, I wanted to go right after it, but Mama told me I shouldn't frighten the wild life. Boy, did she have a lot of rules on these camping trips.

One was that I had to be checked for wood ticks every night. Now I didn't mind this one bit. That's because either Mama or Papa would go over my entire body, searching for bugs. Let me tell you, I thought of it as a great massage. I especially loved it when they rubbed my tummy. Why I'd just twirl my paws in the air and get this really contented expression on my face.

Another thing I had to tolerate on our camping trip was paw washing. Every time I wanted to go into the tent trailer I had to have my paws washed. That's because Papa didn't want to get dirt and rocks in his bed, things he thought I might carry inside on my paws. And boy did I hate having wet paws! But I soon realized it was that or sleep outside. Outside meant coyotes, cactus and cold, so I quickly accepted the wet paw alternative.

And there was one night I actually didn't mind the idea of wet paws at all. That's because I had my first 'deer hunting' experience. It was in Zion National Park. We were walking along the river just before sunset and I saw a deer drinking from the stream. Papa wasn't holding my leash very tight and so 'off I went' right after that deer, Papa chasing after me. Why before I could get to him, the deer heard me bark and up went his head and off he went. I managed to catch up with him, even though I heard both Mama and Papa screaming after me. When I was just about to grab his tail, the deer fooled me. He jumped into the water and swam right across it! I was so startled, and without thinking, jumped in after him. By this time, I could really hear Mama and Papa screaming as loud as they could. I didn't even care. I was about to have me a sample of deer meat – venison to be exact. But then it came to me – I was in deep water and I didn't even know how to swim! And I hated water! And it was cold! I could barely stand, and the current was strong against me. I quickly forgot about the deer, certain that my 'doggie life' was about to come to an abrupt wet end. I tried to turn around, but I couldn't. The water was pushing me downstream. I heard a big splash beside me and there was my papa. I've never been so happy to see him in all my 'doggie days'. He wrapped his arms around me and pulled me from the water. Mama was standing on the bank crying.

"Oh, Lucky, you poor little thing!"

Papa carried me to Mama. I was shivering real hard. She took off her coat and wrapped it around me. I looked up at both of them, real thankful-like. In fact, I even forgave them for spoiling my deer steak dinner.

The final night of our Utah camping trip was at Grand Staircase of the Escalante National Monument. It was beautiful there, so peaceful and quiet. Our campground was beside a small, clear stream; one that didn't frighten me half as much as that big river in Zion or that deep Grand Canyon.

During the day it was hot, so Mama and Papa decided we should hike up to a waterfall, several miles from the campground to take a swim. I was all for the hiking, not at all for the swimming. About an hour up the trail, it became unbelievably hot. I started to pant and Papa poured water from the canteen over my head to keep me cool. Now this I didn't like one bit. They even doused my red and white camping neckerchief with water and put it around my neck. But I was starting to feel real sick. I could tell Mama and Papa were worried.

"It's too far to carry him back to camp," Papa said. "But I think Lucky's suffering from heat exhaustion."

Mama looked real scared, like I was going to die or something.

"We've got to cool him down."

Oh, oh, I know what that means . . .

But by this time I was breathing so hard and feeling so bad that I didn't care what they did to me. In fact, I had collapsed by the side of the trail.

So they both took one end of me and dashed down to the creek and dunked me right in. Boy, did that wake me up in a hurry! But it did make me feel much better. So Mama and Papa made me stay there for quite a while until I cooled off. And let me tell you, this was not a 'pooch seat' that I particularly liked, and I soon convinced them we should get out. Still we sat by the streamside watching the rainbow trout swim in the clear, cold water until the sun started to go down. Mama and Papa barely talked. I knew they were really worried about me. Finally I was able to make the hike back to camp.

Of course Mama and Papa were very happy campers that night. In fact, they were so happy that they sat in the stream beside our camp and drank a *margarita* – a real Mexican drink – in honor of my still being alive. And once again I proved what a lucky dog I was.

CHAPTER 23
SNOW BOUND

After we returned home from our camping vacation, I was totally exhausted. While I had experienced a 'good old doggie time,' I came to realize more than ever that there's no place quite like home – specifically 'home' on San Raphael in Dana Point, California. Now, don't get me wrong, I loved camping and most of what went with it, like that great camp grub and our nights under the stars and sleeping right next to Mama and Papa. But I've reached the conclusion I'm not 'heat crazy' at all. I'm just no 'desert rat,' not me. I have to admit I much prefer 'beach life.'

Another thing I'm not too crazy about is cold, which I also experienced plenty of on our camping trip. I was certainly thankful for that little heater beside my bed, let me tell you. I suppose I'd had my fill of cold nights during my street-dog days in Mexico and every time – even to this day – that I get cold, it always brings back those horrible memories to me. Nightmares, that's what they are.

I think Mama and Papa knew when I was having one of them as they said I'd moan and groan in my sleep and kick my legs in the air. I'd never realized that we dogs have dreams, but I guess we do. I'm 'barking proof' of them.

Anyway, except for my occasional nightmare, life was totally a 'bowl of Purina' for me, except that I don't like dry dog food much, so I suppose I should say that life was like a 'great big bowl of Mama's spaghetti' for me.

Each day I was becoming more 'American.' We celebrated all the American holidays like Memorial

Day, Labor Day and the Fourth of July, which I especially enjoyed. That's because it was very much like *Dia de Independencia* in Mexico. In America everyone sang patriotic songs and stuffed themselves just like they did on that holiday back in the 'old country.' But in America everyone wore red, white and blue instead of red, white and green like in Mexico. So you know what that meant in the 'wardrobe department' for me – a red, white and blue scarf with little American flags on it. I had finally won 'my stripes.'

Now in Mexico on Independence Day they drank plenty of *tequila*, but in America they drank lemonade and beer. But of course it was the food I liked best about this holiday. Why Papa would fire up the old barbecue and make so many hamburgers that we could have invited half of Dana Point. That was okay with me, for it meant there would be plenty of leftovers and you know where they went – to yours truly.

One thing I didn't like, however, were those loud noises they called fireworks. They totally disrupted my *siesta* time, and they went on long into the night. But they didn't scare me one bit. Why, some of our neighborhood dogs were big boobs and they barked and cried all night, just at the sound of them. Of course, this further complicated my 'napping' time. In Mexico fireworks are a very common thing indeed – practically the national pastime. Let me tell you, more than one time in my street dog days I had to speed away from a stray firecracker headed in my direction.

We celebrated other holidays, as well, and before I knew it I had spent my second Halloween and Thanksgiving in America. Of course all these holidays we shared with friends and family and this made them even more special. One thing I didn't realize, however, was that my family extended beyond California.

220

"We're going to Salt Lake City for Christmas, Lucky," Mama told me one day, "so that you can meet the rest of the family. You remember Granny, of course."

Of course I did. She was the cute little lady that always rubbed me behind my ears real good, and told me I was in need of a shave.

But Salt Lake City . . . where's that? I was hoping it did not mean another camping trip as it had been raining almost every day for over a month. The thought of hiking around all those cactus in muddy muck did not sound at all enticing to me.

But before I knew it, off we went in the Jeep again. Now I didn't complain, I loved road trips – especially those on which I was included. For when Mama and Papa went on them alone I was not one happy pooch at all, as you may recall.

The first night we spent in a place called Las Vegas. Why, I've never seen so many lights in all my 'doggie days.' I bet Papa wouldn't like to pay that electricity bill one bit, as he was always telling Mama to "turn off the lights." And there were so many people walking on this street called 'The Strip' that I thought I must be back in Mexico for sure. Except that they weren't all speaking Spanish – they were speaking many languages that I couldn't understand even one little bit. Believe me, I was kind of frightened, so I stuck real close to Mama and Papa. It was also much colder than California and I was wishing for my camping sweatshirt.

As always, Mama came through and out popped my cute little red, white and blue sweater from her bag. Boy, was I one 'proud pooch' in that. Why, just about everyone looked at me and smiled as Papa led me down The Strip. And were the smells ever good. Why there were so many great smells: hot dog, prime rib, French fries and steaks – my favorite. I was getting hungry, so I decided I'd go inside one of those 'casino' places, as Mama and Papa called them.

"Oh, no, Lucky, you're not twenty-one. No gambling for you, Old Boy."

Silly Papa, I don't want to gamble – I just want to eat.

Papa must have read my thoughts, for we were soon in our room and he was cooking me up a Cup of Soup, which had become my 'special' hotel food when we were on the road. Of course, Mama always added some chicken or turkey and some pieces of bread, so it wasn't too bad at all.

The next day we kept driving and driving and driving. I was certain we had to be heading back to Mexico. But we weren't. We were headed north to Salt Lake City, Utah, and the first sign of that was all this white stuff beside the road. I kind of remembered seeing a tiny bit of it at the top of the mountain in Mexico so long ago, but still, I wasn't at all sure what it was.

"Look at all the snow, Lucky," Mama said. "Don't you just love this drive? It's so beautiful here in the mountains. Polly used to love to make this trip."

Oh, no, not the 'ghost dog' again. It had been some time since I'd heard her name.

Soon Papa stopped the Jeep, as I was giving my 'I need to pee' signal. That means a little whine and whimper.

"Okay, go do your thing, Old Boy," Papa said, as he opened the back of the Jeep. I looked down, not knowing whether to jump or stay right where I was. It was indeed cold out there and this white stuff was practically up to the rear bumper of the Jeep.

Well . . . I don't know about this. Should I jump or should I stay?

I decided to jump. As soon as I hit the snow, I quickly changed my mind, but it was too late. Papa had already closed the door. *Papa, my feet are cold! Open up that door! Where's the grass?* But it was not to happen, so I just pushed my way through that cold white stuff, trying to find a dry place. No such luck. And I really needed to pee. Have you ever tried to lift your leg when it's buried in snow up to your neck? Let me tell you, it's no easy job. Imagine, there I was balancing on three legs, the other high in the air, my snout buried in the snow. I felt like a Popsicle! I was certain I was about to be buried alive, never to be found.

But Papa saved the day. He pulled on my leash and up I popped, my entire head still covered in white fluff. Now I didn't care for that even one little bit as it reminded me of my bath, except I couldn't smell Mama's flower-scented shampoo. I started to shake as I never had before and soon all three of us were covered in snow. Mama and Papa thought it was funny and we started running around and they threw snowballs at each other like a couple of little kids. They looked like they were having so much fun, I decided to get in on the action, so I raced around in large circles as fast as I could. Of course, a couple of times I got the 'old dunk' – but snow didn't seem nearly as wet as water, so I decided I liked it.

Good thing. I was about to experience its whiteness for an entire week. That's because we were headed to Granny's house in Salt Lake City and she had lots of snow in store for us. Mama said it made Christmas very special. I was about to find out.

The lights of Salt Lake City sparkled in the distance as we approached it late in the evening. When we arrived at Granny's house, little red and green Christmas lights lined the gables.

"I hope Mom didn't get up on that ladder again," my mama said, shaking her head.

"At 97, I hope not either," Papa added, pulling into the driveway. "But you know her, she's apt to try anything."

Oh yeah, I remember Granny. She's the one that walked me all the way down to the beach and then took off her shoes and went wading.

Papa opened the rear of the Jeep. "Come on, Lucky, let's go see Granny."

Believe me, I was more than ready to jump out of the Jeep after more than an eight-hour *siesta*. Needless to say, I was also very perky after all that sleep. As seemed to be the norm in this part of America, I jumped out into snow. Why, it was so deep only my snout showed above it. And it was cold, let me tell you. But it was also beautiful, soft, and very white. In fact I loved it so much, I rolled and rolled until I looked like a 'snowdog' – that's a dog kind of snowman.

After I made a few 'pee stops' in the front yard, we knocked on the door.

Granny answered and hugged Mama and Papa so hard I thought she was going to squeeze the life right out of them. I was not about to become an orphan again, so I squished between the three of them and tried to get in on some of the action.

"Oh, Lucky, *hola*," Granny said. "It's good to see you up here in snow country, so far away from Mexico."

I'd forgotten what a happy little lady she was. I wanted to hug her, too, but since I was not capable of that, I jumped up and placed my paws on her legs, hoping she would bend down and kiss me or something.

"Oh, no you don't, Lucky! No jumping!" Papa scolded.

Well, he kind of ruined my greeting, but Granny didn't seem to mind. She bent down and gave me a nice pat on the head which made my tail move faster than the windshield wipers on our Jeep.

Then I went to work on checking out her house. The Christmas tree was nice with lots of *regalos* tucked underneath. And I knew from past experience it was not a place for us dogs to lift our legs. There were lots of good smells at Granny's house, like a pork roast cooking in the oven. I also thought I sensed a cat smell and frantically checked out the house to find its owner. No such luck. I later found out the kitty belonged to Uncle Gary and that Granny only tended it once in a while. Disappointed, I found myself a good spot in front of the fire and curled up.

It wasn't long until I was eating pork scraps and mashed potatoes for my supper. And this was just the beginning of a week-long feast for me. For everywhere we went, somebody wanted to feed me. Of course, I didn't mind that one bit – or should I say 'bite.' Uncle Jerry, why he made great sour dough bread and these little peppers stuffed with melted cheese, which I loved, even though they gave me heartburn. Aunt Janette whipped us up some great spaghetti sauce. At Uncle Gary's and Aunt Norma's, there was a spread which covered the whole table – and guess what? I was the lucky pooch sleeping beneath it! Uncle Gary didn't let me meet their big white cat called 'Blanky," as he said he would tear my eyes out. I could tell he was crazy about that cat when he was telling Mama and Papa how Blanky would sleep all night right on his belly. I think my uncle was afraid I would eat his precious kitty or something. Of course I wouldn't. I just wanted to check him out, maybe chase him around a bit. But I could sure smell him all over the house.

Then at Michael's apartment – he's my older brother, which I suddenly learned I had – why he made us a barbeque right in the middle of the snow. Can you imagine cooking in the snow? Papa said he used to do that when he was in college in Utah. It was difficult for me to imagine my papa barbecuing in a blizzard. Michael also told me about his big black dog, Apollo. He was also a street dog of sorts and Michael found him when he accidentally ran over him. It was kind of a story similar to mine, and I liked Apollo immediately, even though Michael no longer had him. That's because he got loose one night and wandered off, never to be heard from again. Why, I thought my big brother was going to cry when he talked about that dog of his. It really made me feel bad, so I gave him a quick lick on the hand. Still I wondered why that Apollo was so stupid to run away from such a good thing. *Certainly not what this perro would do.*

* * * *

Christmas came and went. I was in 'pooch heaven' all week long. And to top it all off, all the family gave me more *regalos* for Christmas than I had seen in all my 'doggie days.' Why I got rawhide chew toys, squeaky fuzzy teddy bears, red and white rubber candy canes and even a yellow plastic pussy cat, which I was supposed to chase around. The only cats I was interested in were real ones, however, and that dumb toy I quickly put aside. There were also some food gifts. Aunt Norma even gave me a can of tuna fish, as she said that was their cat's favorite. Not mine. But I was polite and ate it anyway. And Granny, why she was always feeding me. I think I gained about five pounds that week and Mama was sure Dr. Saunders would be very upset the next time I went to see him.

Another thing Granny did was let me outside about every fifteen minutes. Now I thought this was just great as I loved to play in the snow. But Mama and Papa were certain she was spoiling me and they kept telling her not to do this because then I would want the same kind of 'in and out' treatment at home. They couldn't convince Granny about this, however, since she claimed she always let her and Grandpa's dog, Pasha, out any time he wanted. I looked around, and wondered where Grandpa was, especially after Granny went on to remind them that Grandpa also gave Pasha vanilla ice cream every night at ten before he went to bed. Now things were really starting to sound interesting, but Mama put a big halt on that practice. I did finally figure out one thing, both Pasha and Grandpa were no longer with us – that they were of the 'ghost variety.' *Darn, I think I would have liked that grandpa of mine.*

Mama and Papa also spent a lot of time on the ski slopes during our visit – that meant I got to stay home with Granny. Even though I missed Mama and Papa, staying with Granny wasn't so bad at all. That's because she'd spoil the heck out of me. Why I must have gone outside to the back yard about a hundred times a day. And she also cheated, but just a little bit, by giving me a spoonful of ice cream one day. I didn't get off on it all that much, however. It was cold and stung my tongue. So she decided instead to give me tidbits of roast and bacon bits. Boy, would Mama have loved that!

We also got to visit Utah friends that had dogs, but I wasn't allowed to go inside their houses as Papa was

227

afraid that I'd do a little marking, just to personalize their homes to my own 'doggie' preferences. So I never did get to meet Priscilla's dog, Mooshie – who I understand is one pampered pooch, nor did I get to meet Shaytoon and Zooey, Nicole's miniature Greyhounds, whom I suppose must be gray. But from the way Nicole and Priscilla liked me, I quickly figured out that Mooshie, Shaytoon and Zooey were spoiled little pooches. But then I don't have much room to 'bark,' now do I? In fact, I soon learned that they never had to go to the kennel. Why I couldn't imagine for the 'doggie' life of me how that would feel.

Sometimes I got to go along on family sightseeing trips while we were in Utah. That also required a bit of waiting on my part as dogs were not especially appreciated, whether we peed or not. We visited "This is the Place Monument," and I thought what a strange name it was. Of course 'it was the place,' why did they have to name the monument that? Then there was this giant hole in the ground that looked almost like the Grand Canyon, but Papa said it was filled with copper, whatever that was.

One night we went to this big park-like place in the middle of the city, which Papa called Temple Square. It looked like a regular old park to me, except that dogs were not allowed. There were many trees and some big white buildings. Practically every inch of the place was covered in millions of tiny Christmas lights. It reminded me of the stars on our camping trips. But since I wasn't able to go inside, I had to be satisfied with viewing it all from the Jeep.

"They don't want you to pee in there, Lucky," Mama said. "It's a special place to people here in Utah."

Fine with me. . . I was more than happy in my bed in the rear of the heated Jeep.

* * * *

When it was time to go home to California, I actually felt kind of bad. I wanted to take Granny back with me. But she said she couldn't go with us because her pipes might freeze while she was gone. She did promise that she would come for a visit in the spring. She kept her word. Many times after that Granny came to see us, always more than happy to open the French door to let me out for a bit of fresh air as often as I wanted.

CHAPTER 24
ACROSS THE WIDE ATLANTIC

Boy, was I ever enjoying my 'beach bum dog' life. It went on for two years, in fact, just lazin' in the sun, enjoying the view of the blue Pacific, with a few outings, vacations and family thrown in for good measure. Little did I know there was more than one ocean in the world and that my view of the current one was about to come to an abrupt end.

I could tell something was going on by the look on Papa's face when he came home from work a bit late one night. I knew he was late, as it was long after my 3:00 p.m. '*galleta* time.'

"We need to talk," he said to Mama.

Now that in itself was not so strange, as they were always talking to each other. It was the tone in his voice that frightened me. He didn't exactly sound like my papa. And I was certain he didn't want to talk about me, as I hadn't made any 'boo boos' for a good long time.

"Remember all the great times we've had visiting Europe over the years?"

Mama looked at him kind of funny. "Of course. I love Europe."

"Really love it?"

"Why yes, I suppose you could say that."

By this time I was really curious as to what was going on, so I moved in for a closer listen. Papa was so preoccupied that he didn't even bend down to pat me, so I let out a little 'give me some attention' whine.

"In a minute, Boy. I'm busy now," Papa said. "I got a call from my boss today."

Mama looked concerned. "About what?"

I could tell she was on to something. It was like the time I had an accident in the front room and she went around on her knees sniffing until she found my dirty deed.

"You seem upset."

"No, I'm not, I mean I am, sort of," Papa said. "I didn't know how you'd take the news."

"What news?" Mama's voice was getting louder. "Don't you dare tell me they're transferring us to Houston."

"No, it's not that."

I heard Mama sigh and looked up at her. She was kind of smiling.

"That's good, because I'm not about to go."

"Remember how we've always loved London?" Papa asked.

London? Now where the heck could that be?

"Yes . . . what are you getting at?"

"The company wants us to move to London and Amsterdam, Holland for a few years."

Mama's face had turned to stone and I knew she was going to start crying.

She sniffled a little. "I know it sounds like a fantastic opportunity for us and for you career-wise, but we've only been home from Mexico for two years."

"I know I promised you we wouldn't move again for a while, but this just came up and I . . ."

"I know, it sounds like a dream come true. But I love this area so much . . . " She shook her head. "Although Europe is great, too."

By this time she had a sort of smile on her face.

Papa looked a bit more relaxed, although he still hadn't bent down to pet me.

"Well . . . what do you think?" he asked Mama.

"Oh, what the heck. Let's go for it."

231

Boy did Papa look relieved. And there I was waiting for somebody to start crying. They never did. One thing I did conclude from watching them – that my parents are just gypsies at heart, the way they like to travel. *And that must mean that I'm a gypsy, too – of the 'dog variety' of course.*

Then Mama got this concerned look on her face. "Hey, wait a minute, we can't move to London. They have quarantine in the United Kingdom. There's no way we're going to put Lucky through that for six months."

By the look on Mama's face, I knew quarantine was something I wasn't going to like even one little bit, so I started to whine real loud.

Mama bent down and patted my head and gave me one of her great big warm hugs. "No, Lucky, we would never do that to you. You've already been through so much in your life."

"But I've got that all figured out," Papa said. "We don't need to put Lucky into quarantine. I've been doing some research."

"Now how would we avoid that, if it's the law?"

"There's this new policy within the European Union. If we live in one of those countries, like The Netherlands, for example, for at least six months, then we can take Lucky to the U.K. and not have to quarantine him. Simple as that," Papa said in his best 'engineering voice.'

Boy was I getting nervous, with the mention of my name so often. And I got this feeling that my beach life, as I had known it, would soon become a thing of the past. And I didn't care for that idea even one little bit.

"Don't they have quarantine in The Netherlands?"

"Nope. The Dutch love dogs and would never do anything to harm them. They aren't worried about rabies as much as the British are. And besides, they're not an island country like the U.K., one that has never had rabies."

I was soon to learn that the Dutch are indeed 'animal lovers.' But that's another story.

* * * *

Before I knew it, in came those old movers again. And away went my 'beach bum' life.

My poor mama did a lot of crying those next few weeks, as she went around the house putting little stickers on everything. 'By Sea,' 'By Land,' 'By Air,' 'For Storage,' they read, whatever that meant. And each time the movers took a picture off the wall, or packed a dish, or boxed up a piece of furniture, Mama got this really sad look on her face, like someone had died, or I had pooped right in the middle of her favorite Persian rug. In fact, she was so sad that I just wanted to lick her all over, hoping to make her feel better. But I was too busy keeping a watch on my *cama* as I wasn't about to be 'bedless' again. In fact, each time one of those mover men got anywhere near it, I growled at them and 'off they went' like 'Speedy Gonzales.'

Of course, I should have known that Mama wouldn't let them take my bed, even though she didn't even have to growl at them. Instead she just smiled and told them to please not pack my bed and dishes. Wow, was I relieved. But I didn't like the idea of them packing all my Persian carpets any too much. *Where am I going to roll?* I decided the back lawn would have to do. *Now, they're not going to pack that, are they?* I thought of the stash of giant rib bones I had buried out by the spa and wondered if I could take them along.

Before I knew it, the only things left in our house were my bed and dishes, some suitcases, and me and

Mama and Papa, of course. Oh, it was so sad when the three of us stood in the empty living room and looked out at the Pacific. I had this awful feeling I would not be seeing it again for a good long 'doggie' time.

We spent our last two American nights at Vacation Village Hotel in Laguna Beach, where I always received a 'royal dog welcome.' Raphael was my friend there and he always had a handy supply of my favorite *galletas*, which he kept in a special jar on the registration desk, just out of 'dog reach.' But he knew what I wanted each morning when I placed my paws politely on the counter, let me tell you that.

After my morning snack, Mama and I would kiss Papa goodbye and off he'd go to work and off we'd go to Main Beach for Mama's cappuccino on our favorite bench. Afterwards we always went on a stroll through Heisler Park. Why, I could barely contain myself, waiting for her to finish her coffee. Believe me, I tried to be patient, but I was just too excited. Those were special times between Mama and me. Of course, she did have some 'teary eye' times as we walked along the pathway on the cliffs above the Pacific. It was so beautiful and quiet there as we watched the seagulls dip in and out of the surf below. I knew Mama was very sad to leave and I tried to comfort her as best I could, but since I couldn't say, "I'm sorry, Mama," I often looked up at her with my big brown eyes and did a little whine.

I think she got the message because she kept saying, "Oh, Lucky, you are about to have a great adventure." I wasn't so sure she believed it herself, however.

* * * *

And then before I knew it, there we were back at Los Angeles International Airport once more, about to fly off to Europe, wherever that was. By the looks of the stack of luggage we had, I figured it must be some place very far away, and that we were going to be gone a good long time. One thing in the luggage pile I especially didn't like the looks of was my dog kennel. I hated that big green plastic thing with all those bars. And Mama had filled its water dish with ice cubes, so that meant I was about to go on a long, long journey. And it wouldn't be sitting in the back of our Jeep. I had a pretty good idea it was going to be in the cargo hold of an airplane. But I was starting to feel a bit sleepy, so I didn't fuss too much when the man at the Lufthanza airlines counter made me go inside my kennel. In fact, I seriously wondered if Mama and Papa had slipped a little 'something' in my food that morning.

They had. By the time I woke up, I had a feeling I had been sleeping for a good long time. My legs were really stiff. I couldn't do my usual morning stretches as the kennel was too small, but I could stand up and turn around. The ice cubes had melted, so I quickly drank the water. *I've got to pee! What am I gonna do?* We dogs are just not into wetting our beds, no sir, not me. So I just decided I would have to hold it. The only way I could do this, was to go back to sleep. That's what I did. And by the time I awoke again, I felt the plane bounce onto the runway. We were at our destination, wherever that was. I wondered if we were back in Mexico. All I knew for sure, was that it was the beginning of another 'new life' for me.

When they finally unloaded my kennel from the plane and put it on the conveyor belt, boy was I one happy pooch! All I could do was bark and bark for Mama and Papa. *Where are they?* I looked around and around but could not find them. I kept barking nonetheless, hoping they would find me.

Soon two men lifted my kennel off the belt and put it on this cart filled with suitcases, golf-clubs and lots of boxes, like I was merely a 'piece of luggage.' I showed them a thing or two. I wasn't about to sit there like a stupid suitcase or set of golf clubs, so I started to bounce against the bars of my kennel and barked at them to open the door. They didn't. They just looked at me and talked in a language I had never heard. You see, I didn't realize I was in Frankfurt, Germany, clear across another ocean, across the world almost. I looked around. The sky looked the same blue. But the air smelled different. It did not have that fresh 'salty' smell of home. But it didn't have the smell of Mexico, either.

Inside the luggage reclaim area there were lots and lots of people. The men unloaded my kennel in a place labeled 'Oversized Baggage.' *Like I'm a giant or something? Where are Mama and Papa?*

Everyone in the area seemed to be talking at once, but I didn't understand even one word. I barked just the same, hoping someone would pay attention to me. I also watched the conveyor belt across from me go round and round, as suitcases spilled from this little hole. I was hoping Mama and Papa would come out of it, too, but they didn't.

Then I heard familiar voices.

"Lucky! Lucky, here we are!"

It was Mama and Papa! Boy, was I ever happy to see them and I barked and barked and everyone turned to look at me. I was so happy in fact, that I accidentally peed in my kennel. But Mama said it was okay, as she had covered the bottom with lots of newspaper. They got me out right away and about hugged the 'doggie daylights' out of me. Of course I didn't mind at all.

"How was your flight, Lucky Dog?" Papa said, attaching a leash to my collar. *Oh boy, oh boy, we get to go on a walk!* I tugged on it just as hard as I could.

"Wait a minute, Old Boy," Papa said. "We need to clear Customs first."

Didn't he realize I needed to do my 'big number' after such a long flight? Come on, Papa. I gotta get out of here.

Mama came to my rescue. "Be patient, Lucky, we're going to leave just as fast as we can." She pulled a dog treat from her purse and that got my mind temporarily off my other need.

When we got up to the Customs desk, this big blond man looked at me kind of strange, like I should be a German Shepherd or something. He didn't even smile at me, like almost everyone I met did. Instead, he just waved us through without even looking at my official papers.

Now Papa wasn't surprised by the 'no smile routine' of the Custom's official as he had told me that Germans are not of the 'smiley' crowd like Californians. He said it was because they don't see enough sunshine in their country. But Papa did say that they are very efficient people. Let me tell you, I certainly learned that in the next twenty-four hours.

"Can you believe they don't even want to see his papers?" Papa said, as we walked through the opening. "After all the expense of going to the vet and getting all those letters and filling out the forms. And I always thought the Germans were very into papers and detail."

Mama just smiled. "Guess Lucky looks harmless enough to enter Germany," she said. "We need to get him out for some fresh air and a 'potty stop.'"

No kidding, Mama! Let's go!

"Why don't I take him and you bring the luggage and we'll meet you out front?" she told Papa, knowing very well that he would much rather carry around suitcases than my poop in its little pink plastic bag. Mama didn't need to repeat her suggestion. I raced from that building like a Greyhound and found every cement support post at Frankfurt airport to pee on. I was one relieved dog, let me tell you that, especially after I found that nice little private area near the parking garage where I could do my 'big deed.'

Before I knew it, I was in my very own *cama* in the back of a very big van, which was loaded with all our belongings. *Now, this isn't so bad, is it? We're all together again – just a different car – and in a different place.*

It certainly was, as I soon came to find out. But for the time being I was perfectly happy to be riding down the *Autobahn* with Papa at the wheel, the radio playing what Mama called German *oompah* music. It sounded kind of like those Mexican 'Selena' songs to me, so I was just in my element. Or so I thought.

CHAPTER 25
HAPPY DAYS IN GERMANY

I couldn't figure out why I was still so tired, even though I'd had a twelve-hour nap 36,000 feet above the Atlantic ocean. Can you imagine that? Napping at 36,000 feet? I figured out that must have been a 'doggie first.' Even though I wanted to check out all the new scenery in this place Mama and Papa called Germany, I kept falling asleep. It was like my days and nights were all mixed up. In fact, they were. Mama said I had 'jet lag,' a feeling I didn't mind too bad as I had always been a *siesta* taker at heart. But boy, I hated missing all that beautiful German countryside.

It was covered with green hills and dotted with villages full of gingerbread houses with red-tiled roofs. Each village had a cute little church right in its center. In fact it looked like the pictures Mama had shown me of Disneyland, or like the book she had read to Nico and Isabella. I was sure Gepetto and Pinocchio must live in one of those villages. But no matter how hard I tried, I couldn't find them. For you see, at the time I didn't know they were Italian and lived far down the *Autobahn* from Germany in a place called Italy. Since the sun was shining, many people were outside walking along the streets or sitting in the parks and beneath the trees drinking beer. Some were digging in their small gardens, which were lined one beside the other.

We stopped at one of the villages to rest and buy some cherries – that always meant a 'potty' stop for me. Cherries were a specialty in this part of Germany and about the size of ping-pong balls. Mama and Papa gobbled them up like they were red rubies, but they didn't much appeal to my 'doggie taste.' I've always been more into the 'meat' side of things.

One thing I quickly learned. Almost all the streets other than the *Autobahn* were made of what Mama called cobblestones and she thought they were just so quaint and cute.

Mama, if you had to walk on them with bare feet, you wouldn't think they were cute at all.

I found that out fast when we stopped for lunch in a village on the Rhine River called *Rudesheim*. It was 'fairy-tale cute' and all the people seemed happy. At the time I didn't know that's because they were coming out of the *weinstubs*, the wine cellar restaurants. I was soon to experience one of them myself. Can you imagine, a dog in a restaurant? Impossible!

For you see, we went up this tiny little cobblestone street called *Drosselgasse*, which wound through the village. It was filled with small restaurants, gift shops and wine cellars. There was no way our van would fit here so we had to 'hoof it' as Papa sometimes called walking. Why, I didn't mind one bit as I had been in my kennel and in the car for so many hours that my legs felt like they had been cemented in one position. That was until my paws kept getting caught between some of those cobblestones. Ouch, did that ever hurt! More than one time, Mama had to stop and help me out.

"Poor Lucky," she said. "Maybe Papa should carry you."

Papa quickly vetoed that idea.

Anyway, we soon stopped at one of the restaurants, which we entered down several steps into kind of a cellar. It was sort of dark and cool in there and the smooth stone floor felt real good on my sore paws. At first Mama and Papa didn't know if I'd be allowed, but quickly the man at the front desk motioned all of us inside. And guess what? They even brought a bowl of water for me. Now this wasn't so bad at all – cool water and a cool floor! What a lucky dog I was.

Before long, Mama and Papa were pretty happy too, just like all those other people. That's because they had a *romer* – in German that's a wine goblet with a green stem filled with the Rhineland's local wine. They also ordered what is called *saurbrauten*, that's a big pig knuckle boiled in a special sauce and served with *sauerkraut* and special German potatoes. Boy did it smell good. Every time the waiter passed by carrying a tray of those *saurbrauten*, I wanted to jump into the air and grab me one of them. It didn't happen, however, because Papa kept a tight hold on my leash as he soon figured out what was on my mind.

"You have to be a polite doggie in the restaurant," Mama said. "I can't believe they actually let you come inside. In the U.S. that would definitely be a big 'no no.' Why, the Board of Health would go crazy if they saw a dog inside a restaurant."

"Not in Germany," Papa said. "They love their dogs and wherever the people go, their dogs go right along with them."

Now this idea sat very well with me, of course. Perhaps I was going to like this new life. It meant I would never have to be away from Mama and Papa. Boy, was I in for a big surprise. But as I've said before, that's another story.

Anyway, when Mama and Papa had finished eating and I had finished starving, they took me outside and Mama pulled a leftover pork knuckle out of her purse. It was wrapped in a napkin and she placed it on the sidewalk in front of me. Was I ever one happy dog! Why I chowed down on that thing like I hadn't eaten in a month! And that's how *saurbraten* became my favorite treat whenever we visited Germany.

Then it was back in the car again and up the *Autobahn* toward *Koln*, that's Cologne in English. Here we would spend the night on our way to The Netherlands, our new home, as I was soon to find out.

Koln was also a special place. That's because it had this great big Gothic church which could be seen several kilometers – that's kind of like miles – from the city. It stuck up in the sky like a huge jagged mountain and even I took notice. I wondered if we were going to climb it.

"Lucky, look at this big church," Mama said, as we stood beside it. "Isn't it beautiful? And it's so old. It was started in 1248, even before the Aztecs were in Mexico."

I have to admit that I've never been much into history, Mexican or otherwise, but I was still impressed. It was about a million times taller than me and I felt smaller than a Chihuahua gazing up at it.

"This cathedral was about the only thing in Cologne not bombed during World War II because the bomber pilots had so much respect for it, being a church and all," Papa said.

Well, that was all nice, but I was ready for a walk and a nap. I had both when we checked into a small hotel in the *Alstadt*, the old town. It was stucco with wood beams and looked very different from anything I had ever seen in Mexico or California. A big fireplace sat right inside the door and let me tell you, it looked like a perfectly good place for napping. But I didn't get that opportunity as we were quickly ushered up these carved steps by a very big lady in what Papa called 'total German efficiency.' Our room had lace curtains and two beds with big fluffy down comforters on top. I wondered if one of the beds was for me. Not to be. Papa soon produced my *cama* and put it between the two beds, so I was only a bit disappointed.

After a nap and a shower for Mama and Papa, we went out into the streets again.

Papa seemed excited as he told us we were going to a beer festival, whatever that was. I soon learned that Papa had lived in Germany for a year when he was a student and he still remembered how much fun he had in the beer gardens. So I figured out I would enjoy it, too. Now, Mama, I don't think she was too excited as she doesn't like beer, but she's a good sport and went along just for the experience.

What an experience it was! When we entered this big square in the old town there were blue and white flags and banners everywhere, and long tables, row after row of them. They were filled with people singing and waving beer steins in the air. I have to admit I was a bit worried that one of them was going to fall and bop me on the head, so I quickly sought refuge beneath the table where Mama and Papa finally found a spot. I decided to settle in for a nap. But I couldn't sleep even one little bit as there were more *oompah* bands around that square than I could have ever imagined. It was more noisy than Garibaldi Square in Mexico City where all the *Mariachi* bands played on Saturday nights. And people here were doing this funny dance called 'The Chicken Dance.' They didn't look like dancing chickens to me, and one thing I knew for sure, I wasn't about to try it. I was hoping Mama and Papa wouldn't do it either and they didn't. They were too busy eating these giant pretzels dipped in spicy mustard, which I didn't like even one little bit. Then Papa bought Mama this big gingersnap cookie that hung from a piece of pink ribbon. It was decorated with colorful frosting, which said 'I love you,' in German. I thought for sure Mama was about to cry. Why she even thought it was so special that she wouldn't even eat it, but hung it around her neck instead. Believe me, I kept an eye on that cookie all night long, just in case the ribbon broke and it fell down to my 'neck of the table.'

And there were all these German ladies dressed in ruffled white blouses and puffy skirts who carried around four steins of beer in each hand. I wondered how they drank so much beer, until I discovered they were putting them in front of all the people, including Mama and Papa. Papa took a big gulp of his, but Mama, she just sat there and smiled at hers, probably counting the calories that it contained. As for me, I totally kept my eye on those 'beer-toting' ladies, not about to be the recipient of one of their steins on my head.

In the meantime, I took in all the other good smells in the beer gardens. It wasn't long before I had sampled my first *bratwurst*, that's a big German veal sausage. They were Papa's favorite and it didn't take me long to understand why. And the funny thing was, the instant people saw me with Mama and Papa, down would come another piece of *bratwurst* right off their plates, especially for me. Now that made me feel like a really special pooch. But by the end of that night my stomach had never been so full. Papa and I were both miserable on the walk home and Mama said we looked like a couple of stuffed Germany sausages ourselves.

So ended our first day of life in Europe. It had been good, so I wasn't too worried about the times ahead of us. Like I've said many times before, all days are good for me as long as I'm with my Mama and Papa.

CHAPTER 26
DOING IT 'DUTCH'

"Lucky, *mira*, look!" Mama said.

I jerked up from my nap because I thought maybe Mama had seen a whole bunch of rabbits or something. Boy, was I disappointed – only more green countryside with lots of trees, just like I'd been seeing for the past two days in Germany. *Now why would she bother to wake me for this?*

"We're in The Netherlands, you know, Holland, that's where the Dutch people live," she added, like I would certainly understand. "Maybe we'll see a windmill soon."

Whatever that was, Mama seemed pretty keen on finding one. So I perked up a bit, thinking perhaps it was a new kind of Dutch rabbit or something. Nope . . . nothing like that, just more green, except that now the countryside was not as hilly. It was downright flat. Papa said it was even below sea level. That had me scared. Not being a water dog, I was absolutely afraid we would all drown.

I had to admit, however, that the Dutch farms were beautiful with their gabled houses and barns, all in perfect order and freshly painted, as Mama was quick to point out. There were lots of cows and sheep grazing along the roadway in these grassy places called *polders*, but those kinds of animals didn't bring me much excitement anymore – not enough of a wild scent for my 'doggie' taste.

"You know these sheep like the grass because it's salty in these *polders*, which are lands reclaimed from the sea," Papa said, pointing at the grass-covered dikes that bordered them. "So I don't think you'd much like it, Lucky Boy."

Even though I was a grass grazer – but only when I had an upset stomach – I didn't much think I'd care for this salty Dutch grass. So I went right back to sleep and continued to enjoy my 'jet lag' for a few more hours.

That's until we got to a place called Haarlem. It would become my home for the next eight months because I wasn't allowed to enter the UK without going into quarantine – that dreaded word that brought tears to Mama's eyes – unless I first spent six months within the European Union. For some reason, I suppose the British thought dog immigrants would be a-okay if they lived in another part of Europe before coming to their country, like it would rid us of any rabies we might have. Why I'd be one dead dog long before seven months had passed if I had rabies, now wouldn't I? Oh well, what the heck, I decided I'd just have to settle into a new life – a Dutch life, that is.

Haarlem was a pretty town. It was just outside of Amsterdam and even older.

"Can you believe this town is nine hundred years old?" Papa said. I figured that was pretty old by the look on Mama's face. Now while Amsterdam is famous for all its canals and 'red light' district, whatever that was, and some artist guys by the names of Rembrandt and Van Gogh, Haarlem is known for other things. It didn't have too many famous artists except for one by the name of Frans Hals, and had only a small 'red light' district. In addition to being old, it had lots of gabled Dutch houses and big ancient churches. It even had a couple of windmills – extremely important in Mama's eyes, although I never could see much in those 'twirling houses.' Haarlem was also full of canals, and we were about to live right beside one of them.

Something else about Haarlem – there were so many dogs being led on leashes that I couldn't believe my 'doggie' eyes.

"The Dutch do love their dogs," Papa said, noticing that I was totally alert and looking out the window. "I've heard they're considered the 'sacred cow' of Holland."

Whatever that might mean, I had no idea, but it wasn't too long until I got the 'complete picture.' But that's another story, as well.

Anyway I really perked up when we entered Haarlem, somehow knowing I was going to be spending a lot of time here. We crossed over a couple of small bridges, which broke in the middle to let boats pass by. Now these boats kind of looked like the ones I remembered at Dana Point Harbor, except they were filled with Dutch people, who were mostly very big and very blond. We crossed canal after canal and I wondered on which one we would live.

"We're going to the Carlton Square Hotel for a few days," Mama said. "Until our house is ready."

Hearing the word 'hotel' I got really excited, as staying in one has always been one of my favorite 'doggie' pastimes. Now this hotel was quite nice, except that the rooms were stacked one on top of the other – the kind of hotel I had never experienced. The lobby had dark flowered carpeting, which perfectly showed off my shedding summer fur. Mama was embarrassed and kept me very close to her, like I wouldn't shed as much or something. There was a big green park right across the street – perfect for doing my thing – and a small canal with little Dutch houses behind the hotel.

A nice girl named Kera worked at the front desk. She immediately came out to greet me with a dog treat. Now this I could get used to, even if they weren't as salty as the ones back home. But for a moment it saddened me as I thought of all my *galleta* treats from Raphael at Vacation Village in Laguna Beach. In fact, I think I was a bit homesick already. But then again Mama and Papa were right there in Holland with me, so I figured out everything would be okay.

We were assigned a room on the fifth floor, so Papa loaded the suitcases into this big square box with a door and then Mama and I went inside and the door closed. I just couldn't figure out for the 'doggie' life of me what the three of us were doing in this big box. In fact, I wondered if they were going to put us inside an airplane and ship us someplace else. And when it started to move, let me tell you, I didn't care for that even one little bit. *A moving box! Where on earth are we going?*

After about a minute, the door opened and I was the first to jump out just in case it closed again. Then off we went down the hallway to our room. It was Dutch size and decorated with lots of flowers – flowered bed-spread, flowered chairs, flowers in a vase, you got the picture. You see, the Dutch love flowers almost as much as they love dogs. Why, they're all over Holland, both real and otherwise. There were lace curtains at the window – typically Dutch, you see – and they opened onto a nice balcony overlooking the canal – perfect for swan watching, I was soon to find out.

The next morning, Papa went to work and Mama to the lobby to change our room for one with a better view of the canal and the distant church. Now that didn't bother me at all as I've always been into vistas. When she came back to move the suitcases to the other room, she left the door ajar with a small suitcase holding it slightly open. Even though she told me to *"la guardia, por favor,"* – that means 'watch the room, please,' I decided I would venture out into the hallway for a quick peek. I squeezed through her makeshift fortress and off I went to explore Carlton Square Hotel.

First thing I ran into was a Russian maid. Why I thought she'd jump right out of her flowered uniform when she saw me. *Was I having a 'bad hair' day or something?* She acted liked she'd seen the ghost of Dracula. Why she started screaming, and raced down the hallway and into a room and slammed the door. That's the last I saw of her.

But in other ways, my hotel exploration really paid off. For right in front of the doorway to the room next to the elevator was a tray on the floor. A tray complete with a plate of lamb bones! Of course I certainly couldn't just pass them by now, could I? I quickly grabbed two of them and hurried back to our room for my mid-morning snack. Boy were they juicy! I didn't mind eating those salty Dutch sheep even one bit.

Now when Mama came back to the room she had a funny expression on her face.

"Lucky, have you been a good boy?" I heard her say when she entered the room. "Because I just noticed that the lamb bones on the tray beside the elevator are missing."

I couldn't exactly deny her accusations since two bones were hanging from my mouth, so I just gave her a little possessive growl and continued my feast.

"Shame on you, Lucky!" she said. "Stealing food!"

But then I saw her laugh and knew everything was okay. "Once a scavenger, always a scavenger," she said. "But just don't do it again. This isn't Mexico City, you know. And besides, you're not supposed to eat bones."

Okay, Mama, I promised, finishing up my bone, and wondering if I'd have a chance to go after the rest of them.

I didn't. For Mama had completed our move to the new room and then off we went to explore Haarlem. What a beautiful day it was. The sky was a Dutch Delft blue and the sun was shining – very unusual in Holland, we soon discovered. In fact it wasn't long until I was the proud owner of a yellow vinyl raincoat, complete with four rubber boots. (Little did I know Mama had actually bought it in America as they didn't sell such a thing in Holland – not for dogs anyway.)

I was soon to find out that those Dutch dogs loved water in any old form, including the 'rain' variety – nothing like me as I only liked the 'drinking' variety of water. Of course most of them were Labradors – water dogs, you know, and they'd jump into those canals and cool off just for the fun of it. One thing I quickly decided – I wasn't about to turn into any Dutch dog. But that's another story, as well.

As we wandered along the street leading to the 'old town,' first thing we noticed was that there were lots of people walking on the cobblestone streets beside us. They were pushing these little canvas carts. Why, we seldom saw people in California walking, except at the harbor and beach. And the people certainly didn't have any carts there. It was more like Mexico, except I didn't get the idea that these 'walkers' were maids. We quickly concluded that cars weren't allowed in this part of town, only people – and bikes, we were soon to find out. Why I had never seen so many bicycles in all my 'doggie days' – hundreds of them. And one of them about ran us right over! If we hadn't jumped quick, we would have been about as flat as those *pankoeken*, the famous Dutch pancakes covered in powdered sugar and molasses – not to my 'doggie' taste at all, incidentally.

"*Het is niet goed! Nee! Nee!*" the bikers kept saying to us, waving their arms. Mama figured out we were doing something wrong, that we must be in the bike lane, so we quickly got out of the way before we became 'biker victims.' Then all became perfectly fine and we began enjoying the sights.

One thing that quickly caught my attention were all the flower stands, perfect places for 'letting loose,' or so I thought. Mama and the vendors quickly changed my mind in that department. But I did enjoy all the smells and colors. And here was my Mama, the perfect "flower lover." Why Papa even called her a 'leftover flower child' sometimes. She just loved them, and by the time we went back to our hotel, Mama was carrying six bunches. Now what she intended to do with them, I had no idea. I wondered if Papa would be upset seeing all those posies in the bathtub when he returned. But then again, that's another story, and one we all became used to here in the 'land of flowers.'

Soon we reached a great big square called the *Grote Markt.* Whatever its name, I liked it just fine. Mama said it was Medieval. It was circled by beautiful old buildings like the *Stadhuis* – that's the town hall where couples get married and everyone throws flowers at them when they come out. Then there was the old meat market, now unfortunately a museum, with not even one piece of meat. For a moment I thought of my days in Mexico at the *carnaceria*, begging for meat. *Nope, don't have to worry about that any more.* And then we saw Haarlem's famous landmark. It was a great big church, the *Grote Kerk*, officially called the Church of St. Bavo.

"It was built in the 1300s," Mama told me, like I would certainly be interested in that fact. "It's where Mozart and Handel even played the famous pipe organ."

But I was much more interested in things other than organs and who played them.

251

For you see, there were also lots of restaurants and shops around the *Grote Markt*. The restaurants had tables outside and people were sitting at them eating. It was quite the feast for my 'doggie eyes,' all those neat little Dutch sandwiches stacked with meat and cheese. I could taste them already, and was dying to sink my teeth into one of them. But Mama pulled on my leash and I never got close enough to snag a *toastie* for myself.

There was also something else I liked about the *Grote* Markt. There were lots of dogs. In fact, I'd never done so much dog greeting and sniffing in all my 'doggie days.' Of course, all of them except for me and a couple of little 'yappers' were Labs, so I was kind of short. In fact even Mama and Papa were short compared to the Dutch. Why we looked like some of Snow White's dwarfs in comparison to the Dutch and their great big dogs.

One thing I knew for sure, I wasn't about to get into an argument with one of those Labs, even over the grandest and most delectable bone. But they seemed friendly, so 'a sniffing I did go.'

Needless to say, Mama and I had a great day, and she wasn't even too disappointed that we only saw one windmill. It was in the center of Haarlem on the Sparn Canal. She was sure there were many more throughout the country, and I could tell by the tone in her voice that we would be locating each and every one of them.

One thing we did find in Haarlem were things to buy, and believe it or not, I even got to go into the shops with Mama. Why I couldn't believe my 'doggie ears' when the shop owners said, "*Hullo, hoo-der duk,*" that's 'hello, good day,' and motion for Mama to bring me inside. Now I didn't need a second invitation, and into the shop we'd go. I do know Mama was always nervous

252

about taking me inside and she kept me tight on my leash and very close to her, like she was afraid I was going to pee or something. Now I'd never do that, would I? But I never could quite convince Mama of this.

After Mama bought her own Dutch shopping cart, she certainly didn't take very long to fill it. *Oh, oh, Papa's gonna come to hate this cart.* In fact, I didn't like it so well myself, as she was always running me over with its wheels. But now that we were the very proud owners of our own pull-cart, first thing Mama bought were some brightly painted wooden tulips and a pair of yellow and blue wooden shoes, since she thought both were 'very Dutch.' She said the wooden shoes were for the kitchen window and boy, was I ever glad. I couldn't imagine her actually wearing those great big blue and yellow clogs and, worse than that, me being accidentally kicked by one of them. Come to think of it, I was glad the Dutch didn't go around in those wooden shoes like they did in the 'old days.' Imagine the kicking they could have done with those things. But then again, I didn't have to worry. I remembered papa's words about how the Dutch love animals, especially us dogs. And I knew I could depend on anything my papa said, so I quickly reached the conclusion that the Dutch were definitely not 'kickers.'

After a while, Mama got tired of shopping – actually I think she was having a little 'jet lag' herself, but wouldn't admit it – so we went and sat at a table in a cute little sidewalk café right beside *St. Bavo.* It had checkered tablecloths and flowers on every table. It was so beautiful looking up at the huge church with its many spires and bell tower. The waitress didn't even tell Mama dogs were not allowed as she placed the menu before her. Now this we couldn't believe! Dogs allowed in restaurants? No way! But we quickly concluded it was 'the way' in Holland, after seeing several other dogs lying beneath the tables.

Mama ordered a sandwich and shared half of it with me, and the blonde waitress quickly brought me a big bowl of cold water and even gave me a nice couple of pats. Was I ever having a 'doggie good' day! As I settled down for a little snooze while Mama enjoyed a cup of cappuccino, I had definitely determined I was going to like this place called Holland, even if the dogs were bigger than me.

CHAPTER 27
CANAL LIFE

Several days later, we moved into our house at 67 Schoter Singel, which, lo and behold, was on the Schoter canal, one of the most beautiful in Haarlem. It also had lots of swans, much to my liking. Our place wasn't exactly a house, it was part of a big old house that had been made into four 'little' houses. They were not 'dog size' by any means, but they were not nearly as large as our house in California. Needless to say, our place was very Dutch, with wooden floors, very steep steps, lots of wood trim and lace curtains. The thing I liked best about it was the front room bay window – it looked right out onto the canal and park, which were directly across the narrow street. I could already imagine the fun walks Mama and I would take in this park and all the 'swan spotting' I could do. But for the time being I loved nothing better than standing on my hind paws and staring out the window, watching the 'Dutch world' go by.

One thing for certain, there were lots of bikes in it. Even the old lady upstairs, Mrs. Van Leeuen, who was 91 years old, did a lot of peddling. Mama and Papa thought that was very funny and couldn't even imagine Granny peddling off to the store every day. I was seriously hoping Mama and Papa wouldn't get any ideas about my learning to ride a bike, but since I hadn't as yet seen any 'dog peddlers' in Holland, I figured I was safe. For walking, the streets of Haarlem seemed perfectly fine to me, even though the Dutch mostly rode bikes on the special bike lanes designed for just that. I wondered if Mama and Papa would buy bikes. Of course, that would mean I would have to run awfully fast behind them, so I was hoping they wouldn't. Anyway, Papa seemed more interested in the business side of biking and always said he'd like to own a bicycle shop in Holland, as he could not only make money selling bikes but repairing them, as well. Somehow, I couldn't imagine Papa fixing bikes in his suit and tie.

Something about the Dutch bikes that I quickly noticed, however, was that they were not as fancy as the ones I'd seen in California – no gears, no fluorescent colors, no designer seats nor chrome wheels. Mama said it was because the Dutch are very sensible, and Papa said it was because they don't like to waste money, which brought a big smile to his face. I think it had something to do with the weather, as many of the bikes were pretty rusty. That's one thing it certainly was good at in Holland – raining – much to my 'doggie dismay.' Nonetheless the rain didn't stop those Dutch, and they would peddle away, sometimes with umbrellas in hand, sometimes not. I was certain they must be related to ducks since they enjoyed the water so much. Even their little babies didn't seem to mind biking. Why, they'd put them in a little pouch in front of them – rain, sleet, or snow, and away they'd go! Not for me, thank you very much, so I was sincerely hoping Mama and Papa wouldn't buy a bike pouch to put me in even if they did buy bikes.

One thing I decided very soon into our Holland stay – I wasn't about to get anywhere near those bikes, rusty or otherwise. I knew for sure that they were extremely capable of running over little old me, even in my bright yellow raincoat.

Oh yes, I'll never forget my yellow vinyl raincoat for the rest of my 'doggie days.' The first time Mama got it out of the closet I wondered what on earth it could be. When I noticed it was 'dog size,' I quickly got the feeling that I would be the dog wearing it. Now this I didn't like even one little bit, as scarves were about as far as I cared to go in the 'clothing department.' But I couldn't convince Mama of this.

"Look, Lucky, a raincoat just for you!"

That's okay, Mama, you can have it. I'll be more than happy to share.

That idea didn't work out at all, as Mama quickly put on her own yellow raincoat. *Oh no, the raincoat twins!*

Then she went to work on me. And let me tell you, not without a fight.

"Come on, give me a big 'doggie' smile," she said, slipping the hooded coat over my head before I had time to react. Why that hood was so big that it completely covered my eyes and I couldn't see a darn thing, so off I went, racing around like a blind bat! I even bumped into Mama's favorite vase and it went crashing to the floor. Now she wasn't a happy mama about that, but what's a dog to do? I thought one of our roles was leading the blind, not being blind.

Next came these stupid yellow boots. Yes, boots – now why on earth would a dog need to wear boots? Mama quickly answered that question as she said it wouldn't be healthy if I got wet feet because I might get sick. Personally, I think I'd rather suffer from the sniffles than the humiliation I was about to endure. But on this issue, I figured I was not going to come out the winner. You know how mothers are when it comes to health issues – they always win.

Anyway, after a bit of a bout between the two of us, Mama finally convinced me that I would be wearing my raincoat and boots if I wanted to go out walking if it was a rainy day. But she did do a bit of 'hood altering' so I could at least see where I was going. Then off we went into the rain – totally prepared from snout to paw.

But then bad things started to happen. Why everyone looked at me like I was a purple dog from Mars or something. Then they would start to laugh and point me out to everyone around. Why, I've never been so embarrassed in all my 'doggie days,' especially when those big black Dutch Labs just stood there in the rain gawking at me and enjoying the weather just fine. Of course, that didn't surprise me at all, as they also loved jumping into the canals and swimming. Now how crazy can a dog get?

"Lucky, you're really making a hit around Haarlem, aren't you?" Mama said. "They're all jealous because they don't have a cute raincoat like yours."

Yeah, right, Mama. Can't you see I'm totally embarrassed?

Mama didn't see it all, and she proudly paraded me throughout Haarlem, certain that one day my photo would grace *The Haarlem Times*. Can you imagine – me in my glowing yellow raincoat on the front page of the local newspaper? Now how 'low' can a puppy dog go? But that's a story I will fortunately never have to tell.

Thank goodness the Dutch also liked to look at things other than me in my yellow raincoat. They also like to peer into other people's windows. Now that's not because they are rude or 'peeping Toms,' but they like to see who has the cleanest house. And that's another thing they like to do – clean, clean, clean. Of course Mama thought this very nice. And they also loved to wash their windows, even in the rain. Mama couldn't understand this habit at all, and she was very surprised one day when she washed the windows after several days of rain and someone left a 'flower of appreciation' right on our window sill. Oh, was Mama embarrassed – you know, kind of like I felt in my raincoat. She hadn't realized she was offending our neighbors with our rather dirty rain-splattered windows. Personally, I didn't care whether our windows were clean or not, just as long as I could see out of them. I'd rather Mama spend her time taking me for walks.

And that we did plenty of. Each morning, rain or shine, off we'd go shopping, with Mama's little cart in tow. Now I didn't like that cart too much, as it often got too 'close for comfort' as far as my paws were concerned. More than once it ran right into me when I'd stop for a pee. Of course, Mama always apologized profusely and kept a close eye on the cart for a while so it didn't do a repeat operation on her pampered pooch. But at least it was better than racing behind a bike.

First stop we'd make was the bakery, that's the *bakkerij*, where the lady behind the counter would always tell us "*hooder moorhen* – good morning," and Mama would answer the best she could. I think Mama must have spoken funny Dutch, for it always brought a big smile to the woman's face.

And Mama had a horrible time deciding which bread to buy as she thought they all looked delicious – would it be *en tarwer brote, en krenter brote, or en stok brote*? I really didn't care. For you see, I was much more interested in the big fat orange cat that sat in the bakery's front window. It always looked out smugly at the two of us as we were approaching, then the second we entered the door it would disappear like a flying fairy. Boy, did it make me mad as a dog can get without having rabies. I would have loved to chase it around the bakery, scrambling over the many loaves of bread. It was never to be, however.

"*Tot ziens*, bye bye," the bakery lady would say, and then off Mama and I would go toward the *Grote Markt*. And let me tell you, our adventures there resulted in lots of 'doggie' experiences, even when I wasn't wearing my raincoat.

Actually, there was only one thing I liked about rainy days, even if I did have to wear that darn coat. We got to rest more often. When we got to the train station, which was about halfway there, we cut through the building since it was dry inside. Well, sort of. Even though it wasn't raining inside, it was very slick because of all the rain tracked in by bikes, dogs and people. Sometimes it was like an ice skating rink and I had to do my 'doggie best' just to stay upright. In fact, one day Mama and I did take a tumble, but we quickly regrouped before anyone saw us. In Holland one doesn't just trip for no reason at all, you see.

We also got to stop at my favorite coffee shop for another quick rest and a hot drink on rainy days, except we were not allowed to call it a coffee shop like we would back home, but instead a café. That's because coffee shops in Holland are where they sell marijuana, and I didn't think my mama wanted any of that. In fact, in the coffee shop, oops, I mean, café, where we stopped there was a sign that said, 'We Do Not Sell Drugs.' But they did sell cappuccino, so Mama was happy.

When we reached the *Grote Markt*, we sometimes went to McDonald's for lunch, as we got tired of Dutch food, and Mama said it reminded her of 'back home.' So the ancient McDonald's in the middle of the square kind of became our 'homesickness remedy place.' Of course I also liked the smell of the hamburgers and such that permeated the air, even if they were never to come my way.

Afterwards it was on to Vroom En Dreesman – V&D, as the locals called it, and Mama's favorite department store. I'll never forget the first day we went there. Before I knew it Mama led me onto these shiny stairs and 'off they went,' just like that. Why it about scared the 'doggie daylights' right out of me! And the faster those stairs moved, the more scared I became. Why I almost peed in the middle of them. But then Mama bent down and held me close to her, so I tried to be brave until we reached the top. Then I jumped right out of her arms before those moving stairs sucked the tail right off of me! I never did get used to those moving stairs all the time I was in Holland. But they did have interesting things in V&D, like a Dog Department, where I always got to choose a special 'doggie treat,' as it had all kinds of things for us canines. So you see, I had to put up with those stairs, no matter how much I hated them. *Oh, the things we dogs do for treats.*

Next we'd go to Albert Hein, that's the grocery store in Haarlem. This was about the only place in town where I was not allowed inside, so I had to wait out front with all the other dogs tied to some special dog posts. While I didn't care so much for Mama leaving me, it did give me the opportunity to do some 'doggie socializing,' so it wasn't too bad. There was one brown female Lab that I took a liking to, even though she was about twice my size. But she had beautiful brown eyes and a wonderful smelling rear, so I fell madly in love before Mama came out of the store and spoiled it all – and another one of my love affairs came to an abrupt end.

Then there was the 'quality time' I believe it's called – that we spent at home. Each night we sampled different Dutch foods. My favorite was the *rijsttafel*, the rice table. Actually it was Indonesian, but considered the Dutch national dish since the Dutch used to own Indonesia or something like that. It consisted of about twenty or so different dishes of meats, fish, rice and sauces. Of course my favorite was a mound of rice with some chicken tossed in, but please, Mama, leave out the coconut and that horrible peanut sauce. Mama and Papa also liked the *erwtensoep* and *tomatensoep*, that's pea soup and tomato soup – probably because it was the only can label they kind of understood. But neither were suited to my 'doggie taste.' And then there was the *saucijze broodje* – sausage roll, which I definitely loved, but Mama thought they were fattening, so my intake of them was severely limited. Oh yes, what I believe to be the most popular food in all of Holland – *nieuwe* haring – that's herring – yuk! Why the Dutch swallow it raw and whole like goldfish. Mama and Papa never did try them, so I didn't get to, either. But in that department I was not too disappointed.

Since there wasn't much we could watch on TV other than CNN with our limited Dutch, and the fact that Papa didn't want Mama and me to become 'CNN Addicts,' we listened to music in the evenings and my parents played with me a lot. Boy, did we have great fun. I loved that time of my life when it was cold outside and we were nice and warm and cozy in our little Dutch house.

Of course, out came the candles each night and Mama would light each and every one of them. I have to admit it was kind of romantic, even if I didn't have a girlfriend. Of course, Papa was sure Mama was going to burn our two-hundred-year-old house right down, but she didn't. Why, I've never seen so many candles as we did in Holland. For you see, burning them is another favorite Dutch pastime and there wasn't a window in all of Holland that did not have them shining at night. What a wonderful welcoming beacon we thought they were here in the land of tulips, wooden shoes, bikes, windmills – and Labradors, of course.

CHAPTER 28
NIGHTS ON THE TOWN

So life went on in Holland. It was good for the most part, even though I have to admit I had many more 'yellow raincoat' days than I would have preferred. But summer in Holland was 'sweet,' although winter – it was nothing but 'sleet' – and rain and sometimes even snow. Now you can imagine how much I didn't enjoy that.

But we had lots of fun times, especially at night. And especially during the summer months when it stayed light until eleven o'clock. Now at first that really confused the 'doggie heck' out of me. As tired as I was, I thought it would never be time for bed because it wasn't dark outside. I'd just keep going to my *cama* and hoping it would get dark. But it didn't, so out I'd jump in search of Mama and Papa. Of course they had different feelings about those long nights – they loved them – and they didn't understand my 'early-to-bed' ritual even one little bit. Finally I gave it up myself, and learned to enjoy the long summer days of Holland – because in the winter it was totally the opposite – hardly any days at all – mostly darkness and gray, the sun far below the horizon.

On summer days we would sit out in our garden and enjoy the flowery scent and listen to the church bells. Why we had more blooms in our little garden than I could count, which probably cost more Euros – that's like dollars in America – than Papa would care to count. There was hardly a spot for me to squeeze in for a good pee without a petunia or cosmos up my snout, as well as in 'other' places. But Mama was always happy when we were out there, so I made the 'doggie' best of it.

Sometimes we would take our folding chairs and sit beside the canal. Now this I really liked. While Mama and Papa enjoyed a glass of ice tea, I enjoyed watching my favorite swan. We called him 'Big White' as he was one giant bird, let me tell you. I didn't even attempt to bark at him since he was bigger than me and had one huge beak. I didn't think he'd be someone I'd like to tangle with. Instead I satisfied my need for 'fowl interaction' by watching Big White glide by on the still water, his reflection gliding right there beside him.

I well remember the day Big White got caught in a fish hook and Mama and all the neighbors were so upset. But someone called the emergency number and a nice man came in a big truck and unhooked him. I've never seen a swan swim so fast after that – it was like a motor had been attached to his behind. We never saw him again.

In addition to ducks and swans, there were also lots of people on the canals. And no, they weren't gliding along like swans, they were in boats. As I've said before, those Dutch loved water and anything to do with it. Papa said they were so happy it was summer that they stayed out long into the night, eating *Gouda* cheese and drinking *Heineken* beer.

Papa thought that was a pretty good idea, too, so sometimes we'd just walk across the park to the train station and take the train to Amsterdam. Now the train was okay, although I didn't much care for the way it swayed back and forth. Besides, the windows were too high for me to see out of, so I stuck very close between my papa's legs. And then when we reached Amsterdam a few minutes later, I couldn't wait to escape my confinement and was always the first off the train. But it wasn't over for me yet. There were all those bikes to deal with, loads of them! I mean they were practically piled all on top of one another. Why I'd never seen so many bikes in all my 'doggie days.' Mama said it reminded her of when they visited China, wherever that is – but it reminded me of a good deal of danger, just dodging them.

Bikes excluded, Amsterdam was a pretty city, filled with many tree-lined canals and old Dutch gabled houses. There were also these glass-topped boats which people seemed to like to ride in, but I wasn't permitted on them, so we usually walked or took the streetcar. You can guess what I preferred, so walking alongside the canals toward our favorite hangout, *Rembrant Plein*, that's Rembrandt Square, is what we usually did.

Enroute we'd pass by a famous house called the *Anne Frankhuis*. It was a tiny place on *Prinsengracht* Canal where a family stayed inside the attic for over two years. Now that seemed like an awful lot of time to be inside the house in 'doggie time,' especially when they lived in such a beautiful tree-lined city. Mama said they had no choice.

Next we'd stroll through Amsterdam's famous flower market. Here I was absolutely not allowed to lift my leg, even one little time. Why they'd have all those flowers if a doggie couldn't even lift or sniff at them was beyond me. But Mama certainly enjoyed them, and she always ended up with at least one bouquet.

Papa would just shrug and say, "What else can a man do when surrounded by all these flowers?"

Mama was quick to agree and into his pocket he'd dig.

Sometimes we'd also pass through Amsterdam's famous Red Light District, where all the tourists seemed to want to go. There were also lots of coffee shops around there – remember what they sell – and the sweet aroma coming out of them about knocked me for a 'doggie loop.'

"Lucky, are you stoned?" Papa said, when I started to sway a little.

No, Papa, I'm just fine, but let's hit the pavement a bit faster – I just happen to hate this smell.

Personally, I didn't see too much to the Red Light District at all – just a bunch of ladies wearing tiny lacy things sitting on these stools in front of big windows with red lights above them. Why they didn't even pay any attention at all to little old me. But they sure would pucker their lips at Papa, and Mama would give him a dirty look and he'd just laugh. Of course, I joined Mama's team, so I did plenty of leash tugging, anxious to get to our destination.

Rembrandt Square was nice. There was a big grassy place in the middle where vendors sold ice cream and balloons. Of course I was into it more for its 'rolling' potential, and round and round I'd go. Then we'd go find a table at one of the many sidewalk cafes and watch the world stroll by – a popular European pastime I must admit. My mama and papa enjoyed this very much, as well. As for me – I spent my time snoozing beneath their table. Of course I really couldn't sleep much because of all these off-key musicians who kept coming by. Papa sometimes paid them some money and it seemed like they would stay forever – awfully hard on my sensitive 'doggie' ears, let me tell you.

After Mama and Papa had ordered their food, I'd just wait there patiently, hoping for a few accidentally-dropped morsels. They seldom came my way, except when we happened to be seated next to a family with small children – then it was an absolute 'doggie smorgasbord' – a night not to be forgotten. By the time we got up to leave, I could barely move, stuffed full of more *broodjes* and sausages than I could have imagined.

Then we'd continue our walk clear back to the train station, which was several miles. Often we'd walk by the famous *Rijksmuseum* or Dam Square or the Van Gogh Museum, even though they were not on our way. Let me tell you, I was one tired pooch after those Amsterdam 'nights on the town.' But Mama always told me that we'd never been in such great shape.

"If you'd just stay away from those sausages," she'd warn me.

Most weekend nights, however, we'd spend in Haarlem. Sometimes we went to this little Dutch pub at the *Grote Markt*. On summer evenings, the people that were not floating on the canals seemed to be congregated at the huge town square, listening to music, sitting at sidewalk cafes and just plain having fun. Our favorite pub was very very old and had windows with tiny panes. It had big heavy beams inside and an old carved wooden bar, and one very steep Dutch staircase that led to the 'WC' – the water closet – that's the bathroom. But since I didn't have to climb those steps, I didn't much worry about them. But my mama certainly did complain.

The barkeeper, Pieter, just happened to like me. Well, actually he happened to like all dogs.

"*Hullo*, Lucky!" he'd say when we walked in. "*Mag ik u iets te drinken aanbieden?* Can I offer you a drink?"

Before I could reply, down would come a nice big bowl of water right before my paws. Then he'd ask Mama and Papa what they'd like to drink. They always thought it was so cute that Pieter served me first. Why he liked me so much that he even had dry dog food for me. And he'd taste it beforehand, just to make sure it wasn't too salty. Now that put a funny look on both Mama and Papa's faces, and I didn't think they'd be sampling dog food any time soon. Of course Pieter didn't know I wasn't into dog food – especially the dry kind – but he was just so nice to me that I forced myself to eat a bit of it, although I much preferred the food at our next stop – *Restaurant Torenvalk.*

It was our favorite place to dine in Haarlem. It, too, was old and tiny and had a stone fireplace right in the center of the dining room where they cooked the meat over the flames. Talk about 'doggie heaven!' We always tried to get the place next to it – a perfect 'dog lounging' spot in my opinion, especially on cold winter nights when my snout would be about frozen off before we got there. One thing I know for certain; a winter night in Holland is truly a winter night. It's when one wants to wear every sweater and hat he owns all at once. Why the wind would blow off of the North Sea, which was a few miles from Haarlem, and about take us with it. My ears would fly out like sails and I can't tell you how many of my parents' umbrellas were bent upside down. In fact, I didn't mind wearing my red, white and blue turtle neck sweater even one little bit – and sometimes it was with my yellow raincoat on top. And since Mama and Papa were wearing their boots, I was happy to wear mine, as well.

In fact, some nights were so cold that we'd just stay home and enjoy our candles and watch skaters on the frozen canal. On nights like this our neighbor, Toby, would often come over. She was a lonely widow, so Papa and Mama felt sorry for her. Besides, we really liked her. Although she couldn't speak much English, she liked to tell us about Holland during the war, which happened to be many years before 'my time.' She said those Nazis were right in Haarlem, roaming the streets with their tanks and guns. From the look on Mama and Papa's faces I didn't think I'd like to run into any old Nazi anytime soon.

At first Toby didn't much like me, very strange for a Dutch person, as they're all such 'dog lovers.' But after I turned on my 'doggie charm' she decided to love me, especially after she'd had a glass of *jenever,* a fiery, colorless Dutch liquid that made people act real funny. Mama and Papa didn't like it at all, but they had to choke a little down when Toby came for a visit, as she'd often bring some. You should have seen the look on my parent's faces when they took a sip of that stuff. Why, I was certain they were about to explode! And Toby, why she'd just watch and laugh and make sure they swallowed it. It's the one thing I didn't even come close to begging for.

And it was Toby who came to our house crying after the 2001 terrorist attacks in America. I knew something was very wrong the second I saw her. And then Mama and Papa started crying, too, and I couldn't imagine what horrible thing had happened. Since we didn't as yet have a television, Toby took us to her house, sat us before her TV and served us warm tea, all the time crying and hugging us. It was the one time during our stay in Europe that I could tell Mama and Papa really wanted to be back home in America.

The next day the streets of Haarlem were almost silent – only the sound of the many church bells could be heard throughout the city. Everyone put out their Dutch flags, bent downwards in a symbol of mourning.

I know Mama didn't feel much like walking, but since Papa had to go to work, I think she needed to get out of the house. We walked for several hours – probably about the longest walk I'd ever taken. Mama was kind of in a daze – she barely talked to me, and that was very strange for my mama. Many of the shop windows displayed American flags and anything else 'American' that the owners could find. There were t-shirts with flags, and posters of the Statue of Liberty and the Grand Canyon – even one of the New York skyline. Everyone we met on the street – and who knew we were Americans – bowed their heads and told us how sorry they were. They didn't even laugh at my raincoat that day. I could not imagine what terrible thing had happened, but I hated seeing my mama so sad. Although I kept giving her my special 'butterfly kisses' on her hand that she's always loved, I just couldn't seem to cheer her up. She'd just pat me on the head with this faraway look.

We ended up at the *Grote Markt* and sat on a bench for a long time, looking up at the great cathedral as the bells tolled and tolled. It was the one time I didn't once tug on my leash. I only knew my Mama needed me right there where I was right beside her – her best friend.

CHAPTER 29
OUT AND ABOUT 'DUTCH STYLE'

It took Mama and Papa a while to get over those terrorist attacks in the U.S., and believe me, I tried as hard as I possibly could to cheer them up. Why I'd give them all kinds of 'butterfly kisses' whenever their hands were at the optimum height. I tried not to spill any of my food when I ate. I didn't pull on my leash when we went walking. I didn't snore when I took a nap, and I didn't even fuss all that much when I had to wear my raincoat. Why I was the best little doggie they could have ever wished for. What more could they want from me?

I think my efforts paid off. For day-by-day they started to smile and laugh again. Boy, was I ever one relieved pooch! I was beginning to think they were going to toss me out or something; that perhaps they really didn't love me any more. While I have to admit that living on the streets of Holland would be 'a hound dog' better than the streets of Mexico, I was perfectly content to be right where I was.

One day when I was having a nap, Mama came up to me and bent down.

"Lucky, you bring so much joy into our lives," she said, just giving me the best old scratch behind my ears. "I'm sorry we haven't been very attentive to you these last few days."

I looked up at her with those big brown eyes that she loves so much.

Mama, that's okay. I know I bring joy to you – except of course when I poop on the rug. And, by the way, I love you, too.

Soon we were once more out and about on our 'adventure tours' of Holland, much to my 'doggie delight' and boy did we have some fun times. And I have to admit, we found more than our share of windmills, as well as other very Dutch things.

"How about let's go to *Zaanse Schans* and check out some windmills for Mama," Papa said one Saturday morning.

Now you know me – no need to ask twice. I was 'up and ready' immediately, my tail wagging full throttle. And even better – it was a beautiful day, so that meant no yellow raincoat. Boy was I in a 'doggie' good mood. So we jumped into the car – at least I did – Mama and Papa weren't too good at jumping in the car, they just stepped inside and sat down like people tend to do. Now children, they're another story when it comes to getting in the car. They like jumping in. And the funny thing about them is that they just keep jumping and jumping and jumping, instead of settling down for a good old nap like I do. I sometimes wonder about kids and their lack of 'sleeping ability.'

In Holland we had a little Ford – that means no SUV – so the viewing wasn't as good from my 'doggie perspective.' Didn't matter to me, though. I was perfectly happy sitting in the back seat.

But Papa used to get in a bit of a tizzy when I went along because it was a company car and my shedding made for some pretty funny-looking Dutch suits when Papa had to take clients out for lunch. That's because some of them had to ride in the rear seat. Although he cleaned and cleaned after I got out, I always managed to leave some remnants of little old me, which were passed onto Papa's clients, which did not make Papa very happy at all. Well now what could I do? I couldn't exactly keep my fur from falling out, now could I?

"Darn you, Lucky," Papa would say. "I'm going to have to shave you bald one of these days so you won't shed."

Oh sure, Papa, I'd look pretty funny without my fur coat now, wouldn't I? Do you want to go around leading a sausage on a leash?

Our first stop that day was the village of *Spaardam*, which was on the canal just a few miles from Haarlem. It was a cute little town surrounded by dikes. There was a bronze statue of this little boy named Young Pieter. Mama said he plugged the dike with his finger and saved all of Holland from flooding in a book called *Hans Brinker and the Silver Skates*, like I was supposed to be impressed or something. Well I wasn't – until she told me he was the symbol of the everlasting courage of the Dutch people. Now this I could sort of relate to – I liked the Dutch. They were good to me. Still, I would have preferred it if the statue was of some famous Dutch dog. Nope, unfortunately I never saw one of those in all my travels throughout Holland. And believe me, we put on plenty of kilometers – that's what the Europeans call miles, remember – except that they are not as long as miles.

After we finished looking at the statue, down the tree-lined road we drove through all these perfect little farms. Many of the houses had thatched roofs, which Mama really loved. Personally, I couldn't see much to them. Then it was onto the car ferry which took us across this very wide canal. This I really liked as it reminded me of the car ferry in Newport Beach, California – thus home.

By the time we reached *Zaanse Schans*, I was one excited pooch. That's because there's lots of good things for dogs to do there, when I could persuade Mama and

Papa to stop shopping for *klompen* – that's wooden shoes. You see, there was a place that made them while you watched, and I can't tell you the number of wooden shoe demonstrations I must have witnessed while in Holland. Papa was just fascinated at how the carpenter could take a block of wood and turn it into a pair of shoes in a matter of minutes. So you can imagine what all the folks back home got for Christmas, can't you?

Worse than watching them make those shoes, was posing for a picture while sitting in this giant wooden shoe outside the shop. I might as well have been wearing my yellow raincoat to top it all off. Why, my parents must have taken twenty or more pictures of me in that thing. I was lucky I didn't have a girlfriend they could show them to.

"Smile, Lucky, smile," Mama would say, snapping my picture. But I have to admit, I've never been the photogenic type. For some reason, the second anyone points a camera at me, I almost always look the other way. It's not that I'm 'camera shy,' it's just that I don't like to waste time posing for photos. I much prefer peeing on a bush or sniffing out some treat accidentally dropped on the ground.

But finally we were off to explore the windmills, Mama's favorite part of *Zaanse Schans* since there were twelve of them. One was used for cutting lumber, another for making vegetable oil, one for churning cheese and even one for making the famous local mustard. And, of course, Mama insisted that we visit each and every one of them. I would have been perfectly happy to wait outside for my parents, but no way – Mama said I had to check them out first hand.

"After all, who knows when you'll be living in Holland again, Lucky," Mama told me, like I was suppose to just smile and jump right inside the windmill

274

like a good little dog. Now going up those very steep steps when one has four feet instead of two can be very tricky; especially when each of the steps is about half my height. But I have to admit, that when we got to the top, the view was beautiful. It looked out over all the little canals and other windmills, and the village with its cobblestone streets. The only thing I didn't like was this great big wooden paddle that kept going by me round and round and round. Why I thought it was going to grab me and take me right up to the sky with it. It about scared the 'doggie daylights' right out of me! I think Mama and Papa finally figured that out, so I didn't have to go into the windmills any more. And Papa didn't mind waiting outside with me even one little bit.

Some weekends we went to some very old Dutch villages called *Volendam* and *Marken*. They were located on the *Ijsselmeer*, a great big lake that used to be the sea. Now how that works, I have no idea at all. Anyway, the people there still dressed in the old Dutch way – long skirts and white pointed hats for the women, dark captain hats and trousers for the men, and wooden shoes for all. Just looking at all those wooden shoes with so much 'kicking' potential certainly gave me the 'doggie creepies.' But then I remembered that the Dutch don't kick, so I got into watching them making cheese and eating herrings, so visits to these villages turned out to be fun. One thing I certainly enjoyed were all the outside cafes beside the moored boats where we'd sit and have Mama and Papa's favorite – now you can guess what that is – cappuccino! By this time in my life, I was pretty much getting used to this routine, so I'd settle in for a little 'doggie' snooze.

Afterwards they bought me this red, white and blue Dutch kerchief, complete with a tiny wooden shoe that cinched it around my neck.

"Now you look like the locals," Mama said.

Nope, Mama, sorry – not tall enough for that. Not blond enough either.

Then there were our visits to *Gouda* and *Edam*, where they were really into the cheese, let me tell you. Not being much of a cheese *aficionado* – especially with the smell of that cheese – definitely 'old sock' – which, incidentally came in blocks bigger than me – I just made the best of our visits. At least I was with Mama and Papa. But I did get kind of bored when the Saturday morning cheese auction started, and I'd have to do a bit of 'leash tugging' to get Mama and Papa up and at em' again.

We also liked to visit the town of Delft, where they make the famous blue and white pottery. Now Mama loved it – Papa hated it. Guess what? Mama bought a big pot anyway and my papa didn't do a lot of smiling that day, even though I did my best to cheer him up. *That's okay, Papa, it's only a piece of pottery that could be easily broken by a swish of the tail, if you know what I mean.*

And then on we went to *Den Hague*, where there is this famous world court, whatever that is. It's also where the queen lives. But we didn't even get to visit her. Instead we went to a museum where the painting of a girl who liked to wear pearl earrings was displayed. I didn't think it would be such a big deal to meet up with such a girl, but my parents certainly did. Why when they came out of the museum where I incidentally, was tied out front waiting – they had great big smiles on their faces. So I merely wagged my tail just as hard as I could

276

and greeted them, sure that they would forget about that girl and her earring soon enough.

But the best time of all in Holland was "Tulip Time" – that means late April. The entire country turned into a rainbow of color. We used to drive this road called 'the Tulip Trail.' It's in the *bollenstreek*, that's the bulb district, which was very close to Haarlem. Even from a 'doggie point of view,' it was one of the most beautiful things I had ever seen. Why everywhere we looked there were fields of blooming tulips and hyacinths – some purple, some pink and others orange, yellow, red and white. I can't even begin to tell you how many times I had my picture taken in those tulip fields – probably at least a hundred. Why we even bought a garland of tulips to put on the hood of our car, just like the Dutch did. And if you really want to see bikes in Holland, go during Tulip Time. Why, I think that every Dutch that ever thought of owning a bike was out there riding alongside the fields, enjoying the blue sky and sunshine. We sure did.

Mama even packed us a lunch and we sat beside the car and ate it, watching the tulip parade go by – that's a parade where all the floats are covered with tulip petals and some of the Dutch girls go around dressed as great big tulips. I have to admit it was nice, but I didn't even see one dog on any of those floats – just a bunch of flowers, so soon I got bored. I was one happy pooch when we moved on.

Then it was on to Keukenhof Gardens. The Dutch call it "Holland's Gift to the World." Mama simply called it 'beautiful.' Why there were more tulips there than any place in the world, just gardens and gardens of them. I was certainly happy they let us dogs share in all that beauty – but I was certainly not happy that Papa would not let me lift my leg, even one time.

Oh yes, what wonderful memories we were making. We had so much fun traipsing throughout Holland, enjoying its woods, canals, villages, beaches, flowers and such. But little did I know that these fun times would soon come to an end – at least for me.

CHAPTER 30
LONELY DAYS

"Come on Lucky, rise and shine," Mama said to me early one morning when I was just in the middle of a great 'doggie' dream – bone and all. *Now why is Mama waking me up this time of morning? She knows how I love to sleep in.*

Slowly, I opened my eyes and glanced up at her. She looked kind of sad, which was strange for my mama, so I knew something was up.

"We've got to get going. We need to check out your new kennel," she said, bending down to pat my head. At the word "kennel," I closed my eyes again and wound into my 'street dog' curl. I wasn't about to go to any kennel – not ever again. In fact, I was surprised there was such a thing in Holland, being the great dog lovers that they are.

It's not that I think kennels are all that bad. It's just that they don't come with my mama and papa included, and that was enough to make me not like them.

"I said we've got to go, Lucky," Mama repeated, nudging me gently by the collar. Now my mama seldom did this, so I knew she meant business and reluctantly I got up.

Of course, I did my usual morning stretching exercises, first one leg and then the other stretched way out behind me. Afterwards I hurried to the kitchen door so Mama could let me out for my morning 'pee' time. Boy, did I need to go.

She opened the door for me, still looking kind of sad. "I sure hate to do this to you," she said. "You don't deserve it, but we can't take you to England until you've been in Holland for six months, and unfortunately Papa

279

and I have to be in the UK by next week, so that means 'kennel' for you, Lucky Boy."

Like I'd understand her whole speech. But I did understand one word and that was enough to make me run. But I quickly found I had no where to go but our tiny rear yard, and I had already discovered there was no escape route there.

An hour later we were on the A9 heading for *Alkmaar*, the 'big cheese' place. But I had a funny feeling we were not on the way to buy cheese – we were heading for the kennel Mama had been talking about, and I seriously doubted they sold even a slice of cheese there. When Mama exited the freeway at *Beverwijk*, I knew this for certain. There was no cheese smell.

Well, we drove through all these pretty tree-lined roads and little villages with Dutch style houses until we got very near the North Sea. Mama seemed to be looking for something the entire time, so I decided to join in her search although I didn't have the slightest idea what she was looking for. *Nope, no conejos around here.* The only thing I saw were lots of fields, woods, and people riding bikes on the bike paths which ran alongside the road – typical 'Dutch.'

Suddenly she turned into this tiny lane, after she saw a big sign with a dog on it. *Oh, oh, I know where we're going now. She can't fool me.* She stopped the car in this place with a fence all around it. There were lots and lots of trees inside and outside the fence and I could hear dogs barking. *The kennel – has to be the kennel.* Promptly I plopped down into the seat hoping I would disappear or something. No such luck.

"Here we are at *Torenvalk*, Lucky," Mama said, getting out of the car.

I was not about to budge, and if I could have locked the car, I would have done so. But that's one trick this puppy's never mastered.

Mama proceeded to hook the leash to my collar and urged me from the car. Even though I didn't want to get out, I had no choice. And besides, I did need to do 'my thing.'

Just as I was about to lift my leg on a nice green bush, Mama screamed.

"No Lucky, not on that bush! It's stinging nettle!"

Whatever that was I had no idea, but quickly decided it must not be a good spot.

Instead Mama led me along this little trail through the trees. Still more of that stuff that Mama didn't like. *Mama, I've seriously got to pee.*

Finally, we came to a clearing and there I got to do 'my thing.' Boy, was I one relieved pooch.

Then it was back to the kennel, much to my 'doggie dismay.' *No, Mama, please, please, I don't want to go there.* I pulled hard on my leash, but it didn't seem to do a bit of good for Mama was just as determined that I would be going inside with her.

"It's okay, Lucky, we're just here to look today. You don't have to stay."

For some reason, her words sounded reassuring, but still, I wasn't so sure about this place in the woods.

Mama read the sign and then said a few words that I won't repeat. "They're only open for visitors between noon and three." She looked at her watch. "That's two hours from now. Those Dutch and their schedules," she moaned. "Guess we'll just have to take a good long walk, Lucky."

Of course, that didn't bother me at all, so off we went into the Dutch countryside for a hike. Now this was really what I liked – a heck of a lot more than a kennel tour, let me tell you. We crossed over several little canals on tiny bridges until we came to the sand dunes, which were near the coast. They were beautiful and I was hoping Mama would let me go free, so I could have a good run on them.

"No, Lucky, you have to stay on your leash. The sand dunes are protected in Holland. They don't want you digging up all the growth that keeps them stable."

Oh well, at least I tried. But the path was okay, and soon we reached the beach and the North Sea. Even though the day was sunny, the sea looked gray. It always did. Nothing like the California ocean. It was certainly not a place I'd want to go swimming, even if I did like water, which of course I don't. So Mama and I simply walked along the beach and didn't say a thing to each other for quite a while.

Finally, Mama decided to go test the water, but her test was very short-lived when she found out how cold it was. "Can you imagine swimming across this sea like the British like to do?" Mama asked. "They must be nuts."

Mama looked at her watch again. "Gotta get back to the kennel before they go and close on us again," Mama said, turning back.

Darn, I was hoping we could spend the day on the beach like we used to in California. Remember our favorite bench in Laguna, Mama? But she didn't pay a bit of attention to my thoughts.

When we arrived back at *Torenvalk*, the gate was wide open, so in we went.

Right inside the door was a great big glassed-in room where lots of cats were roaming around, napping and licking themselves. Boy would I have loved to jump through that glass and scare all those cats, but I wasn't to have the chance. Instead I barked as loud as I possibly could and they all woke up and got in their rounded snarly-cat positions.

A large blonde Dutch woman stood at the front desk and gave me what I thought was a disgusted look.

"*Goede middag*," she said, eyeing me suspiciously, like I was a spoiled brat or something.

Mama smiled at her and quickly asked if she spoke English.

"*Ja*," she answered, which meant 'yes' in Dutch.

"We're here to tour your kennel," Mama said. "This is my dog, Lucky, and we recently moved to Holland from America."

The woman looked at me kind of funny, like she was trying to determine what kind of American breed I was. Silly her, she didn't know I was a Mexican. But at least she had warmed up a bit. Wanting to find out more about my gene pool, she came around the counter to check me out. I noticed that she wore these huge clogs, so I crept up real close to Mama.

"*Hallo,*" she said, scratching me behind the ears. *At least she's not a kicker.* I let out a little moan and enjoyed her touch. "So you will be staying with us at *Torenvalk*?" she asked me.

Not if I have a say in the matter, Mrs. Dutch lady.

Then she proceeded to give Mama one of those colorful brochures featuring her kennel, complete with all those 'happy' dogs running around. Yeah, right. I bet those dogs are about as happy as if they'd been kicked by a pair of clogs. Oh, I know. They were probably her dogs and this was their home. Yes, that's it. You know – it was all the usual pitch.

"Come, I will show you our animal hotel."

Yeah, right. As far as I could see, it was just about like any other kennel. Lots of rows of pens that smelled like antiseptic.

"These are our kennels," she said. But they looked more like 'dog prisons' to me. Each had two bowls – one for food and the other for water, a hook for a leash and a bright flowered cushion for sleeping.

I started to feel really bad. I just didn't want to stay in this place, clean or not.

Next the woman took us outside to what she called the 'yard for exercise.'

"Every day we exercise de dogs," she said, a big smile on her face.

"That's great," Mama said, trying hard to smile.

Yes, the kennel was nice all right, especially the exercise yard. It was large and had a bunch of trees for peeing on. But still, I wanted to go home with Mama and not stay at this kennel, nice or not. And believe it or not, I did get to leave with her! Why, I couldn't believe my 'doggie' good luck. *Mama, oh how I love you!*

I think Mama sensed my mood, and she reached in the rear seat and gave me a warm touch, her eyes tear-filled.

"You don't have to stay this time, Lucky, but I'm afraid you're going to be coming back here."

I pretended I didn't understand a thing she said and just let her keep right on patting.

Soon we pulled out of the drive of *Torenvalk* Kennel and headed down the road and back to Haarlem, much to my 'doggie delight.'

"Hey Lucky, look, a shortcut back to Haarlem," Mama said, pointing at a small sign by the roadside. Now we won't have to take the freeway."

She turned beside the sign and off we went on this rather tiny country road. Why it was so narrow I was afraid a tree was going to reach right inside the car and whack me on the head. But then we got to this great big meadow full of those 'salt eating' Dutch sheep. I relaxed a bit. Still something seemed wrong. I think Mama thought so, too.

"This sure isn't a very wide road," Mama said, becoming a bit nervous. "Maybe we should have taken the freeway."

Then before we knew it, all these bikes were coming at us – in front of us, behind us, all over the place. Why I thought they were going to run us right off the road!

Mama was beginning to panic, so she jammed on the brakes and brought the car to a screeching halt, like she was about to run over a skunk or something. Why, I almost bumped my head on the back of her seat! She just sat there and shook her head.

"*Nee! Nee!*" the bikers yelled. "*Nee, beslist niet snelweg! Het es voor filetspad!*"

"I'm sorry," Mama said, but I don't speak Dutch."

"It's for de bikes," one man shouted at her. "Bike path – do you understand? Not for de cars."

I think by then Mama had gotten the message, and she turned bright red. "Oh, I'm so sorry. I thought it was a road."

"A picture of bicycle is on de sign," one man said.

"I'm sorry. I didn't notice it."

Of course all the Dutch bikers had gathered around our car by then. They shook their heads, and then gradually started to laugh and point at us, the 'stupid' Americans. It's a good thing I didn't have on my yellow raincoat that day. We would have been laughed right out of Holland.

Mama was so embarrassed, and about out of choices, so she put the car in gear, waved them a 'good-bye,' and drove right across the meadow towards a distant road, much to the shock of the Dutch observers.

Let me tell you, my mama never drove on a bike path again, which I must add were a very frequent sight in Holland. At each and every intersection she always studied the sign to make sure there was no bike of any kind on it.

* * * *

The next week I was not so lucky. For back we went to *Torenvalk* Kennel. This time I had to stay.

Mama and Papa both gave me a big long hug and I stuck to them like Super Glue. *Please Mama and Papa, don't leave me here.* I even whined, but it didn't do a bit of good. The big Dutch lady put a lasso on my head and off I went to my cell – oh, I mean my kennel.

The last thing I remember were Mama's tears and Papa saying, "It'll be okay, Boy. We'll be back for you in two weeks. We've got to go to London and find a place to live."

I just didn't want them to leave at all, but I had no choice. Remember, I was on the end of the Dutch lady's lasso, and as hard as I dug in my paws, the harder she pulled on the lead. I finally gave up and followed her, my tail between my legs. But I knew my mama and papa would come back for me. For they had never broken that promise. I just had to be brave.

The first few days I just lay in my bed at the kennel and thought of Mama and Papa. I thought of our bench in Laguna Beach and of the cat next door at Norma's house. I thought of our camping trips and all our great outings to Dana Point Harbor. I thought of my brother. Boy was I homesick and lonely.

When the Dutch lady came to take me out for exercise I did my thing and then moped under a tree. I didn't feel like playing with the other dogs. I only wanted to play with my mama and papa. *Why don't you come back for me? I hate this place. I'm so lonely.*

So I called and called for Mama and Papa until I was totally hoarse. But they never came. This I could not understand. My mama and papa had always been there for me.

I didn't eat either, and this really got the Dutch lady nervous. "Lucky, you must eat," she told me over and over again, each time adding something different to my bowl. Didn't matter – I missed my rice and pasta – especially the way Mama and Papa made it. I merely looked at that Dutch dog food, gave it a sniff and went right back to my cushion. *I'm not about to eat a thing.*

The lady looked worried. Soon she showed up at my kennel again, this time with a pile of raw meat, which she placed in my food bowl. Now this I couldn't resist, so I gobbled it up.

Raw meat became my diet at the kennel, even though the kennel lady complained how much it smelled each time she gave it to me. "You American dogs are too fussy," she told me over and over again. "Why don't you like Dutch dog food? It is good for you."

Frankly, I didn't care whether it was good for me or not. I wasn't about to eat it. This battle I won. But I have to admit, my raw meat diet really made my poop smell bad. Of course, my Dutch kennel lady reminded me of that, as well, each time they had to clean my cage because of the 'runs' the meat gave me.

"You must drink water," she said, coaxing me to drink.

I took a sip and then went right back to my cushion. I could tell she was worried about me.

"You must be missing your mama and papa, little dog," she told me, giving me a quick pat on the head.

I seriously wondered if she would call my parents to come and get me.

No such luck. I figured out I was doomed to this place for life. Now, it's not that it was a bad place – it was as good as a kennel could get. Everything was perfect there. It was like a summer camp for dogs – most of which played happily with each other. *Why was I being so stubborn? Couldn't an old street dog like me handle being in a nice clean pen for a few days?*

I finally decided I had no choice, so I buckled down and tried to be happy, reminding myself that sooner or later Mama and Papa would come and get me.

And they did! Boy was I one happy pooch that day. In fact, I heard their car pull into the gravel parking lot out front. You know, us dogs are really good at knowing the sounds of our owner's cars. Each engine sounds different, you know. And when I heard the sound of their engine, I let out a 'doggie whoop' like I never had before. Let me tell you, my Dutch keeper about flipped right out. I think she thought I was having a heart attack or something. But I was just fine. I only wanted to see my mama and papa.

When she came to the kennel with my leash in hand, I didn't even wait for her to put it on. I raced right between her legs and to the front desk. Mama and Papa stood there with the biggest smiles on their faces. Why I about wagged my entire bottom off I was so happy to see them. *Mama! Papa! I love you!*

We all hugged each other and I contributed a bit of licking to each of their faces, then off we went back to our place on *Schotersingel* canal. Boy, was I one happy pooch!

* * * *

Unfortunately, this kennel experience was one I had to go through many times in the next six months, much to my 'doggie dismay.' But then again, life can't be totally a 'bed of roses' now, can it? Sure I'd led a 'dog's life' for the past several years, even though I was a street dog at heart. And those days were what I'd call really tough times. So putting up with the kennel really wasn't so bad at all. I'd been through much worse times. So finally I concluded that I would have to adapt.

CHAPTER 31
ACCIDENTAL CAMPING

Of course, all my days in Holland were not spent at the kennel, thank goodness. We had lots of great times, especially on the weekends when we'd pile in a rental car to explore the European countryside. And, much to our surprise, we even got to go camping in Europe. Unfortunately it was not by choice.

It was on a long holiday weekend in August, shortly after our arrival in Holland. A 'bank holiday' is what they called it in Europe. In fact, that's what they call all holidays, and I often wondered if the banks were going to run out of money since they were on holiday so much of the time. Anyway, this first 'bank holiday' Mama and Papa decided it would be nice to drive to the French coast, which turned out to be lot farther than we thought.

And boy was the weather hot, something very strange for Holland. The Dutch were all out on the canals in their boats and drinking beer, dressed only in their bathing suits. And there I was dressed in my fur coat, which I couldn't do a darn thing about except for panting.

But my papa saved the day since he had decided it would be a good idea to rent a station wagon with air conditioning so it would be cool and have more space for little old me.

"You'll enjoy looking out the window, Lucky Boy," he told me as we drove into the car rental garage at the airport. "It'll be nice for you to see the countryside."

Whatever, Papa. I'm just happy that I'm going along.

Like I needed a good geography lesson on Europe, but you know my papa – he didn't want me to be a dumb dog, you can bet your 'doggie diddles' on that.

When we arrived at the car rental agency, they had a station wagon reserved for us all right, but it did not have air conditioning. Now my papa without air conditioning in hot weather was not a particularly happy papa. I was not a particularly happy pup, come to think of it, anticipating the long hot ride ahead of us.

"We do not need the air conditioning here in Holland," the huge man at the counter said. "It is usually cold and rainy."

Papa knew better than argue with any Dutchmen, so off we went in our hot rental car, me panting away the kilometers. The traffic was really heavy, kind of like the 'great getaway' weekends in California.

"Thank goodness we have a reservation in Ghent, Belgium for tonight," Mama said. "But I'm really worried about tomorrow night on the coast of France. We should have made a reservation there, too."

"Don't you worry," Papa assured her. "There'll be plenty of places to stay in the beach communities."

I remembered how busy it used to be in Laguna Beach in the summer with all the tourists, and I was hoping my 'doggie' best, it wouldn't be like that in France.

Mama only shook her head. I have to admit I was about as worried as she was, but not too much, because at least I was traveling with my own bed.

We arrived in *Ghent*, a very hot two hours later. It was certainly a different world from Haarlem. Papa said that's because it wasn't Holland, but that we were in Belgium, a country I hadn't visited before. *Oh boy, another stamp in my official European Union 'Pet Passport.'*

I have to admit, however, that Ghent looked very similar to Holland, except more Medieval. That's because there was an old wall around the city with spires every so often. I thought it was pretty neat – especially when we got to walk on top of it. One more thing – the people didn't speak Dutch. They spoke what's called Flemish, which is kind of like Dutch with different words thrown in. *Oh no, not another language to learn.* But I was soon to find out we were only there on a temporary visit, so there was no need bothering to understand what people were saying. All that mattered to me was that they seemed to like dogs.

We stayed in this hotel called *Sint-Jorishof.*

"Built in 1228," Mama was quick to point out. "It's where Napoleon Bonaparte used to stay."

So . . . . who the heck cares? Little did I know that Napoleon was one short but very important French guy who used to conquer places. I didn't much care – all I wanted to do was put on my outdoor 'doggie' gear and get exploring.

That we did. Why I was so tired when I hit my *cama* that I barely stirred all night, even though Mama and Papa complained about the noise from the revelers below our window, which faced the main square.

They were both kind of groggy the next day, but I was as 'peppy a puppy' as ever and off we headed toward France. Little did I know – nor my parents for that matter – that it was going to be a seven-hour drive to *Deauville.* At least it was getting a bit cooler as we neared the French coast.

Late in the afternoon we began hunting for a place to stay. Nothing. Why we checked out every inn and hotel in several towns and not a room was to be found. By this time it was early evening and we were all tired and grouchy and hungry. I seriously wondered how Mama and Papa were going to heat my Cup of Soup for dinner. I could tell Mama was thinking about pointing the 'I told you so' finger at Papa, but she didn't. She just had this kind of smirky smile on her face.

"It looks like we're going to have to spend the night in the car," Papa said. "And I'm not looking forward to that even a little."

"We should have taken the room over the stable at that hotel in the Loire Valley," Mama said, "but no, you thought it would smell like cows, so here we are on the street and we'll just have to make the best of it."

I wasn't about to get involved in their argument, although I couldn't find a thing wrong with smelling cows all night – in fact I kind of liked the idea.

Well, we drove all over *Deauville* looking for a safe place to park. Just as Papa drove up to a parking lot next to the Holiday Inn, Mama pointed to a sign on the road.

"Look, it says campground. We can go there!"

Papa looked at her kind of funny. "Can you see a tent trailer behind our car?" he asked her. "How in the heck are we going to camp?"

"We've got a station wagon. We'll just have to make do. At least there will be bathrooms there, and security."

Papa nodded his head. "I suppose you're right."

Now I know my papa hated admitting he had made a mistake, but he was very brave about it this time because I think he thought Mama was going to hit him over the head with her guidebook or something. And I was really getting hungry, so the camping idea sounded great to me. Like I said before, I had my bed right there in the car with me.

So we drove to the campground, which was a few miles out of town. The lady at the gate told us to find a place anywhere on the large grassy area where we could pitch our tent – I suppose she thought no one in their right mind would go camping without a tent – so off we went to find our little patch of 'camping paradise.'

She also told us that the gates closed at nine and it was already eight. We soon discovered there was not a grocery story or a restaurant in the campground. Boy, was I getting worried, for by this time my stomach had really started growling.

Of course Mama's camping idea was all good in theory, but since we didn't have a tent to pitch or one of those cute Dutch fold-up tables, nor the little plastic picnic dishes that all of Europe loved, we couldn't exactly set up camp.

"We don't even have any bedding," Papa grumbled.

"It's too hot for blankets anyway," Mama answered. "We can use our garment bag for a pillow. "It'll be fun."

Let me tell you, Papa didn't look as if was going to be any fun at all, but I had to agree with Mama. I thought we were going to have a 'doggie good time,' just as long as I got to eat. And while my parents re-arranged the back of the car I explored our camping spot, careful to mark each and every bush and flower.

"Hey, what are we going to do for dinner?" Papa asked. "I'm starved."

Back from my exploration, I seconded his comment by letting out a big 'let's get out of here and go find some chow' kind of bark. I looked around, but there was not a plug in sight for Mama to plug in an electric tea kettle, even if we'd had one with us, so there was no way she could prepare my Cup of Soup.

So we quickly drove back into town and picked up a pepperoni pizza and soft drinks at a take-away place, and back we headed to camp as it was dark and almost time for the gate to be locked. In fact, when we arrived, the lady was just locking it, but after some pleading from Mama, she grunted, grumbled, and then opened the gate so we could get through.

Back at our camping spot, we opened the rear of our station wagon and had ourselves a very merry little picnic in the dark. Let me tell you that pepperoni pizza tasted darn good and Mama even tore mine into tiny little pieces so that I was able to easily chew it as I don't have a great deal of teeth. It was the first and only time in my life I was ever given the chance to enjoy pizza. I had to admit I'm still a rice or pasta type of guy – but in our circumstances that night – pepperoni pizza ruled.

Come on, Mama, be a sport. Please give me another slice

"No more, Lucky. It will give you diarrhea, and we don't want to deal with that since the three of us are sleeping side-by-side tonight."

"Hey, just you wait a minute," Papa said. "Lucky's not sleeping with us. He never has and he never will. We'll just have to think of another option."

Mama gave him kind of a dirty look.

"I'm sorry," Papa said. "I suppose it will be kind of fun camping. Something we'll always remember about our time in Europe – but Lucky's not sleeping with us."

As for me, I thought this sleeping arrangement was much better than that 'Napoleon place' where we had stayed in Ghent. At least it was quiet and the stars overhead were beautiful.

Mama reached down and patted me. "This is nice. It reminds me of our great camping trips in the Rocky Mountains and Southern Utah. I miss that so much, don't you two?"

Papa nodded and gave Mama a hug, so I knew all was well between them.

*Of course I miss camping, Mama, but as long as I'm
with you and Papa, I'm one happy doggie.*

That was before I found out that I 'really' wasn't
going to be sleeping in the back of the station wagon
with the two of them. For Papa had been serious about
what he said.

"We're going to have to put your bed outside near the
car," Papa said.

"You've got to be kidding?" Mama said. "You know
Lucky will take off. He's always been a wanderer."

"Not tonight. I think I can take care of that. I've got a
good idea."

And being the engineer that he was, Papa got our
great big red suitcase from the back of the car and put it
right next to my bed. "We'll just attach Lucky's leash to
this suitcase and he won't be going anywhere tonight. It
weighs a ton."

I gave Papa a really dirty look when he led me to my
bed, right next to that big old suitcase. Why I was so
upset that I wanted to pee right on it. Then Mama and
Papa got into the back of the car and off we went to
sleep in the peaceful quiet.

Mama later told me that in the middle of the night
she heard this *clickity, clickity, clickity* sound that woke
her right up. "What's that noise?" she said, shaking Papa
awake.

"What? What's the matter?" he said, swatting at a
bug on his bare leg.

Mama jumped out of the car in her nightgown and
looked around. "Lucky's gone!"

Of course Papa jumped out, too, dressed only in his
underwear – the ones with the Dutch tulips all over
them. "Where is that darn dog? I tied him right next to
this suitcase." He pointed at the spot where the suitcase
had been. It was gone. "Why that little bugger!"

Mama and Papa both raced to the gravel driveway that circled the campground and searched where the clicking sound was coming from. And what did they find? Why little old me, out exploring, their big suitcase trailing right behind me.

What did you want me to do Mama and Papa? I couldn't sleep and there's just so much exploring to do around this place.

But let me tell you something – I had one stiff neck for the next several days. Therefore, I decided I would never go 'suitcase exploring' again, not me, and that I definitely did not want to become a 'bell dog' in some French hotel.

CHAPTER 32
CHRISTMAS – THE EUROPEAN WAY

My neck finally healed. And before I knew it, winter had arrived. And boy, did they know a thing or two about winter in Holland. Why it was nothing like the California or Mexican winters I remembered. This was 'real' winter – the kind with ice and sleet and snow. I know my Mama was always talking about having those things in Utah, where she grew up. And she said she never wanted to have them again. So I wondered what we were doing in Holland. Oh yeah, I think it had something to do with Papa's work.

Anyway, every time we went out of our house, it was on with the sweaters, coats, hats, boots – the whole *tostada*, if you know what I mean. Why it took Mama so long to get all her things on, and then my sweater and boots, that I thought I was going to have to do my deed right on the floor – and believe me, I knew from past experience where that would get me. *Nope, not going to do that again.* In fact, I rather liked being on Mama's 'good doggie' list, so I waited very patiently for her to put on my winter doggie-wear. The only thing my mama didn't cover on me was my tail. And believe me, when we were walking toward the *Grote Markt* on some winter days – the wind blowing so hard that we could barely walk – I was seriously wishing for a 'tail sweater' of some sort. I thought my tail was going to freeze right off and that I'd have to go around looking like a Bull Dog or some other tailless breed. Now how embarrassing would that be for a *macho* guy like me?

But winter also brought beauty to Holland. I loved watching the snowflakes fall outside our front window, and the skaters as they glided across the canals, some doing twirly steps, others holding hands. I wondered where all the ducks and swans had gone as I didn't see any of them wearing skates. I was sure hoping Mama wouldn't get any ideas about skating for me, but fortunately the Dutch dogs didn't seem to be doing it, so I considered myself safe.

When December rolled around, up went this giant tree in the *Grote Markt* right in front of the church. It was a real beauty. There was nothing more I would have liked to have done than run right up and give it a big 'mark,' but believe me, Mama wouldn't let me get within a leg's reach of it. The tree was especially pretty at night. Covered entirely in white lights, it looked like it was sprinkled with a million stars. The children of Haarlem made decorations to put on the tree, and then gathered to sing Christmas carols around it. I didn't mind the cold at all when we headed to the square at night to listen to the carolers.

"Prettige Kerstdagen en een gelukkig nieuwjarr," said the family standing next to us. We figured out that it must have meant 'Merry Christmas and Happy New Year," so we nodded and smiled.

At this time of year, the Dutch children were waiting for a man called *Sinter Klaus,* that's Santa Claus to Americans, Saint Nicholas to us Mexicans. As far as I could tell from my 'doggie' observations, they were all the same guy. All of them dressed in red and brought lots of gifts to the good little kids, except in Holland *Sinter Klaus* arrived on St. Nicholas Eve, December 5[th,] not on December 24th, like in most of the world. Instead of arriving on a sleigh pulled by reindeer, he came via boat on the canal, which we thought to be 'very Dutch.' And instead of stockings hung by the fire like in America, the Dutch children put out wooden shoes for him to fill. I certainly thought that was also very Dutch, since they loved their wooden shoes so much. And another thing strange about *Sinter Klaus*; he didn't have any of those short little guys helping him. Instead he had this tall guy they called 'Black Pieter.' But I think Black Pieter must have multiplied as we'd see him running all over town in his striped suit, colored tights and puffy hat with a feather on top. In 'doggie' terms, he looked pretty funny, I must admit. But since I didn't have any wooden shoes – thank goodness – I didn't get too much into the *Sinter Klaus* thing.

Then there were the candles. Now I knew the Dutch liked candles, but during the Christmas season, they liked them a whole lot more, let me tell you. Why they had so many candles in their windows I thought the whole town was going to burn down. So did my papa. But Mama thought they were absolutely beautiful, so you can imagine what our front window was filled with. That and all these other wooden Dutch Christmas figures, all painted in red, white and green.

Why we even had a little Christmas tree about a foot tall, but every time I looked at it, Mama gave me the sign of 'don't you dare, Lucky' so I kept my distance.

* * * *

One afternoon Papa came home from work and suggested that we take a trip around Europe to experience the Christmas season first-hand. Now Mama and I didn't need to be invited twice. We were packed and in the car wearing our boots and sweaters before Papa could barely take off his tie and change his clothes.

"I meant we can leave tomorrow morning," Papa said, coming out to the car. Well, since we couldn't sleep in the car, we had to go back inside and wait until the following morning to depart.

I have to admit it was beautiful driving around the European countryside at that time of year. All the fields were covered in snow and the trees were frosted with ice. Mama said it reminded her of a Christmas card picture, whatever that was. Of course every house had candles and a Christmas tree in the window and we felt very 'Christmassy.' Many of the squares in small Dutch towns were lit by – what else – thousands of candles, and, of course, we stopped to admire each and every one of them.

"I seriously wonder where the Dutch get all that wax," Papa told us.

Mama just laughed at him.

The first night we stayed in Bruge, another Medieval city in Belgium surrounded by walls. Now this place was something else, let me tell you. Even from a 'doggie' point of view it was 'fairy-tale-like,' and I quickly understood why it is considered one of Europe's most beautiful cities.

"It's like going back in time. Everything is so Gothic, Romanesque, Renaissance, baroque, rococo," Mama went on and on, telling us all about European architecture, as we walked down the cobblestone streets. "Listen to all the church bells."

Come on, Mama, I listen to the church bells each and every hour in Haarlem.

As for me, I was more intent on watching the swans swim in the canals that were not quite frozen over. I really didn't give a 'doggie diddle' about what she was talking about, but I was sure enjoying the environment in Bruge.

Papa seemed to be enjoying himself, too, and we soon stopped at a sidewalk café in the main square where my parents ordered some hot mulled wine to warm them up. They also ordered *des pome freet,* that's French fries, and I did manage to get a bit of their warming potential when Mama 'accidentally' – yeah right – dropped a couple off of her plate. Of course I didn't need much to warm me up – after all, I had my own built-in fur coat, as well as a sweater on top, so I just cuddled close to Mama and Papa and took in the lovely scene before us.

At about this time it began to snow. The flakes drifted down from the sky and quickly covered the steep rooftops of the buildings and the church spires. It collected on the wood-paned windows just the way Mama used to put that fake snow on our windows in California at Christmas time.

"Now this is really what I call Christmas," Papa said.

"*Noel*, as it's known here," Mama added. "It's just like a Christmas card, isn't it?"

I didn't care what it was called. This special moment was good in any old language, including 'doggie lingo.' There were good smells and sights all around, and I was there with Mama and Papa. What else could a dog wish for?

Then it was off to Brussels, the capital of Belgium and also the European Union.

"It's kind of like Washington, D. C., our capital city, except that here they speak French," Mama said, like it would be a big 'doggie deal' to me. I really didn't care. I was much more interested in viewing all the snow-covered parks outside the car window and wondering if I was going to get to romp in them.

Nope. Instead we went to this huge, huge cobble stone square called the *Grand Place.*

302

"Wow," Papa said as we walked to its center. It was surrounded by old gabled guild houses in Gothic architecture.

"They represented all the different kinds of workers," Mama said. "Look at that one with the big hammer sign."

"Must have been the carpenters' guild house," Papa said. "And that one with an anvil must have been for the blacksmiths."

Whatever . . . this dog was much more interested in the nativity scene on the square's far side, in front of the *Hotel de Ville* – the town hall. It was very big and had all the holy family figures just like in Mexico. But instead of people dressed as animals, there were real animals – a donkey, several cows, and some sheep, in fact. Of course I wanted to get up real close to get a good sniff, but Papa kept me tight on my leash, as usual. I figured out I'd better not bark as he might try to strangle me with my own leash if I made too much of a commotion, so I sat there like a good little dog and just panted at all those other animals from a distance.

I seriously wondered if they were going to have a *posada* like they did in Mexico. *Thank goodness they have real sheep, so I won't have to dress like one again.*

We walked around the square a bit and looked at the famous Belgium lace and all the chocolates in the shop windows. Of course everyone was speaking French, so we barely understood a word.

"*Joyxus Noel,*" all the people were saying to each other. I figured it either meant 'hello' or else 'Merry Christmas."

"Those chocolates sure look good," Mama said, smiling at Papa.

I looked at the candy which was arranged in colorful tiers while Papa went inside the shop. But they didn't

303

much entice me. Now if it would have been bones or steaks in piles like that – well now that's another story. Why I would have followed Papa right into that store.

After that we went to this small restaurant, where, of course, dogs were allowed.

Mama went on to tell us how much the French love their dogs. For a moment I thought of our good friend, Monique. She lived in Holland, and she was the only French person I had ever met, even though she never spoke French to me. But I now knew for certain she was French because she sure loved us dogs. She told me she once had a doggie named Cleopatra that she loved very much, so I think that was why she was so crazy about me. Why she'd always bring me plenty of doggie cookies whenever she came to visit, and one time she brought some dried rice stuff that I didn't much care for at all. Of course, I forgave her as Monique always had lots of hugs, pats and belly rubs for me, and she even forgave me for the time that I accidentally peed on the cuff of her pants. *And, no, I didn't think she was a tree – she just happened to be standing in a place where I was doing a bit of 'marking.'*

"Oh, Lucky, I love you just the same," she told me. "You are a very lucky dog."

As if I didn't know that!

Yes, it was nice to think about Monique again. It had been several weeks since I'd seen her and I was missing her. *Besides, isn't it about time for my Christmas present?* But for the moment, I decided I'd better concentrate on all those dogs in the *Grand Place*. Why, many of the poodles and other small 'lap' dogs were actually sitting in their owner's laps, right at the tables. *Now that would be nice – eating at table level instead of under it. I bet Monique's Cleopatra got to do that.* I didn't get the chance to experience it first-hand, however, since I knew the prospects of my sitting on Papa's lap and eating my dinner were not all that great. Anyway I wasn't much interested in the menu items. Mama and Papa had some mussels in a tomato broth and some *escargots* – that's snails. Yuk! *Why would anyone like to eat a big plate of snails?* I wondered if they were still alive and crawling and kept a close watch on them. The only thing I had known about snails before this dining experience was that Mama was always going around poisoning them in our garden back in California so they wouldn't eat her flowers. Now here she was having them for lunch. I could not figure this out at all.

"Let's go visit *Manneken Pis*. He's just around the corner from here," Mama said, after they had finished slurping up their slimy snails. Believe me, I didn't do even a little bit of begging during 'that' meal, and I was more than happy to get out of the restaurant just in case the owners got an idea about serving up some 'puppy steaks.'

Now who the heck we knew here in Brussels, especially by the name of *Manneken Pis*, I had no idea. Oh well, visiting him was good for a nice walk in the cold afternoon sunlight.

When we got to him, boy was I ever in for a 'doggie surprise'. Why there, right on this corner was this statue of a young boy, completely naked. And guess what he was doing? Why he was peeing a stream. And funny thing was, all these people were standing around taking pictures of him doing his deed. Now Mama and Papa never took a photo of me when I whittled, but they sure liked to snap that bronze kid. I just thought it was the funniest thing.

But I didn't get a chance to dwell on him for long as Papa said we needed to get heading for Flanders Fields and then France, where I was sure I'd been before. But I just figured it was all part of our Christmas tour.

We stopped for the night in *Ypres*, a city made famous in World War I according to Papa. "Almost 55,000 British and Canadian soldiers died here," he said. Now that was an awful lot of people and it made us all feel very sad.

We spent a while walking through the graves at Flanders Fields and Mama got all teary-eyed. I didn't even think about lifting my leg, of course. It was such a quiet place, with not even the song of a bird.

"In Flanders Fields the poppies grow," Mama said reciting an old poem about the cemetery. Well, I didn't see any poppies – all I saw was snow. And my feet were getting cold, so we headed for a little inn to spend the night.

It was warm and cozy inside. We ate our dinner beside the fireplace, me curled beneath the table, hoping for a bit of meat. Unfortunately, I had to settle for a 'Cup of Soup.'

The next morning we crossed into France, but this time it was not sunny and we were not at the beach. It was full of snow-covered rolling hills and tree-lined roads, although the trees had no leaves. The houses were mostly brown and didn't have those gabled Dutch roofs. I was seriously hoping we wouldn't be doing any camping again like we had in the summer.

"It's so stark but beautiful," Papa said. "We're almost to Normandy."

Whatever that place was, Mama and Papa looked serious. Here the houses were made of limestone and dark wood. They even had grass roofs, which I thought very strange. Now *how was a doggie supposed to get up*

306

there to romp around? Didn't matter – I didn't get the chance.

Instead, we drove along the chalky cliffs of *Arromanches* and looked out onto the cold Atlantic Ocean. It was snowing a bit and I was thankful to be nice and warm and sitting in our car.

"Omaha Beach," Mama said, pointing to the stretch of sand below us. "The place where the Allied D-Day invasion took place."

We got out and looked down at the beach in *Colleville-sur-Mer* from our cliff-top location.

"Imagine climbing up those cliffs with all that German artillery firing at you," Papa said. Mama looked real sad and I snuggled close to her leg and gave her a warm loving look.

"This is the place that changed the course of World War II," Papa went on. "The place where so many Americans, British and Canadians died, trying to save the European continent from Hitler."

Whoever that Hitler was I didn't even want to get to know him. Mama and Papa certainly didn't seem to like him even one little bit.

We drove down the road a ways and came to this big – I mean huge – cemetery. Row after row of cement crosses and Jewish stars filled the entire snow-covered lawn as far as we could see, clear down to the cliffs above the beach. Why it was just about the saddest place I had ever seen, and I didn't even know why. All I knew was that Mama and Papa were very quiet as they stood at the edge of the cemetery and looked out at the rough sea. It was very cold, but I didn't even make a whimper, although we stood there for a long time.

Actually, I was glad to finally leave Normandy. It was just too sad there. I was happy we would not be spending the night. I was ready to get back to our happy Christmas experience.

"I think you'll like where we're going next," Mama said. "It a big old monastery called the Abbey of *Mont-St. Michel* and it's in Brittany – another area in France."

Wherever that was, I didn't care. If Mama said it was a place I'd like, then I was sure it must have something of interest for us dogs.

It did. Why it was really cool. This big old abbey sat way up high on some cliffs and was surrounded by water. It looked just like a castle. We drove across this long bridge until we reached it. There was a village just below the fortress, where we checked into this tiny hotel. Boy was it ever old.

"Bonjour, Comment allez-vouz?" the man at the front desk asked us. *Oh, oh, more French. I think he must have told us hello and asked us how we were.* Boy, was I ever getting good at languages.

Our room was way up under the eaves with lots of stairs to climb. Of course, this I didn't mind a 'doggie bit' as I loved stairs, and I raced up them as fast as I could, tugging Mama after me. Our room was small, just big enough for a bed for Mama and Papa and a place for my *cama*. The bathroom was way down the hall, but that didn't bother me as I wouldn't be using it anyway, as I always had to go outside to do 'my thing.' Let me tell you, Mama and Papa were not too happy about that, but I thought it was a good lesson for them as to how I feel when I need to go and have to go clear outside. At least they only had to go down the hall. But the room had a perfect view of *Mont-St.-Michel* so that made them happy.

As soon as we unpacked, we went out to explore the village and fortress. Were those cobbled streets ever steep. And slick. Why my four paws about went right out from under me as we were climbing toward the abbey. Mama and Papa also struggled to keep on their feet.

The climb was worth it. When we got to the entrance of the abbey it was closed for the day, so we walked all around the outside of the huge fortress, just inside its tall stone walls. Luckily for me there were little windows about every ten feet and they were just at 'doggie' height. Now I didn't know they were meant for cannons in the old days – I thought they had been built especially for 'doggie sight-seeing.' Why, you can't imagine the view from there – I could see clear across the Atlantic Ocean. Believe me, I checked out every one of those holes while Mama and Papa followed behind. They always thought it was so funny that I liked to take in views. Well, why not? I'm about as curious a tourist as a doggie can get.

After that, we shopped in the village for some Christmas presents. All the shops were filled with special French hand-carved toys and things with pictures of the abbey. The clerk wrapped our purchases in flowered paper and tied them with red bows.

"Au revoir," she said, waving good-bye.

The next morning, it was very foggy up on the hill; so foggy that we could barely see the abbey.

"Gotta go," Papa said. "We need to make it to Germany before dark."

Germany? Haven't I been there before?

I was right. For it was in Frankfurt, Germany that I first entered Europe. But this time we weren't going there, we were going to a small village on the Romantic Highway – *Romantische Strasse* – called *Rothenburg ob der Tauber.* It was in the foothills of the snow-clad Bavarian Alps. Now this I really liked. The mountains reminded me of Utah, where I had gone to visit Granny for Christmas. But when we arrived in the village there was no Granny to greet us. Only a bunch of German people who sounded kind of like they were speaking Dutch.

"It's the best preserved Medieval town in all of Germany," Papa said, as we drove through the main gate, right beneath a big old clock and watchtower. Of course all the streets were cobbled – what else is there in Europe? The houses were made of plaster with wide timbers running crosswise from top to bottom. The roofs were steep and gabled. I wondered if we'd be staying up under the roof again, but Mama interrupted my thoughts.

"Wow, this place looks just like a fairytale," Mama said. "And it has one of the most famous Christmas markets in all of Europe."

Oh, oh, more shopping. That ought to make Papa happy.

And boy, was it some Christmas market! All these little wooden houses had been especially built around the squares just for the Christmas season. Groups of people were singing carols and there were lit trees everywhere, so I couldn't help but do a couple of 'leg lifts' while walking by. The wooden houses sold all sorts of things. Some had these giant gingerbread cookies, decorated with flowers and such, just like Papa had bought Mama at the beer festival. This time I think they said, "Merry Christmas," and Papa bought Mama another one, and gave her a great big kiss. It's not that I wouldn't like a kiss from Papa, but I was seriously hoping he wouldn't buy me one of those giant cookies. They looked pretty darn heavy.

There were also stands selling hand-made wooden toys and Christmas decorations. Let me tell you, we spent a lot of time there. But I didn't care, even though my paws were freezing. But there were lots of good smells in the air and I wanted to get to where they were coming from. Papa had the same idea, so off the two of us went, leaving Mama to buy all the Christmas decorations she wanted.

We stopped at the first *bratwurst* stand we came across. Here a man dressed like Santa Claus was roasting these big giant sausages over an open fire. Now, this was what I call 'doggie heaven' – big sausages, complete with a fire to warm my paws. Only thing missing – my Persian carpet.

Papa bought two sausages and some mulled wine in a cup that said, 'Rothenburg." I watched real closely as he ate the sausages, just in case he happened to drop a bit before my very paws. Well, I'd have to gobble it up, now wouldn't I? I looked at him real hungry like, so he bought another and put it right in front of me on the ground. Why I couldn't believe my 'doggie eyes.'

"It's Christmas, so I guess I can spoil you just this once," he said. "But please don't tell Mama that I cheated. You know we don't want you to become a begging dog."

Oh, don't worry Papa, I wouldn't think of telling her. Of course I quickly destroyed the evidence in about two bites. Just in time, as we saw Mama coming into view, her arms filled with packages. Oh, how I liked these Christmas trips. I wished we could take them each and every day.

Of course when we got back home to Haarlem we were completely exhausted. Why we were so tired that we even went to bed without dinner. But we sure had enjoyed our holiday trip. Yes, the Christmas season in Europe was very cool – even in 'doggie terms.'

311

CHAPTER 33
MOVIN' ON

A week later, the 'real' Christmas finally arrived – but I was not to be a part of 'the Christmas decor.' That's because Mama and Papa flew off on a big jet to California, while I was nicely deposited at the kennel for two weeks. Now this I wasn't happy about at all – in fact I was downright 'doggie' mad – and I don't mean in the 'rabies' sense of the word.

For me, Christmas day meant more of the same raw meat, the same flowery cushion, and the same old sleet out in the 'doggie' play area. Only one thing was different – the kennel owner put a bell with a red ribbon on each of our kennels – well, wow, dee wow!

All day long I thought of past Christmases with Mama and Papa – our prime rib Christmas dinners, complete with Yorkshire pudding – the *posadas* in Mexico – unwrapping my presents beneath our Christmas tree (using my teeth, of course). Why I became so homesick I thought I was going to cry. But since we dogs don't have tears, I merely whined and whined and whined some more.

Mama! Papa! Where are you?

Why I think I whined for two weeks straight until the whine was right out of me. I don't think the kennel much appreciated my 'whining' efforts, except for the fact that it put an end to my barking, so I saw my big Dutch caretaker smiling a lot more. But who knows . . . maybe it was because it was the Christmas season.

Finally one day I heard the sound I had been waiting to hear all those days – Papa's car engine in the parking lot. Let me tell you, I let out one of the biggest nearly silent howls that I had ever let out in my entire 'doggie' days. I suppose it was a good thing, as I was about out of sound. Otherwise, I think my loud barking would have scared the 'doggie daylights' out of all the other dogs. And it would have scared the wooden clogs right off my Dutch caretaker.

Besides, I quickly found out I would be bidding her *au revoir*, whoops, I mean *'tot ziens'* as they say in Holland, and that it would be for good. That's because I was about to be 'un-Dutched,' for we were moving to England. Actually Mama and Papa already lived there part-time, and now I was about to become part of their happy twosome. For you see, I had completed my six months of waiting in Holland so that the British would let me into England. It's officially called 'The PETS Travel Scheme,' which Papa thought sounded very British. Whatever scheme it was, I didn't like the waiting part of it at all. And why they were afraid of letting a little old street dog like me into the U.K., I had no idea. Did they think I was going to bite the Queen or something?

"You're going to like London," Mama said. "We live right by Hyde Park and it's one of the largest parks in the world."

Frankly, I didn't give a 'doggie diddle' about some old park. I just wanted to be with my Mama and Papa in a full-time ownership position, just like it was before.

"Remember when we first came to Holland and we took you to Dr. Aukema to have you micro-chipped? He also gave you a new rabies vaccine, even though you'd just had one in California, which I couldn't understand for the life of me," Papa said, like I would perfectly get what he was saying. But at the mention of micro-chip it quickly came to mind.

313

Oh yeah, my 'Certificaat Uuitsluitend Bestemd Voor Rabies Vaccinatie,' how could I forget about that? You dumb dog.

Oh yes, and I also remember when my Dutch *dierenart,* that's my veterinarian, planted that micro-chip right into my shoulder with one great big needle. *No need to make me relive that one, Papa.*

But Mama kept on telling me it was so that if I ever got lost I would be found. Now how stupid a dog would I be to ever get lost from the good thing that I'd come across? No way! I was around to stay.

"Anyway, we've got to take you to see a special International Veterinarian first, so they can be doubly sure that you don't have rabies."

Why with all the talk I'd heard about rabies over the years, I'd decided it was something I definitely didn't want to have, even if I didn't know exactly what it was. The only thing I knew was that it had something to do with 'mad' dogs, so I really tried to keep my temper under control for the next few days so Mama and Papa would take me with them to England.

But it wasn't that easy. Several days later, we went to Amsterdam to the International Vet's office to get his *handtekening officiele functionaries* – that means his oath that I was in good health. Boy was I one excited pooch. You would have thought Mama and Papa were taking me to a bone-eating contest or something.

Of course it took us a bit of time to get there as Papa had the driving directions in Dutch and we got lost a couple of times. But we finally ended up at a building with the appropriate name.

When we entered, I finally knew what was up – no fooling this puppy – it was a regular vet's office, even it if was in a big tall building. The antiseptic smell said it all. I could already feel those needles piercing my

314

bottom, that cold long thing inside my ear, and someone plopping me on some shiny metal table. At least one thing I knew for sure in Holland – it would certainly be antiseptically clean.

Just as I had predicted, once we were in the examination room in came the vet – this giant-sized guy – Dutch, after all – dressed in a blue scrub suit. He gave me a pat on the head and said:

"*Ja, he's goode.* Where is de form?"

Why, he barely examined me, and for this I was one happy pooch.

Before he could ask any more questions, Papa quickly produced my 'RabiesVaccine Certificate' and the 'Veterinary Health Certificate for Entry of Pet Dog or Cat into the UK from The Netherlands' for this official vet to sign.

So that was it, the end of my Holland vet experiences, or so I thought.

But two days before I could be transported to the U.K., I had to go back to my own vet to get some more treatments and be issued a 'Pet Travel Scheme Certification of Treatment Against Ectoparasites and Endoparasites,' whatever they are. I sure didn't like the sound of them one bit and was thankful I was being treated for them. Why, in my 'doggie' lingo, they sounded much worse than rabies.

Boy, these British sure are fussy. There sure must not be many dogs in England – especially foreign dogs. I seriously wondered what they'd think if they found out I was from Mexico. Why perhaps they'd hold 'one big *fiesta*' to welcome me. But I didn't think so since Papa had already told me the British were more into pubs than *fiestas*.

* * * *

At 5:00 a.m. on the morning I was to fly to London, we had to unfortunately pay another visit to some more inspectors. Why I'd never been inspected so much in my entire 'doggie' days. I guess they wanted to definitely make sure that I was 'rabies free.'

These final inspectors were also the same ones that would take me to Schipol Airport to board the plane, like they didn't trust my mama and papa or something. What were they worried about? Did they think my parents would switch me for some Dutch Labrador? Not a chance – I knew my mama and papa better than that. They loved me, that's for sure, even when I cost them some 'big bucks.'

"In addition to all these inspections, it's unbelievable how much all this transport stuff has cost us," Papa said, in his usual 'concerned about money' voice. "I can't believe they charged us three hundred Pounds – that's six hundred American dollars – just to take Lucky on this forty-minute flight!"

He scratched his head and looked at me. "And to think we only had to pay a hundred and twenty-five dollars to get Lucky all the way to Europe."

"Go figure," Mama said. "But you know how expensive things can be in the U.K." She smiled at me. "I hate to think of what it will cost to take Lucky to the vet there."

Papa didn't even smile back, but he did bend to give me a quick pat on the rump, so everything must have been a-okay with him. "Yeah, Lucky, I guess you're worth it. But you'd better stay healthy."

You can bet your darn Dutch clog I'm worth it, Papa, I thought, at the same time hoping he was not bringing his clogs along to England.

316

Before I knew it, I was airborne once more, green kennel and all – this time in a shiny silver British Midlands jet – flying across the English Channel.

But this time the Dutch vet had said. "No drugs – not good for *honds*."

So instead of 'sleeping' the flight away, I 'barked' it.

Afterwards Mama told me they could hear me up in the cabin, and that everyone was looking around the plane for a stowaway dog. More like a 'prisoner' dog in my point of view. Believe me, I would have much preferred to be up in the cabin eating little British tea sandwiches – as long as they were salmon, of course. But I was where I was – so thank goodness the flight was short.

My inspections didn't end upon landing, however, and it was a good long time until I got to see Mama and Papa again. That's because the British – at least they spoke English so I could understand what they were saying – whisked me off the plane real fast and on to three other offices for more inspections. Why I was 'inspected right out' by the time they finished with me, and certain that not even one old flea or tick or rabies, or whatever, could have possibly made it across the English Channel with me.

Finally Mama and Papa showed up on the scene, and was I ever one happy pooch to see them, let me tell you.

"Guess you passed the British test," Papa said. "Now you're an official resident of the U.K., Old Boy."

Well, whoopee . . . But what I really need about now is a good old poop.

They must have read my mind, for Mama immediately trotted me around the parking lot to do my

317

thing. Then it was into the extremely small rental car for our drive into London Town.

For a new day had begun.

CHAPTER 34
WELCOME TO LONDON TOWN

The drive into London was nice, except for the fact that Papa was driving on the wrong side of the road and, believe it or not, from the wrong side of the car! I thought maybe he was the one who had picked up rabies! Why I just couldn't get used to this driving fact, even though Papa did it wrong for the next three years while we were in the U.K. Now if I'd gotten my 'pooping' habits all that wrong, I would have been one very unlucky dog indeed.

Oh yes, I've added a new word to my 'doggie lingo' in case you haven't noticed. That word is '*indeed.*' Why, the British use it all the time, so I decided if I wanted to fit in with the local culture, I would have to use it, as well. Of course they also used other words in the U.K. very differently than we do in the U.S. For example, '*cheers*' means 'see you later' or 'hello' and '*collect*' means 'I'm going to come and pick you up.' And you should have heard them talk in Scotland, Wales and Ireland. Why I could barely understand a thing they said. Neither could my papa. Mama seemed to catch on pretty well, however, so she translated for us. But, of course, that will have to be another story.

Anyway, back to our drive into London. It was a beautiful day. The sky was blue – very strange for these parts, I was soon to learn – and there were lots of rolling green hills and big black bubble-topped taxi cabs. Little did I know I would be doing more than my fair share of riding in them, much to the cabbies' dismay – you know, me and my 'runaway' fur. But I had to admit, they were a darn sight better than riding in that 'Tube' thing – that's the London Underground, which is actually a train that runs beneath the streets without one little view whatsoever. And then there were those big red double-decker buses that swayed like crazy when we sat upstairs. But for the time being, I wasn't thinking about the different forms of British transportation, however, I was purely interested in getting to my new home. Let me tell you, though, London was nothing like Dana Point, California – not a darn 'doggie' bit.

First of all, it had started raining by the time we made it into London from Heathrow Airport – definitely not like Dana Point, but typical British weather, of course. That's one thing I quickly discovered that the British and Dutch have in common – rain, rain, and then more rain. I was certain I was going to wear my trusty little rain coat entirely out by the time we returned home.

There were lots of beautiful old brick buildings crowded very close together lining the streets. They all had chimneys on top, which to me equaled many pleasant nights lying before the fire. There were also lots of people walking the streets of London, all topped by umbrellas. The people were close together, as well. I hadn't been in such a large city for a good long time, and wondered how I would manage not getting squished by all those people when Mama took me out walking. Briefly I thought of my brother Buddy, and how he'd been run over in Mexico City. *Nope, I wasn't going to let that happen to me. My life was too good to lose under some big old red bus.*

"Look, Lucky, The Victoria and Albert Museum," Mama said. "We're almost home."

Now that word I could understand and I wagged my tail so hard I thought it was going to fall right off. Boy, it was good to be out of the kennel and airplane and on my way home again.

"The Bunch of Grapes Pub," Papa said. "It's our '*local*,' and it's a real trip into the past. There's nothing like having a pint there."

"Yeoman's Row," Mama said. "This is our street."

I stood up on my hind paws and leaned against the window, making a smudge right across it with my snout. *Oh boy, I'll bet the guy at Hertz is going to love this.* The tiny narrow street was lined with old town homes, all hooked together. I seriously wondered how I was going to get to our back yard to do my thing. I looked up. *Definitely too high to jump over.* Why the houses must have been four stories tall. I wondered which one was our house.

"Twenty-seven Yeoman's Row," Papa said, parking the car. "We're home, Lucky Boy."

Our new home looked like all the others. Old, old, old. And boy was I surprised when there were no balconies for ocean viewing across its front – but then again, there was no ocean to view, so what did it matter? Instead it had a couple of what the British call '*window boxes*,' which were filled with colorful flowers. I had a feeling Mama must have had something to do with that. I didn't see any palm trees out front either. I wondered where I was going to pee. One thing I knew for sure – it would be a bit tricky getting up to those window boxes to do it.

"It's a 'Mary Poppins' house, Lucky," Mama said.

I wondered if Mary Poppins was someone I would be meeting, and hoped she was not a vet. Believe me, I'd had about enough poking and sticking to last me another ten years.

Like all the others, our house was made of bricks and it was very narrow – I'd say about eight dog lengths – and I'm not talking about 'Grayhound lengths' here. But it stretched way up to the sky and I was certainly hoping it wouldn't have an elevator, or even worse an escalator, the thought of which absolutely made me get the 'doggie' jitters, as I much preferred stairs.

When Papa unlocked the door, of course I had to be the first inside. Why it didn't take me more than five minutes to sniff out every inch of our new home – all four floors and forty-three steps of it – with no escalator or elevator in sight, thank goodness.

The best part about it, however, were the familiar things. Our California sofa was there, even though the movers had to cut it in half and nail it back together again just to get it inside. The coffee table that I used to like to crawl under for a quick nap was also there. But best of all, right before the fireplace was my very favorite Persian rug! Now how lucky can a pooch get?

And when I went down the stairs to the kitchen, there they were – my favorite *cama* and my three blue china bowls. I just couldn't wait to gobble up my dinner from them once more and to sleep in my very own *cama*.

As a special homecoming treat, Mama made me my favorite capellini for dinner. It was complete with marinara sauce and tiny pieces of meat tossed in. Boy, were my parents ever spoiling me.

After dinner, I went for my very first London walk, one of many, many London walks I would participate in. Why I think we must have walked the entire city about a thousand times before we left. My old joints can certainly attest to that, let me tell you. Why I even wore my rain boots completely out. But that's another story.

Anyway this first London walk was a rather short one. And best of all, it had stopped raining, so I didn't have to wear my raincoat and get laughed at. I was hoping Mama had forgotten it in Holland, which I seriously doubted. No such luck, for the next time it rained, out came my yellow hooded vinyl raincoat. Still I thought that if I was really a lucky dog, maybe she would buy me a black or tan London Fog raincoat like all the British wore. Then I wouldn't stand out so much. No such luck in that department either. Oh well, a dog just can't have everything he desires, now can he? But on this first walk I wouldn't have to worry about such things as raincoats, and I was really excited to explore my new world.

The end of our street didn't go anywhere, as there was a house right in the middle of it, so we turned around and walked the other way. Papa called it a 'dead end,' but it didn't look very dead at all to me. There were lots of growing things. And even though there were no palm trees or the Pacific Ocean in London, I kind of liked my new home town. It had a 'doggie' good feeling to it. For there were lots and lots of big old trees for doing my 'thing' and many very old houses that Mama said were historical, whatever that means. There were also many tiny shops filled with interesting window decor that I liked to check out on my hind paws – you know me, always the curious doggie. However, the British shopkeepers on Walton Street didn't seem to much appreciate my nose print on their shiny windows, so Mama tried her best to keep me on all 'fours.' Best of all about the shops, however, were the good smells coming from many of them, although I had yet to be introduced to shepherd's pie or good old greasy British fish and chips.

And guess what? Right next to the Bunch of Grapes Pub on the corner of our street was a coffee house. Boy, did that make Mama and Papa happy. No, it wasn't a Starbuck's, it was Costa Coffee, but it did have cappuccino, and barely a day went by that the three of us didn't sit at one of their outside tables and order one.

Now this I didn't mind so much because it gave me a chance to rest my old legs for a bit. The only thing I disliked about it was when this gray-haired lady with her sneaky dog sat next to us. Her dog fooled me every time. Just as I was about to drop off for a bit of a nap, this snarly little Terrier would jump from inside her coat and across her lap like a ghost and about scare the 'doggie daylights' right out of me! Why I thought that dog was going to snap one of my floppy ears right off! It about scared the 'people' daylights out of my mama and papa, as well, so we soon learned not to sit anywhere near that lady and her mean dog. From this 'first' experience with British dogs, I wasn't so sure they would be as friendly as Dutch dogs. But I soon changed my mind after I got around a bit more.

After we returned home, there was yet another discovery I had not as yet made. Why, we had our very own 'secret garden' at the back of our house, complete with a tiny glassed in porch – which the British incidentally call a '*conservatory*.' It led out to our tiny garden. It even had a fountain and a stone statue of a naked girl, which Papa seemed to take a special interest in. The walls were ivy-covered and there was a small stone patio. It had two large trees in planters that were unfortunately above 'peeing' reach, but they created a canopy over part of the garden, which made it nice and cool on hot days – which was about once a month, I'd figure – and that was in June, July and August.

The three of us sat out there for a long time. There wasn't so much to explore – you know, no rabbits, cats, squirrels or such – so I curled up beside the tiny wrought-iron table and looked up at the stars. I think they were the same stars as we saw back home except that there were not as many of them. But there were lots of birds in all the surrounding trees and we listened to them bed down for the night. Come to think of it, I was tired, too. For it had been a very long day indeed.

After a while it got quite chilly, so we went back inside the house and Papa lit a fire in our fireplace, which was surrounded by a carved wood mantle and bookcases. Of course you can guess what I did. I curled up on my Persian rug right before it and thought how happy and content I was. It didn't bother me even one 'doggie' bit that the floor was kind of slanted. But my Papa, the engineer, was certainly bothered by it. All I cared about was that the three of us were finally together again, which made for one very happy doggie indeed. Yes . . . London was going to be an okay place.

CHAPTER 35
A WALK IN THE PARK

The next day was Saturday. And a beautiful Saturday it was indeed, the sky a cobalt blue. It was also a day in which I was to learn what 'walking' our Knightsbridge neighborhood in London was really all about. It started out simple enough – cappuccino at Costa Coffee – snarly dog included, of course. But this time I was prepared with my own snarl for that nasty canine, and I about scared the wiry hair right off him! In fact I was so proud of myself that I went around with a 'doggie' of a smug expression for several hours.

Then it was off down Brompton Road to check out some of our local sites. First stop – Beauchamp Place. It was mostly full of dress shops and what Papa called 'high-end' restaurants, whatever they are. The smells coming from them were pretty darn 'doggie' good indeed, but the dress shops didn't interest me too much. My mama seemed to like Beauchamp Place, however, especially since it was once Princess Diana's favorite shopping street.

"Now please don't go and get any ideas about becoming a regular shopper here," Papa told her, just as she was about to enter one of the shops.

"Oh, don't you worry, I'm just going to look."

Yeah, right, Mama. I'll bet you're going to 'buy.'

Of course, Papa and I waited outside, but it was only for a couple of minutes – just long enough for me to get into a comfortable napping position – before she rejoined us.

"Don't think I'll become a 'regular' here," she said. "The shopkeepers would barely talk to me – guess I'm not dressed in the 'correct' brand."

Let me tell you, my Papa looked very relieved indeed, especially when Mama pointed out the dress in the window that cost twelve hundred pounds.

"Why that's twenty-four hundred dollars!" he gasped.

As for me, I was far more than ready to get on walking than worrying about numbers. So that's just what we did.

Next it was on to my first view of Harrod's, probably the most famous department store in the whole wide world. It looked like any old department store to me except it was very fancy and covered with all these white lights, which really lit up our part of town at night. And I was certainly thankful that they had NO DOGS ALLOWED signs on each and every one of its more than twenty entrances. For me that meant 'no escalators,' and was I ever relieved. I just hated those 'moving steps' every time Mama and I went shopping at V&D in Haarlem. And since I had managed to hang onto my tail thus far, I wasn't about to take any more chances of parting with it in London.

Even from my 'doggie' point of view, I had to admit that the windows at Harrod's were beautiful. Why they were full of all these Mazzarattis and Jaguars and long-legged pretend ladies, which Papa liked. Of course they had lots of clothes and other gadgets Mama 'goo-gooed' over. There was even a great big window filled with animal stuff, can you believe that? But there were no fake dogs there. But they did have the fanciest fur-lined dog beds I have ever seen, and silver dog dishes and even dog collars studded with diamonds and such. I wondered if I would be sporting one of them in my future – no such luck. That's okay. I'm not a 'jewel type' of doggie. Too 'street smart' for that, I must admit.

After Harrod's, we cut through a little lane beside this great big church called Holy Trinity Brompton, and ended up in what was to become my favorite place in London. You guessed it! Hyde Park! Why it was the biggest park I had ever seen in all my 'doggie' days, even larger than *Parque de Chapultepec* in Mexico City. And it was filled with all these giant trees and flowers and lakes and bridges and fountains and little restaurants and horse trails, the whole *enchilada*. Why there was even a bronze statue of a guy called 'Peter' – 'Pan' that is. He was a guy who never got old and Papa said he would enjoy a little bit of his 'eternal youth' once in a while.

"Peter Pan could even fly," Mama told me. "Imagine that."

I didn't want to imagine that at all, as I had experienced more flying that I cared to. In fact, I hated airplanes. I'd just have to leave flying up to that Pan guy.

There were also lots of other dogs in Hyde Park. Why, I think about every dog in London must have been at the park that day. There were big ones and little ones and in-between ones, just like me – size-wise, I mean – as I seriously doubt there were any other Mexico City street dogs. But there were plenty of Jack Russell Terriers and Scotties and English Sheep Dogs and Bull Dogs, and even an occasional Labrador or two thrown in. But I quickly figured out that most of the Labs had been left in Holland.

Wow, what a place this Hyde Park was! I just couldn't wait to explore it. So I pulled on my leash just as hard as I possibly could and about took Papa's arm out of its socket, a favorite pastime of mine, incidentally, as I'm sure you've already noticed. Actually that trick works even better with Mama as she's not as strong, which gives me way more 'pulling power.'

"Hey there, Old Boy, wait up," Papa said, struggling to keep hold of my *lead*, as they call a leash in the U.K.

"Maybe we should let Lucky off his leash," Mama said. "All the other dogs are free, so I guess it's okay."

Papa looked at me hard, then at Mama. "Are you sure you feel up to the chase?"

Mama glanced at me and smiled. "Oh, how fast can he run? He's getting pretty old."

Oh, Mama, that's a challenge you're going to regret making.

Anyway, Papa decided to give me a try at freedom and unfortunately I did prove them right. Why I took off like someone had stuffed a firecracker right in my 'you know what,' my floppy ears flying out behind me. I couldn't believe I was really free, and right in the middle of Hyde Park! It had been such a long time since I had felt the real 'rush' of freedom – clear back in my Mexico City street days. Why I could have run for miles and miles. But before I got too far ahead of Mama and Papa – who incidentally panted after me – I took a quick look back to make sure they were still in sight. Yep, they were there all right, no where near to keeping up with little 'old' me.

Ha, ha, fooled the both of you! But then I began to feel a little guilty, especially after Papa started whistling for me to come. After all, they were getting kind of old, too. They were no '*Peter Pans,*' that's for sure. I didn't want to be the cause of their 'end,' now did I? So I decided to slow down. *How long can I make poor Papa whistle for me? And they're both panting so hard.* Besides, I didn't want to be deprived of this 'freedom' opportunity again, so I put on my good little 'doggie' disposition and trotted right back to them. Boy, were they happy. Why you'd think I'd been gone for a week, the way they hugged me on my return.

After that, each time we visited Hyde Park and they let me off my lead, I tried to be a good dog and stay close to them. Papa contributed to this fact by not actually removing my leash, but just letting go of it. That way I couldn't run too fast or I would get tangled up in my own leash and trip. That engineer Papa of mine just always figured everything out.

So our exploration of 'Hyde,' as we fondly came to call it, continued. Before long we were crossing over this wide dirt path which went all around the park. It smelled pretty darn good to me and I quickly came to realize it was the scent of horses I was enjoying so much when two British ladies dressed in these little black hats and red jackets came trotting right by us. And funny thing is, the British ride horses as strangely as they drive cars – totally the wrong way. Why they sit with both legs on one side. Now how are you going to hang on to a horse like that – especially when there's a doggie around and the horse decides to make a run for it? Guess what? Off they popped. And all because of me! Actually, they didn't really fall off, they kind of just slipped off, like they were going down a slippery slide or something, and landed on the padded bottoms of their puffy riding pants. Nonetheless, I knew I was in trouble. Why Mama and Papa were so embarrassed as they helped the poor ladies to their feet. Needless to say, that was the end of my Hyde Park freedom for that day.

But still it wasn't so bad being on a leash as Mama had bought me one of those leashes that are magic. You see, the faster I went the longer it got. Boy was it cool! It didn't have all that much 'magical ability' however. At about fifteen feet, its magic just plain stopped – thus so did this 'puppy.' However, I still managed to get into a bit of trouble with it hooked to my collar.

You see, I came upon another awfully good smell – something like horses, but not exactly the 'real' thing. That's because it was the leftover from the horse – you know, its poop. And I just couldn't help but taste a little sample of it. Why when Mama saw what I had done, you'd have thought I was chewing on a piece of arsenic by the scream she let out.

"Lucky, you spit that out and I said right now!"

Papa ran to where I was and pried open my mouth, like he was my vet looking for cavities.

Papa, I'm just having a little tiny taste! Give a dog a break, would you?

I wasn't able to finish my sample, for soon it was in a pile on the ground before me and my magical leash was closed up to within a foot of Papa's arm. Oh well . . . I tried, now didn't I? But I have to admit, it was the last of my 'horse poop' sampling for quite some time, and it really hadn't tasted too bad – kind of like the pieces of dried up salad that I used to find under the kitchen table on occasion.

I did do some other sampling at Hyde Park, as well. Now all those ducks and swans swimming along in the Serpentine Lake following the row boats didn't do much for me at all. They were 'old stuff' to me – often seen and chased before. Besides, Mama quickly pointed out the signs all over the place that reminded us not to disturb the wildlife. *Okay, Mama, don't you worry. I'm not going to eat any old ducks – too many feathers for my taste – and I promise not to bother them in any other way.*

But there was one more smell that I just had to 'bother' myself with. I wasn't sure what it was, but it sure did smell very fine and wild indeed. So good in fact that I just had to roll in it over and over again. Why at first Mama and Papa just thought I was doing my grass rolling/back-scratching exercise and they stood there and watched me, talking about how cute I was.

"Hey, wait a minute," Papa said. "What in the heck are you rolling in, Lucky?"

Me Papa? Oh, nothing . . . .

I had to admit I was fibbing. I had latched onto an unbelievable wild smell and I was going to make the most of it, whether my mama and papa liked it or not.

"Look, Lucky's back is all black!" Mama said.

Papa raced up to me. "And does he ever smell! You're not coming into our house like that, you damn dog!"

They proceeded to get some napkins from a nearby restaurant and soaked them in the lake and tried to clean me up. Didn't help much – I managed to retain that wonderful wild smell. Only thing I was worried about was that they were going to dump me in the lake entirely and you know me and water – yuk! However, no need to worry as NO SWIMMING signs were about as frequent as NO BOTHERING WILDLIFE signs. Later Mama and Papa found out that my discovery consisted of red fox droppings. Let me tell you, that was the end of my 'fox hunting' days. Every time I even looked like I was going to take a roll in the grass at Hyde Park, Papa stopped me in my 'doggie' tracks. Oh well, guess I can't have it 'all.'

Needless to say, we had to cut our walk short for a bath stop at home, much to my 'doggie' dismay.

"Why if our landlady, Mrs. Watts, knew that we were bathing a dog in her perfect porcelain bathtub, I think she'd absolutely throw a 'tizzy' fit," Mama said, as

Papa scrubbed me down with this floral scented shampoo.

"Oh don't worry, she must like dogs or she wouldn't have rented this place to us," Papa said, as he continued to scrub on me like he was scouring the frying pan after dinner.

I just sat there in the tub soaking wet and feeling very sad indeed.

Mama, what kind of a machismo dog am I gonna smell like now? I much preferred that delicious 'fox' scent.

But Papa kept right on scrubbing away.

I was finally rewarded for my suffering. That's because we got to go out walking again once I was dry. No more Hyde Park for me that day, however, and at this I was more than a little disappointed.

It wasn't the last contact I would have with that red fox, however. That's because it must have been one of the red foxes that lived in the park that liked to visit Yeoman's Row about 2:00 a.m. every Wednesday morning when all the trash bins were put out. Let me tell you, I smelled that thing coming from the end of our street and I made darn good and sure Mama and Papa knew about it, as well. Why the first time they thought someone was breaking into the house or something as I had put up such a racket. They both raced down the stairs in their pajamas, Papa holding his hammer right in the air. Why, I thought he was going to hit me with it in order to shut me up. Nope . . . he was only after the 'imaginary' burglar. When they found out it was red and that it was a fox, they both laughed and Mama raced after her camera. The many times I called them after that when Mr. Red Fox appeared they didn't think it funny at all, and Papa quickly made me return to my *cama*, which was down in the kitchen.

But back to our neighborhood tour. After my bath, I was feeling very good *indeed, even if I did smell like a wild Irish rose* (see, I was getting a feel for the British language.) We were hungry, so decided to go on over to Pret for one of their tasty sandwiches. But bummer, I didn't even get to go inside with Mama and Papa – and I didn't get to participate in the sandwich eating either, so it wasn't as neat as I thought. Oh yeah, they did save me one crust, but what's the big 'doggie' deal about that?

Didn't matter, I was more in the mood for walking than eating and I knew for certain that my mama would make me a wonderful pasta dinner that night or that Papa would prepare me some of his famous Basmati rice. So we went on over to the V&A – that's the Victoria and Albert Museum. Now it was a grand old building named after some English Queen and her husband, but as is the general rule in London – No Dogs Allowed. That referred to me, so on we went, past the Natural History and Science museums, where the same applied. Right then and there I decided I was going to be more of an 'outside' dog here in London – the Netherlands it was definitely not where we dogs are concerned. Oh yeah, I got to go inside an occasional pub out in the countryside, as long as there was no food served – but then why the heck would I want to go into a pub with no food? That makes not one bit of 'doggie' sense to me. I was also not permitted in any restaurant nor in the stores – except for dog shops, of course. The theaters were also a 'no dog go,' but what good I'd get out of some live theater production is beyond me, even though Mama and Papa certainly seemed to enjoy them.

In spite of all these inconveniences, London was still one great town. In fact, I didn't mind being outside a bit, except when it was raining and I had to wear my 'you know what.' But I especially loved it when we were together at our little house, me right there sitting beside my mama and papa, a warm fire in the fireplace. And that's exactly what I did, day in and day out, rain or shine.

CHAPTER 36
THE 'A' TO 'Z' (ZED) OF LONDON

I very soon came to realize that London was really a wonderful town for exploring, rain or shine. It was also filled with more walking opportunities than this little old pooch could have ever imagined. Why, I'm downright surprised I didn't manage to wear the thick skin right off the bottom of my paws. I probably would have if I didn't have to wear my little boots on so many rainy days, that's for sure.

Each and every Saturday, the day when Papa didn't have to go to work, and we were not traveling to some other place of 'doggie' interest, we explored our new home town. Why I'm sure we must have walked at least twenty miles most of those days. But the idea of that didn't bother me one 'doggie diddle,' or so I thought. But that's another story.

Now my mama had this little book of London maps called "A to Z," (but the British pronounce the 'z' as 'zed.' She said it contained a map of each and every street in the entire town. And as I would find out, we were about to sample almost each and every one of them during our time in London.

Our first all-day walking marathon took place on a very warm Saturday in March – St. Patrick's Day, to be exact. St. Patrick was this Irish guy, so everyone was dressed up in green. Why Mama even put a little plastic shamrock on my collar as she was sure I must have a little Irish somewhere in that 57 varieties of mine. Naturally our first stop was the St. Patrick's Day parade, which seemed to be meandering all over town, as we ran across it several times that day. But a parade is a parade, so we quickly moved on toward Notting Hill and its famous Saturday market; something which we incidentally did every Saturday as Papa loved nothing better than to paw through all that green stuff.

Now Notting Hill was nice and Mama had already told me that a famous movie was filmed there, but there were so many people walking around I was sure I was going to be one squashed dog by the time we got out of there. Besides, who wants to look at all those piles and piles of bananas and broccoli, and artichokes – certainly not to my 'doggie' good taste at all. And then there was the antique section, which I really hated. Nothing to eat there, unless one likes chewing on old brass door knockers or copper spoons. Not this pooch.

I much preferred the excitement of Camden Locks market, which was very colorful indeed. Besides, they had veggies, too, so that made Papa happy. But I've never seen so many people with spiked pink, purple and green hair in all my 'doggie days,' and I was sure hoping Mama and Papa wouldn't get any ideas in that department. I just couldn't imagine my papa with purple spiked hair. All these young people also circled their eyes in black and they had these tattoos and wore great big black leather boots, which I was sure were perfect for kicking me clear to the moon – especially us smaller dogs. But I was soon to find out that they liked us doggies very much – so no need to worry about the kicking potential of the Camden Locks folks. These kids were more into buying this loud crazy music, which was sold everywhere. But Mama and Papa didn't like that music very much. Instead they were more into the fresh produce that was for sale on the streets, so I had to sit obediently by their side while Papa sorted through every piece of cauliflower, every green bean and each head of lettuce.

Of course what I liked best about Camden Locks were all the food stands. Why I had never seen so many places selling Chinese noodles and rice in all my 'doggie' days. So you can imagine the spilled leftovers I just managed to snag as we made our way along the sidewalks fronting the canal. Only one bad thing – Papa kept tugging on my leash and I had to really 'eat on the run,' so I couldn't enjoy it as much as I would have liked.

Afterwards, we would walk along the canal and watch all the little boats go by. But it was nothing like walking along the River Thames. For it was a great big mud-colored river with lots and lots of big and little boats. I was hoping Mama and Papa wouldn't get any ideas about going on one of them – but they didn't seem too interested, so I was safe. Instead we walked along this big tree-lined path that ran beside the river, which certainly provided many 'perfect peeing moments,' let me tell you.

There were also lots of famous buildings to see. Why the first time I saw Parliament and Big Ben – you know, that famous London clock – even I was impressed. I never did understand why one would name a clock Ben, especially since it was named after an old neighbor of ours that I didn't like so much. Of course we stopped to take a picture next to the big clock, and Mama assured me that it would be on our next Christmas card.

"What a cute little doggie," said a lady from Kansas who had volunteered to take our picture.

Oh, oh, I know what that means – here comes Mama's famous Lucky story.

"Oh thanks so much, Lucky was once a Mexico City street dog. . . "

See what I told you.

338

As usual, the lady looked as if she had seen a ghost, and then she shook her head and smiled, listening to every word of Mama's story, although I'm sure she would have much rather been spending her time at Westminister Abbey – looking at all the famous graves and such – which was right across the street. Fortunately, I didn't get to go inside the big old Gothic church, but I did enjoy it from the outside – another British landmark indeed.

Then it was on to one of the most famous British landmarks of all – Buckingham Palace.

"This is where the Queen lives," Mama said, as we joined the gathering crowd.

"We're going to watch the changing of the guard," Papa said, finding a spot for us right next to the black and gold gate.

Now I seriously didn't know what guards were, but when I saw all these guys marching around in red coats and black tall furry hats that looked like curled up raccoons, I decided they must be the ones who were going to change something. I certainly hoped it was their hats, as it seemed far too hot a day to be wearing fur hats. I know that wearing a fur coat wasn't particularly easy for me as it must have been around eighty degrees.

Well these furry-topped guys marched around for a while until I got kind of bored, so I put my legs up on the fence to get a better view, and let me tell you, this other guard came over and told me to get them down. Mama was so embarrassed.

"Lucky, you've got to stop being so curious!"

Sorry, Mama, I didn't know it would bother those furry guys.

Finally, they changed places with each other and then back to the River Thames we went, which I much preferred. Across the Waterloo Bridge there was a great big round circle which went round and round. Papa called it the London Eye – didn't look much like any eye that I had ever seen, and Mama quickly explained to me that it was a Ferris wheel with little glass cages which allowed everyone who rode it to get a spectacular view of London.

Oh, oh, I hope that's not where we're headed. For you see, hanging around in some glass ball high above the River Thames was certainly not what this old doggie had in mind. Escalators were frightening enough. *No thanks, not me.*

Fortunately, this time I was in luck, for we headed right up the path until we got to Trafalgar Square – one of Mary Poppin's hangouts, I was soon to learn.

"It's where she used to feed the birds," Mama said.

Well, there were certainly enough pigeons all over the huge square with its lion fountains and statue of a Lord named Nelson. And they were certainly doing their 'thing' all over him. Why, we could hardly make out the old lord's face. Boy, was I one happy pooch to get out of there before they did their wicked deed on me. Rolling in fox doo-doo, now that was good – but bird doo-doo, no, I don't think so. It was just too white and lumpy in my 'doggie' point of view.

So up the river we went until we could see this great big square bridge with little towers on each side. It looked very 'fairy tale' according to Mama.

"There's the Tower Bridge," Papa pointed out.

No kidding, Papa. I can certainly see why it's called that.

"And the Tower of London is right behind it," Mama said.

After she explained that it was the place where they used to keep famous prisoners and chop their heads off,

I had no desire to see that tower place even one little 'doggie' bit. Especially after I learned that they keep a bunch of ravens there for good luck. Personally, it didn't sound like a very lucky place to me – especially if one was a prisoner there. Besides, I'd about had my fill of birds for the day, and there was also the famous NO DOGS ALLOWED sign right beside the entrance. But no big problem for us, as Mama and Papa had already been there and seen the Crown Jewels and all the *bloody* towers and all. Hmm . . . I had finally figured out why the British use the word 'bloody' all the time. It was all because of those towers. Can you believe that? And all along I had thought it had something to do with a nice rare steak.

We did get to walk across the bridge, however. At first I was a bit nervous, walking on this big bridge which stretched clear across the river, and I stuck very near to Mama and Papa. Why it was as close as I ever wanted to get to walking on water, let me tell you, and I was one thankful pooch when we reached the other side.

There was Shakespeare's Globe almost right in front of us. It was round indeed, but I had no idea that it was where a famous British guy called William Shakespeare liked to do 'his thing,' so Papa said. Boy did 'my mama, the English major' give him a dirty look. For you see, Shakespeare's thing was nothing like 'my thing,' if you know what I mean. For his 'thing' was acting and writing plays, and I was later to visit his birthplace of Stratford-Upon-Avon – which was far away from London – to see where he started all of it. Of course, Mama loved Shakespeare and during our time in the U.K. we seemed to do a lot of things associated with that Shakespeare guy.

By then it was late afternoon and boy, was I ever getting tired. I was wondering when we were going to stop for our cappuccino as I was definitely in need of a nap. Believe it or not, my wish was granted. For there in front of us was a Costa Coffee – not that this was strange in London as there was some kind of a coffee house on about every corner. Anyway, we sat at one of their little tables right beside the river. And best part of all, there was no Mr. Snarly Dog to jump out at me, so I got in a nice fifteen-minute nap.

Believe me, I was going to need it for the walking I was about to endure. Why I thought it would never end. I honestly thought we must be walking clear back to Holland or something. I could tell by the angle of the sun that it was getting late and for me, that meant it was about time for my 'dinny,' – you know, my dinner. But unfortunately there was no rice or pasta in sight. There was a sign that Mama read, which said, LONDON UNDERGROUND, and little did I know that it was exactly where we were headed.

"I think we'd better take the Tube home," Mama said. "Lucky looks exhausted."

Well, she got that one right. But that was before I realized what that old Tube was all about.

"Would you like a ride home, Old Boy?" Papa said.

I wagged my tail in agreement, thinking we would be getting into a rental car, or maybe even a taxi. But no such luck. That's because before I caught on, we were going through this little gate and then down an escalator. Why I was rolling right along before I even realized it, much to my 'doggie' dismay. And worst of all, we were headed way down into this pit far below the sidewalk, which I didn't like even one little bit.

"I'm going to have to carry you, Lucky," Papa said, reading the sign, which said that animals had to be carried. I had to admit it was better than risking my tail to be gobbled up by that old escalator, so I didn't complain too much when Papa scooped me up just as we were about half-way down.

Mama helped to hold me, as I wasn't exactly a light weight, if you know what I mean. I think it probably had something to do with all that pasta and rice I'd been eating all those years.

I was still really scared and boy, did I ever cling to Mama and Papa. For you see, it was not one escalator that we had to take down into the pit, it was three! Why I thought I was going to have one heck of a 'doggie' breakdown before it was all over.

We finally reached the bottom and then walked along this path to a big long hole in the ground where I saw some gray mice running around. Now why they'd want to live down there in the dark was beyond my 'doggie' belief. I much preferred Yeoman's Row.

Then the strangest thing happened. Along came a train. Now how a train got way down in that hole was a real mystery to me, but when the doors opened, I was the first one to pop inside, knowing I had to get out of that hole one way or another.

We found a spot at the rear of the car so I would have a place to sit on the floor without getting squashed, as, of course, dogs were not allowed on the seats. Let me tell you, after riding that Tube, I certainly know how all those sardines feel to be squished into one little can. Why, I'd never seen so many people in such a small container.

Finally, the train started and I about fell over in my tracks. That's because it wobbled from side to side as it sped along the track. I just didn't know what to do. There was no way I could sit as the motion of the train and the vibration of the tracks below me scared the 'doggie' heck out of me. Thus, I decided I would stand. But when I about fell over several times, I settled on another form of travel. I spread my four paws out real far apart so I had better balance.

Papa laughed at me. "Lucky looks like a new-born baby calf the way he's standing."

Well I didn't think it was very funny at all, as I was shaking around like some 'hip-hop' artist.

And Mama, you know what she did? Why she got that digital camera of hers from her purse and took my picture! Now how humiliating can that be?

But suddenly the train stopped and was I ever one anxious doggie to get out.

"Not our stop, Old Boy," Papa said. "We get out at the Knightsbridge station."

Ten stations later, I was finally led to freedom. Let me tell you one thing, riding on the London Underground was certainly not on my favorite 'doggie' to do list. Why when we went up the escalators and out into the setting sunlight, was I ever one relieved pup.

All in all it had been a great day, however, and London was beginning to feel more and more like home.

CHAPTER 37
SPRING BREAK – UK STYLE

Now, mind you, we didn't spend all our time in London. You can bet your 'doggie' diddles we didn't. For the United Kingdom was one big country from my 'doggie' point of view. No, not as large as America, but it covered more space than I'd care to trot, let me tell you. And we were soon to discover some of its very special spots.

That's because it was Easter time. Here in Europe that meant 'trip-time,' and boy do those Europeans love to go on 'holiday' as they call it. Why Papa always said they were planning their next holiday as soon as they got back from the one they were on. My mama didn't think that was a bad idea at all, and neither did this pooch.

Anyway, our first Easter in London we decided to go 'all out.' First we headed to the Cotswolds – a very pretty country region a few hours from London. Of course, Mama had to stop at famous Oxford University – which is actually several colleges – and check out some of them. She said they were built in the tenth century. Now that sounds pretty old from my 'doggie' point of view, since we canines don't live to be old and retired like humans, with all that Medicare and Social Security and stuff that Mama and Papa are always talking about.

As we walked the tree-lined streets of Oxford that connected the campuses, I seriously enjoyed checking out about every bush and tree, leg held high, while Papa told us that famous people like Samuel Johnson, Sir Walter Raleigh, William Penn, and Lewis Carroll had studied there. But it didn't matter a 'doggie' diddly bit to me, as long as there was greenery around. After all, I wasn't about to go to college and earn a Ph.D., now was I?

After seeing the dining room where Harry Potter and his friends ate dinner in the movie, it was on the road again, and this time it was one tiny road indeed. Why I was afraid our rental car wouldn't even fit on it, and if we met up with a car going the other direction, by 'doggie golly' I didn't even want to think of the consequences. So needless to say, I didn't sleep a wink as we went through villages with such names as Stow-on-the-Wold, Wotton-under-Edge, and Moreton-in-Marsh. Then there was Upper and Lower Slaughter, Chipping Campden and Painswick.

"These names are really something," Papa said, jamming on the brakes when he saw a car coming right at us. No wonder I couldn't sleep. Why I was one 'doggie' nervous wreck by the time we got to a village called Bibury, where we would spend the night. But to tell you the truth, it wasn't really so bad missing my afternoon nap as the countryside was the greenest I had ever seen. Of course with all that British rain I could certainly understand why, and I quickly wondered if Mama had managed to tuck in my yellow raincoat. Why of course she had – I knew my mama better than that. But this day was very sunny with a bright blue sky, and the surrounding hills were rolling and covered with big oaks, bright yellow daffodils, and fluffy white sheep with little new-born lambs. Boy, would I loved to have sunk my chewers into one of them. Of course, Mama and Papa didn't give me even one tiny bit of an opportunity to accomplish that dream. I'd just have to rely on my nightly Cup of Soup with bread crumbs and some deli ham for the trip – something I became quite used to when traveling, by the way. That's because they have a tea maker in every room, as the British can't survive without their tea, and it proved to be a perfect device for Mama to heat my portable 'noodle' water in.

Now Bibury was a perfect little storybook village. All the houses had slate roofs and were made of Cotswold stone, which is kind of a honey-brown, yellowish color, about the color of my pee, actually. Mama said they all looked like 'Hansel and Grettel' houses and that they were built in the 1500's.

"Can you believe we're right here in the middle of history?" Mama said, pointing out the leaded glass windows of a tiny cottage. "It's as if we've gone back in time."

Papa nodded. "Well I hope the inns we're staying in at least have king-size beds. The houses seem pretty darn small to me."

She smiled at him. "Don't worry, whatever we sleep in will be fine. Just think 'history' instead of 'comfort.' "

But Papa didn't have such a smiley face at that thought. As for me, I didn't care one little bit what size of bed our room would have as I had my very own *cama* right along with me in the car. The thing I was most excited about was sleeping in the same room as Mama and Papa, something I just adored.

The village sat on the banks of the Coln River, which, incidentally, was totally filled with local trout – something else I would have liked to sample. I looked longingly into the clear cold water as we walked beside Arlington Row, a group of old gabled houses that were originally built for weavers. *How was I ever going to snag me one of those fish?* I think Papa must have read my mind, as he gave me a quick jerk on the leash.

"You're not going fishing, Lucky Boy," he said. "I don't think the local folks would like that one bit as they're very much into the preservation thing."

But Mama surprised us both when she went into this little shop and came out with a nice big piece of smoked trout. And believe it or not, she even shared it with Papa and me. Boy was it good. I would have preferred the whole fish, of course, but it wasn't to be.

The Bibury Court Hotel, our home for the night, was just down the lane and when we drove up its long gravel drive, Papa let out a big sigh.

"Looks really old to me," he said. "But at least it's big. By the way, how much does this place cost?"

Mama ignored his last comment, so I figured out it must be pricey. "That's the whole idea, dear – we're here to experience 'old.' It was a manor house built in 1633 for Sir Thomas Sackville."

I had to admit it looked pretty cool indeed from my 'doggie' point of view. The great big stone and brick house had a very high gabled roof. The river ran through the property and there was a huge lawn out front where a couple of brightly-colored pheasants were feeding. Believe me, I knew how I could interrupt their lunch break quite quickly. But just as I was about to head their way, Papa pulled on my leash real hard. Oh, how I sometimes hated being connected to that thing. It totally robbed me of all my 'doggie' liberty.

"Oh no, you don't, Lucky. Leave the wildlife alone, Old Boy."

Oh, Papa, you always have to ruin my fun.

Inside everything was very old, too. It had wooden plank floors, a great big fireplace, perfect for lounging beside I was soon to find out, and lots of antique furniture.

"Dinner is at seven," the desk clerk told us as we wound our way up the oak staircase.

Our room was under the eaves and had windows all the way to the floor, perfect for 'doggie' viewing. It looked out to the lawn and river, and I quickly settled in for a good view since the pheasants were still there. My patience was further rewarded. It wasn't long before I saw several rabbits nibbling away on the grass, and then a bright red fox ran right across the lawn. Boy did those feasting pheasants and rabbits do a great big 'let's get the heck out of here' routine. *Oh . . . a perfect 'doggie' smorgasbord*, I thought. Did my mouth ever start to drool. Why I just wanted to run down and join all of them on the grass so badly that I started to do my 'whining' thing, but Mama insisted I needed a nap, and that was that. *You're just no fun at all, Mama.*

It wasn't too long until I was fast asleep, dreaming of rabbit hunting no less; that is until I smelled the aroma of my simmering noodles. Boy, was I ever hungry. Must have had something to do with my dream. After wolfing down my chow, Papa took me out to the lawn to do my deed. Then we went into the sitting room to await Mama and Papa's call to dinner.

We found a place right next to the big stone fireplace, where a log fire roared. It was just what I needed after a long day in the car. Why the warmth of the fire took every one of the old aches and pains right out of me, and I was in a very deep sleep when the waiter called Mama and Papa's name.

"Sorry to wake you Old Boy, but you're going to have to wait in the car while we have our dinner," Papa said.

Why I was totally insulted, even though I knew we doggies were not allowed in dining rooms in the U.K.. That's one thing I missed about Holland – going out to dinner all the time. Still I could tell Mama felt bad having to leave me in the car.

"We'll only be a while, Lucky, so just take a nice nap."

Yeah, right, while you're dining on pheasant and duck there in that nice cozy dining room.

Let me tell you, I was not a particularly happy pooch at that moment. But my bed was nice and warm. To insure my further warmth, Mama insisted that I wear my wool turtleneck with red, white and blue stripes before we went outside. I suppose things really weren't too bad so, as usual, I had to forgive my parents.

The next morning we were up at the crack of dawn and walking along the river in the mist. It was really beautiful. There was even an old mill wheel with water spilling over it, and Mama and Papa watched it go round and round. To tell you the truth, I was more interested in checking out the wildlife and growled deeply each time I saw a movement in the bushes alongside the stream.

Since it was Easter, we went to the service at the tiny stone Romanesque church next door which Mama told us was built in the 1300s. Of course, dogs were not allowed to go to church in England either, so I waited patiently, tied to a post beneath a tree out in the graveyard. I would have much rather checked out the old tilted headstones, but was certain Papa thought I would pee on one or something. Why I'd never think of doing that, now would I? Instead I decided to settle down and take a nap, while I listened to the beautiful Easter music played on the old pipe organ inside the church.

After the service, we went to a village called Bourton-on-the-Water, for lunch. Guess where it was located? On the water, of course. In fact, it sat on lots of water, as there were all sorts of little creeks running right through the small town. We sat at a picnic table beside one of them and had the best greasiest fish and chips in all of England.

Then it was onto Shakespeare country and his birthplace, Stratford-Upon-Avon, where we would spend the next night. Of course it was filled with tourists, especially during Easter week, as Mama said that everyone wanted to see where Shakespeare was born. I suppose that included us. I had to admit it was a pretty place, filled with Elizabethan buildings made of plaster and timber – 'Tudor style,' Mama said. Some of them even had grass roofs like in Holland. But I didn't see any sheep grazing on top of any of them, hard as I looked. The River Avon flowed through the town and there were swans swimming on it and lots of little row boats. Of course I paid no attention to the swans whatsoever, after living right next to them in Holland all those months, and I had already calculated there was no way the three of us would fit into one of those boats, so we were not about to have a 'water' experience.

We also went to visit the house where Shakespeare was born and the thatched-roof cottage of his daughter, Anne Hathaway, but they all looked pretty much the same from my vantage point – outside, that is. I really didn't care to see the bed where the old playwright was born anyway, but Mama sure got all excited about it. I wondered if she'd get as excited over the leaf-filled hole where I was born in The Gully. It had been a long time since I'd thought of my 'puppyhood' in Mexico.

That night Mama and Papa went to the Royal Shakespeare Theater, which was beside the river. Guess what I did? I slept in my *cama* right in the car. *Bummer.* On such a beautiful moonlit night, I wanted more than anything to be out walking beside the river. But Mama and Papa rewarded me with a nice stroll when they came back from the play. I think I must have peed about a hundred times I was so happy. Afterwards we went to bed in this old inn called the White Swan, can you believe that? But I didn't see any swans wandering around its pub. But that's okay, you know me and swans. A few of them in my life are quite enough.

The next morning off we headed for the Yorkshire Dales, way in the northern part of England.

"You're going to love the dales and the moors," Mama told me. "It's where the famous vet James Herriot lived." At the mention of the word 'vet,' I personally didn't think I was going to get too excited about this area at all. I was wrong. Why it was beautiful country with steep rolling hills and lavender heather-covered moorlands and tumbling streams. Of course there were more sheep than I could ever count with my limited math experience. But I'd given up chasing them, so I just enjoyed the view from the back seat of the car.

We stopped for lunch in the Pennines hills, home of the famous writers, the Bronte sisters, and of course Mama got excited all over again. But from my 'doggie' point of view, it looked very dreary indeed since everything was covered in this foggy mist.

"England's a perfect place for you, dear," Papa told Mama, sensing her excitement.

"It certainly is. I love *Wuthering Heights* and *Jane Eyre.*"

I wondered briefly what and whom Mama was talking about, but I quickly turned my 'doggie' attention to the views – what I could see of them, that is.

My mama thought it was a perfect place for all of us – lots of sheep, footpaths and trout-filled steams and cute little inns with fireplaces. I thought about it for a moment – yes, it was perfect out here in the country – especially with my mama and papa.

Before I knew it, we were in a little town called Thirsk. It was a nice place with a small square and some stone houses, one of which had a sign which read 'Veterinary Clinic.'

Oh, oh, what am I in for now? I could smell it already.

"This is where James Herriott had his veterinary office," Mama said, "although he often went out into the countryside to treat sick animals."

Papa's face brightened at his name. "He's the one who wrote *All Creatures Great and Small*, isn't he?"

"Yes," Mama said, and *All Things Bright and Beautiful*. They're both books about animals," she told me, like I could read or something. "Let's go take a look at his office. I'm sure dogs are allowed here."

Guess what, Mama? It's one place this old dog doesn't want to visit.

I didn't have much choice, however, as we were soon inside the small waiting area, much to my 'doggie' dismay. I soon came to discover it wasn't so bad at all because there was no vet in sight. No wonder. Mama hadn't informed me that the famous vet was dead. So instead of getting shots, they just snapped my picture by the photo of the dead vet and bought some of his famous licorice, his books, and a doggie treat for me. Then off we went again. Wow, now that was the best vet visit I ever had in all my 'doggie' days!

Except for the fact that Mama tried to get me to taste her black licorice.

No, thank you very much indeed. And on this, Papa and I wholly agreed.

Back in the car, we proceeded farther north to the Lake District, in search of some of Mama's famous poets, whatever they were. I had a feeling it had nothing to do with eating, so I just took myself one good long nap.

When I awoke, we were driving through some mighty big mountains indeed. We were clear up by the border of Scotland. We stopped for the night in this town called Windemere right by a lake with the same name. I seriously wondered how many fish lived in the depths of the big blue lake. I wasn't about to go swimming and find out, however. You know me and water – never to be a match. I was perfectly fine sitting out on the hotel lawn at sunset while Mama and Papa had a glass of wine. They gave me one of my doggie treats to chew on, so that made it a very beautiful sunset indeed.

The next day we checked out the many authors who had once lived in the Lake District. Why my mama had the biggest smile on her face that I had ever seen, even when we didn't run across William Wordsworth's *field of golden daffodils* or his *lonely clouds*. We did get to see the cottage where he wrote all his poetry and the places where poets Keats and Tennyson liked to hang out. Mama also said something about Beatrice Potter and *Peter Rabbit*, and for a moment it got my attention, until I found out Peter Rabbit was only the name of a book and that there would be no 'real' rabbits running around.

By the time we were finished, I think we had visited the places of interest of about every old English writer there was, and I seriously wondered if we were now going to look for places where famous engineers lived to please my papa.

As if she had read my mind, Mama said to Papa, "It's too bad there aren't any famous engineering sites around here or the birthplace of a famous engineer."

Papa laughed. "They're all in Germany."

But my papa made the best of it and sure seemed to enjoy the beautiful countryside, as did Mama and this lucky old pooch. That's because we were soon off 'footpath trooping,' as we came to call it, and believe me, it was one of the very best things we did during our time in Europe. Let me tell you, it was one 'doggie' paradise. For you see, the British have all these paths out in the countryside which connect the villages. So instead of driving between villages and to the pubs, they just walk. And boy did that suit this little doggie just fine. Why the three of us must have walked about two hundred miles during our Easter week holiday. Why we saw so many sheep, green rolling hills, and wildlife. Of course, I was especially fond of all the rabbits. Why they just made my mouth water. Believe me, I was one slobbery mess by the time our trip came to an end.

Too soon that came to pass and it was time to return to city life, so down the road we headed back to London. Was I ever a disappointed pooch. But then Mama got this brilliant idea that we should take the long way home along the British Coast so that we could stop in Brighton for lunch and then go on to Dover to check out some white cliffs that had something to do with the war.

Now lunch in Brighton was nice because I got to share my parents fish and chips, but the beach I wouldn't recommend at all since it was nothing like Laguna Beach, but consisted of big rocks, about the size of my paw.

Then there was Dover. I didn't care so much for it either. While it had a great hiking trail along these white

355

cliffs that Mama had been talking about, we were all very disappointed when we didn't get to see any bluebirds, like the song about that place said were sure to be there. But worse than that, there was a very strong wind. And when one is 'dog size' wind speed really makes a difference. It pushed me right to the edge of the path, and for once I was more than thankful to be hooked to the end of my leash. Why my ears flew right out like two sails and I was sure I was about to fly across the English Channel and right back to Holland, 'no thank you, very much.' I have to admit that it was the only British footpath walk I did not enjoy, and I was one happy pooch to be back inside the car again.

So over fifteen hours after our departure from the Cotswolds and due to Mama's extra-curricular activities – like about half-way around England – combined with all the holiday traffic, we arrived back in London. That's when I decided I was one happy puppy to be back home again on Yeoman's Row. I think my papa agreed.

CHAPTER 38
CELTIC COUNTRY

Two weeks later we were on the road again. Why, I just couldn't believe my 'doggie' good luck. Two vacations in one month! Wow! Once more, we traveled to the far north of England, then over the border to Scotland, a separate country for the most part, but still part of the United Kingdom, which certainly made no sense to me. All I knew was that I was really excited as I thought for sure we would once again be doing the 'footpath routine' through the sheep pastures. It was something this old dog totally enjoyed.

Was I ever wrong! Instead Papa drove our rental car into this big city called Edinburgh, which kind of reminded me of London. But still, I was lovin' it – just as long as the three of us were together.

Well, we checked into an old hotel – the Hilton wouldn't allow dogs, if you can imagine that – but it was the kind of European hotel we really liked best anyway. It had those leaded glass windows that Mama loved; wooden beams and sort of slanted floors, which Papa didn't particularly care for, being the engineer type. But best of all, a giant stone fireplace took up the entire wall of the lobby. I definitely loved this fact, already imagining my nighttime snoozes before it.

Edinburgh is Scotland's capital, and it's an old Medieval city with a castle on a big hill right in the middle of town. Looking up at it, I quickly concluded I was about to do some hiking, as Mama had her eye on it first thing when we entered the city. But this time our hiking would not be through sheep pastures, unfortunately.

Let me tell you, the hike up to that castle about wore out my old 'doggie' legs. The steep cobblestone walkway made us slip, and I almost fell right on my snout. I knew there was no use in complaining since with Mama as our guide, we would see each and every castle in all of the U.K. during our stay. It was like we saw each and every windmill in Holland. I was certain we would continue our hike to this particular castle no matter what, even if we slipped all the way to the bottom and had to hike up again. So upward we went. Why I was so huffin' and puffin' that I didn't even jerk on my leash.

Now Papa just didn't know what to think about Scotland. That's because he couldn't understand a thing anyone said. Frankly, neither could I, so we both waited for Mama to translate for us.

"I can't believe you two," she kept saying. "They're speaking English, after all. Only a portion of the people still speak Celtic."

"You could have fooled me," Papa said. "Just tell me how to order a pint."

We did that in the Café Royal Circle Bar, and then my papa was very happy indeed. But he didn't think too much of the bagpipe music, and to tell you the truth, neither did I. It about burst my 'doggie' eardrums. And the fact that many of the men were dressed in plaid skirts called *kilts* really confused me, and I think it confused Papa, as well. But he didn't say a thing because I think he was afraid of what Mama would have to say about that. He didn't have to worry for long, as we were soon off to our next destination, St. Andrews.

"This town's the Home of Golf," Papa told us. "Your Uncle Gary – our family golfer, incidentally – would sure like to visit here."

I had to admit St. Andrews was a pretty little town, very old, all the buildings made of this gray stone. It was built right on the bay of guess what? St. Andrews – which was on the North Sea.

"I'll bet they get a lot of rain here," Mama said.

Oh, oh, raincoat time.

But I was to be proved wrong, for the day was perfectly sunny and beautiful.

"This is where Prince William goes to school." Mama pointed out the famous old university as we drove by. "It's the oldest college in Scotland."

Now why a prince would want to live here where it rained day after day was beyond me, but then again, it rained a lot in London, too. And, after all, he was British, and those folks know a thing or two about rain.

Of course Papa was much more interested in checking out the town's famous golf course, the St. Andrews Links. Sounded like a good peeing spot to me, so I was more than happy to go along with Papa's idea.

It was a beautiful golf course and sat right beside the ocean above a white sand beach. An old club house and hotel, stood beside the course. We had to walk across the famous turf for a bit, of course, and I was more than happy to put my mark on it, much to Papa's dismay.

"Uncle Gary would chop your head off for that, Old Boy," he told me.

And then when I did my 'big deed' right beside the first tee, I thought Mama and Papa were both going to drop dead right there on the spot. Why I've never ever seen them scramble so fast to find a doggie clean-up bag as they did that day. Why, you would have thought we'd committed a high crime and were about to be arrested when all I did was a little 'poop.' Boy, these humans . . . sometimes I think I will never understand them.

359

Needless to say, we didn't hang around the Old Course at St. Andrews for long, just enough time for my parents to buy some golfing memorabilia for the golfers back home and then it was 'on the road again.'

Next stop – the Scottish Highlands. Now this was a place a dog could really enjoy. It was wild and rugged, filled with mountains and glens – that's valleys – and seashore and lochs – that's a lake in Scottish – and all kinds of wild animals, even a monster, if you can believe that.

We stopped the first night in a fishing village called Plockton, and stayed in a tiny cottage right on the water where we could watch the colorful fishing boats go in and out. I was hoping fish would be on the menu for me that night – but no such luck – just another Cup of Soup, this time with beef chips. Boy oh boy, how about that? Of course, Mama and Papa chowed down on the freshly-caught local fish and then, surprise of all surprises, I was rewarded with their fish skin, so my meal wasn't as boring as I had anticipated. After dinner, we walked down the cobbled street to this old pub where a bunch of locals, their fiddles in tow, had gathered for a live folk music sing-along. We enjoyed this very much, even though we didn't understand even a word they said as it was all in Celtic. Didn't seem to bother my parents a bit, however, so I settled in on the stone floor next to the fire and listened to the sweet, sad music.

The next morning we slept in a bit late, then sat at a picnic table and Mama and Papa ate the famous Scottish tea snack, Walker's Shortbread cookies, with their coffee, and I just sat and watched them eat. Now what do you think of that? But to tell you the truth, I don't care for either cookies or coffee, so it didn't bother me all that much.

It was then on to Loch Ness, where the famous Lochness Monster, Nessie, is supposed to live. Well, I didn't see any old monster in that great big lake, but there were a lot of old castle ruins surrounding it. Besides, I didn't really want to see a monster anyway. I know it would have scared the livin' 'doggie' daylights right out of this old pooch. There were, however, quite a few boats on the lake monster hunting. Mama and Papa didn't seem too interested in looking for monsters, so we headed to   Glen Coe, the "Valley of the Weeping." What a beautiful mountain valley indeed; set between some very high peaks on the shores of Loch Linnhe.

"This is where the MacDonald clan lived and were killed in a huge battle by the king's troops," Papa said.

Mama didn't seem too excited to visit such a place until she discovered it was where the movie, *Braveheart*, was filmed, so then she became more interested. As for me, I just went along 'for the ride.' And let me tell you, it was a very steep, twisty one indeed.

But I was rewarded at the end because we got to hike up through the gorge. It was beautiful and steep with rocky crags on both sides and a rushing river below the trail. The first wildflowers of spring were just opening and a slight mist rose around us.

Something else seemed to be rising around us, as well – Scotland's famous midges (pronounced mid-gees). If you take my advice, you'll never want to meet up with these spec-size gnats that liked to gnaw on everything in sight, including us. Why my flea repellent didn't even help a tiny bit. They were so thick they created a black cloud around us. My papa, the famous mosquito hater, wanted to dash back to the car right away, but Mama and I voted him down. If it hadn't been for the mosquito nets Mama had made to put over all three of our heads, I'm sure we would have been beheaded on the spot by those biting little menaces. Thanks to our netting hats, we were the only ones on the trail able to finish the hike. But can you imagine me, this Mexico City street dog, dressed in mosquito netting? Why the boys on the street would have laughed me right out of town. Oh well, the things we have to put up with when we're adopted by humans. But I was thankful for one thing. At least it wasn't raining and I didn't have to put on my yellow raincoat. Why, I would have probably been slaughtered right out of Scotland by those tough Scots.

Early the next morning, while I was still enjoying my 'doggie' beauty sleep, Papa about pulled me out of bed and said we needed to get on the road.

"We've got to make it clear down to Wales today," he said. "So we'd better get moving, Old Boy."

Since I didn't have much say in the matter and had no idea where this place called 'Wales' was, I did my stretching exercises and headed for the door of the room so I could go outside and do my routine 'pit stops.' Then off we headed into the early morning Scottish mist.

It seemed like we were driving forever that day, back again into England and through the Lake District, where we didn't get to take even one little hike. Then it was on through the Yorkshire Dales, where we barely had time to stop for fish and chips. Next stop, Liverpool, England where the Beatles got their start, but it was only to gas up the car.

"I'd love to see the club where the Beatles first sang," Mama said, but Papa was in his 'driving mode,' and during those times nothing stopped him but an empty gas tank or my need for a good old poop.

Besides, what Mama saw in a bunch of singing bugs was beyond me, so I just continued my long spring-time nap.

We didn't reach Wales until after dark, because it's way out west of England. I was soon to learn they spoke Celtic there, as well, so naturally Papa and I were in for more upsets in the language understanding department. Mama told us they actually speak what is called Welsh, but that they are a Celtic race. Whatever. . . it sounded pretty Celtic to Papa and me. And we barely understood a word.

When we awoke the next morning and I looked out the window of our room, boy was I ever in for a 'doggie' good surprise. For there were mountains and hills everywhere – all a bright green. And it wasn't even raining! Why I couldn't believe my good luck. We were in this place called Snowdonia National Park, but I couldn't even see one bit of snow from our window. There was a huge mountain, however, and it was called Mount Snowdon, the highest mountain south of Scotland. I was hoping we'd get to climb it.

But Papa said, "No, we don't have time."

Boy was I ever disappointed, as I hadn't climbed to the top of a 'real' mountain since *Nevada de Toluca* in Mexico.

Mama said it's called *Yr Wyddfa*, in Welsh, but little did I care since I wasn't going to be climbing it anyway. But I did get a lot closer look at that big old mountain. That's because we traveled through the mountains and forest to Betws-y-Coed, which just so happened to be a popular tourist village. Guess how I figured that out? There were more tour buses than I could even begin to count. Then we took this miniature railway to the top of Mount Snowdon – at least almost to the top. You just can't imagine how much I wanted to get out and run right up to the summit, but no such luck. Papa was really being firm on that decision, much to my 'doggie' dismay.

But we did get to check out some cool castles in Wales. Why Castle Caernarfon was very Medieval and also scary indeed, especially after Papa told us about all the bloody battles that had taken place there, just so the British could take over Wales. Of course, I wasn't about to go wandering around in that big stone place after that, so I waited beside the huge wall which surrounded it and visited with the guard. Not bad at all, because he just happened to share his Welsh lamb sandwich with me. And it was perfectly clear to me after that why Welsh lamb is the best in the world, so I was very anxious to get out in the meadows to chase some of them.

Then the worst thing happened during our entire holiday. It started to rain. And it rained and it rained and it rained. Of course I really needed to pee and all I could think of was 'yellow raincoat' so I held it for as long as I possibly could. When I finally started to whine, Mama knew darn well what I needed to do and out it came – my precious little raincoat.

"Come on, Lucky," let's get your coat on and take you for a pit stop," Mama said, pulling the hood up over my snout so that I could barely see the end of my nose.

Out we went into the downpour. I was hoping I would not run into any other dog as it would be totally embarrassing. We did see some people holding umbrellas, and sure enough, they took a good long look at me, laughing all the time. *Oh, Mama, why do you do this to me?*

364

Once I had finished, I did one very fast 'doggie' trot back to the car, jumped inside, then shook like crazy.

"Hey, Lucky, what the heck do you think you're doing? You're getting everything all wet!" Papa yelled at me.

Sorry, Papa, it's the only way I can dry off my precious little rain coat.

That night we stayed at an inn in the stone town of Dolgellau and watched the rain from its pub. Why, I was sure it would never stop and that we would have to hire a boat to get back to London.

But the next morning the sky was pure blue, not a cloud in sight. So you can imagine what a happy pooch I was as I bounded out the door to do my thing, hoping at the same time to snatch me a little Welsh lamb for breakfast.

Since the weather had improved, Mama got into her shopping mood, so Papa got into his 'not so good' mood. In Brecon, Mama bought love spoons for my brothers, just in case either of them decided to get married. Now why anyone would need a spoon to get married was beyond me. But Mama told us these carved wooden spoons with hearts and stuff, were the ones like the Welsh boys once carved and gave to their girlfriends as a sign of love. Papa even bought one for Mama and that made her very happy indeed, so he decided to be happy as well. Then I decided I might as well be, too, so I wagged my tail like crazy at both of them.

As we made our way down to the Wey River Valley, Mama stopped off in every village searching for antiques as we drove through Brecon Beacons National Park. We reached the town of Tintern at sunset, where we would spend our final holiday night. There she bought an old Welsh milking stool and a piece of blue porcelain pottery, both of which fit nicely beside me on the rear seat of our rental car. But then things got complicated. We stopped right outside the famous Tintern Abbey, which was once a beautiful church, now pretty much a ruin. Since a famous poem had been written about it, all the tourists came to see it. Personally, I didn't think it was much to look at from my 'doggie' point of view – pretty much a bunch of rocky pillars with the roof missing.

We didn't stay there for long, however, as Mama had her eye on an antique shop beside the river across from the abbey. And guess what? They ended up buying a grandfather clock. Now that's all nice and fine, but not so great when it has to share the back seat of the car with you all the way back to London, let me tell you! Now some love spoons and a stool I could put up with, but a clock that was about as tall as Papa, now just a minute!

As you can imagine, my ride back to London was not the best. Why that clock rattled the whole way and kept me from napping. It also leaned against my bed and I was more than certain it was going to fall and make a 'doggie' pancake out of me, even though Papa promised me they had it tied in place. Of this I was not sure, so I kept one eye on that darn clock all the way home.

I arrived home 'crush-free,' thank goodness. But I had this feeling that my luck was beginning to turn in the opposite direction – away from 'good' if you know what I mean. That's because Mama was being very quiet.

"We've had such a good time the past month, traveling all over with Lucky," she whispered to Papa, thinking I was asleep – even with that old clock hanging out over my head. "I just hate to do this to him."

"We don't have much choice," Papa whispered back.

Oh, oh . . . I couldn't imagine what they were talking about but I had a feeling that my 'doggie' good times were about to come to an abrupt end.

CHAPTER 39
MOSSBANK FARM –
OH NO, NOT ANOTHER KENNEL

As I'm sure you must have noticed by now, we're real travelers, like of the 'Marco Polo' variety, as my papa always says. But unfortunately all of the family travels did not include a threesome, much to my 'doggie' dismay. That's because sometimes I was no where to be found in the vacation family photos. Now this didn't make me one little bit happy, but since I couldn't talk and defend myself, I ended up 'you know where' – in the kennel.

I started getting suspicious when Mama spent an entire day on the phone calling what I was sure were vets, or even worse – kennels. That's because she kept mentioning my name and asking lots of questions.

And low and behold I was right, because when the weekend arrived and we rented a car I knew something was different. I was certain I would not be going along on any trip, even though my *cama* was sitting by the front door ready to go. Mama's eyes were all teary, which meant I was in trouble. Finally Papa told me I was going to a place called *Mossbank Farm* in Hampshire, and that it was way out in the English countryside, very close to the famous Stonehenge. He told me I was going to like it there as Mama had really checked it out.

I don't want to go there, Papa. I've already been to Stonehenge. And just to try and pacify me, my parents delivered me to Mossbank the first time, just to make sure Mama's feelings about the place were correct.

"You're going to like Mossbank Farm," Mama assured me, her face still tear-stained.

Mama, I know better – we're not going to any farm; we're going to a kennel now, aren't we?

She looked the other way and dried her eyes.

And if I'm going to like it so much there, why the heck are you crying? And why aren't the two of you staying there, as well?

I just knew I was right – we were headed straight to a kennel. Why last time I went to a place with a fancy sounding name with lots of dogs in sight, I ended up at *Torenvalk* Kennel in Holland, and the time before that at *Camp Laguna*, which certainly turned out to be a kennel, and then there was *Canino Hacienda* in Mexico – yes, this old dog knows a thing or two about kennels, that's for sure. And he doesn't particularly care for them one 'doggie diddle.'

I had to admit it was a nice drive out to Mossbank – all 80 miles of it. Once we got off the Motorway past Heathrow Airport, it was one country road after the next, and they all wound through the always-green English countryside – this time of year with bright yellow canola oil flowers interlaced with the green. Of course Mama didn't talk much on the way and Papa mainly complained about how far it was.

"I can't believe we have to drive 160 miles round trip to deliver Lucky to the kennel," he said.

"Just relax," Mama told him. "They have a pick-up and delivery service into London twice a week."

"I'll bet that must cost a few Pounds," Papa answered, "with prices the way they are in this country."

"Actually it's a good deal considering the distance, but I didn't want to put Lucky through another boarding facility experience without first checking out the place ourselves."

See what I said – they were taking me to a kennel! Boarding facility was just another fancy name for it that she thought I wouldn't recognize.

After that I didn't sleep one little bit, wishing I could stop the car right then and there and turn it straight away back to London. Wrong! One thing I hadn't mastered was 'doggie driving.' For a moment I really wanted to bite both Mama and Papa, but no, I couldn't do that – I just loved them too much. Instead I looked out the window and did a little whimpering routine, which I knew would bring those old tears to Mama's eyes again. It did. And then I felt guilty, so I tried as hard as I could to take a nap, but I couldn't fall asleep. For by this time the road had become more and more 'countryside' and in England that meant winding. My 'sniffer' told me we were definitely in real 'animal' country. Why there were more sheep than I could count, and some horses and pheasants thrown in, as well. *If only we are going to a bed and breakfast for the weekend.* But I knew we weren't since Mama and Papa had no luggage. I was no dumb dog and it didn't take me long in my adopted life to figure out that any sign of luggage in our front hallways meant 'travel.' But I still hadn't figured out whether or not it meant travel 'with' or 'without' doggie in tow.

"Here's the road we need to turn on – Picket Piece," Mama said as we circled a flower-filled roundabout near Andover.

"This really is out in the country," Papa said. "It's not far from Winchester and Salisbury with their famous cathedrals."

"And ancient Stonehenge where the early English practiced pagan worship as early as 2800 B.C.," she added.

Oh, Mama, please say we're going to Stonehenge today. I well-remembered the giant circle of upright stones and those old towns with their great big churches. Maybe I had been wrong about going to a kennel – we were just off on another sight-seeing trip across the U.K. *Oh, don't get yourself all excited – you known 'doggie darn well' you're going to a kennel.*

Papa made the turn into Picket Piece. Now this was one small road, let me tell you – even in 'doggie' terms. It was about wide enough for a tractor, and I was certainly hoping we wouldn't be meeting up with any old semi-truck going in the opposite direction. Tall grass and trees grew on each side, along with some bright yellow canola flowers. As I was sniffing out this new environment, I picked up a scent I knew and loved very well – *conejos!* Well, at least I'd be able to do a little rabbit hunting out here in the countryside.

"Here's the gate Wendy told me about." Mama read the sign. "Mossbank Farm – you turn in here. It's really a pretty place, isn't it?"

Papa drove up a long gravel drive with trees on both sides and stopped in front of a garage where a big white van was parked. Little did I know I would be riding in the back of that van many times between Mossbank and London in the days ahead.

Across from the garage was a farmhouse, surrounded by a white picket fence. A lady with short blond curly hair with a great big smile on her face came out the door and toward our car.

Oh, oh, that's it for me – I hope she's not another one of those 'training ladies.'

Close behind her followed a man with shoulder length hair, wearing a plaid wool jacket.

371

"Must be Wendy and Howard," Mama said, appearing to like what she saw. "They look like real nice down-to-earth folks."

I don't care whether they're down to earth or not, Mama. I don't want to stay here.

"Hello there, glad you were able to find us," Wendy said in a Scottish accent.

Oh, oh, Papa ought to love this. And I won't be able to understand a word she says, so we'd best be getting back to London.

Mama and Papa said 'hello' and shook hands with Howard and Wendy.

As for me, why I tried to disappear into the back seat so they would forget to drop me off. But no such luck. Papa soon opened the rear door and they all peered down at me like I was going to be in a beauty contest or something; or like they were trying to pick out a good steak to barbecue.

"Why, this must be Lucky," Wendy said, stooping down to pat me. "Welcome to Mossbank Farm."

Howard did the same thing, and even gave me a good old scratch behind the ears, which I had to admit I quite enjoyed.

I'm not sure why, but I just couldn't keep myself from liking Howard and Wendy right from the start. They were kind people who loved animals – I was sure of it. And believe you me, we dogs have a real knack for recognizing nice people as soon as we hear their voice and get one sniff of them.

"Come on, Lucky," Wendy said. "Let's show you around the place." She took hold of my leash and led me from the car.

I had to follow. What else could I do? Besides, there were some dogs barking in the distance and I sort of wanted to find out who they were.

We followed Howard and Wendy up this path past a little stone house, which I soon learned was the kennel kitchen. It quickly earned a 'Lucky Seal of Approval' from me as it was where Wendy would make special food for us dogs.

Then we went through a gate, which Howard closed behind us.

Oh, oh, 'Maximum Security.'

I'm sure that must have made Mama and Papa very happy as they knew what an 'escape artist' I could be. Now I was certain there was no way I would be walking back to London to find them.

"This is our play area, Lucky," Wendy said. "All the dogs come out here to play and go potty four times a day, 8:00 a.m., 1:00 p.m., 5:00 p.m. and 9:00 in the evening."

Well, whoop de do! I thought, when I just wanted to get back in the car and return to London with Mama and Papa. But I knew this wouldn't be so, as Howard had my bed in tow.

"That's great," Mama said. "Lucky will love playing with the other dogs."

Oh yeah, Mama – what makes you think so? By this time I was a little put out with her, but still curious to meet my other kennel inmates.

It wasn't long until I did. For as soon as Wendy opened the next gate we were inside the kennel, which consisted of a long row of runs much like others I had frequented. *Oh no, not another cage.*

But these were nice runs and very clean indeed. Why, I could smell the cleaning liquid from outside the doors. And when we got inside, there was a red-haired girl wearing great big black rubber boots. She had a mop and a bucket of good smelling dog chow. I would later learn that she would also be spending lots of time with me.

She bent down and gave me one great big heavy-duty pat. "Hello, Lucky, I'm Sarah. Now don't you go pooping in your kennel, okay?"

I was just about to go and poop right there on the spot to show her a thing or two, but I didn't want to disappoint Mama and Papa, so I held it.

Then this great big golden retriever came rushing toward me and about scared the 'doggie' daylights right out of me, let me tell you.

"Bill, this is Lucky," Wendy said, grabbing him by the scruff of the neck. "Don't frighten poor Lucky."

She turned towards Mama and Papa. "This is our dog, Bill. He can be a bit overly-friendly."

I looked up at Wendy, at the same time keeping a close eye on Bill, hoping he wasn't going to take a big chunk out of my back leg. No, he was okay, just a bit on the friendly side. He gave me a good sniff and wagged his tail. I wagged my behind right back at him. And we both decided right away we would be friends.

"Here's your kennel, Lucky," Howard said, placing my bed inside. "And look, it has a door, so you can go outside and nap in the sun whenever you want."

Now this I liked – the fact I could go inside or out whenever I wanted. No, it wasn't Hyde Park – but it wasn't too bad. It was clean and at least I had my very own bed. Now if only Mama and Papa would stay here with me . . .

That wasn't to be. Before I knew it, Mama bent down, kissed my head, and told me "*Adios*." Papa gave me a good old pat and then off they went. Boy was I feeling bad, even if I was at what Mama and Papa called my new 'home away from home' – Mossbank Farm.

Let me tell you, I spent many lonely hours in my kennel. Oh, how I missed Mama and Papa. Often I would whine for them, but they never came. But Howard, Wendy and Sarah knew I missed my parents and somehow, when I was feeling most sad, one of them would just happen to come by my kennel and give me a special dog biscuit or a big hug or fluff my bed cushion. They knew just what to do to make this old pooch feel better.

I remember one night the first week I was there. It must have been quite late as all the other dogs were snoring away, but I was wide awake and whining for Mama and Papa. Well along came Howard. He came inside my kennel and bent down beside me.

"How are you Lucky? I couldn't sleep either. He looked kind of sad, too. I didn't know at the time that he was ill. All I knew was that it was good to have someone right there in my kennel with me at that moment and that he was giving me a great tummy rub. Why I even found myself dozing off.

Oh, thank you, Howard. That feels so good.

After that, either Howard or Wendy seemed to make a special effort to check on me quite late at night, usually with a nice little doggie treat. Why, I really came to love Wendy's red coat. She always had treats tucked into its pockets.

But finally I learned to pass the long nights and actually sleep quite well, especially after Howard cut a big piece of carpeting to put under my bed so I could get out and do my street dog stretches when I felt like it.

During the day, things were not too bad. Playtime at Mossbank was really fun. All of us dogs got to be together several times each day. At first Wendy had me go out with the 'big dogs,' but when she sensed their size frightened me, she changed me to the 'small dog' schedule. That way I could be the 'big doggie' on the block, which suited me just fine. For you see, from my days of getting attacked by other dogs on the streets of Mexico City, I still knew that size mattered – for the big guys always ended up with the bones, the little guys with lots of bites and no bones.

And it was in the dog play area that I met my good friends Rupert and Rusty, who were both from London, as well. Rupert was a King Charles and he also lived in Knightsbridge, like me. But he was what the British called 'posh,' – which I think means very rich. He was also very well-mannered, something so important in British society. Why he was even delivered to Mossbank in a chauffer-driven limousine. Can you imagine that? My papa would have loved paying that bill!

My friend, Rusty, was also a King Charles, but a Red and White King Charles. To tell you the truth, I didn't know those king dogs came in so many colors. I wondered what color of 'king' dog Queen Elizabeth had. Even though he was a king, Rusty was a bit more 'down to earth.' He was also from Knightsbridge and lived at a dress shop very near our house. Sometimes Mama and I used to run into him on our way to Hyde Park.

Oh, and I can't forget my best friend, Barney, a black and brown Jack Russell terrier. He was known as the 'local wise guy' at Mossbank Farm. He was one funny pooch, let me tell you. Why he even liked to wear sunglasses. Picture that – a sunglass-wearing canine.

Why Rusty, Rupert and Barnie were about the best little pals a doggie could ever have. We had so much fun together. We'd chase each other across the grass and then roll and bump into one other and have pretend dog

376

fights. We also liked to go to the fence on the property line and bark at the horses next door. And then there were our attempts at rabbit hunting, which were always a failure as those darn *conejos* were much faster on their feet than we canines. But we sure did have a 'jolly good doggie time' together.

Of course I had other 'doggie' friends at Mossbank, as I think they all thought I was pretty cool, being so well-traveled and all. They included Harry, who always ended up with muddy white paws, and Wooly and Tahta and Fritz, all regulars at Mossbank.

Yes, playtime at Mossbank was always special and I will never forget my buddies there. Mealtime was also pretty darn good. No, they didn't have pasta or Papa's Basmati rice, but they did have good home-cooked meat with rice and dried dog food tossed in. Was it ever tasty! Why I scarfed it up in about thirty seconds. And boy oh boy did it plump me up. In fact, my parents always said I looked chubby when Wendy delivered me back to our house in London. That meant lots of extra walks. Of course that suited me just fine.

One thing was certain. I always knew when I was going to go home from Mossbank. That's because Sarah would give me a bath. Then Wendy would pull the van out of the garage, which I could hear from my kennel. Before long they loaded my *cama* into the van, and I was all leashed up, smelling like a rose, and ready to go home. Why, I was so excited I couldn't sleep all the way back to London, which took two hours. And I couldn't sight-see either, as there were no windows in the back of the van. But I didn't mind; for all I did was think of being with Mama and Papa once more and of the great pasta dinner I would have that night.

As it turned out – and lucky for me indeed – Mossbank Farm was a good place. I was loved and cared for in the very best way. In fact, Howard and Wendy became my substitute parents and I grew to love them almost as much as Mama and Papa. I know they loved me. Why it wasn't very long until I was a member of their family indeed. In fact I spent lots of hours inside their little farm house, both Bill and myself, lying before the fire taking some very long and warm 'doggie' snoozes.

"There's always room for Lucky at Mossbank," Wendy used to tell my mama. And I believed her.

CHAPTER 40
THE 'OTHER SIDE' OF LONDON
FRIENDS, FAMILY,VETS, ETC.

Of course, I was always one very happy pooch indeed when I returned home to London and our house on Yeoman's Row, whether it was in Wendy's big white van or Mama and Papa's rental car. After all, isn't 'home where the doggie heart is?'

And believe it or not, we were not always on trips or out and about in London the three and one-half years we were there. We spent lots of hours in our cozy little house, listening to classical music and lounging before the fire. This was especially true during the dark winter months when it never seemed to get light or stop raining. Those were definitely 'fire nights' at home, let me tell you. Why Mama even had a bit of a time getting me to step outside in our back garden to do 'my thing,' let alone getting me to go out the front door for a long walk. But from my 'doggie' point of view, a walk was a hard thing to turn down, so eventually I'd surrender, and wait like the dutiful good doggie while she proceeded to put on my raincoat and boots.

Boy, I hated those boots! Why they were so slippery I thought for sure I was going to fall flat on my snout more than once. And they made my ankles ache when Mama cinched up that Velcro so tight like she was never going to take them off.

Anyway, we did do our winter walks, but they were much shorter than during the other seasons. The wind whipped right into our faces, and Mama tried to hold on tight to her umbrella. In fact, sometimes the wind was so strong I thought it was going to take Mama and me right up into the sky with our umbrella, just like that Mary

Poppins lady. Now can you imagine that – a flying dog? And a mama attached to an umbrella? Sounds more like a 'doggie' nightmare to me actually.

Of course, we didn't always spend all of our time at home alone. That's because we even had some family in London. They consisted of our niece, Sheila, and her husband Peter and their two daughters Lindsey and Sophie, both incidentally 'dog haters,' much to my 'doggie' dismay.

Why, the second they knocked on the door and I went rushing to greet them as loudly as I could, those two little girls screamed and screamed and screamed. I thought I was having a very bad hair day indeed, the way they looked at me. Why I wondered if they thought I looked like a monster or wild animal, not some *guapo* Mexico City street dog.

Even though their mama and papa told them that's how doggies say 'hello,' there was no convincing Lindsey and Sophie of this fact. And when I tried to reach out and lick them, why holy moly, you'd have thought I had rabies or something, the way they carried on.

So guess what happened to this old dog? Well every time they came over for dinner, I got sentenced to my bed in the kitchen, which was downstairs out of their sight; or, if I was really lucky, Papa would tie me on my leash on the stair landing so I could barely see them in the living room having a good old time without me. But the girls didn't care too much for me within eyesight, so it was back down to the kitchen again. Was I ever one unhappy pooch when this happened, which was every few weeks.

But guess what? I finally did win Lindsey and Sophie's hearts, but it was not in London. It was several years later when they came to visit us in California.

Against their wishes, Mama and Papa finally agreed to put me at Camp Laguna during their visit, much to my dismay. Imagine having to go to a kennel when your mama and papa and family were having all kinds of fun at home? I was not a happy puppy, let me tell you.

Anyway, I ended up staying at the kennel for one day. Then suddenly Lindsey decided she wanted me to come home, so, of course, her little sister agreed. Frankly, I think it's because Mama had bought our nieces some little plastic dogs that didn't happen to bark. Of course they had been playing with them since their arrival, so maybe they decided dogs were not so bad after all, and that I was no longer a 'barker.'

Anyway, their parents agreed I should come home, so Mama picked me up at the kennel after the girls had gone to bed. She later told me she couldn't sleep all night because she was afraid Lindsey would come downstairs in the morning, take one look at me and have what Mama called a 'hissy fit,' whatever that is. Anyway, I had a feeling I didn't want to be a witness to it, even though I was getting old and couldn't hear too well anymore.

Guess what happened? Early the next morning while I was still snoring, I thought I heard small footsteps on the stairs. I opened one eye very slowly and saw Lindsey and Sophie creeping ever so carefully down the steps. I quickly shut my eyes and pretended to be asleep. Well they came nearer my bed and when I didn't move, they both sat down a short distance away and held hands. Slowly I opened one eye and then the other. Then I wagged my tail. They both looked startled for a moment until I let out a very soft whine and wagged my tail again. Then lo and behold, Lindsey decided to touch me – just for a moment, of course. I stayed very still and let her pet me, so Sophie gave it a try. And believe it or not, by the time their parents came downstairs, the three of us were jolly good friends indeed. Boy, were their parents happy. They told me over and over again that I had performed a miracle, whatever that is. Why I can't imagine that me, a lowly little Mexico City Street dog, was able to do such a momentous thing just by being 'me.' But let me tell you, I was one happy pooch for the rest of the week and very proud of myself indeed, even though Lindsey about wore the fur off my back with all that petting. In fact, last I heard Lindsey was begging for a puppy for Christmas.

But back to London. In addition to family, we also had many friends. There were Jack and Barbara, and Peggy and Paul, Kathy and Dave, Esperanza and John, Emma and Sergio, Chris and Pattie and Faye and Kahan. Wow, I'm about out of breath! What a lot of fun parties we had. And they all liked me just fine – at least most of them – the ones that spoke Spanish, well, I wasn't quite so sure whether or not they liked me. But they didn't try to kick me, so I suppose they did. Even better still, none of our friends even cried when I barked my greeting to them at the front door. Thank goodness. Besides, Barbara and Peggy were real animal lovers and they always gave me lots of good pats and hugs, and believe you me, I was tossed a few bits under the dinner table when Mama and Papa weren't looking. Why Peggy even wanted to tend me when Mama and Papa went out of town, but my parents were worried she had too many stairs in her flat for me to go potty easily. Besides, dogs were not allowed and they didn't want her to get into trouble. So 'poof' went my chances to avoid kennel time. Sorry, Peggy.

Then there were the Watts, who owned our house and the one next door. Now they were very rich people who lived out in the country and only came to London on occasion. Papa said I was lucky because Mrs. Watts liked dogs – in translation that meant I could live with Mama and Papa in London. Boy, was I one happy pooch to learn this, as I was definitely not too excited to go out on the streets to live again. True, there were a lot of homeless in London – mainly people – and I for one did not want to become a part of that life again. Street walking was not for me.

Of course Mama was careful to put an extra rug under my bed so as not to soil the carpeting and she always kept my dishes in the kitchen with a plastic mat with a picture of a bone on it beneath them. She also cleaned up my poop in the garden just about as fast as it came out. In fact, sometimes I was afraid Mama was going to scoop me right up into the poop bag, as well.

"Let Lucky finish for heaven's sakes," Papa would tell her. "You're neurotic."

When it came to my poop, I had to agree. *Mama, don't worry, my poop's not going to go and disappear on you.*

Needless to say, when Mrs. Watts came to inspect our house with Dahrain, the estate agent, they were both very pleased indeed.

"What a fine little doggie tenant you are, Lucky," they always told me. "In fact, the best doggie tenant we have ever had."

Whatever that meant, it must have been something good, as it certainly brought a smile to Mama's face.

Of course, they didn't know I'd had a couple of accidents in the house when my parents left me for too long and I couldn't hold it any more, but my accidents, too, were cleaned up 'lickety-split' the second my mama got home.

One other thing the Watts were not exactly aware of – Papa sometimes had to give me a bath in their beautiful porcelain bathtub. Now my parents felt really bad about this, but they had no other choice when I went rolling around in fox doo-doo at Hyde Park, now did they? Of course, Mama cleaned it up like Mr. Clean just as soon as Papa finished bathing me, so I guess what our landlords didn't know didn't hurt them. After all, they wouldn't want a dirty pooch roaming round their house, now would they?

There were two other friends in London that I liked to visit – the homeless guys who lived in front of Valerie Patisserie. Why they would always ask Mama if they could pet me when we walked by and she'd always stop, even though they sometimes didn't smell so good. Their names were Edward and John and we used to take them extra food and clothes, especially during the winter months. I was glad we did this. I remembered too well how cold and lonely days on the street can be and I was glad we were helping them out.

Oh, yes, I nearly forgot about Auntie Chrissie. She was known in London as an 'Animal Aunt.' These were older ladies who tended animals in their flats when their owners were out of town. Mine was named Chrissie, but she preferred that we called her 'Auntie.' I would stay with her when my parents went on short trips because she was right in London. I enjoyed it there because there were usually several other pooches, and we dogs had the 'run of the flat.' We could also sleep any old place we pleased. I preferred her squashy old sofa and never used my own *cama* when I was there. Why my mama and papa would have had a fit. I think they were kind of suspicious, though, because when I got home, Papa said my bed never smelled like me. Of course, I had no idea who had borrowed it during my stay.

Auntie Chrissie was very kind to all us dogs. The only thing I didn't so much like about her was that she liked to sleep in late. It wasn't easy for an old doggie like me to hold my pee and poop far into the morning, let me tell you. But when she'd get up and take all five of us to Regent Park walking, her lack of early rising made up for it. We had a 'doggie' of a good time.

I had one other friend in London. It was Kevin, our veterinarian, as they say in the U.K. You see, in the U.K. doctors are called by 'Mr.' and vets – oh, excuse me, veterinarians, by their first name – no doctor titles for either one at all. The first time I went to the Brompton Veterinary Clinic I had been pulling at my ear. Mama found his name in the phone book and pronto, off the three of us went. Of course, Papa was worried that vets in London would be extremely expensive. Of course they were, but Kevin turned out to become a very important person to us indeed. He saved my life. But that's another story.

The first time we went to Kevin's office, I knew we were at an animal hospital. No fooling this doggie in that department, let me tell you. You know the smell – dogs, cats, antiseptic – the same old thing the world over, believe me. Of course the usual smiley girls dressed in their animal-print uniforms were always behind the counter. There were always photos of dogs and cats galore pasted on one of the walls, as well as a bowl of doggie treats somewhere in the vicinity, which, incidentally, I quickly came to recognize, no matter what veterinarian office I was in, and no matter what country.

As was normal, there were other dogs in the waiting room. This time there was a young black woman holding a tiny Yorkie in her lap. She looked real sad and I could tell Mama felt bad for her. Soon they went into the examination room and came out a few minutes later.

The woman was crying, holding tightly to her little dog. I wondered what was wrong and started to whine myself.

Then the receptionist went over to the lady and told her, "It should only be another fifteen minutes."

I've never seen such a sad look on Mama's face. "Oh, no," she whispered to Papa, "They must be putting her dog down. How sad."

I knew my mama was going to cry at any minute, but she didn't have time as we had been summoned to the examination room. I certainly hoped my experience inside would not be as sad as it was for that other little dog.

Of course, it was much the same as other animal examination rooms – shiny metal table and all.

"My name is Kevin," the vet said. "And this must be Lucky." He bent down and ruffled my fur, melting the old fear right out of me. Immediately I liked him and knew I could trust him. And I didn't think he would mind a bit if we called him a vet.

After he determined I had an ear infection, Kevin checked me out in other areas and told my parents I needed to have my teeth cleaned, but that they would have to put me out in order to so. What that meant I had no idea, but I don't think it had anything to do with putting me 'out' to go potty. Mama and Papa talked with him a little more and a date was set for the following month.

When we returned to the waiting room, the woman was still holding her little dog, but it looked like it was asleep. She was crying even harder. Why, I felt so bad for her and I just didn't know why.

My mama looked very sad and she moved beside the lady and put her hand on her shoulder. "I'm so sorry."

The woman looked up at her, her eyes overflowing with tears. "Thank you. He was old. But I loved him so much."

"I'm sure you did." Mama squeezed her shoulder. Then we walked quietly from the office.

"Too bad about that little dog," Papa said, bending down to pat me. "I dread the day we lose Lucky Boy."

Was I ever feeling bad about whatever they were talking about. Something just didn't seem right to me at all.

Mama really started to cry then. "Please . . . don't even talk about it . . ."

CHAPTER 41
NOT ALWAYS A BED OF ROSES

December was soon upon us. The Christmas season turned London into a fantasy of tiny white lights in all the windows and the lamp posts were topped with Christmas trees. Street vendors were selling roasted chestnuts, and everyone was snuggled up in their hats, scarves and coats, including 'little old me.' As usual, the windows at Harrod's were a rainbow of colors and animation, this third Christmas season for us in London featuring fairy tales and James Bond scenes, complete with Ferraris.

The three of us took many walks this time of year, just to share in the festiveness of the season. And one night it even snowed, strange for London.

"Lucky!" Mama called, waking me up from my usual morning sleepiness. "Look outside!"

I lifted my head ever so slightly and opened my eyes. Why Mama looked so excited that I decided I'd just better move my old bones over to the dining room window to see what was making her go *loco.*

Why I couldn't believe my 'doggie' eyes! Our entire garden was covered in white fluff.

"It's snow, Lucky. Remember you saw it in Utah when we went there for Christmas."

Oh, yes . . . I remembered that white, cold stuff. It sure did make my paws about freeze right off, let me tell you. But I think I liked it. It was lots of fun to roll around in and take in a bite or two.

So guess what we did? Mama piled on her parka, hat, gloves and boots. Then came my turn. She tugged my red, white and blue wooly sweater over my head, and afterward out came the good old boots – which she proceeded to push my paws into, even though I let out a little groan. Then we headed for Hyde Park.

"We can build a snowman, Lucky," she said. "Just like I did when I was a little girl."

Now I'd never heard of any man by the name of 'snow,' but I was a pretty friendly sort of pooch, so I decided I wouldn't mind meeting him.

"This is perfect, and so close to Christmas," Mama said, stomping along the snow-filled path beside Holy Trinity church on our way to the park. The church was beautiful, its eaves covered with snow, which sparkled in the morning sunlight.

I did my fair share of 'doggie' exploring, as well, and discovered a surprising tidbit of information – that my pee is actually yellow! Why I'd always thought it was just extra water pouring out of me, but when I let loose in the snow, it turned this bright yellow color. Surprise of all 'doggie' surprises!

When we reached Hyde Park, it was like half of London was there, especially those of the 'kid and dog' variety. I could tell right away we were about to have one heck of a 'doggie' good time. And we did.

I soon learned what a snowman was. That's because there were about a hundred or more of them all over the park – great big balls of snow stacked on top of one another with carrot noses and rocks for eyes. Why they were like no other kind of man I'd ever met. But they didn't talk or move or have any good people smells, so I quickly lost interest in them.

Personally, I found chasing after snowballs much more exciting, except they kept falling apart in my mouth whenever I picked them up. Actually, what I enjoyed most about the morning was rolling in the snow. Why I had a heck of a 'doggie' good time.

First, I'd race across the snow-covered grass as fast as I possibly could, Mama chasing behind me. Then I'd stop suddenly, so both of us would topple over and roll in the snow. Mama also made marks in the snow, which she called 'snow angels.' As for me, I just rolled around over and over again until I was all white, even my black nose.

"Oh, Lucky, you look so cute, all frosted like that," Mama laughed.

Of course, she took my picture – actually about a hundred of them.

"Papa will love this one," she said, when I buried my snout in the snow.

But all 'doggie' good times have to come to an end, so we headed back home. I have to admit that by this time, my feet were totally frozen and my boots had not done a darn bit of good. In fact, I was hoping this fact would convince Mama so I wouldn't have to wear them ever again. Wrong!

After taking off all our wet clothes, Mama lit the fire and we spent the remainder of the day beside it, Mama sipping hot chocolate and reading, and me enjoying one very cozy 'doggie' nap indeed.

In fact, there was only one disappointing thing about the entire day. After our afternoon nap when I looked out the window, the snow had totally disappeared. And to make it even worse, that was the only time we saw snow that year. Well, so much for snow in London.

Now the next day in my life wasn't nearly so neat. That's because I had an appointment at the vet's to have my teeth cleaned. Of course, I liked Kevin and visiting his office, but I wasn't so sure I would like to have him messing around in my mouth all that much. Like I had any choice in the matter, right? I suppose Mama and Papa thought I should have a bright and perfect smile –

like I did a lot of smiling, if you know what I mean. Smiling just doesn't happen to be a 'doggie' specialty. And I didn't plan on making any toothpaste commercials. But just the same, Mama convinced me that tooth cleaning was a good thing because if I didn't have it done, I would loose my teeth and then I wouldn't be able to eat as I wouldn't be able to chew my food. Now 'eating information' I could totally understand, so off we went to Brompton Veterinary Clinic.

"Like I told you," Kevin explained to us. "We'll have to put Lucky to sleep so that we can work on him."

Mama nodded. "Yes, I understand, but I do worry about putting Lucky under as he's quite old."

"He'll do fine. Don't worry," he said. "Why don't you come back late this afternoon and Lucky will be here waiting for you with very clean teeth indeed."

Boy, I hated to see my Mama leave me there, especially when I saw all these cutting tools and a shot-giving needle on the side of Kevin's examination table. I let out a little whine, just hoping Mama would stay and, for a moment, she hesitated. I certainly noticed she was not wearing one of her 'smiley' faces, so I was seriously wondering what I was in for.

In fact, she ran her hand slowly down my back, bent over me, and gave me a kiss on the head. "*Adios,* Lucky, I'll be back for you soon. Be brave."

Then she walked right out the door and boy was I one upset pooch, my mama abandoning me like that to a doctor with a shot needle in his hand! I wasn't so sure I could forgive her for that one. But I didn't have much time to think about it since Kevin had proceeded to stick me with his old needle, and I felt my eyes closing real fast-like.

When I woke up, my mouth hurt. Why, it felt like someone had taken an axe to it, let me tell you. But I quickly forgot my pain when I heard Mama and Papa's voices outside the operating room.

"Lucky's still quite drowsy. You'll need to take him home in a taxi," Kevin said. I could tell there was something more he wanted to say, but didn't seem to quite know how to say it.

"Of course," Papa said. "No problem."

Mama didn't say anything, but I could tell she was not herself. She just patted me and looked at Kevin. "How did it go?"

"Well, the cleaning went fine. Lucky's teeth are in fairly good shape considering he's had distemper and all but . . ."

He hesitated and both Mama and Papa looked concerned.

"What's wrong?" Papa asked.

"Actually, I don't think anything is wrong, but we did find three small masses inside Lucky's mouth during the cleaning. One was on his gum next to a tooth and two others were on his lip."

Why I thought Mama was going to faint right then and there, and Papa looked pretty white, as well.

"I think they were probably benign growths, but we cut them out and will send them to the lab for a biopsy, just to make sure. It will take about five days. Don't worry, Lucky will be fine."

Now even I didn't have such a good feeling by the looks of Mama, Papa and Kevin, but I was still dizzy from the stuff they put me to sleep with, so I just slouched down to the floor and fell asleep. I knew that Mama had stooped down beside me because I could feel her massaging my neck. I also heard her sniffling.

"Thank you, Kevin," Papa said. "We'll wait for your call. Hopefully it will be back soon, as we're scheduled to depart for America in four days to spend Christmas. In fact, we're going to be moving back to California soon."

"I'll see if I can rush it," Kevin said. "And please . . . don't worry."

Mama and Papa carried me outside and Papa hailed a taxi. Since I looked all sleepy, and we were right in the front of the veterinary office, the first taxi stopped – no questions asked.

The next morning, I was off to Mossbank Farm for a couple of days as Mama and Papa had to go to Amsterdam for a company Christmas function. Mama didn't want to go, but Papa convinced her I was fine, although I got the feeling he really didn't think I was. But just to be nice to Papa, she finally decided to go along.

"Besides, Lucky's in good hands at Mossbank, you know that, and there's nothing we can do until Kevin receives the biopsy report."

"I suppose you're right, but still I hate leaving him . . . for some reason, I'm really worried."

Papa squeezed Mama's hand. "Just don't you forget it. Our Lucky is a fighter."

"I know he is."

"And he's always been very healthy."

"Yes, you're right."

Mama and Papa returned two days later very late in the evening and rented a car to pick me up at Mossbank Farm. As usual, I was very happy to see them. I didn't know I'd be coming back in three more days and that it would be for three weeks and that we wouldn't be spending Christmas together.

What a bummer.

When we entered our house, the telephone answering machine was beeping. Mama and Papa looked at each other.

"You'd better get it," Mama said. "I'm too nervous."

Papa went over and picked up the phone. There were three messages, all from Kevin.

"Hello, this is Kevin at Brompton Veterinary Clinic. I need to speak with you regarding Lucky's pathology results," he said.

Mama and Papa both looked pale and became very quiet.

The second message was from Kevin again. "This is Kevin. I am hoping that you have not departed for America as yet. I need to speak with you regarding Lucky."

Mama and Papa looked even more frightened.

They played the third message, which had come in only an hour before. "This is Kevin at Brompton Veterinary Clinic. It is urgent that I speak with you about Lucky's laboratory results. Please call me right away."

Of course by now Mama was crying really hard and Papa was holding her. "Don't worry, everything will be okay. We can't call Kevin until morning as he's closed by now, but I'll leave a message on his answering machine."

Papa dialed his number while Mama sat beside me on the floor. "It's okay, Lucky. You're going to be just fine. You have to be."

Mama held me so tight that it really hurt, but I knew she needed to hold me tight, so I didn't try to pull away. Whatever it was that was upsetting her, I knew it must be darn serious.

After Papa left a message for Kevin, we sat in the living room.

By this time Mama was really upset. Papa even looked like he was going to cry. Why I'd never seen him look like that before. When the telephone rang a short time later, they both jumped and Papa ran to answer it.

"Hello," he said, putting the phone on the speaker mode so Mama and I could hear.

"Oh, thank goodness I was able to reach you," Kevin said, on the other end of the line. "I thought you had left for America."

"No, we're still here for three more days. You said you needed to talk to us about Lucky's lab results."

"Yes, I do. I'm afraid I have bad news for you," Kevin said. "The pathology report showed melanosarcoma – cancer . . . If I may, let me read the report to you: *Three small masses were found in Lucky's mouth – one on the gum next to the tooth, two other separate masses growing close to each other on the lip. Both of these masses are probably part of a melanosarcoma/malignant melanoma. His prognosis is guarded to poor.*"

Mama started to sob and Papa's eyes filled with tears and his voice choked up.

"I'm so very sorry," Kevin said, his voice cracking.

"Oh, my god . . ." Papa said, "It's just so hard to believe . . . Lucky has always been such a healthy dog."

"I know," Kevin said. "But these things happen. But, please don't give up. We're going to hope for a miracle." His voice sounded strained and sad. Mama and Papa both seemed to pick up on that.

In fact, by this time my poor Mama was in total hysteria. "Please, let me talk to Kevin," she said. "There must be something . . ."

Papa handed her the phone.

Kevin explained the same thing over again. "I'm so very sorry. I know how you love Lucky."

"Oh . . . . yes . . . . we do. He's like a child to us. Isn't there something you can do to help him? Anything at all?" Mama sobbed.

"I know it's risky at his age, but I'd like to perform some more radical surgery and remove more tissue. There's a slight chance we can get all the cancerous cells. But the surgery has to be performed right away."

"Oh, thank you, Kevin, we'll take any chance to save Lucky's life," Mama said, trying to control her sobs.

"Then why don't you bring him into the office first thing tomorrow morning and I'll do my best. I'm so glad you're still in London. I've been beside myself all day long, worrying about Lucky."

"You're a good man," Mama choked. "I really think you can save our Lucky."

The next morning it was off to the surgery room again for me, much to my 'doggie' dismay. But I sensed something was terribly wrong, and that I had better cooperate fully. I'd even overheard Mama and Papa talking and crying way into the night, so I crept up to the landing outside their bedroom and tried to sleep, but I couldn't.

"I just can't believe this is happening to our Lucky," Mama sobbed. "He's always been such a healthy little dog and he's survived so much – distemper, pneumonia, living on the street for so long. We just can't lose him now."

"You have to realize we might."

"No, please don't say that. I love that little dog more than I can ever say."

Papa wrapped his arm around her. "I know you do, believe me, so do I, but we have to be realistic. I was just thinking . . . You know we're going to be moving back home the end of February and if Lucky's really sick he won't be able to travel by then, so maybe we should take him back with us this trip and he can stay with Matthew until we return."

"I just don't know what to do! I can't stand the thought of him dying or having to leave him here because he's too weak to travel. I'll never desert Lucky."

"I know you wouldn't. So maybe we should take him to California now while he's feeling okay. At least he'll make it back home."

By this time Mama was crying so hard that they didn't even hear the door creak when I pushed it open with my snout. I went inside and lay by their bed. I didn't know what else to do. Boy, was I one frightened pooch. I didn't know what was about to happen to me, but I knew it wasn't one bit good. Yet somehow lying there right next to them made me feel better.

"I think we should talk to Kevin and see what he thinks. He sounded like Lucky should have the surgery immediately if he is to have any chance at all," Mama said, crying so hard she could barely speak.

"I'm with you. Somehow in my gut I have a feeling that Lucky's going to make it."

"We can't give up on him. We just can't," Mama cried.

"Definitely not. He's our boy. Come on, let's go downstairs and make him some pasta."

"Good idea. I think it will make all three of us feel better."

Why Mama almost stepped on me, and about squashed me flat as a piece of pasta when she jumped out of the bed so quickly.

She bent down, gave me the biggest hug ever. "Oh, Lucky, you're always there for us, aren't you? And you always will be."

The next morning this old doggie was 'under' Kevin's scalpel again, and this time he took off half my lower lip and a good big chunk from my mouth. And when I awoke from the surgery, I had one heck of a sore mouth, let me tell you. I was also wearing what they called an Elizabethan collar, which was this big white plastic thing that stuck out about a foot and wrapped right around my neck like a big cup. And here I had always thought wearing my raincoat was bad. I promised myself to never complain about it again. Why with this thing, every time I moved it banged into something, so that I could barely go any place at all.

But I got used to it, as I did all things in life. Before I knew it, my Elizabethan collar had become part of my new attire and Mama told me I looked like a long-ago queen named 'Elizabeth.' Why I even learned that a dog could take a nap wearing it quite well indeed. All I did was hang my head over the side of my bed, Elizabethan collar and all.

"It's okay, Lucky, the collar's not so bad," Mama would tell me. "It's so you can't claw out all your stitches."

Yeah, right, Mama. Would you like to try it out for a while?

Of course my mouth was so sore that I could barely eat the first few days, but Mama made me lots of soft foods like overcooked rice and pasta and even garlic mashed potatoes dripping with butter, which I totally loved. But let me tell you, eating it with that collar on required quite the feat as my mouth barely hung out the end of it.

Of course with Mama and Papa's coaching and tender loving care, I soon started to feel much better. *Hmm . . . maybe being sick wasn't quite as bad as I'd imagined. Mama and Papa sure are spoiling me.*

At the same time, Mama and Papa were still very worried, as the second lab results had not yet arrived. Each day they called Kevin's office and each day they were told they were still waiting for them. I could tell this result was one they were very anxious to get, because each time the phone rang, one of them raced for it.

Even though Mama and Papa had postponed their trip by several days, it soon became necessary for them to leave for America. Howard and Wendy had generously agreed to become my nurses. Howard assured them that having had cancer himself, he knew just how to take care of me and that I would be residing right inside their house the entire time. Of course, my mama was still very reluctant to leave, but Papa assured her I was in great hands and that she needed to go back and prepare our house for our move back to California – Lucky included. Of course that brought a quick smile to her now always tear-stained face.

Why my poor mama was so upset, that every time she talked to anyone on the phone – especially her close friends, or Howard and Wendy – and my name was mentioned, why she'd burst into tears. Let me tell you, that really had this old dog worried.

Of course I hated to see Mama and Papa leave, and seriously wondered if I would ever see them again. I know it was very hard on my parents, as well, but I did manage to have a "Happy Christmas" as they say in the U.K. That's because I celebrated it with Howard and Wendy and their dog, Bill. Of course, Mama had left lots of little gifts for all of us to open, and fortunately none of mine included a new yellow raincoat.

Mama and Papa later told me they arrived home in California just two days before Christmas and that they received their Christmas gift early.

"At four o'clock in the morning our cell phone rang," Papa said. "Of course we both raced for it."

It was Kevin, so they didn't care what time it was. It didn't matter a 'doggie diddly' that he had forgotten about the greater time difference between London and the west coast of the United States. Now four a.m. was really early in my particular 'doggie' terms, as I've always loved to sleep in, but I know my parents would have answered that call at any time, day or night.

"It's Kevin," he said. "I have some very good news for you indeed. It looks as if Lucky is going home to America with you when you depart in February."

Mama and Papa both gasped and held their breath.

"He's going to be okay. The pathology report came back negative for cancer. I was able to get all of it. I'm so glad for the three of you. Let me read you the lab report. *None of the eight blocks taken from the submitted tissue show any neoplastic tissue. There are small areas of epidermal hyperplasia, probably a response to the previous surgery or to the mass. Complete removal of the mass should improve the prognosis, although Lucky needs to be regularly checked for regrowths.*"

Mama and Papa both started to cry. But this time they were happy tears.

"Kevin, thank you so much," they both echoed. "You are one wonderful vet! You couldn't have given us a better Christmas gift than our Lucky Boy."

"Happy Christmas!" they both said, holding each other.

And once again I proved myself to be one lucky dog.

CHAPTER 42
HOMEWARD BOUND – AGAIN

Was I ever happy to see Mama and Papa when they returned after Christmas – almost as much as I was to get rid of that darn Elizabethan collar, which I had to wear until Wendy's vet took my stitches out. I knew my parents were about to arrive, the second Sarah took me to their dog shower. Believe you me, I was smelling pretty bad after almost a month in the kennel, even though I had spent the first part of it right in Howard and Wendy's house while they were nursing me back to health. I never did figure out what it was that I had, but I was certainly glad I didn't have it any more, let me tell you. Why I was feeling just 'doggie' peachy keen.

"Lucky! Lucky!" I heard Mama crying from out in the yard. "We're back."

It's about time . . . But I couldn't stay mad at Mama for long, so I answered her just as loudly as I could. Of course that made all the other dogs in the kennel start to bark, and we had a very merry welcoming dog chorus indeed, all for the benefit of my mama and papa.

"How ya doing Old Boy?" Papa said, ruffling the fur on my back. "You look great!"

Of course, I look great, Papa. I'm always great when I get to go home.

Mama got all teary-eyed when she saw me, and had a hard time letting go of me. But to tell you the truth, I didn't mind one little 'doggie' bit as I was more than happy to stay right where I was, curled there in her arms.

"We've missed you so much, Lucky," Mama said. "And you look so good. Howard and Wendy took such good care of you."

She turned to them. "Thank you so much. I don't know what we would have done without you these past four years, especially this time, when Lucky was so sick."

"We were happy to help out," Wendy said. "We love Lucky. You know that."

"Yes, and we were so worried about him," Howard said. "But we knew this old lad would make it. He's a tough one, that he is."

During their talk, Mama and Papa still kept petting me and I just sat there on my haunches in the cold afternoon air and soaked up every bit of their love, even though my old bottom was about frozen right off.

"There's something else we need to tell you," Papa said.

Both Howard and Wendy looked very nervous, as if Papa was going to tell them I was going to drop dead at any second.

"What? What is it?" Wendy asked. "Is Lucky really okay?"

"Yes, Lucky's fine. It's something else."

They both looked puzzled.

"We're going to be moving back to America – the end of February, to be exact," Papa said.

"Oh . . . no . . . that means we won't get to tend Lucky any more," Howard said, his smile fading. "We love him like our own."

"We know you do," Mama said. "And I'm sure Lucky is going to miss you terribly, too. You'll just have to come and visit us in California."

"We've never been to America. Maybe we will some day."

"We'd all love that," Papa said. "Especially Lucky."

Two hours later, we returned to our somewhat peaceful life on Yeoman's Row. But by the time Valentine's Day and mid-February rolled around, we were on the 'go' again. And it wasn't a short 'go' either, like in 'trip;' it was a long 'go' – way back to California, USA. Now mind you, going home sounded good to all three of us. We missed our California friends and family, and to tell you the truth we were really quite tired of being waterlogged. Of course I was hoping against all 'doggie' hope that my little yellow raincoat wouldn't be accompanying me. But was I ever wrong! Mama told me she just couldn't part with it because of all the special memories it brought to her about our time in Europe.

Hey, Mama, you weren't the one wearing it all the time, just think of that. You weren't the one who was totally embarrassed right out of his 'doggie' pelt, let me tell you.

Oh well, on this subject it didn't matter one 'doggie' diddle – the raincoat would accompany us home. There was one thing good about this fact, however – I wouldn't have to wear it. That's because it "never rains in Southern California," just like the old song says. Wrong. It does rain sometimes, but when it does, we just jump in our car and drive, and the rain doesn't bother us one little bit. So I just figured out that Mama probably wanted to put my raincoat in a picture frame and hang it on the wall so she could look at it every day and think of all those special memories of our time 'continent' traipsing all over Europe. Hopefully she would not be hanging it by the front door as a reminder that maybe she should put it on 'little old me.'

Of course, moving meant that the movers would be coming again, much to my 'doggie' dismay. But this time they were not Mexican, so that meant they would most likely not be into kicking. They consisted of three British blokes who spoke English with a Cockney accent so thick, even Mama had a hard time understanding them. But they were nice chaps and gave me plenty of their tea cookies, much to what would have been my mama's dismay – that's if she had seen them sharing with me.

For you see, my mama didn't want me having any cookies, except of the 'dog biscuit' variety, but I liked the English shortbread cookies just fine, and I was right there begging at the moving men's tea time.

It took them only one day to pack our belongings as most of our things were already in the U.S. in storage. And needless to say, I kept a very close eye on my *cama*, jumping into it every time any one of those movers went anywhere near it.

"Lucky, they're going to pack you right with your bed if you don't watch out," Mama told me. "I don't think you'd like to spend six weeks traveling across the Atlantic Ocean in a freighter, now would you?"

You're darn right, I wouldn't, Mama. I don't even like the thought of spending another long flight in the airplane, believe you me. I'm not there sipping champagne and eating caviar like you two – nor lounging in a reclining seat with a puffy pillow.

But it turned out the movers didn't pack all of my *cama*, only the outside of it, so I was left with my cushion in its usual place on our slanted dining room floor. Now staying on that cushion without the sides of my bed was a real 'doggie' feat in the middle of the night, let me tell you. Each time I rolled off, it woke me right up, so I had to jump back on it and try not to move at all. Even if I snored a little, off I went onto the floor.

It got to the point that I was almost looking forward to having the cushion in my traveling kennel so that at least I could spend the night in one place.

Well the next day the movers showed up again, this time with a great big truck that filled up the entire width of Yeoman's Row. Now some of the neighbors didn't go around with smiley faces at all that day since they couldn't get their cars out, but I wagged my tail at them just the same. One thing I knew for sure, I was going to miss our little street and all the wonderful times we had in London. But I wasn't enjoying the thought of moving or not moving at the moment because my tummy really hurt. I had a feeling that it had something to do with all those cookies the movers had been giving me. *And then again, it could have something to do with those two juicy frozen beetles I ate in the garden several hours ago.*

It only took a couple of hours to get the stuff that we would be taking back to America loaded. We gave some of our appliances to the movers, who refused our electric alarm clocks because they said that expats moving back to America gave them electric clocks every single day since they were 220 volt, whatever that means, and the movers said they didn't know what they were going to do with all those clocks. It didn't matter anyway, as the Notting Hill Charity truck came right after the movers left to collect the rest of our belongings. Believe you me, this pooch was keeping a good old 'doggie' eye on his cushion, as it was about the last thing left in the house except for my two dishes, Mama and Papa's suitcases and several bags of coats, hats, gloves and umbrellas.

"We won't be needing these any more," Mama smiled. "Let's go take them to Edward and John, our homeless friends. I think they could use most of them. Besides, I'd like to take a final walk in Hyde Park."

Now Mama didn't need to ask me twice about that one, as it was my favorite place to walk in the whole entire world, even though my stomach still didn't feel so good. It was the one place I could really be free since my days on the streets of Mexico City, and I would never forget our great times there.

I have to admit that even though we were excited to go home, it was sad walking beneath the barren trees that cold February afternoon for the final time. The park was almost empty, so Mama let me off my leash for a last good run through the park.

"Now don't you go and find yourself any fox droppings," Mama warned me. "Papa would ring both our necks and then we wouldn't be able to go home to California, now would we?"

Don't worry, Mama, I just want to get in a little run.

And run I did. Why my ears flew out behind me so far that for a moment, I thought I was going to fly, just like Peter Pan. I peed on every possible tree that I could find, and even did a little barking at the ducks which were floating on the Serpentine. I even forgot I wasn't feeling good.

My mama chased after me as fast as she could and when she started to cough with her asthma, I felt sorry for her and slowed down. Suddenly I realized that my stomach still hurt and I was sure I was about to lose my lunch. During my 'near vomiting' dilemma, Mama caught up with me and grabbed my leash real quick-like before I could properly get rid of it whatever was in my stomach.

We shared the rest of our walk together, passing through Kensington Gardens, then by Kensington Palace and on to the Princess Diana Memorial. Finally we walked clear around the Serpentine again to bid farewell to Peter Pan, where Mama rubbed the bronze statue for the very last time. It was all kind of sad, and I was certain that at any moment she was going to start crying. In fact, she did sniffle a little.

"We've had so many good times here, Lucky. I will never forget them."

I knew I wouldn't either, so I snuggled up to Mama real close and gave her a quick kiss. But suddenly I felt my lunch coming up in my throat and I spit it out real fast-like. Why it almost went all over my mama and her brand new red coat. And it was filled with little black pieces of 'you know what.'

"Lucky, what's wrong with you? You've eaten something black!"

Of course since I couldn't talk, I couldn't tell her about the hundred or so cookies that I had been eating the past two days and those two delicious beetles, so I'm sure she thought I was dying again from cancer.

"You're never sick like that! I just can't imagine what you've been eating?"

Of course not, Mama. I looked up at her with sad brown eyes. I really wasn't feeling good at all.

"I think we should call the vet."

Oh, no, I don't think so, Mama.

But as usual, I had no vote on the matter.

"Why don't you watch Lucky overnight and see if he vomits again. And make sure you keep him hydrated with plenty of water," Kevin told her.

Unfortunately, I did vomit – eight more times, in fact, and Mama and Papa were really two upset humans, let me tell you.

"Look, it's white and puffy! Lucky must have pneumonia!" Mama said. "And his nose is hot – he has a fever."

Personally I don't think I had any fever, even though I still didn't feel so good. In fact, I felt like I had a pile of rocks in my belly, even though there was nothing left there.

Papa examined me carefully, when I rolled over on my back. "Lucky's stomach is very hard."

"Oh, my god, what if he's got a big tumor that's obstructing his bowels and causing him to throw-up," Mama said, starting to cry.

Papa looked at her hard. "Don't get so charged up – Lucky will be just fine. Remember, he's a survivor, right?"

Mama looked relieved. "That's right. Yes he is."

At that, she bent down and gave me a big kiss on the head. "You're going to be just fine Sweet Pea."

Still my mama stayed up with me all that night, dressed in her robe, curled in a ball beside my bed. I have to admit I kind of liked this, having her so close and cuddly. Except for the drowning part. That's because every few minutes she made me drink water from her hand, and I was sure I was going to die because she was going to drown me. When I spit up some yellow stuff a couple of times, why I thought she would go crazy. She even went in and woke up Papa.

Early the next morning, we were off to Kevin's office *muy pronto*, let me tell you, even though I was actually feeling much better. But there was no convincing my mama of that.

Well after five hundred Pounds of testing – one thousand dollars – according to Papa's calculations, they found nothing wrong.

"Thank goodness," Mama said, about squeezing the life right out of me.

"I think it must have been something that Lucky ate," Kevin said.

"I hope he enjoyed it," I heard Papa say, under his breath, giving me this kind of dirty look, like I could do something about what I had done.

"But the tests did discover something," Kevin continued.

Both Mama and Papa turned pale as Kevin put the x-rays up on the lighted screen in the examination room. I think they still remembered the last thing Kevin had discovered.

He pointed out my body parts on the x-ray and said they all looked fine, so Mama and Papa both looked a bit more relaxed. Personally I didn't get why they were huddled together looking at this black and white thing on the wall in the shape of a dog – that dog being me.

"Lucky definitely does not have pneumonia," Kevin said. "His lungs are clear. But there is one thing that bothers me." He pointed to a place on the x-ray just below my right lung at a small oblong object. "It looks like a bullet to me."

Mama and Papa both looked totally shocked. I wasn't shocked one little bit for I knew that Kevin was right.

"A bullet?" Papa said. "Are you saying that Lucky was shot? He hasn't had any wound that we know of. And where on earth could he have been shot?"

Mama nodded in agreement.

"Well, I checked him over thoroughly and there's only a small scar beneath his fur where a bullet could have entered a long time ago. Anyway, it's not giving him any problems, so I think we should leave it right where it is. He was very lucky it didn't puncture his lung."

Here I was living up to my name once more. And believe you me, I knew exactly where that bullet had come from. And it wasn't from out in the English countryside as if I'd stepped into the middle of a fox hunt or something. It was a little souvenir from Mexico.

* * * *

I remembered the day it happened quite well. I was on my head and forepaws scavenging through the garbage containers at the Japanese restaurant near The Gully. Suddenly, I heard this loud bang and felt something hit me with a stinging sensation, which soon turned into a sharp pain.

Of course I yelped real loud, scrambled out of the bin and ran just as fast as my scrawny legs could carry me. By this time I was becoming very weak, so I stopped, turned, and looked at my side. It was very red indeed. But I knew I couldn't stop running until I made it back to my dug-out hole in The Gully.

When I got there, I collapsed. I was bleeding pretty bad by then, but I just licked and licked at the wound in my side until the bleeding finally stopped an hour or so later.

I didn't move from my spot for several days. Why, I was so weak and in so much pain that I thought I was going to die. But I didn't. Somehow I recovered. But let me tell you, I didn't go out scavenging at the Japanese restaurant ever again. For I wasn't about to test my luck one tiny bit more.

When I finished with my memory and wishing I could somehow explain 'the bullet mystery' to Mama and Papa, they were still talking to Kevin. They seemed in a much better mood.

"Then you're sure Lucky will be all right?" Mama said.

"I'm sure he will be if he's been carrying around that buckshot this long," Papa said. "We'll just call you a 'cow dog' Lucky – right out of the 'Old West.'"

Kevin laughed. "Yes, I think you're correct about leaving the bullet in place. It would be much safer to leave it where it is than to try and remove it after this long. I've seen several dogs that have been hit during fox hunts and some of them still have their bullets to prove it."

"Then Lucky will keep his too," Mama and Papa both agreed.

By this time my mama was hugging me real hard. "Oh, Lucky, you really are one lucky dog."

On this point, I had to agree.

The next morning there was a smaller van in front of our house – Howard and Wendy's van. Boy was I ever surprised. It really scared the 'doggie' heck out of me.

Does this mean I'm not going to go back to California with Mama and Papa? It's not that I don't love Howard and Wendy, but I want to go home . . .

Papa seemed to read my mind. "Don't worry, Old Boy," Papa said. "You're going to be spending a couple of days at Mossbank Farm while Mama and I finish things up in London. We have to stay at a hotel and they don't allow dogs. We'll pick you up on our way to the airport."

Whew! Did I ever let out a 'doggie' sigh of relief. Since I wasn't going to be staying at Mossbank forever as I had feared, I figured it would be nice to spend a few farewell days with Howard and Wendy, and, of course, Sarah and Bill. I owed them that much.

Howard loaded me into my kennel in the van. "Come on, Lucky, climb in."

Of course, I didn't want to, but I figured out I might as well get into practice as I had the feeling I would be spending lots of hours in my traveling kennel the next few days.

I whined a goodbye to Mama and Papa, knowing that it was the last time I would see the two of them standing together in front of our Mary Poppin's house on Yeoman's Row.

* * * *

Three days later, Mama and Papa came with a driver in a great big van to pick me up. I had said my 'goodbyes' to Wendy an hour earlier and she had cried and cried.

"I just can't say goodbye to you, my Lucky Lad. I'm going to go out for a while so I don't have to see you leave us." She bent beside me and gave me about the biggest 'doggie' hug I had ever received.

"Lucky, are you ready for the big jet ride?" Papa asked me, when Bill and I ran up to greet them. Papa patted us both on the head. "Sorry, Bill, you don't get to come along." He wagged his tail at Papa pleadingly.

Howard brought out my kennel and put it into the back of the van, which was already loaded with lots of luggage. "I cut several pieces of carpet to put under his cushion so that Lucky will be comfortable on the long plane trip," he said.

We all saw the tears in Howard's eyes and we felt so sad. Yes . . . we were going to miss these kind people in our lives, that was certain.

Howard gave me a great big hug and then Mama hugged Howard.

"Thank you so much for what you have done for us," she said. "We really appreciate you and Wendy so much."

"Yes, we sure do," Papa agreed, shaking hands with Howard and patting him on the back.

"I'm so sorry that Wendy is not here to tell you 'farewell,' but she just . . ." His voice cracked. "She just couldn't say goodbye to the three of you."

"We understand," Mama said. "But please, give her our love. And don't forget, we'd really like for you to come to America and visit us."

As we pulled from the drive at Mossbank Farm, I sat on my hind legs and stared out the window and watched Howard wave. Bill stood right beside him. I would miss them all. For I loved them as only a pooch can.

Before I knew it, we were back at Heathrow Airport for the last time. At first I thought maybe I had gotten lucky since Mama and Papa hadn't made me get in my kennel. *Maybe I'm going to get to ride with them in the top of the plane this time. Now that would be something, wouldn't it?*

No such luck. For when we reached the front of the line, Papa made me get into my kennel.

"Come on, Lucky, in you go." He pushed me on the rear as I stood stubbornly before it, my four legs spread apart. But Papa kept pushing, and in I popped, and down went the kennel door like a streak of lightning. "Sorry, Old Boy, won't be for long. It only takes a little over an hour to get to Paris."

Paris? I thought we were going to America.

I think Mama knew I looked confused, so she explained. "We have to stay in Paris overnight since Air France won't let you fly for too many hours at once, and since the trip home tomorrow is another eleven, they think you need a break in between."

I agree, Mama, fifteen hours in this old kennel? Holy moley, what a drag that's going to be.

"Guess it's a good thing that the French love their animals so much," Papa added.

No kidding, Papa.

But the flight to Paris wasn't too bad at all. When I woke up from a nice little afternoon snooze, we were there and it wasn't long until I was put on the conveyor belt, even before the rest of the luggage was loaded. That's because I was a very special piece of luggage indeed.

As usual, Mama and Papa were at the baggage area to greet me. I wasn't one bit surprised, as I had gotten used to this routine by now. What did surprise me was that we were going to spend the night in the Paris airport at the Sheraton Hotel.

Now this was pretty neat as it was a very nice hotel indeed, except that they spoke French there and I didn't understand a thing they said.

"*Bonjour,*" the girl at the reception desk said. It sounded kind of like 'bone' to me, so I perked right up. But then she realized we were not French, so she started to speak English.

"*Pardon . . .*" Mama tried to speak French, but where does the 'doggie' go *le toilette*?

The girl smiled. "In the parking gaaaa-a-ragee," she said in a heavy French accent. "It is thee only place."

So that's the direction we proceeded in before heading to our room on the tenth floor.

"That garage ought to smell nice," Papa said. "I hope they don't have too many dog guests at this hotel."

Mama laughed. "I'm sure they keep it clean. Besides, I brought some of Lucky's pink 'poopie' clean- up bags with me," she said, digging into her pocket.

Believe you me, it didn't take me long to do my deed and put Mama's bag to good use. I wanted to get out of that place fast as I could. It was cold and kind of dark in that parking garage and it reminded me of my days on the street. Besides, I was hungry and wondered what I was going to get for dinner. I had a sneaking suspicion it was going to be Cup of Soup.

I was right. The second we entered our room, which looked to have a very giant cushy bed indeed, which I was sure that I was not to have the pleasure to sleep on, Papa got to work heating up some water in the in-room teapot.

Mama took my bowl out of a suitcase and proceeded to crumble up some bread and then, surprise of all surprises, she took out a great big long thing from her purse wrapped in brown paper.

"Surprise, Lucky! I brought one of your favorite Harrod's sausages for you to have in your noodles."

Boy was I one happy dog, let me tell you! That sausage really put some life into those boring noodles and crumbled bread. Was I ever really ready to chow down.

As soon as I finished, I was in for another surprise. I wouldn't be spending the evening in the room when Mama and Papa went to dinner as I did at home in London. I would be going with them. Now this I liked. It was going to be just like it was in the Netherlands. Wow, was I one excited pooch.

So we took the elevator down to the lobby area –
which, incidentally, I have never learned to enjoy –
especially since this one was pure glass and it about
frightened the 'doggie' diddles right out of me. I was
afraid I was going to fall right to the ground. Boy, did I
stick close to Mama and Papa.

Reaching the lobby, we went into this fancy French
restaurant.

"I thought we might as well enjoy our last night here
in Europe," Papa said.

"I can agree with that," Mama seconded.

Of course I came in with the third positive response.
Dining at a French restaurant didn't hurt my 'doggie'
feelings one diddly bit – even after that delicious
sausage I had just devoured.

This nice man dressed in a tuxedo greeted us and
took us to this big cushy booth, with live flowers on the
table, which Mama loved. Of course I wasn't allowed to
sit on those big fat cushions, but I was permitted to lie
on the carpet beneath Mama and Papa's feet. I soon
noticed, however, that the table across the aisle had a
miniature French poodle, and that it was sitting in the
woman's lap, so I let out one of my little begging
whines.

"Don't get any ideas, Lucky," Papa said. "You're not
about to sit on my lap. Just take it easy and enjoy a good
nap while we eat."

"That's right, Lucky," Mama said. "You be a good
dog."

*Okay, Mama, if you insist . . . but the food in this
restaurant sure smells fine.*

Before I knew it, the waiter bent down and gave me a
nice big bowl of water. I thought that was pretty neat
indeed, and I wondered when my *filet mignon* would be
coming. No such luck – it never did.

I just had to lie there below the table and smell their French onion soup, all that warm crusty baguette, Papa's rosemary lamb and Mama's duck. Now that wasn't very fair, now was it? But I didn't complain, as it was a heck of a lot better than staying in the room and watching CNN International, let me tell you.

In the end, I did get lucky, however. That's because I was fortunate enough to get Mama's leftovers when we returned to our room. Why, I hadn't had such a great piece of *duck al la orange* in all my 'doggie' days. Yes, this second time in France was very nice indeed. And what a wonderful way it was to say *au revoir* – that's good-bye – to Europe.

CHAPTER 43
HOME AGAIN – NATURALLY

The next morning we were up at the crack of dawn – and not my kind of 'doggie' dawn, let me tell you, as my getting up time was usually about 9:00 a.m. I mean it was the kind of 'dawn' like in 'people' time – like in those that have to go to work every morning time.

"We need to hit the tarmac," Papa said, "It's six o'clock."

I opened my eyes briefly, gave him a dirty look, and went right back to sleep.

But Mama came over to my *cama*, rubbed behind my ears. "Come on, Lucky, it's time to get up. We're going home to California."

Now that I liked the sound of, so I bounced right out of my bed, did my morning 'doggie' stretches, and headed for the door of our room. *Boy, do I need to pee.*

Papa quickly got the idea and put on my leash. "Lucky, you have the best bladder of any dog I've ever known. Let's get you down to the garage."

Oh, no, not that glass elevator again. I wondered how long I could hold myself, and thought of taking the steps, but decided against it, as it was a long walk to that cold garage from the lobby and I 'really' needed to go by this time.

After Mama and Papa's breakfast of *cappuccino*, French bread and *brie* cheese – none of which they shared with little old me, we proceeded to the front desk to reclaim our stored luggage. And what a pile of it there was. It looked like we were going to be traveling around the world about a hundred times. At first I didn't see my green traveling kennel and boy, I was seriously relieved. But then out came another porter with a luggage carrier full of our boxes. And there it was, my shiny green kennel right on the top! No such luck in getting rid of that thing! I wondered where my yellow raincoat was. I was hoping Mama had packed it in the very bottom of her biggest suitcase.

Boy, I hope I don't have to wear that thing through the Paris airport. The French would really get an 'ooo-la-la' out of that.

Fortunately my little coat did not appear, even though it was raining outside, or sleeting, or snowing – something like that. All I knew was that it was awfully cold in that airport with its marble halls and glass walls, as we walked what seemed mile after mile through it.

"Lucky, you act like you're cold," Mama said.

I'm just fine, Mama, no need to get out the old raincoat.

"Maybe I should get out your sweater from my carry-on."

I let out a little 'doggie' sigh of relief – which was a quiet whine – and she smiled at me.

"Yes, you want your sweater, don't you?"

Now I didn't mind my red, white and blue sweater with the stars on it one little bit. In fact, it made me feel very American. And since we were about to depart for America, why it made perfectly good 'doggie' sense for me to wear my patriotic sweater. And besides, maybe it would help keep me warm in the cargo area of the airplane, which the airlines always told us was perfectly well heated – but usually not hot enough for my 'Mexican' taste, unfortunately.

When we arrived at the Air France check-in counter with our two hotel porters following us, there was a great big line. But when the employees saw that I was with my mama and papa, they took us right to the front

420

of it. They probably thought I was going to bark or poop on the floor or something.

Of course my cage was the first thing to be unloaded from the cart, and a fat little airline man proceeded to coax me inside it. But he wasn't too successful with all that fancy French he spoke to me as I wasn't about to get into that traveling kennel again, no matter what language he was talking.

Papa finally had to come to his rescue. "Lucky, are you being a bad boy? Come on, you need to get into your kennel if you want to go home to California."

Papa gave me a little pat on the rear end. "Come on, in you go."

No I don't want to get into my kennel, Papa. I'm not getting in that green thing ever again.

Papa took hold of my collar and urged me inside, while the French man pushed from behind. I pressed my paws to the floor as hard as I could, but it was so polished and slick that I slid right into my kennel.

Bummer! I don't want to spend the next eleven hours in this thing!

Then Papa and the man picked up the kennel and put it on the scale – like I had gained a bunch of weight since the day before, right? Didn't matter – rules were rules.

After my weigh-in, was I ever in for a surprise. They let me out of my kennel!

Oh boy, oh boy, I must be going First Class instead!

No such luck. I was going outside for one last 'potty' stop before our departure. And then it was back in the old kennel and onto a cart, while two airline employees rolled whining little old me, through the sleet and snow to our plane. Why, I was sure glad Mama had persuaded them that I could keep on my trusty sweater or I think I would have frozen into one great big 'doggie' ice cube.

Boy, oh boy, was that California sunshine ever sounding good.

* * * *

I suppose I could say that the flight home was okay. I had several good dreams and thoroughly enjoyed Howard's cushy carpet on the bottom of my kennel carrier. The inside of the animal cargo space was nice and warm and even had a small light. The food was not so great however, so I was seriously hoping Mama and Papa were not enjoying all that *filet mignon* they must be eating. That's because my airline meal consisted of a tiny plastic dish attached to my kennel which was filled with dry food and some ice cubes in another attached dish to serve as my drinking supply. Of course, most of it splashed out after we hit the first winter air turbulence so I was one 'bone dry' doggie. I quickly decided I'd just have to 'bark and bear it' and I did just that – for at least two hours. When I finally realized Mama and Papa were not going to come down and get me out of the cargo area, I decided to take a nap – a long nap – and hoped that we would be back in America by the time I woke up.

Of course, this was all nice in theory except that the Bull Dog in the kennel next to me snored about as loud as the airplane engines, which both served to keep me awake much of the time. And then when the dog wasn't snoring, the cat on the other side of me was snarling and hissing. Oh, the joys of travel. I finally concluded I was more than ready to settle down in one place and stay there.

* * * *

Twelve hours later, when we finally touched down on the runway at Los Angeles International Airport, was I ever one happy dog. Why I barked and barked and barked until everyone on the airplane was wide awake indeed, Mama later told me. We were home in America after more than three years! Boy was I feeling patriotic to be on American soil again. I could tell that Mama and Papa were, as well.

This time we whisked right through Customs as I was barking so loud that I think the Customs Agent wanted to get me out of there, so he didn't even bother to inspect any of our luggage, including little old me. And did I ever need to go potty, so Mama rushed me out the door of the baggage area while Papa got our stuff.

I think I must have peed for about five minutes. Then it was into the rental van and off we headed down the San Diego Freeway toward home sweet home.

That evening Mama, Papa and I sat on our front balcony and watched the sun set into the Pacific Ocean. The sky turned orange, then a bright pink and finally a pale golden color that matched me.

"Isn't it great to be home?" Mama said.

Papa nodded and squeezed her hand, and then reached down and patted me.

I looked up at both of them and wagged my tail.

What a dog's life I have. . . . I certainly did win the 'doggie lotto.'

THE END

OR AS THEY SAY IN MEXICO, '*ADIOS*.'

EPILOGUE

Believe it or not, five years have passed since we returned home. I'm still with Mama and Papa and we're still here in California enjoying our beach life once more. Each night I chomp on my pasta or rice, but with fewer teeth. And we often take long walks on the beach and down to the Harbor. Yes, we've all gotten a bit heavier around the middle and my old joints are acting up a bit. Because of this, Papa finally had to make me a ramp for getting in and out of our Jeep. And sometimes I do unintentional splits, where all of my four legs go in different directions. Of course, my hearing is about gone, but I seem to manage. And there's one thing I'm more sure of than ever. I still consider myself the luckiest little street dog in the whole wide world.

SynergEbooks

Taking Books to New Heights